Advanced Praise for *The Book of CarolSue*

"In *The Book of CarolSue*, Hugo deftly combines whimsy and longing, old grief and newfound joy. With her unique and compassionate voice, she writes about loss and redemption in a way that makes you laugh out loud one minute, tear up the next. Either way, you're sure to experience tender feelings for her engaging cast of unforgettable characters." —Diane Chamberlain, bestselling author of *Big Lies in a Small Town*

"Sparkling prose, wry humor, and timely, relevant themes abound in this genuine story of two sisters, a son, and the unexpected arrival of a small, immigrant child. Hugo writes about internal conflict with sensitivity, and compassion, making for a compelling page turner about personal loss, perseverance, and rediscovering the heart of family." —Donna Everhart, USA Today bestselling author of *The Moonshiner's Daughter*

"Lynne Hugo writes down to the bone of family complications, grief, and shattering loss, while also offering miracles of rescue in *The Book of CarolSue*. The author walks a perfectly balanced tightrope as she illustrates how political conflicts are woven right into the heart of an Indiana farm family. I lost hours of sleep as I raced to finish this extraordinary novel." —Randy Susan Meyers, bestselling author of *Waisted*

"The ability to take tough issues and get others to truly see them is nothing short of magic; Lynne Hugo expertly wields that wand. In *The Book of CarolSue*, the plight of today's immigrants, a mother's sacrifice, and a family's grief reveal the vulnerability of love, and its incomparable strength. Delivered with humor and heart by way of those delightful characters readers have come to expect from this author, *The Book of CarolSue* will echo long after the last page is read." —Terri-Lynne DeFino, author of *The Bar Harbor Retirement Home For Famous Writers (And Their Muses)*

Praise for *The Testament of Harold's Wife*

"Grief can make a woman a little crazy, but it can also make her very entertaining! *The Testament of Harold's Wife* is part romp, part suspense, but above all, a love story. I adored this fun yet poignant book." —Diane Chamberlain, *New York Times* bestselling author of *The Stolen Marriage*

"*The Testament of Harold's Wife* is a glorious—and unique—tale of tragedy, resilience, and one kick-ass grieving widow and grandmother. I laughed, cried, and cheered as Louisa talked to her pet chickens, splashed bourbon in her tea, hid 'Glitter Jesus' around the house, and wrestled with revenge. Louisa captured my heart, and I will never forget her." —Barbara Claypole White, bestselling author of *The Perfect Son* and *The Promise Between Us*

"*The Testament of Harold's Wife* is a richly told tale that explores the human/animal connection and the journey to get past tragedy. Louisa, the spunky, elderly narrator delivers a tender hymn of hope and rebirth that stays with you long after the last page." —Kim Michele Richardson, *New York Times* bestselling author of *The Book Woman of Troublesome Creek*

"At the center of this moving, transcendent novel is the unforgettable Louisa. Perceptive, wry, full of righteous fury, and enlarged by deep compassion . . . I promise you will miss her when you turn the last page. The story itself—flawlessly written and genuine to the core—takes an unflinching look at how we survive shattering tragedy and pointless cruelty and continue to love the world. Its startling life-affirming conclusion will haunt me for a long time." —Patry Francis, award-winning author of *The Orphans of Race Point*

"Perhaps the toughest and bravest way to survive tragedy is by bearing up. In *The Testament of Harold's Wife*, after losing her husband and grandson, Louisa weathers catastrophe through hard-fought wisdom, humor, and revenge served cold—fueled by a side of hot bourbon. I never left her side as she proved reinvention is possible at any age." —Randy Susan Meyers, bestselling author of *The Widow of Wall Street*

"Lynne Hugo's delightful page turner, *The Testament of Harold's Wife,* is fast-paced, unexpectedly poignant, and fun. Louisa's utterly winning voice propels us at breakneck speed. As a woman who has seen it all and lost it all, Louisa will take her place in the pantheon of unforgettable characters. You may never see an older woman in quite the same way again. This gorgeous new book, with its swiftly moving plot and subversive humor, will stay with you long after you have finished the final page."
—Laura Harrington, bestselling author of *Alice Bliss* and *A Catalog of Birds*

"Hugo's latest is a sweet, sad, funny meditation on the nature of aging and grief . . . This is a novel that would fit right in on the shelf next to novels like *A Man Called Ove* and similar books that balance humor and heartbreak." —*Booklist*

"Suspended between heartbreak and hilarity, readers are sure to find emotional common ground in this story of an engaging elderly widow who sets her sights on revenge after the devastating loss of her husband and grandson, but unexpectedly finds hope, healing, and the possibility of a happy future . . . Lynne Hugo's character building is superb . . . The plot is propelled forward at a good pace, and readers will be compelled to turn the pages as Louisa speaks with candor, wisdom and keen insight about her thoughts on life, The Plan, and her relationships with those around her . . . A winning and wonderful novel, with a unique and distinctive storyline, there is a little bit of magic for everyone within the pages of this book." —*The New York Journal of Books*

"I found a kindred spirit in Louisa, a somewhat eccentric, aging, bereaved woman who finds solace in conversing with her chickens. Her heart is empty and her rage is full. Relatable. Loss does that to you . . . The warp and the weft of Lynne Hugo's characters in *The Testament of Harold's Wife* are woven into a rich tapestry of life, where the irreverent, unconventional, quirky 'flaws' become the very thing that make it absolutely perfect, and fills one with a sense of hope." —Delilah, *Delilah's Book Club Pick*

"*The Testament of Harold's Wife* comes with a bounciness and light touch that surprises and delights . . . [as it] takes on the theme of survival, of hanging on . . . The results are poignant, but Hugo delivers a fresh blend of pathos and humor. The text is leavened by Harold's wife, Louisa's, tart observations on life and the failings of those around her, bless their hearts." —*Wilmington StarNews*

The Book of CarolSue

LYNNE HUGO

KENSINGTON BOOKS
www.kensingtonbooks.com

KENSINGTON BOOKS are published by

Kensington Publishing Corp.
119 West 40th Street
New York, NY 10018

All Kensington titles, imprints, and distributed lines are available at special quantity discounts for bulk purchases for sales promotion, premiums, fund-raising, educational, or institutional use.

Special book excerpts or customized printings can also be created to fit specific needs. For details, write or phone the office of the Kensington Sales Manager: Kensington Publishing Corp., 119 West 40th Street, New York, NY 10018. Attn. Sales Department. Phone: 1-800-221-2647.

Kensington and the K logo Reg. U.S. Pat. & TM Off.

ISBN-13: 978-1-4967-2568-4 (ebook)
ISBN-10: 1-4967-2568-9 (ebook)

ISBN-13: 978-1-4967-2567-7
ISBN-10: 1-4967-2567-0
First Kensington Trade Paperback Printing: September 2020

10 9 8 7 6 5 4 3 2 1

Printed in the United States of America

For Alan, Brooke, and Ciera, with my heart

And in memory of my son, David Alan deCourcy

"... *When all the birds have flown to some real
    haven,*
We who find shelter in the warmth within,
Listen, and feel new-cherished, new-forgiven,
*As the lost, human voices speak through us and
    blend*
Our complex love ..."

—May Sarton

Chapter 1

CarolSue

Charlie was already dead when I finally hung up with my sister and came in from the porch. The twilight had settled around me like a sticky damp quilt, but the sky had held the glowing embers of the day and was lovely, so I'd stayed out. "Charlie, honey," I said as I glanced at him, irritated as any wife would be, "you've dropped a hunk of pie into your lap. I can't get blueberry out of khaki. Don't touch it while I go get napkins."

Even when I came back from the kitchen, stopping to turn down the roar of our Atlanta Braves against Milwaukee from the television—Charlie never would put in his hearing aids—I didn't catch on. "Pay attention, will you?" I said. That man could find a way to spill hard candy on himself. *I* was the one who should have been paying attention instead of being pleasantly surprised that for once he hadn't made a mess worse after I told him not to touch it. *I* was the one who dropped the rest of the pie on his khaki pants when I picked up the plate, realized, and screamed. "No! No! No!"

I'm usually the calm one, but I must have been still screaming when I called 911 because the dispatcher kept asking me to repeat myself. It took them almost fifteen minutes to show up. I could hear the sirens rising, falling, rising, falling, well after I'd made a total mess of things, after I realized that no, CarolSue, you really can't even attempt CPR on a body that's sitting in a recliner, you have to get him prone. Here's a hint I hope you never find useful: If a 225-pound man has his legs up in a recliner, you can't just shove them down. You have to use the lever. Well, I couldn't get to the lever without sitting on his lap. As my sister would say, please don't picture how that covered Charlie's fly and the rear of me in blueberry pie, or the whispering it doubtless prompted among the ambulance and hospital personnel.

Charlie was way bigger than I am. I had to drag him from the recliner by his ankles to get him onto the floor. I banged his head so hard I thought if he wasn't already dead, maybe I'd just killed him and I'd end up in jail. It was then I remembered that I don't know the first thing about CPR. It was my sister, Louisa, who had to get certified in it because of some law in Indiana where she used to be a teacher that they all had to know CPR, even though not a single elementary school student in the state had ever had a heart attack at school. So, naturally, I called the expert.

"Louisa! How do you do CPR?" I shouted. Possibly I could have been more clear about the nature of the problem.

"What do you mean?"

"HOW DO YOU DO CPR?"

"I don't know. I'm retired, remember? Take the class. Why?" My sister can be like that, bless her heart.

"It's Charlie, he's dead. How do you do CPR?"

"You call 911!"

"Tell me what to do!"

"Listen, honey. I used to think Harold was dead if he wasn't snoring, before he did die, I mean, but . . ."

I was going to jail even if I hadn't already killed Charlie with that blow to the head and by failing to know CPR because I had a strong homicidal impulse toward my sister.

"I DID call 911. Help me, what do I do?"

It was as if Louisa suddenly took hold and we switched

places then. I've always been the one to take care of her. I'm the older sister, after all, even if it's only two years.

"Listen to me," my sister said. "Find where the bony center of his rib cage ends. The center. Go up about an inch from that. Put one palm down there, flat. Got it? Now put the other hand crisscross on top of it. Start pumping, hard, fast. One, two, three, four, five, keep it steady, go, go, go, go." And don't you know, Louisa stayed on the phone until the ambulance arrived, her voice like a drum beating out the rhythm for my hands, to tell my beloved husband's heart what to do. But his heart wouldn't, not for me or anybody else on that midsummer night. And wouldn't ever again.

Louisa made it to Atlanta the next noon to shepherd me through the funeral. It was like a replay of how I'd done that for her when her husband Harold died, only I'd had Charlie to help me manage things. Louisa said Gus had offered to come, but that I was, after all, Harold's sister-in-law, not Gus's, and she wasn't about to start letting Gus be Harold's stand-in. I imagine it was Louisa's son, Gary, always overly fond of the internet, who made the quick plane reservation for her.

She warned me that he had the automatic thought that he'd be doing the funeral, being a Reverend and all. Bless his heart, but no way I was going to risk Charlie's soul with Gary's fly-by-night internet ordination. I had no lack of love for my only nephew, him being the closest I came to having a child myself, but I knew I'd have to lie and tell Gary that Charlie had left instructions for his funeral with his will, and unfortunately, it involved his one-time Baptist minister to whom he'd been close. It wouldn't be the first lie I'd ever told and funerals count as a good cause, don't they?

The good-hearted Baptist minister, who'd never previously heard of Charlie, but was kind to help me out, asked Gary to do him the "professional courtesy" of reading the twenty-third Psalm. That line was enough that I do believe Gary thought he'd died and gone to heaven himself, having finally proved himself a good and worthy man in spite of the sins that had cost his family so much.

Louisa and I wore the same black dresses we'd worn to her grandson Cody's funeral—I'd made an emergency run to buy hers—and then, six months later, to Harold's. Then, it had been I who'd dressed her, and she'd been the rag doll.

I would have liked to listen to the service, out of respect if nothing else, but my mind just wouldn't stay in the chapel of the funeral home, though the décor was lovely, a soft peach, like an early sunset—doubtless, I was supposed to think of a new dawn—and the pew cushions heavily padded. That last was a mercy.

I fingered the pearls Charlie had given me for our wedding—they looked nice against my black dress, Louisa said— while my mind zagged from what was I going to do now to how I'd ended up here, where I sounded like a foreigner and people still teased me about my "accent." To me, they all sounded like their words were stuck together with syrup. Well, landing here hadn't been an accident, I reminded myself. Charlie had been as rooted in the South as I'd been in the farmland of southeastern Indiana, and he was still working when we met. I'd never had a real career like Louisa, the educated one. How could I have asked Charlie to relocate? A husband is a husband, even if it is your second one, right? It had to be I who moved. Atlanta was my home now, too, wasn't it? I supposed it was. Fifteen years is a long time. That's what my mind was on instead of whatever the minister was saying. I imagine it was nice. People said it was. Louisa told me that she hadn't heard a word of Harold's service, that she gave herself a grade of A just for sitting through it with none of her special tea, which, she reminded me, I wouldn't let her have in advance.

Well, now I understood Louisa's tea-need at Harold's funeral. I understood a lot. When the funeral meal was eaten, all the crying and hugging and *so sorry, so sorry*, so-sorrying was finally over, Gary was dispatched to his hotel and Louisa and I could finally stop, just stop, I was plain grateful when my sister fixed us both extra-large mugs of it. A body could get drunk on the smell alone. Perfect.

I'd thought I was cried out, but as soon as there was this additional liquid in my body it worked its way out as tears. "I don't know what I'm going to do," I said. We were on the couch in the family room together. It's Louisa's favorite room, I know, because there's some furniture that was Mom's in it, and it's not so formal. "These retirement community— what do you call them? patio homes?—are nice," Louisa said one of the few times she came here instead of my going there. She acted like she was in a museum in which everything has a DON'T TOUCH sign and is surrounded by an electric wire just to be sure. Well, Charlie did pay a fancy decorator, which wasn't my idea, but he thought it would please me.

"What do you mean, you don't know? You're coming home. We're putting this place up for sale and you're coming home. With me."

Home. In my mind's eye, I could picture the corn, how it was silvering in the sun then, shimmering like an inland sea in late afternoon light, rippling when a breeze crossed its surface. Then, when fall came, the combines would crawl across the acres like slow ships heading home.

I hesitated. "I'd need to rent a place there . . . or buy one," I said. "Do you know of something on the market?"

That didn't slow my sister down a nanosecond. "Don't be ridiculous. Your home is with me. We take care of each other, don't we? Good grief, did you think I want Gary wiping my butt when I'm old? And, please don't picture *that*."

"I'm older than you are. We're already old, anyway, and

quite capable of wiping our own butts." I narrowed my eyes at her. "Or . . . uh-oh, aren't you?"

"Pffft." Louisa dismissed that with the wrist flip she'd perfected with years of practice listening to fifth graders. "You're missing the point as usual. I have the farm. How long has our family had the farm?"

"You and Harold bought the farm, not Mom and Dad, they—"

"Good Lord, CarolSue! The *point* is where were we raised? What land is in our blood? You're my family. And *you* are coming home."

I was going home.

Chapter 2

CarolSue

I don't mind telling you that my sister is a bit of a nutcase about making a Plan. And yes, it's capital-P Plan. She got the trait from our grandmother who started each day by asking the nearest victim, "What's the Plan?" meaning a list of tasks the victim was going to accomplish for her with a precise time schedule by which they'd be accomplished. Louisa's version is somewhat different. When she sees something she thinks needs to be fixed, she comes up with a Plan to fix it, and if God has something else in mind, well, I've got to say, it might be too bad for God because once Louisa's head is down and she's got her mind set, you might as well fasten your seat belt because you're going on her ride.

So that night after Charlie's funeral, I knew: Patching up my broken life was Louisa's new Plan and she'd be loaded for bear to take out anything that got in her way. The thing was that I might have put up a token objection, at least for show, if I'd really had one. But I admit, much as I loved Charlie, I'd missed the rhythm of the seasons, although I'd routinely denied it when he asked me. There was that, but more to the point, I didn't have another Plan for myself.

Years ago, I'd fit myself into Charlie's world when I moved that thousand miles from home to Atlanta. Charlie'd been thrilled at how his friends took me right in to their circle. It didn't come naturally; I'd had to play a role at first, though I did it gladly for his sake, and it had become my world, too. Part of me wondered if now I could go back to who I once was, a woman who'd never worn designer slacks with coordinated tops, gotten her hair done, had manicures, even pedicures; a woman who hadn't learned to play bridge two afternoons a week after a ladies' luncheon. Not that I minded the clothes; I've always been the one with a fashion sense. Good Lord, Louisa's idea of a new outfit is whatever she finds in the back of her closet that she hasn't worn in fifteen years. "Nobody remembers it anyway, CarolSue. It's new to them," she actually announced to me when I asked her what she was wearing out to some sheriff's department Christmas gathering last year.

It was while we were packing that I started thinking about how abruptly my life would change. When Louisa asked me where my jeans were, I had to say, "I don't have any."

"No jeans? What the hell do you wear?"

"I'm not exactly out in the coop feeding my chickens. Or running around in a cornfield now, am I?" I'm sure I sounded miffed.

"You have flower gardens. You wear a tiara and floor-length gown when you planted those?"

"I have a skort."

"A . . . *skort*? That sounds like a strong drink. I could use one about now."

I got huffy. We were in Charlie's and my bedroom—my bedroom now—and it had been Charlie who'd bought me my first skort and matching shirt as a birthday present the year we got married so I'd have something nice to wear out on the patio. That was where I'd planted the flower beds, around the edges. The reds and yellows and purples brightened it up so much, and down here, they bloom ten months a year, sometimes eleven. Louisa sure couldn't say that about Indiana farm country. The winters are brutal. Maybe she thought I'd developed Alzheimer's on that subject.

There might have been a touch of sarcasm in my tone when I said, "A skort is a pair of shorts that's fashioned to look like a skirt. As people who don't buy their clothes at Goodwill know." I'd climbed on my high horse and was about to go from a trot to a gallop.

"Well, Miss High-and-Mighty, you can pack your *skort* if you want to, but you'll be needing jeans back home where normal people live."

We were not off to a great start.

Right after I signed the contract to put the house on the market, I met with Charlie's lawyer, who advised me not to make any major decisions for a year.

"Oh," I said. *Now you tell me.* "Why is that?" I asked, glad that Louisa was at my house emptying kitchen cupboards instead of in this thick-carpeted office with the fat mahogany desk and brass lamps and hot to inform the attorney that he was a blazing idiot.

"Always best to get your feet on the ground, get a sense of what you really want. It's too emotional a time, too much adjustment. Give yourself time to grieve," he said kindly. "You're in great shape financially with Charlie's investments and pension. Just wait."

"Thank you," I said, shook his hand and got out fast after he'd ended the appointment with that advice. Charlie had set up a living trust, so everything was already in my name. That good, generous man. I'd made the appointment with the lawyer to change the beneficiaries of my own will. Louisa and Gary. Who did I have now but my people?

When I got home, I didn't tell Louisa what he'd said. Why bother? We'd already gone to the mall here—because there's not one anywhere near the farm—and bought me two pairs of jeans and some "normal people shorts," and they were packed, along with two flannel shirts and two long-sleeve T-shirts and four short-sleeve T-shirts. And a sweatshirt.

"This'll hold you into fall, if it comes early," she said. "If you need anything else, you can wear mine."

"The bag lady look. Save me," I muttered.

"Huh?"

"Thank you," I said.

It was a done deal. It hadn't exactly been a year. I hoped two weeks was close enough.

Gary was going to drive the U-Haul—not that it was one of those huge ones—north to Louisa's farm in Shandon, Indiana, which hardly merits a dot on a map. I would have hired a company, but they are both used to being frugal. As I've mentioned, too, Louisa wouldn't hear of my getting my own place. We decided which of my furniture we'd keep, swapping it out for her much older versions, which she said might have some chicken poop stains on it. "Seriously, Louisa? We'll need to have this treated then, with stain-guard stuff," I said. "Do you know what good furniture costs?" Louisa has a perfectly fine chicken coop behind the house, but in good weather she lets the hens free-range during the day and has been known to leave her back door open. Have they wandered into the house? You heard it here first.

"Not a clue," she said, all blithe like it didn't matter in the least. "But that chair *is* a pretty color. Sort of matches Abigail's tail feathers. And it's comfortable, so we'll get rid of my old blue one." We were surrounded by boxes of my stuff we were getting rid of. It didn't seem like a huge sacrifice on her part.

"Abigail, huh? A new one." I huffed. Louisa started out naming all her chickens and farm animals after characters in *Little Women*, because she'd been named after our mother's favorite writer, Louisa May Alcott. A little weird, I know. I have no idea how our mother came up with CarolSue, probably for a mysterious, differently weird reason. When Louisa ran out of those characters' names after so many chickens and animals, she turned to using names of other Transcendentalists. "Wonderful," I said. "How many others haven't you mentioned?"

"I told you about Abigail!"

"Don't remember. Anyway, I'm asking you about the ones you haven't mentioned."

"You'll love Abigail. And Sarah."

"What else?"

"Well, Rosie Two isn't really new anymore and she's strictly outside. And you know about the puppy."

"So just a dog, the two additional chickens, one you'd forgotten to mention. And being strictly outside would be appropriate for a goat. Wouldn't you say?"

She can make me crazy, Louisa can. I didn't let her see my tears. She'd feel bad, but her Plan was set in cement, immutable, and I guessed it didn't matter if I grieved here or there.

Chapter 3

CarolSue

On the plane from Atlanta to Indianapolis, Louisa sat in the middle and gave me the window seat. She said she thought I'd like to have the view. Bless her heart, does she think I'm too grief-addled to figure out that she just doesn't want an extra person to climb over to get to the restroom? Her bladder is the size of a pea. I told her not to have all that coffee, but did she listen?

I didn't want to wake her to get to the restroom myself, nor the man in the aisle seat who might have been sleeping. Anyway, the man had earbuds stuck in, and it was darn impressive that they didn't fall out since there was so much hair growing wild there. His eyebrows looked like shrubbery, and there was a pretty amazing amount of nasal hair, too, but his head was bald. The point is that seeing him made me miss Charlie because Charlie was so different, kept himself so groomed, and had a full head of hair that was not charcoal shot with silver anymore, but more silver laced with charcoal. If he'd been on the plane, he'd have been sitting next to me, and he'd have asked me which seat I'd like.

Now, though, he wasn't and wouldn't ever be again. Louisa was snoring lightly, and I rested my head back and watched the clouds through the window. Somewhere on a highway below, Gary was driving what remained of my worldly possessions, jigsawed into a U-Haul, to Indiana. My life with Charlie was over. I did not want this to be happening. I couldn't endure this. And yet, from the beginning, I'd known I would. And I'd said, "Yes, yes, I will. Yes."

When I met Charlie, Phillip had divorced me twenty years earlier and I'd sworn off men forever. Good riddance. I'd married him before I turned twenty-one and I miscarried a total of seven babies before I had my last, my stillborn son. Phillip ground me under his heel when he left, claiming *he* couldn't take the pain and grief of so many ghost children. What kind of excuse was that for leaving the mother of those lost babies? In short, I realized I'd been better off before I married, and I'd been smart enough to stay single after Phillip, even if that book about regaining your virginity was fake, and Louisa said she'd meant it as a divorce joke to lighten my mood. She should have known I wouldn't get it at the time. Anyway, I was fifty-two when I met Charlie. Why on earth would I allow myself to be vulnerable again just because The Change was upon me, and of course a man wouldn't expect me to bear him a child.

No, avoiding men didn't have anything to do with children anymore. It was knowing that the person I'd trust to stand by me might break that promise whenever life decided to replace moisture evaporated from the ocean with my salty tears. Best to be alone and know it before a husband could abandon me to cry by myself. I had Louisa, and, back then, our mother was alive. Mothers and daughters and sisters— they were reliable. They might be annoying and give unsolicited opinions frequently, but they'd never leave. They couldn't. Blood was blood, and mine were kindred spirits to boot, especially Louisa.

Then Charlie came along. It was funny at first, when he claimed love at first sight. I used to do that in high school, for heaven's sake, get dreamy crushes on either Fabian (television teen heart throb) or Bobby Willis (football team tight end, and that wasn't referring to the position he played, which I couldn't have identified to save my soul, but how adorable his rear looked in his uniform), or Ted Keefer (biology lab partner, gorgeous dark hair, and eyes under thick sexy eyebrows, who did my lab report for me when it involved testing my blood, which I whispered made me feel faint so he'd hold my hand, prick my finger, and test it for me).

My mother despaired that I was boy crazy. Louisa was the one motivated to go to college; I wanted to get married and set up housekeeping, and Phillip had a handy heart murmur, a 4-F deferment that kept him out of Vietnam but not out of action in bed. Plus he was muscular and cute. Perfect. Except when it counted. "You'll be too soon old and too late smart," Dad used to warn me. He never had warmed to Phillip. Well, crap, he'd been right once, and when Charlie showed up twenty years later, I was for sure not going to let Dad be right again even if he had been dead for ten of those years.

Charlie had come to Indianapolis on business. He worked for some huge Atlanta contracting company that had architects and various kinds of engineers, though he was none of those, but a liaison or coordinator for their huge construction projects in the eastern half of the country. At least that's what I understood about it, which was probably the top two percent, not that Charlie didn't try to explain his job. At the time, I just wasn't much interested in gigantic projects for corporations and didn't tune in with every available brain cell. Charlie was in Shandon because he'd driven his rental car out to the sticks to visit his cousins, who, it happened, were neighbors of Mom's. And Lucille next door had it in her head what a shame it was that poor me had no husband and was always on the prowl for middle-aged widowers or divorced men, she didn't care as long as they were available. Whether or not I wanted a man, which I had been polite but adamant about saying I didn't. "Nonsense," Lucille said, and the really bad thing about my getting involved with Charlie had been that Lucille was so smug about being right, peering over her glasses, eyebrows raised, lips pressed as if suppressing her triumphant *told you so*. I'd never liked Lucille much, and that sealed the deal.

Our initial meeting happened when Lucille dragged Charlie next door because my car was in Mom's driveway, and Charlie asked me out for "a bit of refreshment." He meant a drink, but was too careful to say it in front of Mom—I, of course, refused. Graciously, but firmly. He kept trying. Got my phone number from Lucille, who got it from Mom.

The construction in Indianapolis was an eighteen-month project and Charlie managed to find himself *needed* there regularly to straighten out all kinds of *issues*. And, strangely enough, he had discovered a new closeness with his dear cousins in cow-and-corn country Shandon, Indiana. Which he hadn't visited since his parents had dragged him there as a child, such a shame, he'd loved it so, he claimed. Bless his heart.

It was after I finally relented and agreed to one drink if he'd stop calling me, and then, after we had that one drink (a vodka martini for him, white wine for me) in Paesano's, Elmont's nicest Italian bar and restaurant, and had stayed for another drink and then stayed on and ordered dinner, that I withdrew the condition that he stop calling me. He was such a gentleman and gentle man, dear and kind. It hadn't hurt, either, that he was handsome, his hair charcoal-silver, his nose aquiline, his eyes that unusual green. I liked his height, and his hand on my back felt good when he opened doors for me.

He was a widower; he told me that early on. No children. His wife had had a hysterectomy, but too late. The cancer had spread. After our fifth date, we were in his car, talking in my driveway, he filled in details of what he'd been through. We'd talked on the phone in between dates and had been seeing each other long enough that it was easy for me to take his hand, and I'm sure my face showed my sorrow because he said, "It's all right. I've healed. It was a long time ago. It was the only other time in my life I've had the love-at-first-sight experience. I hope you'll forgive me for being so . . . persistent. It's just that I knew when I first saw her that she was the one, and then, when I saw you . . ."

It was so unlike me. Charlie said that and I didn't object. He kissed me and I didn't pull away. We sat and held hands on an October night, the harvest moon already past, the crickets singing of sleep and death, warning of the earth's relentless turn toward winter and endings. I knew then that if I loved him and let him love me, I'd lose him or he'd lose me. One of us was going to suffer. Isn't that the outcome of every love story, one way or another? Could I bear it again?

It took me months more before I told Charlie everything about the lost babies and my stillborn son. About Phillip, why he'd left. And Charlie took me in his arms, just that. When he finally looked at me, his green eyes were wet. "I'd like to go to your son's grave with you," he said. "Would you take me? When you're ready to share him, I mean."

"Yes," I said. "Yes. I will."

And when he asked me to marry him, and move to Atlanta, I said it again. "Yes. Yes. I will."

Louisa

Déjà vu. That's what it was. No, it was déjà vu all over again, and it wasn't even amusing to mock the poorly taught people who actually said that, because the redundancy was ridiculously appropriate. CarolSue's call about Charlie had jolted Louisa into some two-fisted time warp, back to the first call she'd gotten about Cody, and then the one about her Harold, dead by his own grieving choice at the same spot on the highway where the drunk driver had run down their only grandson. Louisa had known the frenetic panic that was running in CarolSue's veins right then, and how soon it would be replaced by paralysis. So, of course, she'd hung up and sprang into action to take over, just as her sister had done for her both times. They always had each other's backs. If Louisa were Gary, she'd be praising Jesus up and down the glory aisles for that. As it was, Louisa preferred to be simply very grateful, though she felt no need to blab about it on the internet, which Gary was in love with and Louisa didn't use.

On the plane taking her sister home with her, though, with CarolSue next to her like a wilted lily (at first she'd thought *dying* lily, and then, horrified, changed the word in her mind), the ramifications of CarolSue moving in started to become real. She and CarolSue had always told each other everything. But some months ago, Louisa had started omitting certain details. Well, maybe they were more than details. Possibly she hadn't told her something big.

She closed her eyes, thinking she might be able to sleep, but an argument started in her head. *What are you going to do now? You should have told her.* It reminded her of Marvelle, her tuxedo cat, who often swished her tail disdainfully at Louisa's best Plans.

Louisa bristled back, her defense rising over the white noise of the engines: *I was going to tell her. At the right time. How was I supposed to know Charlie was going to drop dead?*

But Louisa of all people did know how people disappeared, here to track mud on your clean floor and laugh when you complained about missing chocolate chip cookies one instant, dead the next, and you don't get two weeks' notice in the mail that it's going to happen.

She tapped the shoulder of the bald man with things in his ears in the aisle seat and gestured that she needed to get out. (Possibly CarolSue had been right about laying off the coffee before the flight, but Louisa was not about to say so.) At home, Marvelle would be waiting for them. She'd take in what was going on, jump off the back of the chair in disgust, and saunter to the back door, wanting to be let out. Marvelle thought she knew everything. Well, Louisa had handled fifth-grade boys, who were a lot sneakier than field mice, and she would damn well make it work with CarolSue there.

The man scarcely moved his knees a quarter inch to let Louisa out. It wasn't exactly pretty, but she made it, straightened up, and sauntered toward the restroom. Her bladder was the size of a pea.

Gary

She wasn't a member of the church, the woman he'd sinned with this time, and Gary wasn't sure if that lessened the offense. It had started when he'd thought her attraction to him might draw her to love what he stood for, the good ways of the church, but then he'd slipped and yielded to temptation again. His motivation this time had been pure, and it was the first time it had happened since he'd been Saved and become a real Reverend himself through GetOrdained-Now.com.

The transgression had weighed on him for months, a worry about whether his intention made a difference. Had he risked his soul? And almost worse, might his trespass be somehow discovered and put the church he'd founded in jeopardy? But then, the Baptist minister called him Brother Gary and asked him to read the twenty-third Psalm at the funeral, as a professional courtesy, and Gary took it as an answer straight from Jesus himself. He was recognized as a man of God. He'd been forgiven.

Gary knew that men stray but that as long as repentance was genuine, there was, indeed, salvation. There were, after all, worse sins than fornicating. He'd yielded to temptation, yes, but when he'd read the words, *Surely goodness and mercy shall follow me all the days of my life, and I shall dwell in the house of the Lord forever*, he'd understood. Mercy. *Mercy* was the operative word in the message to him, and he had been given that gift. He would lie down in green pastures and by still waters. His soul was restored. Forgiven, though it was his task to safeguard his church and the souls gathered in it. Confession would be selfish.

Good works were the key. He needed to show his gratitude, that he was committed to growing the church. After the funeral, he told his mother and aunt that he would drive his aunt's car and possessions home to Indiana, that she needn't hire anyone. Of course, his aunt CarolSue protested that he didn't have to do that for her, but he insisted, telling her that a U-Haul trailer would be far less expensive, and he would take much better care of her things than a stranger. He would load and unload them himself, too, and they could be placed exactly where she and his mother wanted. A much better Plan than theirs, surely. When CarolSue said, "But Gary, that's just too much for you to have to do for me. I'd insist on paying you," he answered, "You know what would really help me? If maybe you could either make a donation to the church or better yet, maybe do a little volunteer work sometime when we need help."

He saw his mother—never a big fan of his work—shoot a warning glance at his aunt, but CarolSue, who could usually be counted on to take his side, hardly hesitated before she said, "Well, I'd be happy to make a donation."

Maybe this was why he'd been tempted and fallen. No telling what greater good might come from drawing Aunt CarolSue in. It was set in motion now, anyway. The women would be home in Shandon well before him, since they'd flown out this morning and he was hardly making sixty-five miles an hour up I-75 in CarolSue's car with a fat U-Haul hitched behind and swaying when he turned; the rest of the traffic was doing close to eighty. It was harrowing, but worth it, even though he really couldn't see what was behind him.

Chapter 4

CarolSue

"The house looks nice, hon," I said when Louisa came in the back door. "You didn't tell me you put up shelves in the hallway bathroom." We'd just arrived from the airport and were opening the house up, and bringing our things in from her car, which she'd left at the Indianapolis airport. It had taken us an hour and a half to get to the farm from there and I was plain worn out, but Louisa had run out to check the chickens and let them out of the coop. The animals always come first with her.

"Oh, you made it in there before you collapsed, huh?" she said, mocking me for being sprawled on the couch.

"Right behind you, Sister. As usual, you were blocking my way. You coulda used your own . . ." I said, meaning the bathroom that was off the master bedroom.

"I, uh . . . don't go in there."

"Huh?"

"I don't use that one."

"What's wrong with it?"

"Nothing, I . . . nothing. Let's get you settled. We need to do Gary's old room over for you. I asked Gus a couple days ago and he said he'll paint it. There's not much of Gary's old stuff in it, so I'll get it packed up and we'll make it really comfortable and all yours. Shouldn't take long at all. I want you to pick out your own curtains and spread anyway."

I knew I was sitting there looking stupid. I just wasn't sure if I was too tired to follow what she was saying or if it just made no sense. If nothing was wrong with her bathroom, why didn't she go in there?

Then she insulted me. "Why are you sitting there with your mouth hanging open? You look like you're trying to catch flies. That's what I have Marvelle for." Marvelle was Louisa's tuxedo cat who was too lazy to catch a fly lying dead on the ground in front of her. Right then, in fact, she was snoring in a late patch of sun on the rag rug, right where she'd be most in the way of anyone who wanted a snack in the kitchen. Like me.

Diversion was one of Louisa's tactics; I'd been on to it for years. "Why on earth wouldn't you use a perfectly good bathroom? You're making about as much sense as Mom used to."

"None of your business," she said, ever the eloquent former teacher. "Let's put your stuff away." With that, she picked up my suitcase and cut from the living room through the kitchen and down the hall.

"How'd you ever come up with such an original line?" I shouted after her. Irritated, I hauled myself up and followed her. Hungry, and done in, I thought, *This all is a mistake. What am I doing here?*

Why can't I just stay in the guest room? I came to my senses with the thought and then immediately said it out loud to her. "Why can't I stay in the guest room? Huh?" She was putting my suitcase on Gary's old bed as I stood in the hall, demanding. I went to the next door, the one to the guest room, which was closed, and turned the knob.

Oh. It was obviously being used. Not at the moment, I don't mean, but someone was using it regularly. Or wait. Two people. A man and a woman. Those pajama bottoms laid on the bottom of the bed sure weren't Louisa's, and neither were those giant brown slippers sticking out half under the bed. But that flowered robe hanging on the hook sure was, and so was the hand lotion by one side of the bed. There were little scattered things around the room, a lot of Louisa's, I saw, but some others that I knew weren't hers: petroleum jelly, for example. Louisa can't stand that stuff. Then, the cincher. A pill bottle on the night table next to the bed. I picked it up. *No!*

Yes. A certain well-known medication for older men afflicted with a condition that affects their romantic functioning.

"Louisa! Oh my God! Are you and Gus . . . *doing it?*" I yelled it out. I couldn't help myself.

"Are you snooping? Get out of there." There's no mistaking it when Louisa gives an order.

I went to the door of Gary's room. "You're doing it!"

"Maybe." She didn't look at me. She was pulling stuff out of Gary's bureau—old sweatshirts—and stuffing them in my suitcase. The clothes in my suitcase had been piled on his bed.

"I don't want Gary's crap in my suitcase."

"I don't have anything to put these in. It's temporary."

Dammit, I got off track. "Never mind. You're *doing* it. And you didn't tell me!"

"Don't picture that."

"Oh my God, you're blushing. You're doing it. Does he . . . live here?"

"Of course not! What kind of tramp do you think I am?"

"Hmmm. Well—"

"Don't be ridiculous. He calls on me and some calls are a little longer than others. We . . . nap."

"Is that what you call it?"

I got her defiant look then. "We nap."

"Right. You nap. And what am I supposed to do while you nap?"

"I don't know. Play loud music."

"I'd think that would interfere with your sleep." Sarcasm

is a talent we both inherited from Mom. Louisa believes she is more gifted than I, but it's only because I practice more restraint. Or I did before I moved in with my sister.

Maybe Louisa thought I'd had enough for one day when she made sure I went to bed before she did. She couldn't possibly have thought I wasn't going to find out. Maybe she figured I wouldn't "overreact," as she put it, if I got a good night's sleep. Well, she could have figured out that I'd have slept a lot better if the teenage boy who works for her, Brandon, hadn't brought her Lab puppy, Jessie, home that night. He'd kept the young dog for my sister because Louisa has an aversion to kennels. Brandon had also come daily to look after the place, feed the chickens, and check on Marvelle, Rosie the goat, and Aunt Peace and Aunt Plenty, the barn cats. (Yes, of course, those last three *are* named for characters from *Rose in Bloom*. My sister had concluded that Louisa May Alcott had given her characters better names than the actual, historical Transcendentalists had, no matter how much she liked their thinking.) But between Jessie's exuberant greeting, which she found necessary to repeat when anything roused her from snoozing, and her decision later that the only place she could possibly sleep for the night was with me, on Gary's bed, I wasn't exactly relaxed and well rested the next day, when I got the next shock.

I saw it with my own eyes in the morning. Thanks to Jessie I was awake before Louisa. I'd used the bathroom and just happened to be on my way out of it when there she was, in her robe, opening the door to the guest room to come into the hallway. Caught barefooted.

"Is he in there?" I was outraged.

"He who?"

"Gus!" I whispered. Maybe it was more like a hiss.

"Don't be ridiculous. You think he climbed in the damn window?"

"Why are you in the guest room then?"

She shrugged, turned sideways to go around me, didn't look at me as she did. "Felt like it . . . bed's better. Did you make coffee?"

"I just woke up."

"Just switch it on. I set it up last night. Can you do it while I pee?" she said as she went into the bathroom.

"Got it," I said, and did. But I'll tell you this. I didn't believe her about the bed.

I waited her out, though, knowing that after breakfast she'd get dressed—yes, she went back into the guest room, which clearly wasn't for guests anymore—and when she came out, dressed in a typical Louisa god-awful getup, she headed out to feed the chickens. It was only because I didn't want to slow her down that I managed not to say, "Tell me you've never let *him* see you look like that."

I watched through the kitchen window to make sure she was engrossed with the chickens. I opened the kitchen window a couple of inches to make sure I'd hear her out there because I knew she talks to them all the time. Then, of course, I headed straight for the door I hadn't opened yet, the one to her real bedroom, the one she'd shared all those years with her husband, Harold, until he'd killed himself, six months after their only grandson Cody was killed by a drunk driver. Harold couldn't go on, believing he carried the weight of failure to find justice for the boy he loved so truly. And, of course, he never got over blaming Gary. Still, nobody really understood Gary's turn to the religious cult, it seemed an obvious scam, but I guess guilt can weigh so much that a body can't stagger another step without a way to put it down. Gary was promised something he needed more desperately than his savings, and though that preacher snaked his way on to his next tent full of victims, Gary was hooked. The internet reeled him in. But all that's Louisa's story to tell, not mine, and maybe you couldn't bear it anyway.

I digressed there for a minute, didn't I? So, Louisa was out with the chickens clucking around, carrying on with the girls as if she's the original mother hen. I realized I was getting testy because I flat didn't know what else she was keeping from me. We'd never kept anything from each other. Not that I knew of anyway. Until her last grand Plan, come to think of it. Maybe that had gone to her head and now she thought she didn't need me. Well, I'd have to show her she couldn't get away with that crap.

I marched to her bedroom and opened the door.

Chapter 5
Gary

Gary knew it was far too late for him to redeem himself with Nicole, even though she'd never remarried. Adultery was too much for her to accept, and who could blame her? He loved her still, and it wasn't devoid of an element of lust. He didn't know what had come over him when he'd had the episode with her sister-in-law, just crazy stupid, he supposed, and pure bad luck that Nicole's brother caught them right in the act. Made it difficult to deny, for one, and for two, he blushed if he remembered it, his own bare ass bobbing up and down in the air like some kind of a carnival target when Rocco walked in on him and Sandra. It had put him at a distinct disadvantage in the confrontation that followed. For three, it was a major sin: Nicole being wrapped up in their son's activities and her job, not absorbed in his problems anymore, was no excuse. Or so he'd been told, and he'd come to see his error. Too late, though, and she'd divorced him and moved back to her hometown long before Cody was killed. His being Saved afterward hadn't moved a last green leaf in the hacked-off thicket of their abandoned marriage; he'd let her know about it, but she'd not responded. He still wondered how she survived losing their son, and if she, too, thought Cody wouldn't have been killed by that drunk driver if he'd been a better father. He'd never know, he guessed.

She'd never been one to lash him with her words when they were married.

The second time he'd fallen was worse because it was after he'd been Saved, thanks to the balm of Brother Zachariah's words, and permission to donate. Then, even though his savings were gone, he'd been able to get himself ordained and establish his own church. There were new faithful now, supporting him and his work. Evangelism was endless and many new members didn't have the funds even to tithe. But Reverend Gary turned no one away, especially not the ones whose lives were broken, as his had been, first by Cody's death, and then his father's. How could he have closed the church door to Rosalina, with immigration agents all over and *Jesus Is The Answer* proclaimed on the very banner he had hanging on the side of the rented white barn that served as his church? She'd spent months making her way up from Honduras, trusting the human smugglers her father had paid. The conditions in the back of that truck must have been brutal. Two died, she said. (The heat. No water. She'd answered flat and matter-of fact, as if he should have known.) Survivors heard it was safer in the Midwest, so after crossing the border, she'd worked her way up from Texas. It wasn't safer anymore. Agents spread out after raiding the warehouses near Indianapolis where immigrants who didn't have good papers could get hired anyway. Some of the undocumented made it from the city into surrounding rural areas to hide, hoping for work, and found it with a convenience store chain that had stores around the city of Elmont. Some nurseries that supplied garden stores couldn't find enough American workers; they paid less and under the table, but it was something.

Gary understood the despair of suffering souls and gave them the same comfort and hope he'd been given. Especially Rosalina. His mistake had been touching her. But she'd been crying, that was how it had started.

At least he'd stopped. He'd come to his senses afterward. Yes, he'd sinned but he counted it as a sign that he'd not been caught, but stopped himself after those few days, repented on his own. How could he not have put money in Rosalina's hand, given her food, a change of clothes from a woman in his flock when he told her she had to go? She'd acted hurt, even though he drove her to the nearest Catholic church. He'd had to stop himself from the sinning. It had been the right thing to do. The sin remained, though, a rock on his chest, as had his failure to minister to the least among them, until he'd received the sign at his uncle's funeral.

It had been the second big failure of his work, after being unable to herd his own mother into the flock. Louisa claimed her fields, woods, and creek were her church, and the creatures that lived there were all holy to her. Now, though, Gary saw an opening with his aunt CarolSue. She owed him. He didn't know what work he'd ask her to do, but he would. And she had money, too. Maybe down the road a bit, she'd join. Support his growing church. Maybe it had all been meant to be. It was another Sign.

CarolSue

I don't know what I expected when I turned the knob on Louisa's bedroom door and pushed it open, but certainly not that time had stood still three-and-a-half years ago when my brother-in-law Harold killed himself by stepping in front of a Dwayne County Waste Recycling truck. Good Lord, and bless my sister's heart, but Harold's pajama bottoms were laid on the bottom of the bed, and his good brown shoes left in front of the dresser. His wallet and keys and what must have been the change from his pocket scattered themselves all casual on the dresser, in front of their wedding picture, and their grandson Cody's framed picture—a different one than was in the living room—right there next to it, plus Harold's spare pair of glasses, as if he might need them again. By his side of the bed, on the nightstand, the *Farmers' Almanac* under the lamp. Harold was more a television man than a reader. A basket with his dirty laundry was next to the wall; I recognized his blue plaid shirt on top, the one Louisa said she loved.

I looked around and startled. Glitter Jesus. Hanging behind me on the wall. He was Gary's creation, a depiction on black velvet that vaguely resembled a blond Elvis, add on a sparkling halo. Utterly sincere, Gary had made it himself as a gift for Louisa after he was Saved. He always did fancy himself to be artistically talented, which was wrong, so wrong. It was as bad as Louisa had told me on the phone. I'd chided her that she needed to hang it anyway, but she'd kept stashing it where she needn't look at it. Other than Glitter Jesus, though, the rest of the room was entirely Louisa and Harold's, as it had been the day Harold died.

I made my way into the master bathroom. There on the counter was Harold's toothbrush nestled in a glass next to what I assumed was Louisa's at the time. His razor, on the sink. Shaving cream, definitely for men. A man's hairbrush, too, gray hair matted at the bottom of the bristles. Prescription bottles lined up with Harold's name on them. It was too much, too much.

I left the bathroom, quietly pulled the door shut behind me. I looked around the bedroom again. This time I scanned Louisa's bureau. Of course, I'd seen the picture of Harold there before. There was an anniversary card standing up. It must have been the last he'd given her. *For My Wonderful Wife*, curly script flourished over a bed of roses. Oh, how those two did love each other. I always knew that. My eyes started to water. I had cards like that from Charlie. They were packed in one of the boxes I'd brought, one that I'd not been able to bear opening.

On Louisa's dresser, I saw a scrap of paper, too, with Harold's handwriting, and picked it up to read. I shouldn't have taken the time. That was my mistake. Otherwise I might have gotten out of the room, shut the door, and she'd not have caught me in there. As it turned out, she was able to tiptoe in behind me while I was engrossed in Harold's last list, which apparently had to do with parts his tractor might need.

I was so startled I jumped and screamed. Which, of course, made me look guilty.

Louisa just stared at me, waiting for me to give it up. I'm the older sister, though, and I know all about the best defense.

"You've let your hair go way too long. If you get some Miss Clairol in town, I'll do your roots for you," I said. It was a decent try, but she just stood there, hands on her hips, narrowing her eyes to slits.

I took another shot, going for a direct hit this time. "So what is this, some kind of crazy memorial to Harold? I thought you had finally moved on," I said. Perhaps I could have phrased that better.

"Looking for something?" she shot at me angrily. "Put that down," she said, meaning Harold's note. I did and took a couple of steps away from his dresser toward her.

"What's going on?" I wasn't about to back down. "I thought you were doing . . . better."

"I. Am. Fine." This wasn't good. She'd crossed her arms over her chest.

"Louisa." I softened my tone. "Honey, it's me. What's going on? You can tell me."

"I told you after he died. I'll always be Harold's wife. This is Harold's space, Harold's bathroom, Harold's bed. I'm not sharing it with another man. Please close the door behind you and keep it closed." Then she turned and walked out.

* * *

After that fiasco, things settled down some. It was a whole peaceful three days before Gus showed up, probably scared to death of what Louisa's big sister might have to say, having doubtless heard all kinds of stories about me, entirely true, since I'm the sensible one of the two of us. I remembered Gus from high school—skinny, acne, undistinguished. When he did make an entrance, it was in an entirely different body ("puffy," Louisa called it, with a gray crew cut, and glasses too tight on his face), and with a peace offering of paint charts, telling me to pick any color for my room I wanted, because Louisa had a charge account at the Supply Company and he was authorized to sign for any improvements she wanted to the house or property. And she wanted my room done to my specifications. She'd already laid out catalogs for me to pick out a bedspread and new curtains once I chose the wall and trim colors.

I wanted a woodsy green with white trim. Louisa rolled her eyes but managed to bite her tongue. She'd suggested hydrangea blue, her favorite color, pointing out for the thousandth time that it would match my eyes. It was a good thing she didn't persist. Maybe she didn't even remember that green and white were the colors of Charlie's and my bedroom, or did she think I'd lost my memory as well as my husband and home?

Oh, maybe that sounds ungrateful, and truly I wasn't. I needed my people, including Gary, who drives Louisa up a tree sometimes. It was that somehow Louisa's mourning managed to fill the available space, like a canvas already fully painted, with the length of her marriage and the magnitude of the two tragedies, that there seemed no room for mine. I kept it to myself, releasing it in private, in my room at night, and when Jessie decided she wanted to sleep with me—though I'd never been a dog person in my former life—I welcomed the familiar comfort of soft, steady breathing and occasional soft snoring, the felt safety of a near body. Charlie, my Charlie. *I've not forgotten,* I'd whisper. *I love you. I miss you. Stay with me. Thank you for our time.*

"I have my own money," was all I said about the bedroom paint colors I wanted, which weren't on the chart Gus had brought. "I want to pay for this." I knew perfectly well that Charlie had left me far better off than Harold had left Louisa, and her own pension, after all those years in the classroom, was shameful. "I insist on paying my share of the expenses around here, too. Or I can't live here. That's the way it's going to be. Isn't Gary going to be upset about losing his room?"

"Gary's in his forties. Don't you think it's time?" Louisa had brushed me off about that, and she had a point there. I didn't bring up the stupidity of Louisa's refusing to use the second bathroom, knowing it was too delicate a subject to argue about. And besides, Gus hadn't been around to crowd the one in the hallway with a man, either, so I knew I didn't have an upright toilet seat to fall into yet. Really, though, I was chafing about my not getting the guest room, which was bigger than Gary's old room and had better light and a queen-size bed. It just seemed silly to me for Louisa not to acknowledge that Harold was gone and that she was sleeping with Gus, that it was perfectly fine for her to go on with her life by redecorating the master bedroom and bath.

I didn't know then what a good thing it would turn out to be that that room was sacrosanct, that everyone knew not to open the door, how badly we—I—would need it for the Grand Plan of my life that would make Louisa look like an amateur Planner. I suppose I should admit, she did assist me, even if she didn't want to at first.

During the daytimes, I'd distracted myself from thinking about Charlie: unpacked, gotten used to Jessie, who'd taken to me like a yellow shadow, and to Marvelle and the girls wandering around. Louisa talked to the chickens and the animals so much I was never sure if one of her comments had been addressed to me. That was a bit of a bump in the road until I caught on that it was best to shut up unless she added, "Sister?" at the end of a question.

Gus showed up the fourth day with new samples, I picked the colors and he left again, pecking Louisa's cheek on the way out in a brotherly manner. *Ha*, I thought. *Don't think you're fooling me, you old lech*. But being, as I've told you, the sensible one, I kept my mouth shut. After all, it takes two to tango and she's my sister.

I helped out in the enormous garden, harvesting vegetables out in the August heat. I remembered about that because Mom used to raise our vegetables. Louisa always cans them for the winter, more heat in the kitchen with the cleaning and cutting and cooking. It seemed unnecessarily labor-intensive to me when there are grocery stores available and I have money, but my sister went on and on about the goodness of the land and the meaning and self-sufficiency of raising your own food. She shook her head at me and said, "It's a lot of work, but it's good work. Did you have a total blood transfusion down South? Have you forgotten?"

I guess I had, some of it, anyway. The backbreaking parts. There's an upside and a downside to every way of life. It was the downside of this life that I hadn't missed when I was in Atlanta.

The next night was when things started to change. Meaning that people started showing up, and I started to realize that it was going to get busy around here, and not just with the animals.

After breakfast, I got dressed for another day in the garden. We tried to get out there early, in the morning cool, saving the indoor work for lunchtime and the afternoon. I thought that I was being helpful and that felt good. "Brandon may be here this afternoon to mow," she said. "Rosie can't take care of all the grass, much as she likes to eat. Such a sweetheart.

Brandon, I mean. Well, Rosie, too. But Brandon, you remember him, he brought Jessie home the first night you were here? I keep a list of barn chores for him to do. He's working for Al Pelley this summer, too, he's my guy who does the plowing and planting since Harold's gone. The field corn, you know. Then he harvests in the fall. He'll have his annual hissy fit about what I keep wild for the deer. Kinda funny. I'll keep him on, though, as long as he does what I want." That's just how Louisa talks. She gets to the point eventually.

"I remember," I said. "I mean I know the name." Then, an afterthought, I added, "Brandon seemed like a good kid. We were so exhausted that night I didn't talk to him, but he was really polite."

"I'm proud of him," Louisa said. "Hard worker, and a reader." Louisa didn't have higher praise than that someone loved to read. Sometime after Harold died, she'd told me that she was helping Brandon plan for college. "He's got those blue eyes . . ." she said, and right then I could tell that he put her in mind of Cody, the grandson she'd lost. I patted her hand so she'd know I understood. Some things are better unspoken.

Louisa waited until that afternoon, when Brandon was there, to spring it on me that Gus would be coming to dinner. "Oh," I said. "Huh. What will we have?" I knew we hadn't been to the grocery store yet. That was supposed to be tomorrow, she'd said, for staples.

"You worried about our dearth of vegetables?" she teased. "Gus'll bring the meat, for you and him. He always does. There's huckleberries to pick behind the barn, and I'll bake a pie. I've got a crust in the freezer already. Brandon's not staying tonight, he's already got plans with some high school friends. You know, getting together with them before he goes back to school." It hadn't occurred to me that Brandon might be included. I had a lot to learn.

"Uh . . . Al?" I was afraid to ask.

"You're kidding, right?" she said disdainfully. "Never. What do you think I'm running here?" *Well,* I thought, *how would I know? There's apparently a lot you haven't told me.* But I kept my mouth shut then, at least while I was figuring things out. I figured I'd use that strategy unless there was something I really had to fight for. I didn't know then that soon there would be.

When Gus came right after lunch, sure enough, he brought pork chops with him and stuck them in the refrigerator as comfortably as if he did it regularly. Maybe he did. It was all news to me. And he had brought extra for me—Louisa had gone vegetarian after Harold died, but said Gus was meat and potatoes all the way. He arrived in paint-splattered clothes and brought a gallon of the wall color I'd picked, plus a quart of the trim for the closet and woodwork, a supply of rollers, a tray and some brushes. Carried in Harold's old ladder from the barn and got to work while Louisa and I continued canning vegetables, which I don't mind telling you I was already mighty sick of doing.

"How many jars of tomato sauce do you figure we'll use this winter? I mean, after breakfast, lunch, and dinner every day, November through April?" I don't even charge extra for subtle sarcasm, which I feel is generous of me. We were standing at the stove "bathing" jar after jar in boiling water until the lids sealed, after peeling, coring, and cooking huge vats of tomatoes from the garden. I've heard that saunas keep your skin looking young. Well, now I wanted to check myself in the bathroom mirror, because I figured I must have reverted to the skin of my thirties. Another day or two of this, and I'd be totally wrinkle-free.

"Don't be ridiculous," my sister said. "It's a basic ingredient in many recipes, and I season it brilliantly. People beg for my recipe. Don't think you can sell it, either."

I decided to try another approach. "You do realize that all the steam in here is going to peel the wallpaper off?"

"Good. Wallpaper is out of style. *You* told me that, remember? Gus can paint it. That old wallpaper is tired. What color shall we go with?"

I was doomed.

Chapter 6

Gary

It hadn't been easy, starting his church, but Gary was positive it was what God wanted him to do. The crowd that Brother Zachariah had drawn to the tent revival was hungry for the assurance and certainty of salvation, the ease of obtaining it. They'd wanted more, Gary had seen that, just as he saw a way to redeem his own life by giving the people what they wanted, letting them donate like Brother Zachariah had let him. Surely they'd bring their brothers and sisters, neighbors and friends into the church, too, and Gary would be the one to baptize their children. He'd Save them all. Well, technically, Jesus would, but Gary would be His right hand man. Sooner or later, he told himself, it would happen. He'd seen it like a heavenly vision.

He hadn't thought the new church would have to meet in the rented barn for several years while the small flock saved money, but he hadn't expected to have to buy land, either. He'd told them he'd have the land, meaning his mother's, but that hadn't exactly worked out. The members didn't blame him, though. He helped them understand, to feel sorry and sad for his poor mother who didn't grasp what God wanted. They were all praying for her and not holding a grudge, even though it meant that now they all had to have their many meetings in a barn which still smelled faintly of manure even

though the Clean for Jesus Committee had done their dili-
gent best with Pine-Sol. (That had set off Sister Rebecca's al-
lergies something fierce and she started skipping services
until they switched brands.)

At least the folding chairs that members had scrounged
from various places were set in neat rows, and he'd fashioned
something like a pulpit in the front. His own art work was on
the wall behind it, a large portrait of Jesus, even better than
the one he'd done for his mother because this time he'd used
both gold and silver glitter in the halo and found a way to
make the portrait suggest both the blood of suffering, by
adding just a few spots of red glitter on the forehead, and
shining salvation, by the use of the silver and gold. Some of
the members were struck speechless in awe of his talent.
When he had more time, he planned to do more art to brighten
up the barn walls, now that it was clear they couldn't afford
to build a new church anytime soon.

Now, back home from Atlanta, Gary thought about how
death led to rebirth. His ministry had been validated by the
Baptist, and not only that, he'd been of true service to his
aunt, who'd always been good to him. His flock needed him,
and there was much to which to attend. Sister Amanda had
misplaced the telephone prayer list, for one, and the Sisters
who worked the daily prayer call team were in such an up-
roar about it that Sister Amanda was going to be in need of
prayers for herself. He was going to have to call a meeting,
that was obvious. It was a plain relief that having received
the mercy message, too, at Charlie's funeral, and knowing
now that he was forgiven, he guessed he needn't avoid the office he'd fashioned for himself, at one end of the barn. It had
been a tack room in the olden days, before the farm changed
hands and the next owners brought in cattle, which was why
it was separate, with a door closing it off from the main part
of the barn. Gary had laid flooring down himself, well, with

the help of some of the church Brothers, who agreed he needed a private place to meet with members of the flock and to prepare the weekly messages and plan revivals.

As it turned out, the old saddle racks had been the ideal base for shelving. Take them down, tack up some drywall, apply some paint, and it had looked downright professional once the members sussed out some used furniture, a couple lamps, and an old desk that had been in someone's garage or barn. He'd hung up his community college associate's degree and his printable certificate of ordination, in Walmart's nicest frames, and his church had been in business.

It hadn't been comfortable to be in his office, though, not since Rosalina, and he'd been doing his work in odd places most of the time. It wasn't that he hadn't tried. He'd sit at the desk and get started, but then his eyes would wander from his laptop screen to the old upholstered armchair, donated by Sister Rebecca and Brother Thomas, which now had an accusatory stain on the seat, which might have been there all along but he hadn't noticed before. He'd see that storm-colored chair, how it looked for all the world like a lap, like his lap, which he'd eased Rosalina onto, and then he had to leave the office every time, before he started looking at the rug—a remnant from the Walmart over in Elmont—and remember that it was five by eight, as if he'd planned to choose something big enough to cushion two bodies, which he swore to God he never had.

Now, though, the merciful message of forgiveness, it was time to realize that when God cleaned your soul, He expected you to move on. He wouldn't have provided the church, Gary reasoned to himself, if He didn't want you working in the building. And so, Gary woke that blindingly bright Wednesday morning after a day of rest following the trip from Atlanta, unloading his aunt CarolSue's stuff, carting away his mother's cast-offs, which of course the church could use, not that he mentioned that to her, a trip to Elmont to turn in the U-Haul, and a twelve-hour sleep in what passed for a parsonage—a room and bath, with kitchen privileges, in Sister Martha's farmhouse—and went to the church. He let himself into his office, took a breath, exhaled, breathed in again and sat at his desk. Cautious, he looked around. *Praise God,* he said. *Thank you Jesus. It's over, it's done. I'm free.*

CarolSue

"Does anyone around here play bridge?" I asked Louisa the next day. I was sweating in the steamy kitchen while I was drying the canning pot and two dozen more mason jars, bands, and lids for the next day's use. After the hot afternoon's work. Yes, the house would cool down a lot with twilight, and, of course, now that we were finished—until tomorrow—with Louisa's manic canning. I was dying to buy her a giant freezer and be done with this ridiculous daily sauna, but she wouldn't hear of it.

"Huh? The bridge will be out again in September. Drives us insane. The detour is way out of the way. Every damn fall some part of it needs repair."

"What are you talking about? I asked if anyone plays bridge?"

"Yeah, it's a game the idiot Great State of Indiana plays with the rural population that can't muster enough votes to get rid of the administration."

"Louisa. Look at me. Bridge. It's a card game." I enunciated as if she were slow-witted or had been drinking her special tea, which I think she had anyway. "I played it with other women. In Atlanta. You remember. I used to tell you. I was in a couple of bridge clubs. We had a fancy lunch. We played bridge."

"Oh. That. No."

"Are you sure?"

"Why would they do that?"

I had another exceedingly strong homicidal impulse right then. What could I do? The puffy sheriff would be along, doubtless, before I could deal with my sister's body, although the notion of digging up all the remaining produce and burying her in the damn vegetable garden was attractive. I temporarily shelved the notion for later consideration and resorted to my nonlethal weapon of choice for the moment.

"Oh, I don't know. Why would anyone want to relax and enjoy themselves in air-conditioned comfort, laughing with friends and doing something intellectually challenging, when they could spend all day every day in a sweat shop slaving to produce what she could easily and cheaply buy in a grocery store? I have no idea."

As you can imagine, I'd gone too far.

"I'm sorry," I said. She'd turned away, facing the sink now, refusing to look at me, staring at the old wallpaper with the little peach and yellow watering cans and flowers she and Harold had chosen many years ago that she said she was ready to take down. But hadn't. I'd moved here, but was clinging to my old life, the one Charlie had brought me to, that I'd shared with him each time I'd come home from those afternoon games. And Louisa: "napping" with Gus, but oh, no mistaking that she was still and ever Harold's wife. How could she not understand?

"I'm sorry, too," she finally said. "We've lived such different lives."

"Until now," I said. "But I need to find . . . I don't know. What do you do?"

"You know what I do."

"I can't tutor," I said. "You're a teacher. You had a career. You have the animals and helping at the school, and now Gus and helping Brandon, and . . . I don't know how to fit."

"You could help supervise at the playground at school? They always need volunteer adults. How about maybe helping the librarian there? Marian loves a volunteer."

"School is your thing. I can't just slide into your life. I should have thought of all this before I came."

Indeed. I should have thought of all that before I came.

Louisa

Louisa knew, she knew all too well that CarolSue was hurting. It didn't matter that she wasn't talking about Charlie; he was all she thought about, all she really wanted when she brought up something like ladies' card games. Because those were part of her Atlanta life and her Atlanta life was her Charlie life, and that was gone. Louisa knew.

Did CarolSue think Louisa didn't understand? Sure, it was different when Louisa lost Harold, but so much the same, too. Louisa knew that given an empty house at night, CarolSue would wander around the rooms like a silent ghost, touching this and that, guessing what Charlie had last touched with his warm hand. Or what was maybe worse: the nights she would keen, a mortally wounded animal. Louisa had been in her own husband-empty house after CarolSue had gone back home, and Marvelle's effort to provide comfort hadn't kept her in her bed. Back in Atlanta, CarolSue hadn't even had a cat, and certainly not her sister, plus Marvelle, Jessie, and the hens to help her go on.

Louisa figured that CarolSue outside working in the garden was the best thing for her. The bounty and the beauty of growing things, the vibrant vegetables and flowers, fresh air and the physical fatigue from the good labor: All this would distract her, and she'd fall into an exhausted sleep at night. Louisa always did. Except the nights that Gus stayed over, not that he'd been able to do that since CarolSue had moved in. Louisa knew CarolSue was up and about and neither she nor Gus felt right about it. "It would be like rubbing her face in sleeping alone all night," Gus said, and Louisa had to admit that was exactly right.

If she could just get CarolSue over worrying about keeping her manicure, and her sister would just give the farm—and the woods and the animals—a chance, they'd help her heal. The animals and the land had saved Louisa's life. They were the lifeblood she had to give the sister she loved. Louisa was sure of her Plan, especially since it was the only one she had.

Chapter 7

Gary

It had been Sister Martha, in a twist about Sister Amanda misplacing the prayer list, who mentioned that a stranger had been looking for Reverend Gary. It was shortly before the meeting he'd called about it, that she'd told him, her voice quivering with the importance of her report. "I saw her twice while you were away. Scared little rabbit, I'm telling you. Looking for the preacher, she said. She's not American, no sir. Ran off. I made sure she wasn't stealing nothing, but she weren't."

Gary's heart dropped, but then he thought no, it's not possible. That was way too long ago, and I've been forgiven. There are all kinds of immigrants around here, all of them in need.

"Not a member in need, though?"

"Not one of ours." Martha's voice, thin and high-pitched, had a whiff of disdain, like she might smell something slightly bad in the air. But her long nose had pinched nostrils and Gary reminded himself that she often sounded that way. Jesus would know her heart and judge her soon enough at the Second Coming, so he refrained from chastising her. Since she was a member, he hoped she wouldn't be among the Left Behind.

"Still, we minister, Sister Martha." Gary tried a mild reminder, just in case Jesus was listening in.

"Didn't ask for nothing. Tried to give her the daily prayer, but she didn't want it. Told her you'd be back today." Sister Martha crossed her arms over her chest.

"That's fine, then. I'm glad you checked the church when you were able. That's doing God's work, Sister."

"Asked her for a donation, but she ran off, like I said."

"Hmm. Well, good try. So we'll get through this prayer-list meeting and then start working on the revival, all right? Do we have a committee going?"

"Got a start on that . . ."

And the woman hadn't come up again. He put it out of his mind.

Sunlight poured as if from a pitcher from the small high window onto Gary's desk now as the morning advanced. It was going to be a good day. He had the praise service to get ready for that night, the Saturday healing service, Sunday's three services, no matter how small the attendance at each, and recruitment plans to work on. The revival. He wondered if his aunt CarolSue would maybe help him talk his mother into letting him use her field for the tent. She'd been pretty mad about it that one time and said never again, but he'd never had Aunt CarolSue maybe in his corner before. Something to think about.

It was two days later, Friday, when he was in his office, revising the Sunday message about the Biblical requirement of tithing, on his laptop. Apparently, some members didn't yet understand the point. He had the door to his office closed as the Clean for Jesus Committee had been in earlier, sweeping and dusting, and those ladies had a pesky tendency to gossip while they worked. Occasionally Gary picked up some useful information by eavesdropping, but today he had too much work to do and couldn't afford the time. They'd been gone for at least a half hour since Sister Amanda had knocked and stuck her head in to wish him good day and tell him they were finished and leaving.

He'd just been thinking that maybe he'd take a break and go get himself some lunch when he thought he heard someone come into the church. He stayed where he was, hoping not to be waylaid by idle chatter, wished the van weren't parked right outside advertising his presence. Unless, of course, he reminded himself, a member was in need of ministry.

Gary was in luck. Or Jesus was smiling on him, he preferred to think, approving of the Sunday message about tithing he'd been polishing as his own shiny offering. He waited in his office but no knock came on his door and a few minutes later he heard the church door close again. Blessed silence. Shortly after, off in the distance, he thought he heard a very old-sounding car—or one in need of a new muffler, perhaps—but it could have been some farm equipment. It didn't matter. His stomach rumbled, not that he'd forgotten the length of time since breakfast. Sure of an easy getaway to a hefty sandwich, he pushed his chair back and left the office.

He made it four steps beyond the office door.

A baby carrier blocked his path. *And, oh Jesus, that's a real baby in it?*

Panic washed over Gary like the Red Sea. "Hey," he shouted. "Hey, who's here?" He ran around the building, looked behind the wooden altar, prayer rail, and tub for immersion baptisms that members had helped either create or rescue from various secondhand sources. It was quite pointless, he knew, but what alternative did he have? Other than in the tub itself, and how would that work since the top was open, there wasn't anywhere to hide in the barn. It wasn't like folding chairs would keep a secret, yet still he got down on hands and knees to look, desperate. Kept shouting, too.

He hadn't even looked, not really, in the baby carrier. Now, from across the barn, he saw movement. A hand waving up was all, then more movement. It was definitely alive. He hadn't been mistaken.

Oh Jesus, oh God.

He walked toward it slowly, as if it were a snake. What was he supposed to do? He figured he'd get back into his office and call one of the Sisters who had a young child. He remembered nothing from when Cody was a baby. Nicole had taken care of him, with help from Gary's mother. Now, though, this was a church problem, obviously. Maybe a member in distress needed babysitting. Gary tried to puzzle it out as he walked, slow and now quiet as cotton through the barn, calming himself.

He approached the back of the carrier, which faced the office, heart pounding as if it might detonate. A small sound, something between a coo and a whimper, came out of it and he startled, less because of that than because a small object hit the floor with a soft ping right after that. He took a step backward, and then when nothing more happened, he leaned over to see what it was. A pacifier, shaped like a nipple. Oh. He wondered if he should give it back to the baby, but then thought it might be dirty. Did it have to be sterilized or something? He couldn't remember.

The baby started to fuss. Not really cry hard, just fuss. Gary walked around to look at it. Oh. There was a bottle tucked next to it—her, he guessed, since the thing she had on was pink, and that meant a girl, didn't it? And two—no three—disposable diapers on the other side. He was afraid to move anything, but he was going to have to, he guessed. She was strapped in at least, so if he didn't drop the carrier, it would be okay. He picked up the carrier, which was gray and looked worn, maybe a little dirty, and then he saw the papers beneath it. Gently, he set the carrier back down and retrieved a folded piece of paper with his name, misspelled in neat childish handwriting: Rev Garry. With it, another folded paper, which he opened first.

Certificate of Live Birth. Female. Mother's name. Rosalina Gonzales. Wait, not the same person, it was a common name probably, she said her name was Lopez.

Father's name. Garry Hawkins. What?

What?

No. No. No.

Gary stood stunned. He studied the birth certificate, willing it to be false, fingered the raised state seal on it. If Jesus had appeared before him in the flesh with a deck of playing cards and challenged him to a game of strip poker with six women, he would not have been more shocked or immobilized. The baby stirred and fussed mildly, squirming. A moment later, she passed gas or worse.

Gary opened the note with his name on it, already limp from the sweat of his hands. *Rev Garry. Gracia is yours, also a U.S. citizen, like you. I give you her proof. I can't take care of her. She must stay with you, a safe American, and get a good education. Please teach her what's right. Tell her that her mama loved her so much. Thank you.*

Then the crying began. By both of them. Gary remembered the pacifier, which he'd put in his shirt pocket, wiped it on his shirt front, praying the Clean for Jesus Committee hadn't used anything poisonous on the floor, and gingerly stuck it in the vicinity of the baby's lips. She rooted for it and then grabbed it hungrily, her pink bud of a mouth closing around it. He stood, staring down, as the infant quieted, sucking fiercely. Closed his wet eyes for a long moment. "Help me, Jesus. Take this cup from me." Opened his eyes. The baby was still there.

He had absolutely no idea what to do.

Chapter 8

CarolSue

I heard tires out on the gravel and looked out the front window. Uh-oh. Louisa wasn't going to be happy. The church van was moving down the driveway. Gary, and it was barely lunchtime. My sister did not appreciate her son's drop-in visits, which usually involved some attempt to draw her into his church—which she wanted no part of. Before you judge Louisa's attitude, you ought to know that Gary's whole sudden foray into religion started with a money-scamming traveling tent-revivalist who plain took advantage of Gary's guilt by promising holy redemption after Gary's son Cody was killed by a drunk driver. Gary had forced the boy to walk the distance home at twilight along a state highway after football practice for some obscure crime, a decision that wouldn't pass anyone's Sensible and Safe Parenting Checklist, so Cody's mother, Louisa, and Harold had hard feelings in the mixed drink of their grief, and I imagine Gary didn't get either an acquittal or mercy from them. Louisa tried to swallow back blame, I know she tried. It's not like she doesn't love him. Perhaps it's easier for his only aunt, just that bit removed, to understand how desperate he'd been for a whisper of forgiveness. He found it, not whispered but shouted, lit by fiery Bible verses, and dangling a hefty price tag, of course. All Gary had to do was empty his bank account for assurance of heaven. That was before he got himself internet-ordained, of course. Louisa and Harold went bonkers.

Anyway, Louisa was out back in the vegetable garden when he drove in. Honestly, I was worried that she was going to get Brandon to bring over a pickup truck and use that to bring her damn vegetables up to the house instead of the garden cart she'd been using trip after trip after endless trip. I kept asking her how many towns we had to feed and for how many years following the nuclear attack for which we were obviously preparing. I seriously wished I knew something about gardening, something useful I mean, like what would kill off healthy vegetable plants that were producing way too much. How many string beans does a body need? How much zucchini and canned tomatoes? I'd come in to use the bathroom and was being as slow about getting back out to help as I possibly could, which is why I happened to be lingering in the living room. I might have been sort of looking at a magazine, in fact.

There was Gary getting out of the car, and pretty soon he'd be at the front door. I wouldn't mind visiting with my nephew, but I knew it wouldn't go over well if Louisa thought that was my idea, so I ducked out of sight and locked the front door so Gary would go around back and find us both diligently working. Then Louisa would avoid him by handing him off to me, I'd be doing her a favor and get out of picking beans, amen.

I sidled back from the door, ducked down again, and scurried—stepping over Marvelle, past Harold's recliner, still there, and through the kitchen to the back door, Jessie at my heels. I moved off the back steps to the garden, dodging roaming chickens with what might have been considered uncharacteristic speed.

"Sorry I took so long, my digestion's not quite right today," I said, and started pulling beans.

"Eating more vegetables," Louisa said. "Good for you."

"Yup. Bless your heart."

"Don't start with me, Sister. They are much better for you than meat."

"I know, I know. Is Gus coming again tonight?" I fervently hoped he wasn't, and I especially hoped they weren't going to take a nap together before dinner, because let me tell you, their naps didn't involve a lot of sleeping as best as I could discern. Seriously, can you fathom? There I am turning the television up so loud you'd think I was Charlie, or taking Jessie for a walk, anything I could think of. Louisa would have some of her special tea, and Gus would have just the Wild Turkey ingredient, straight up, and they'd both have these silly smiles on their faces and be passing secret looks at each other like they were Brandon's age, which must have been eighteen but honestly, he looked twelve to me.

"Might come by, but he had to take the truck in for maintenance or something and so his schedule is messed up. He told me about it but I didn't pay a lot of attention once he started explaining what was wrong."

"Half the time he shows up in the squad car . . ."

"True, but I guess the deputy's squad car is in the shop. So they're down a car. I told you I quit paying close attention. Can you pull those weeds while you're in that row?"

I was hot and hungry and couldn't figure out why Gary was taking so long to figure out that no one was coming to the front door. Why didn't he walk around to the back of the house? He sure knew where to find us. He'd done it before. Louisa plain couldn't hide from him, she'd told me. I admit I was hooked on the notion of sitting in the cool—well, maybe not cool, but cooler—house with iced tea, visiting with my nephew and maybe sharing memories of Charlie with him without feeling guilty. What a welcome rescue he was going to be.

Isn't it strange how we think one thing is going to happen

and something utterly different happens? Inside we are so disappointed and have no idea that life might just have handed us a huge gift. And it's so difficult to remember to be open to that possibility, isn't it? Because we never know when it might be the case.

Anyway, as it happened, I was annoyed with Gary for dawdling because now it was his fault that I was getting fried and still picking beans—and now even being instructed to weed, which was truly adding insult to injury because, I mean, why? Let the fall frost kill the weeds. This ground wasn't going to be planted again before spring, right?

I went into a spin cycle then; teary, I wanted my old life back. I wanted my husband tinkering with stupid stuff out in our garage in Atlanta. I wanted a good game of bridge after a ladies' lunch at the club, all of us wearing colorful slacks with coordinated blouses, necklaces, matching earrings. I'd gotten to be a decent enough player that I was always asked to be someone's partner, never had to go looking for one. In comparison to her own, I thought Louisa saw my life as frivolous, or maybe just overprivileged, lacking depth and meaning. Perhaps she thought easy come, easy go. I only knew that in moments like this when some small disappointment opened a door, I'd be overcome with the giant loss of Charlie and our life together. And I didn't feel like I could cry to her because we were only married fifteen years and it didn't compare to the long shadow of her life with Harold, well over forty years when he died. Maybe I could have, and she'd have understood that even though he wasn't the father of the babies I'd lost, he wasn't the man who abandoned me, either. He never would have, not if he could have helped it. Maybe she would have understood that love isn't measured in length of time, but in tenderness and gratitude. But now there were things she'd not told me, and things I couldn't tell her.

Five minutes turned into ten, and I couldn't stand it anymore. Had Gary left? Was this the one time he wasn't going to, in Louisa's words—snoop all over the place until he sniffed her out? (I've mentioned how he gets on her nerves, haven't I? For the first time, I truly found myself on her side of the fence, except for not sniffing her out, the irony of which wasn't lost on me.) "I've got to go to the bathroom," I said. Perhaps I could have been smarter, since that was exactly what I'd claimed before.

"I'm the one with a bladder the size of a pea, and I'm not running in every fifteen minutes," she said, giving me The Look, the same tilted chin, squinty-eyed Look we both learned from our mother that said I'm Not Buying This Crap.

"Oh, for heaven's sake. I'm not discussing this," I said. "Your hair is a mess. Have you got a box of your color? Let's get those roots done," I said as I dumped the meager pile of green beans I'd picked onto her much larger pile and headed for the back door. I hate it when she catches me like that.

"Go around, not through those! Stop! Those are winter squash and pumpkins."

I turned, trying to grind my shoe down a bit on whatever I was standing on. "Do we have to can them?"

"Well, pumpkin, sure, but not winter squash. Good grief, what do you think we make pumpkin pie with, huh? Tomatoes?" She shook her head at my astonishing ignorance and laughed.

Hoping I was killing a pumpkin vine, I twisted my foot again before dutifully getting out of the garden to make my way to the back door. On the stoop, I stopped with my hand on the knob and looked back at Louisa, surrounded by her neatly planted and tended vegetables, so high and full and lushly green, the purple eggplant glistening on the ground, the bright spots of tomato red-hanging ready, everything offering its goodness and life like my good sister, who I wanted to kill, or at least leave standing there in dirty cutoffs, wild hair, and no makeup, while I went inside and packed whatever I still had to go back to Ladies' Bridge Luncheons at the country club in Atlanta. In that moment, Louisa looked up, waved and me, and called, "Well, go ahead, get on with it," and so that's exactly what I decided to do.

As quickly as I'd decided to move in with Louisa—or she'd decided it for me—I'd decided to move back. And I was resolute about that much. *That's not much of a Plan. Didn't you claim to be the sensible one? You emptied out your house, didn't you? Where exactly are you going to go?* I imagine you're muttering all that right now. I was going to have to come up with a Plan, true enough, and I couldn't see expecting Louisa to be a whole lot of help with that right off the bat, but I'm sensible, and even if I don't lay out a huge Plan the way Louisa does, I don't drink special tea in the late afternoons with Marvelle and the girls—meaning the chickens, remember—although I'll admit it's not bad, and now and then I join them.

Energized by my decisiveness, I marched through the kitchen and thought to check out the living room window. Really, I expected Gary's church van to be gone. It was there, and not only that, he had the back passenger side open and was bent at the waist leaning far into it, his elbows sawing back and forth, clearly working on something, although I couldn't imagine what. I watched, trying to keep back enough to stay out of sight if he looked at the house.

He straightened up and wiped his forehead with the back of his arm, looked sideways at the house. His face wasn't clear, but I thought he looked upset. Then, a moment later, the upper half of his body disappeared back into the van.

Isn't it amazing how we can be completely derailed, slip from one track right onto another? Gary is easier for me than for his mother, so perhaps you've already guessed that I opened the front door and started toward him without another thought.

"Gary? Are you all right? What's the matter, honey?"

"Oh, Aunt CarolSue. I could really use a hand," he called back, pointing into the back seat.

As I got close to him, I saw his face was bleary with sweat, his eyes bloodshot.

"What's happened?"

"Someone has left her baby at the church and I need help taking care of it—her, I mean—while I find the mother and minister to her. So she takes her baby back. Like God wants."

Sure enough, there was a baby in the back seat, in a baby carrier. I heard her whimpering before I saw her, sweaty, overdressed, with a blanket on her in this heat! A pink hat! I pulled off the blanket and saw the problem. Gary had been trying to change a dirty diaper. Clearly he had no idea what he was doing.

"Oh honey. Oh honey. Okay, let's get her cleaned up, and we'll call Gus. Or did you do that already?"

"No! We're not calling Gus. It's not a police matter. It's a church matter."

"Gary, sweetheart. You can't. She wasn't even belted in a safety seat right. You can't do this. What do you have for her?"

"That stuff," he said, pointing to a couple of diapers and a bottle on the seat next to the baby carrier. "Pretty much nothing." Gary's curly hair was sticking to his forehead and neck. The back of his plaid shirt stuck to his skin. If it hadn't been so hot, I'd have thought he'd been crying.

"Don't you see? You can't—" I shook my head and didn't argue more then, seeing how his face turned to stone, glistening with sweat or tears. "Let's change her and cool her down." The baby had to be taken care of. Louisa could talk sense into Gary. "She's a mess. Run into the house and get me two wet washcloths. Ring them out well. And a plastic bag. Make that two old plastic bags. I don't suppose you know her name?"

"Gracia."

"Gray-see-a? Is that like Grace or Gracie?"

"Close enough. I like that," my nephew said.

While Gary jogged for the house, I soothed Gracie as best I could. She was a beautiful baby—well, aren't they all?—but she really was. Tiny, with lots of dark hair and those navy-blue eyes they're all born with. I couldn't pick her up without covering myself with poop, which Gary had done an astonishingly inadequate job of cleaning up with tissues, smearing it hopelessly up her belly and down her legs. I held her tiny fingers and talked to her, stroked her head. She looked at me, right in the eyes it seemed, and quieted. "You'll be all right, honey, listen to me, sweetheart. Everything's going to be fine, don't be scared, it's all right, it's all right," I crooned. I hoped I wasn't lying to her. I so wanted to be telling her the truth. I had to believe I was.

Gary came back with the wet washcloths I'd sent for, having forgotten I'd told him to wring them out well, and not had the sense to think that an infant shouldn't have the shock of cold water on her skin regardless of how it might feel to a grown man. I sent him back. When he reappeared with luke-warm ones, I used the first cloth on Gracie, lifting her legs and cleaning the folds—of course her onesie was dirty. "What else do you have to put her in?"

"Ah, just the two more diapers. Wait, this is with the diapers."

"Bless your heart, you're not serious? That's an undershirt. Give it to me." I bit my tongue. He'd had a baby, lived with one of his own. Had Nicole done everything or had he blotted out all memories of Cody to endure his grief?

I finished cleaning the baby with the second washcloth, after taking off the messy onesie, and put both cloths and the onesie in one of the bags. I put the dirty disposable diaper and all Gary's used tissues—picking them up gingerly from the floor mat he'd left them on—and put them in the second. Gracie waved her arms and fussed mildly, turning her head side to side. "She's hungry," I said. "I think she's looking for a bottle . . . or her mother's . . . um . . . do you know how she's fed?"

"I got one bottle."

"ONE? Bless your heart, how long do you think that's going to last? Oh Lord, let's get her inside, it's too hot out here for this." I picked the baby up, put her over my shoulder, and headed for the front door. "God help you with your mother," I said to Gary, who still stood by the open van door, his mouth opening to say something. "Shut your mouth now, honey, and shut the van, pick up those bags, bring the bottle, and come on."

I was sitting in my own armchair from home, cradling Gracie in one arm, giving her the bottle. Marvelle stared at us suspiciously from her perch on the back of the sofa, but Jessie lay at my feet, her nose on her paws, contented. Outside, I could hear Louisa reading Gary the riot act, doubtless getting the chickens all stirred up, and she hadn't even been inside to see the reality yet. ". . . lost your mind . . . it's not *about* Jesus . . . call Gus . . ." (The business about calling Gus, by the way, is because out here in rural farm country where there's not much of a tax base, the sheriff's department is pretty much the emergency social service system, too.) I caught snatches when Louisa went into her playground control voice. Meanwhile, Gracie was looking into my eyes and I into hers. She was such a sweet little girl. Does it sound like a cliché to say her mouth was like a little rosebud? It was, though, and her eyes searched mine in such a trusting way, the same way the fingers of one of her hands latched around my right pinkie as I held her bottle.

I had to take it away halfway through to burp her, I knew; she fussed a little, but then nestled in over my shoulder, her head in the crook of my neck. I patted her back and sang a little, and she rewarded me with a huge, satisfying belch.

"Good girl, that's my good, good girl," I cooed, before I laid her back and gave her the nipple again.

She was so easy to smile at while outside the argument went on. Her eyes grew heavy and she fought sleep, sucking, stopping, sucking again. I pulled the bottle away with a couple of ounces remaining, and shouldered her again, patting her back softly. "Can you burp for me, sweetheart?" After a while she did, and then again, and she was asleep. I could tell by her weight, how she'd given her body over to mine. She felt safe, and she was.

When Louisa came in the back door, followed by Gary, I put my finger to my lips and glared a warning to them. I pointed to the capped bottle and then to the refrigerator. Both of them had apparently had an attack of total stupidity because Louisa said, out loud, "What?"

I repeated the gestures including the finger to my lips and pointed, also, to the sleeping baby. I ask you, how hard is that for the most simpleminded person to understand?

"What do you want?" said my sister, the college-educated former teacher, louder, as if the problem were one of volume. Again, I had that homicidal impulse.

I worked myself to stand without jostling Gracie, picked up the bottle from the side table myself, and carried it into the kitchen to refrigerate.

Gary and Louisa resumed arguing. I grabbed the baby carrier and headed to my bedroom with it. I didn't want to put Gracie down, but I needed them to be quiet, at least, and I couldn't intervene with her in my arms. In my room, I inched her into the carrier and took the pillowcase off my pillow to tuck it around her, so there'd be something light over her. She slept on soundly, the sleep of the innocent, the sleep of one whose needs still can be met.

"Gus will find her a good foster home. There's a list—all pre-approved by the state," Louisa was saying. She and Gary were both sweaty, but Louisa was a sight in those frayed shorts with dirt on her hands and knees and face (from wiping it with her hands), blondish hair gone wild pinned back, sunscreen forgotten—no matter how many times I remind her these days—Gary in his version of looking professional, collared plaid shirt and khakis with a belt. He does have a certain resemblance to me in the eyes—big and round and what people say is a startling blue, and he's got dark blond, curly hair that he combs to hide that it's receding. Maybe he doesn't know it's thin at the crown, too. I took the two of them in like that for a minute, trying to decide what to do. That was legal, I mean, and wouldn't wake up the baby.

"No. Just give me some time," Gary said. "All I need is some time. I'll find her. You know how the system is, Mom. She'll be judged, and she won't get her baby back. What if she can't even prove it's hers?"

"Gary, don't be dumb. Blood test."

Gary got a funny look. "Mom, I mean, give her a chance. Just keep the baby for me for a little while. It's what God wants."

"Oh, and was it God or Jesus who told you about that? Personal meeting or telephone? Or maybe Western Union." The sarcasm thing, you'll see the family talent. Gary was always at such a disadvantage because he didn't inherit it. Apparently Harold's genes were dominant in that brain area. Unfortunate for Gary.

"Hold up," I said. "Gary, what do you know about the baby and her mother? When and where did you find her?"

"Thank you for asking, Aunt CarolSue. Like I was trying to tell Mom," he said, which probably antagonized Louisa further, "I just found her a little bit ago. Somebody put her in the church while I was in my office. There was a note asking me to help because her mother couldn't take care of her."

"I don't suppose the father is in the picture," Louisa said.

"Yeah, that's rhetorical," she huffed into his silence. "So, let's see the note."

"I can't do that. It would be unethical. It's confidential."

"But you think it's a fine idea for me to keep the baby while you hunt down the mother?"

Gary shifted from one foot to the other. Closed his eyes, then opened them and looked at me for help before he looked back at Louisa.

"Um . . . yes."

Before Louisa could say any more, I inserted myself. "I think we can do that, Louisa. For a day or two. Gary, you'll have to go get formula and diapers, though. And a couple of onesies. And do that right now."

Louisa wheeled and stared at me with as much shock as if she'd caught me naked out by the mailbox while juggling tomatoes, smoking a crack pipe, and guzzling a quart of her special tea.

I shrugged and turned to go check on Gracie. Leaving Louisa speechless was sort of fun. It all fell into place as I opened my bedroom door and looked at the baby, sleeping under my pillowcase. I could wait a day or so to pack up and leave. Of course, Gary was off his rocker about this, but his heart was in the right place, a compassionate place. What was a day or two? And besides. No more picking and canning for me while I worked up a Plan to get me and my stuff back to Atlanta. I'd take care of Gracie, sweet baby Gracie.

Chapter 9

Gary

As he backed the van out of his mother's driveway, Gary couldn't believe what had just happened. It was definitely a heavenly Sign. All he had to do was find Rosalina, explain to her that this wasn't a good idea at all, maybe help her with money, which he'd probably have to borrow. He'd just have to make certain nobody found out. It would ruin his ministry for sure to be known as a fornicator, especially after all the talk when Nicole left him—although that was before he'd been Saved, of course, and his flock made allowances for that. But there was no way, no way, he could let anyone find out or all he'd done to redeem himself, all he'd done to build his church, would be lost. So he'd have to find her, was all. Find her. First, though, he reminded himself, he had to get into town and buy supplies for the baby. Aunt CarolSue had given him a list. And made it clear he'd better do it before he even thought about doing anything else.

He headed for the little grocery store in the blink of a town. It wasn't much to speak of, but they had the basics, he was pretty sure. He'd have asked his mother where to go, but thought her head might explode if he did, and Aunt CarolSue hadn't been back long enough to have a fix on current shopping. The grocery store had the advantage of being the closest, too, and he really wanted to get to work on finding Rosalina. Or on figuring out where to start looking. He felt amped up, as if he'd been drinking too much coffee, which he actually didn't drink at all now because there had been a suggestion at that first revival—if he'd understood it correctly—that it might be sinful. Sometimes it was hard to keep all the Gospel rules straight, like what to eat and drink. Books like Leviticus and Judges—so many of them, really—required many readings and much study.

He parked the van at the IGA in Shandon Center and went in. Not helpfully, there were two different kinds of infant formula. How was he supposed to know which one to get? He was just pulling the one that showed a baby girl on the package—the other kind had a boy on it, so that must be how you knew?—when down the same aisle pushing her own cart, wouldn't you know? Sister Amy! No, no! Gary jammed the formula back on the shelf as if it were a live grenade, turned his back and pushed his own cart down toward canned vegetables, which is where Sister Amy caught up to him as he was putting two cans of sauerkraut into his cart.

"Yes, it's wonderful on a hot dog with some mustard, I find, and an easy supper when I'm busy," he explained after she'd effusively greeted him and examined what he was buying.

"I thought we were discussing in Study Group . . . which Book is it that says pork isn't clean?"

"Sister," Gary admonished. "You know there are even chicken and turkey hot dogs, right?"

"Goodness! That's wonderful. I'd not looked. Now I know! Thank you, Reverend Gary."

They said their goodbyes, Gary paid and left. He'd have to go all the way to Elmont. Shandon Center just wasn't going to work. He hadn't been thinking clearly.

Elmont turned out to be the better choice anyway. There was the big box store there, groceries on one side, home goods on the other. He got the formula with the baby girl on the package, bought a case of it—he could give it to Rosalina to help her out—and then found out, by glancing at the instructions on the back, that he also had to buy bottles with plastic liners, nipples, and caps. Then he searched out disposable diapers. They sold those by the baby's weight. How was he supposed to know? There was a young ponytailed mother in the same aisle with a baby that looked about the same size as Gracia, sleeping in the shopping cart, so he asked her. She asked how much the baby weighed, which was apparently the key to a kingdom that he didn't have. "I'm a pastor, and this is a mercy mission for a church member. I'm afraid I don't know," he said.

"How old is the baby, then?"

Gary had to do a quick calculation in his head. "I believe she's over a month but not two months."

"So say six weeks?" The young mother took a pair of glasses off the top of her head and put them on.

Embarrassed. "Yes, say six weeks."

She scanned the shelves. "These should fit," she said, and took a package off the shelf. "They'd fit my daughter, but I use cloth diapers."

Gary took three more of the same packages. "Um, would you mind showing me what clothes . . ." He consulted his list, "Onesies, I see they're called, would be likely to fit?"

"Those are right over there. It's hot right now, though. You might want to get her something cooler, like this, too," she said, leading him to a circular rack, rifling through some outfits and lifting out a hung-up pink sun suit. "Do you need other supplies, like baby wipes and shampoo? Does the mother have anything?"

"Uh. I don't really know. Maybe it wouldn't hurt to get a few things."

"Well, you probably want some cream in case there's any diaper rash. They sell a layette kit. Maybe that's your best bet.

See that display over there?" The woman's baby was starting to fuss now. He watched how she soothed her.

"I'll get the kit, good idea. Thank you so much for your help, and God bless you," he said, so she'd know she could be done with helping him.

Gary did buy the layette kit, onesies, two receiving blankets, a baby bathtub, a couple of rattles, *Baby's First Book*, and two of the cooler outfits the woman had suggested. It would all go to Rosalina. It was her baby, but he could help, he figured. It was what God wanted.

"Gary! You said a day. Why have you brought supplies for a month?" His mother was already going nuts and all he'd brought in was the formula and bottles. Ha. And she accused *him* of being over-the-top.

"Calm down, Mom. Jesus wants us to suffer the little children, remember? And this stuff is for Aunt CarolSue and you to use for a day or two until I find the mother and help her see God's will. Then I'll give it all to her, to help her. Okay?"

Aunt CarolSue came in behind him then, carrying a load from the van. "Sister! Wait till you see. I peeked in the bag of clothes and Gary got Gracie the cutest two sun suits. Frilly pink, and a yellow one with duckies."

"Great, Merry Sunshine. That's helpful. Do you see the amount of stuff he's got? For two days? Do you see what's going on here? I hope we can't get arrested for this. Gus will—"

"Mom," Gary interrupted then, although he'd been raised not to do that. "Absolutely forget calling Gus. This is a confidential church matter, between me and a person in need. Churches are protected sanctuaries." He was relieved he'd thought of that just then.

His mother was taken aback, at least a little. "Two days

maximum, son. Gus makes a social call here . . . occasionally."

"I know. So? He takes you out to dinner," Gary said. "If you can't manage to wait a day or two, just meet him outside when he picks you up."

His aunt CarolSue didn't say anything, just put down the bag of clothes and went out to get another load. She was different from his mother and the other farm women around here, that was for sure—her streaky blond hair short around her face like something the wind blew, but it was a lucky wind. She wore matching clothes, nice ones, and nail polish, but she was the one to take his side. He didn't have time to ponder that. Gary did not want to see his mother's face when she got a load of the baby bathtub, so he went out after his aunt.

CarolSue

Ha! I thought, as I went back to the van and found, of all things, a full layette kit and a baby bathtub in the back. So Gary thinks Gus is taking his mother out to dinner occasionally. Well, the napping is none of his business, but this could be interesting. Could be amusing to stay here until he finds Gracie's mother. Knowing Louisa, he'd better hop to it.

All I said to Gary was, "How old is she? I forgot to ask you before."

"Six weeks."

"Do you have a lead on her mother?"

"Please don't say anything to Mom, please . . . ?"

I leaned on the van, grateful that this time he'd had the sense to park in the shade of one of the big old maples, though the air still felt sauna-like. Straight to his eyes, I said, "I won't."

"Not a one. But if you'll watch the baby, I'll go get on it right now."

"I'll handle things here. She seems healthy, and I know that now people feed babies when they're hungry, not on a schedule, so that's what we'll do."

He gave me a hug. I felt how hot he was, worry and upset seeping through his skin. "It'll be okay, Gary, you can do this," I said. "I know it's important to you."

"I didn't do right by Cody," he said, his eyes filling. "I carry that."

I wasn't sure what this had to do with Cody, but I said, "Gary, honey, we all do the best we can with what we know at the time. We can't go back. Do the best you can now. It's all we can do. Be brave and honest and do the best you can. Forgive yourself the rest." I admit, I had no idea if this was the right thing to say.

He hugged me again and said, "I don't know if I can. Okay, gotta go now. Thank you, Aunt CarolSue. I love you."

"I love you too, honey. Call us later. I'm sure you'll find Gracie's mother."

"It's what God wants," he said. But then he added, "It has to be."

Puzzling over that one, I followed the stone path from the drive to the front door, carrying the layette kit and the bathtub. Louisa had opened another bag and found more baby things, including two rattles and a book. Predictably, when she saw me with the full layette kit and bathtub, she didn't exactly stay calm.

"How about we have some special tea, Sister?" I suggested.

"I'll make it," she said. "Your version is anemic."

"Yours masks the taste of the tea."

"Exactly the point. What is Gary thinking bringing all this sh—"

"Language, Sister."

"Mom is dead. Beth is the hen who is offended by language because she channels Mom, I swear, but Beth's outside, hunting bugs, as any fool can plainly see. Marvelle doesn't care, and Jessie doesn't know the difference. Rosie, well, everyone knows goats swear like soldiers, so if Rosie was here she'd appreciate it, but she's eating the weeds by the barn." Louisa ranted on while she put the kettle on and got out the Wild Turkey, tea bags, and a jar of honey. "Yes, Marvelle, if you're good, you get a bit too," she added. "None of which has anything to do with Gary bringing all this shit here like the baby will be here for a month, not one day."

"Or two days." I slipped that in. Jessie thumped her tail at that, which I took as support. Pretty soon I'd be dragging the chickens in to bolster my arguments. I winked at Jessie, who appreciates my sense of humor.

"That's the maximum."

"I agree," I said to mollify her. "We can't be doing anything crazy, but you know, Gary is trying to do a good thing, Sister."

"Isn't he always. Let's get this tea before she wakes up. And where are we going to put all this stuff? I wasn't about to say anything to Gary, but what if Gus drops by? Gary would be furious, but Gus would have found out on his own. Problem solved. What do you think?"

"Give Gary a chance. Gus usually calls, doesn't he?"

"Yes, but I don't tell him he can't come—"

"Maybe . . . you could say it's . . . awkward . . . for you, because I'm here and you want to go to his place to . . . nap?"

She paused there in the kitchen, one hand on the kettle, which was just starting to whistle. She turned off the stove and thought about it while she made the tea, then made it "special," which trust me, about that time we both needed it to be. Really special. Even added a slice of lemon and the honey, steps that can be skipped in an emergency, but I guess she figured we had enough time. I stayed quiet to let her think through my obviously brilliant solution.

"That might work," she conceded. "We had to be really quiet because you were here. It was a little awkward for us."

Awkward for you? That was quiet? Bless your heart, I wanted to say, but managed to swallow the words. It required several sips of special tea to wash them down.

Gracie woke and I tended her diaper and showed her the new rattles and book. She waved her arms and legs and I really think she smiled at me. I hoped it was her first smile. What a dear, darling baby. I fed and burped her and she slept again in my arms, content and peaceful. I missed so much, not having one of my own live. Louisa really didn't know how lucky she was.

Gus called that he wouldn't be over that night—he said some police work needed his attention. Louisa and I breathed a sigh of relief, while she told him that was too bad, and that she hoped it would go well and she'd talk with him tomorrow, while giving me a thumbs-up sign. She wouldn't even need my brilliant idea about going to his place, not that night.

I was so busy with the baby all afternoon and into the evening that I didn't do any of what I'd planned, namely call my real estate agent and have him take my house off the market. I also wanted to look into a moving company to come get what I'd brought to Louisa's and get it back to Atlanta for me. I'd hire a decorator to get me some new furniture for the house and place it. I'd learned from Charlie that one can do that, and it's really not difficult. All the appliances were still there. I could hire the help I'd need. It was a matter of making phone calls. Louisa would think I'd lost my mind, but I'd thought that of her on multiple occasions and we'd survived. I just hadn't realized that there wasn't anything for me here; this was Louisa's life, not mine. I missed Charlie desperately, too, and I couldn't find anything of him here.

I'd piled all the baby's stuff in my room, which made it hard to get to the bed, especially since Gracie's carrier was there, too, but it seemed like the best idea since I'd been the one to say we'd keep her overnight. When I got up to go to the bathroom I tripped and woke her up. Then she woke herself, hungry and needing her diaper changed. I didn't get a lot of sleep, but cuddling her with the bottle, sitting in my bed while I fed her, I felt as close as I ever had to any living being. Except Charlie, sometimes. Maybe being soul to soul is something we can only have for fleeting times. It can't last. But it was real. We know we had it and we can reach back for a memory to sustain us.

Chapter 10

Gary

When he left his mother's house for the second time that day, Gary headed for the church, in sore need of spiritual comfort. He was desperately hoping for a Sign, a direct answer to Prayer, because he didn't have the tiniest notion of how to start looking for Rosalina. All he knew was that he absolutely one hundred percent had to find her. It had come to him like the wave of nausea that comes with the flu sometime in the last half hour, the word: *daughter.* As in *Gracia is my daughter?* He strung it together in a sentence, added a question mark, and even then still thought he was going to be sick or pass out.

It felt like an accusation when he first saw the birth certificate and he couldn't absorb it. He'd needed to look at his calendar when he got back to the church, count back the months, add in six weeks. When exactly had she been here? He waved backward through the pages of the desk calendar, looking at the rough outline of his days, not that her name was there, but other events were.

Oh Jesus, oh Lord.

Okay, but how did Rosalina know the baby was his? Gracia should be with Rosalina. Even if she could be his. Because *could* is a big word.

* * *

He'd wasted a good hour in his office, fretting, looking for notes he knew in his heart he hadn't taken or kept, studying the birth certificate for any clue as to where Rosalina might have gone, which he knew was ridiculous, but it didn't stop him. Even trying to remember exactly what she'd told him of her story was difficult. She'd been distraught, he remembered, frightened and needy, and he'd been moved by her plight. Aroused, yes—but it had first been to tenderness, he was sure—by her soft beauty. It had all started out by doing something good. How had it gone so wrong?

There was nothing, no hint of where she might be that he could discern. The birth certificate was signed by a Jennifer Morrow, M.D., and the place of birth was Meyer Memorial Hospital in Elmont. He wondered if someone had taken her there when she was in labor—being a public hospital they couldn't have turned her away, nor called immigration. But the hospital wouldn't release any information, he knew that, having diligently tried to elicit information from the front desk about Brother John, for his distant cousin, and ended up escorted out by a security officer who was unimpressed by what Jesus wanted. He remembered the church he'd driven Rosalina to when he'd given her the money and told her he couldn't give her sanctuary anymore. It was as good a place as any to start. Really, it was the only idea he had.

He tucked in his shirt, smoothed his hair into place, and wiped his face with a handkerchief. The Telephone Daily Prayer Squad was gathering outside his office for their list check, adding and subtracting people as needed. He usually attended, to keep squabbling down, but they'd have to do without him today. They always wanted to know who among them had brought in donations from their calls, and he hadn't checked last receipts yet, which he didn't want to tell them. Getting through them would be like running the gauntlet, but it had to be done.

He hid Rosalina's note and the birth certificate in a manila file marked "possible future building sites," and inserted it in the drawer of his desk and went out to make his excuses.

He drove to St. Peter In Chains Roman Catholic Church near Elmont, where he'd taken her because they also ran something of a soup kitchen certain nights, although it wasn't strictly for people who needed food and shelter, maybe a little more like members' potluck supper, but still, it was free food. But he'd struck out—the Rector had no memory of her by name or description, and no, for heaven's sake, Gary most certainly didn't have a picture of her. So he drove a circuit of all the churches in the greater Elmont area, way beyond the little village of Shandon, asking at each if they'd taken her in. Some, the larger ones, were wary, probably suspecting a trap—but some acknowledged helping undocumented workers hiding in the city when Immigration was in the area, especially women and children—but none remembered anyone of that name. *But who gave their right name?* one church secretary asked him, and of course she was right. She was middle-aged and looked Hispanic herself, with those dark eyes and brows, her black hair laced with gray. "I'm sorry," she said. "It's been bad for the past six months with the crackdown on immigrants. The farmers need the help . . . nothing simple about it . . ." She shrugged as her voice trailed off.

There wasn't a homeless shelter in Elmont—was Rosalina homeless now anyway? And the next big city was Indianapolis. He didn't see a halfway reasonable chance of finding her there. The thing was, he realized, he didn't have the smallest notion of how detectives go about finding someone. He'd done everything he could think of, but surely a knowledgeable professional would be able to figure this out.

In spite of the Gospel message about feeding strangers, sentiment against undocumented people from Central and South America ran like a muddy river through these parts. Louisa had raised him to be unprejudiced about skin color, but that was his mother. Her prejudices were entirely different, although she saw her opinions as based on education and critical thinking. But don't get her going on the subject of trophy hunting, her family always said. Gary didn't have a glimmer of an idea whether there was a secret network that might have taken Rosalina in. Maybe there was no such thing and she was just gone, leaving him with a baby. A baby! What was he to do?

Twilight. He'd missed dinner and he hadn't called his mother. But at least he'd come up with a Hail Mary pass—an expression Cody had explained to him, his lost son, Cody, who'd been so good at football—and now all he had to do was convince his mother and aunt to keep the baby longer.

After coming up empty-handed and empty-brained, he'd been driving the rural roads, brown-edged corn stalks high as the van on both sides, musing about how he didn't know how detectives ever found a missing person. It just came to him like a boom of thunder, which he took as a Sign that Jesus was giving him an answer. His mother had a wannabe boyfriend who was a sheriff. Why not ask him how it's done? Not tell him why, of course. Just get some information on how to do it. He could say it was all a confidential church matter, which was of course the truth, and tell him not to say anything.

Gary felt the burden lift from his shoulders, knowing Jesus was helping him now. Rosalina would be found, and it was going to be all right.

He went back to the church, closed himself in his office, and called Gus. Actually, he called the dispatch number, and—another Sign—Gus himself answered the phone, his voice blasting through the receiver.

"Confidential, huh? Sure, we can make that happen. Do you want me to swing by?"

Gary wondered how anything could be confidential anywhere when Gus seemed to talk through a megaphone. But the specter of a black-and-white squad car parked at the church in front of the giant banner hanging on the white-painted barn (JESUS IS THE ANSWER) was especially alarming. "No, uh, I don't want to put you out. Why don't I run over to headquarters in a bit, if we could meet privately?"

"Sure thing." Gus's voice boomed and Gary jerked the phone away from his ear.

The whole thing had started as a reasonable story, but somehow Gus saw through it. At least partly. "There's a church member who may be in some trouble, and her family is looking for her." An outright lie, God forgive him. "They're not sure how to go about looking for her."

"Where was she last seen?"

"Um, at the church. She came to see me, but I was in Atlanta at Uncle Charlie's funeral."

"With whom?"

"With Mom and Aunt CarolSue."

Had Gus just rolled his eyes? "Who was with the person you want to find?" He left a pause between each word.

"Oh. She was by herself, as far as I know."

"Known associates?"

"I don't know."

"But her family would know, right?"

". . . I guess so."

"What was she wearing?"

"I don't know. I can ask Sister. But I don't know if she'll remember."

"Why do you think she might be in trouble? What kind of trouble?"

"I guess it was Sister's impression. I'm just trying to help. If she maybe . . . didn't have papers, you know, where would she go?"

At that, Gus blew air onto his forehead and this time he definitely rolled his eyes. He pushed his chair back. "Son, what are you asking here? What's really going on?" He was overweight, and his flesh looked like it wanted out of that uniform, pushing against the buttons of the shirt. He pinned Gary like a butterfly, and though his eyes were behind glasses too tight on his face, they weren't hidden.

"Well, okay, she'd come to me before, for help. She came back. I wasn't there. I feel bad about that. She's missing now and I don't know how to go about finding her to make sure she's okay. That's the whole story."

"So . . . *you're* the one who wants to find her."

"Just to make sure she's all right."

"When did you see her last?"

"Me? I saw her last year. But she came looking for me, like I said, when I was in Atlanta with Mom and Aunt CarolSue. Sister said she was real upset. When someone comes for help, Jesus says—" Gary was starting to sweat, trying to avoid lying too much on top of fornicating.

"Yes, I'm sure Jesus says, son." Gus had done security for the church's first tent revival, but he never had joined the church, so Gary didn't know what Gus believed, but he doubted he was Saved.

The office was smaller than Gary's but had a collection of certificates of appreciation framed on the paneled walls, and a jumble of electronic police stuff. There were a couple of windows out into the dispatch area and even a separate area for the deputy. Shelves with stacks of binders. It all looked very official.

"Can you tell me what to do?"

"How about this, instead. Why don't you give me a name and let me see what I can do for you?"

"Oh no, I don't want to cause her trouble. She came to the church. You don't understand. That's sanctuary. That would be so wrong. I was asking you for advice, just unofficially, as my mother's *friend*." The volume of Gary's voice rose, and he started to stand.

Gus gestured him back into his seat with his palm. "Calm down. That's understood. All unofficial. I can't do much with no name, though."

"Oh. Sorry. Thanks. You sure, I mean, nothing will happen to her? You'd just tell me where she is, so I can check on her myself, like I could talk to her?"

"I can't make her talk to you."

"Right. Okay."

"So . . . her name?"

Gary hesitated, but what choice did he have? "Rosalina Gonzalez. At first she told me Rosalina Lopez, though. But I think the Gonzalez is true."

"Why do you think that?"

"Just . . . instinct."

"She didn't say why she gave you two different names?" Gus gave him the police stare, which reminded him eerily of his mother's Look, but Gary just said, "No," and shrugged.

"Odd," Gus said. "I'd have asked about that one."

Chapter 11

CarolSue

In the morning, it was Gracie who woke me up, not Jessie for once, and at dawn. I learned that she could go from an ignorable whimper to a frantic cry in a remarkably short time and could also effectively demand to be taken out of that baby carrier. I was just getting Jessie moved off the bed so I could get a big towel down and change Gracie—diaper and onesie both sopping—before fixing a bottle, when Louisa appeared in the doorway.

"I might as well have a rooster," she muttered. "On the other hand, Bronson always waited for first light." She headed for the bathroom and then, on the way back, said, "I'm going to kill Gary," in a matter-of-fact tone. Gracie wailed on.

The protest stopped, though, the minute she had the nipple. She was, obviously, ravenous. I wondered if I was feeding her enough. Gary was going to have to get her back to her mother, who would know. Gracie sighed then, contented, and paused in her sucking, almost like she was saying thank you, keeping her steady gaze on me. I held her against my body and wondered how her mother could stand being away from her even for a day or two.

She fell back asleep in my arms after I'd burped her twice and let her finish the bottle. I sat there in the recliner to watch her sleep and listen to her breathe. I thought about the babies that had died inside me, and my one beautiful stillborn boy that I did hold until they took him away from me. I didn't think I could go on after that, after burying my son, and I saw no reason to, except for what it would inflict on my mother and sister. It's strange, isn't it? Then I believed that I would never lift my face to the sun and be purely grateful again—not without a bitter sorrow clouding the light. And yet for days and hours like this I have been.

Louisa slept another good length of time. I couldn't see the kitchen clock from where I was, but morning had broken when she came into the living room in her nightgown to ask, "Did you make coffee?"

"Shhh."

"Nothing? You've just been sitting there? Why don't you put her down?" At least she dropped her voice to a stage whisper.

"Tried to, she woke up," I whispered. An outright lie, but harmless. Saying *I damn well didn't feel like it* wasn't likely to go over well.

"You'll spoil her. Good thing Gary has to get her today."

I didn't answer. And Louisa came over and looked at Gracie, sleeping, and I swear she softened, smiling like she couldn't help it. "You want some toast?"

"Yes, please," I said. "Thanks. And coffee."

Gracie was still sleeping in my arms and I was on my second cup of coffee, thanks to Louisa being nice about it all, when Gary finally called.

"You were supposed to call last night," was Louisa's greeting. She knew it was him because he'd had caller ID put on her phone, not realizing that she'd use it more often than not to ignore him. This time, though, she was hot to answer, and picked up on his second ring.

There was a long pause while she listened. She was in the kitchen, so I could hear her side but not see her face. By now, the baby was dead weight in my arms and my legs had gone stiff and numb. I was positive I couldn't get up without help.

Louisa was going to have to take the baby out of my arms and possibly send the six strapping men and the Jaws of Life to get me out of this chair. No way I could get myself in there to get a fix on what was happening.

"How. Much. Longer," Louisa said, significant time between each word. She didn't sound happy. And it wasn't exactly like a question.

"What do you mean you don't know? Bless your heart, how can you not know?" Now she sounded like she was starting to have smoke coming out of her nose and ears.

"Two more days, then. That's two. The number after one and before three," she said finally, and she did not put the receiver down gently. "I'm going to kill him," she said loudly, I assumed for my benefit. "Two more days. Wait till you hear . . ."

In another three minutes when she didn't come in, I was crazed. I couldn't yell for her without waking Gracie, and I couldn't get up. On top of that, I had to pee. "Louisa!" I gave a loud whisper. Nothing. I tried again. Still nothing. I heard her moving around and then, a moment later, a door closed. I hoped it wasn't the bathroom door. Then I heard the shower start.

I was doomed.

After she set a world's record for longest shower, Louisa finally came out again, dressed. Gracie was stirring on her own, so I didn't need to be quiet. "I need you to take her, put her in her carrier, and get me out of this chair before I explode," I said. I might have sounded a little irritable.

"Who peed in your Cheerios?"

"I'm going to pee in more than your Cheerios," I said, "if you don't get me out of this chair, which I'm pleased to say is one of yours and not mine."

"Oh . . ."

She finally took Gracie and hoisted me out of the chair. When I came back, she was cuddling the baby and cooing at her. "So, what's the deal with Gary?" I said, wanting the baby back but not making a move to take her.

"He says he has a lead on the mother and needs more time. He promises, two more days should do it, and says it's the right thing to do. You know all the stuff Gary would say. Fill in the blanks." She shrugged a little, which was difficult, considering she had a baby in her arms.

The sun was mounting the sky and I knew the heat of the day would soon begin outdoors. Louisa wanted to finish picking the beans. "Are you okay with it? I know you were worried—"

"He swears, for whatever that's worth, that the church is doing this, not that I'm a member of the church, so I'm babysitting is all—and that the law has to be kept out of it for the baby's sake, that he can get the baby back with her mother and help them both. You know, that would be better. Foster kids, well—"

"I know."

"She's a darling," Louisa said, looking down at Gracie, then back at me.

"She sure is. What do you want me to do?"

"Can you take care of her while I pull the rest of the beans? They're getting too big as it is. They get tough—"

"Of course," I said. It was exactly what I wanted. Did she know?

By the end of the day, Gracie and I were hitting a rhythm and I was catching on to her little signs. I was also pretty tired. Louisa was, too, from the sun and bean picking, but she was glad to sit with Gracie and shake her rattle, talk to her, while I snapped the stem ends off the beans for her. So we were able to spell each other that way, by swapping tasks, and it was a respite. I could see a change in Louisa. Having relented with Gary must have made a difference, because she seemed to settle in to enjoy the baby. Still, though, she worried about being "caught."

"Well," I said. "Really, we can plead ignorance, can't we? I mean, we're babysitting for Gary, who told us that it's the daughter of a church member. Nothing illegal about babysitting."

"Oh." She chewed on that for a minute. "Hmmm. When it's put that way, it sounds okay, doesn't it?"

"Put it that way and leave it that way. Uh-oh. I think I smell a stinky. And she's on your lap so it's your turn," I teased, fully thinking Louisa would hand Gracie over, but she didn't.

"I do think you're right," she said to me, and then nuzzled Gracie and tickled her belly. "Did you make a stinky, Miss Gracie? Did you do that to Auntie Louisa? Well, that wasn't nice, was it? Let's go get you changed." And with that she put Gracie on her shoulder, holding her there two-handed, and got up from the couch with no assist. I wondered if she was remembering protecting Gary as an infant, and Gary's son, Cody, the same way I remembered folding my baby close in to my own body even the brief time I was given with him, as if our bodies never forget, never ever forget and always long to have our babies back when we can keep them safe.

While she was in using the makeshift changing area I'd set up on my bed, where I'd laid out the baby wipes and diaper cream Gary had thought to buy (I wondered, impressed, how he had thought of so much I'd not put on the paltry list I'd made!), the phone rang in the kitchen. "Get that, will you?" Louisa called. "Could be Gary."

I checked the caller ID, but it was giving a phone number, not a name. "Not Gary," I called in.

"Better get it," she said. "If it's the Daily Prayer Call and Donation Solicitation, ha ha, your turn, you're on your own."

Louisa had memorized the phone numbers of all the people on Gary's God Squad Prayer Team and didn't answer the phone when they called. She said that when she didn't answer for a few days, if Gary was really busy, he'd call Gus and ask him to go check on her, which she and Gus both thought was hilarious, since then Gus could put down his napping time with Louisa as an official call in response to a citizen concern about an elderly parent.

"Hello," I said into the receiver, after I'd turned the kitchen faucet on full blast and leaned over the sink as I answered so I could say the connection was terrible and I just couldn't make out what was being said.

"Just callin' my sweetheart." Gus boomed like a bass drum through the receiver. I jerked away, wondering if my hearing would eventually come back, and then held the receiver three or four inches from my head. "Something wrong with the phone? What's that noise?"

I turned the water off, and said, "Gus, it's me, CarolSue. Louisa is . . ." and wouldn't you know, I couldn't think of a thing to say.

"What?"

"Um . . . in the bathroom."

"Okay, I can chat with you a minute. How are you liking the Great State of Indiana, as your sister calls it? Of course, she often sticks another word between Great and State and sometimes it's not a flattering word, as you might know."

"Oh, I like it fine. You know I grew up here, well, I didn't leave until fifteen years ago, so . . ." I was frantic that Louisa not come in with the baby, who would pick that instant to cry. "Hang on a minute, Gus, will you?"

"Louisa," I called. "Just want to let you know, Gus is on the phone for you."

"Tell him I'll call him back," she yelled. Adamant.

"She says she'll call you back."

"I was going to drop by anyway—"

"She's really tired."

"I won't stay long."

"She's awfully tired, Gus. Worked all day out harvesting beans, you know. Just exhausted. Said she wanted a light supper and to rest up tonight. Maybe—"

He cut me off. "Miss CarolSue, you're the one doesn't want me to come?"

The little watering cans on the kitchen wallpaper were tipped at an angle. I was just as off balance. "Uh, no, I mean, that's not up to me, I just wanted to let you know that—"

"You just tell Miss Louisa I'll be dropping by. She'll be fine. Won't stay long if she's too tired. Just need to see her beautiful face." And he hung up.

"Sister!" I screeched. "We've got a problem."

Louisa and I did a frazzled rush job of moving all the baby's things into the master bedroom, so my bedroom door would be open and everything would look normal in there, as it always did. I'd voted for just keeping my door shut, but Louisa said he would be likely to bring the new hinges for my closet door, and if he had, he'd want to go check that they'd fit, even if he didn't insist on swapping them out instantly, which would be like him. Then we checked the living room and kitchen for baby signs, Jessie following us around, curiously thinking it all a great hide-and-seek game, and Marvelle perched on top of the wingback chair in the living room, being disdainful about all the fuss. Louisa had been keeping the back door shut lately, so the free-ranging girls didn't roam into the house as they had before Jessie's time. Marvelle ignored the chickens, but Jessie was flummoxed as to why they got all riled up when she tried to play with them. Personally, I was grateful that line had been drawn, and didn't much care why they were outside with Rosie. Louisa said there was something seriously wrong with me.

"You're going to need to take Gracie somewhere," she said. "In your car. I'll be rid of Gus as soon as I can. I'll go put the carrier in your car, buckle it in the right way, in the back. You give the house another once-over, make sure everything is in . . . the room." With that, Louisa picked up Gracie's carrier and went out the front door to my car. Carrying Gracie, I hurriedly changed her from a sun suit to a onesie, scanned each room, found my purse, and went out. I thought to take a spare diaper with me, and the bottle with the last few ounces she hadn't finished earlier. Just in case. "Jessie, you stay. I'll be back, I promise," I said, as the Lab tried to come out the door with me. I'd miss her when I moved back to Atlanta.

We'd barely made it out. I guess it had taken longer than we thought to put everything away and ready Gracie. Down the road toward the Athertons' as I was driving away from the house, I passed Gus. I don't think he realized who I was—probably too hot to get his paws on my sister—but I knew him. Needless to say I didn't honk and wave.

I drove around for ten minutes, hoping Louisa was good for her word and Gus hadn't talked her into a quick nap. But when I circled by the house again, there was Gus's truck. That homicidal impulse I've mentioned feeling toward my sister? It was suddenly there again.

I needed a place to go, plain and simple. So, being the sensible one, I went.

Yes, I was careful. I went where nobody would know me, or at least it was very, very unlikely I'd run into anyone who would recognize me. Louisa could just stew, I figured, if Gus left and she didn't know I'd taken Gracie to Elmont, to the big store I could never remember the name of, but knew it has groceries on one side, clothes, home goods, and everything else on the other. I'd put the baby in a cart and walk around. Maybe I'd buy her some toys. For sure, I was going to buy myself a coffee and pastry, because don't you know they have a little sit-down place by the deli part of the grocery store. At least I hoped they still did as I drove there. Gra-

cie was lulled into a happy quiet, enjoying the ride, and I put
the radio on the oldies station and sang to her all the way.

By the time Gracie and I left, we'd had a fine time. She'd
finished up that bottle I'd brought while I had some coffee
and a nice bran muffin, I'd changed her in the bathroom
where there was even a baby-changing place, how lovely, and
then she and I hit the baby department and had ourselves a
grand shopping spree. I could barely push the cart through
the checkout line. "Ha. Wait till Louisa sees what we picked
out! Good thing I'm your fashion consultant and not her," I
confided as I buckled her into her carrier in the car.

I put the toys, the big box with the bassinet, the changing
pad, and clothes in the trunk.

"Now you're a better equipped young lady," I told her.
"And you pay no attention when Louisa has a cow. Let her
have two of them. After all, she's got every other kind of animal on that farm. Why not some cows?" I reached into the
back seat as I said the last and went "Moo, cow, mooooo,"
and tickled her. And I swear, that baby grinned. Her first big,
wide, for-certain grin: eyes, mouth, whole-face-full-of-delight
grin. And it was at me.

"Where have you been?" Of course, I knew it would be
the first thing Louisa said. I have to admit, twilight had
fallen. She called it as she stepped out onto the porch, and
Jessie ran out from behind her to meet me as I got Gracie out
of the car. Louisa waited, a faded figure, outlined by the
lights on in the house, the door standing open behind her.

I walked up with Gracie and handed the carrier to her.
"Went to the big store—what is it, I never remember, and I
was just there—in Elmont."

"Meyer's. Why?"

"Don't know why I can't ever remember that name—"

"Why did you go there?" All impatient.

"I needed somewhere to go. I drove around a while and Gus was still here." I knew I hadn't driven around very long, but she didn't. It was a calculated guess about what had happened. And I must have guessed right, at least partly, because she backed down some.

"Oh. Was it . . . okay? I didn't think you'd be gone that long."

"It was great. She grinned. At me."

"She's young for that," Louisa said, skeptical.

"I think I know what I saw. I bought a few things. I need to get them in. Keep her a few minutes while I unload."

"I've got some dinner ready," she said, motioning to the kitchen. "It's really late now, you must be starving. I sure am. Gus was hinting to stay, big-time, but I put him off. Gary better get this taken care of."

"Yeah," I said. "Or you could break up with Gus." I muttered that last part under my breath as I went out the door to start carrying in baby supplies. I wondered how long it would take my sister's head to explode when she saw what I'd bought.

"What the hell are you thinking? Did you just buy one of everything in the baby department?" Louisa demanded. We were still sitting at the table, and she'd fixed some special tea to go with dessert, which usually meant she was celebrating something or totally pissed off. I was betting on the second. She had managed to hold her tongue until after we ate, but I think it was just because she was too tired, hungry, and wasn't going to fuss in front of the baby. And, this'll shock you, she'd let me set up the bassinet, which was really like a hugely oversized basket, in the master bedroom, because all the baby's stuff was already in there. I put the changing pad I'd bought on the bed, and the big basket-bassinet, which had conveniently come with its own bedding, on the floor instead of setting up the legs that would raise it to the height of my waist and make it look more long-term, which I thought would freak Louisa out even more. I shoved those under the bed.

Now Gracie had been fed, we'd eaten the vegetable (what else?) and pasta casserole Louisa had kept warm until I got home, and Gracie had been washed and changed and put down for the night, easy baby that she was, and Louisa was letting loose. I'd seen it coming, the way you can watch an incoming storm linger in the western sky and make educated guesses about when the thunder and lightning is going to break over your head.

"I wasn't sure it was a good idea for her to sleep in that baby carrier pretty much sitting up," I said. "You know, babies are supposed to sleep on their backs now," I tried.

"Bless your heart, like one more day before she goes back to her mother was going to make a difference? I gave Gary a deadline. To-mor-row." She arched her eyebrows at me and gave her steely teacher-look, the one that says, *And what do you have to say for yourself now?*

"All of it can go with her to help her mother. Whatever her mother doesn't want or need, can be donated to Goodwill. Or Gary's church. There are a lot of people in need."

"Huh," she said, raising and lowering her eyebrows and then narrowing her eyes, clearly wanting to say it again. I never should have taught her the Southern meaning. She couldn't help herself, out it came again, Louisa calling bullshit with, "Bless your heart." She just couldn't quite figure out my angle.

Honestly, I didn't know myself.

Chapter 12

Rosalina

She would not let herself cry, though the milk still leaking from her breasts made her feel as if her body was, despite her will. *What kind of mother would not sacrifice to save her child,* she said to herself. She told herself maybe she could go back to get her baby. When it was safe, maybe. If it was safe.

This was best for now. There were other women who'd crossed alone. What happened to their babies? If their plant was raided, were they given a phone call? Rosalina didn't know the Reverend's number, anyway, only where she'd gone when she'd first made it north. And even if she did reach the Preacher Garry, would he believe her? And meanwhile, what would happen to Gracia, even if he believed her and made the trip to get the daughter he'd never known of? He wouldn't have the papers to claim her. Rosalina had kept Gracia's birth certificate on her own body since she'd received it. That, and now the precious social security card.

The kind, dark-skinned nurse at the hospital who said she was from Haiti "long time ago," had helped her fill out the forms. "Don't be scared, honey. Nobody gonna come into a hospital," Esther said. As if she knew. "It's okay. Your baby's gonna have a birth certificate, and this, see here, it's an application for a social security card—see, she'll have that number her whole life, it's real important. I can help you fill this out, too. Do it all the time." She'd been the one who'd shown Rosalina how to help Gracia latch on to nurse, counseled her to include some bottles if Rosalina was going back to work, "so she'll accept a bottle, don't you know, honey, and won't fuss if she can't have the breast sometimes." She'd held Rosalina's hand, told her she was doing a fine, fine job, and Rosalina had wished so much she could stay and have Esther take care of her.

But then Esther had two days off, and Rosalina was dismissed anyway. Rosalina knew better than to think something that good would last for someone like her, not something she'd lucked into. She wanted to believe in good signs, but she didn't, not really. Nothing happened on its own, she'd learned, despite what the priest had always said about God's will being done. If a person didn't make it happen, it didn't, for good outcomes and for bad, which was why she'd been willing to take her chances crossing the border when her father said she had to escape. The rapes, beatings, killings. Women had no chance, he said. Not even in her own home. It was his only way to protect her. Even her own brother was gone to drugs, to a gang. "Do it, go. Go. Go. I have paid," he'd said. He made it happen. He used to toss her in the air when she was small, and she'd scream with laughter, never fear. He would always stop her from falling to danger. Even if it meant never seeing her again.

She couldn't do less for her own child.

She'd had to leave her beautiful Gracia the way she did. Gracia's father must be a good man, yes, a man of God. A man of faith, who would see a girl to safety, give her school, a home. Gracia wouldn't live week-to-week in a dark apartment shared with recent strangers in a strange land, all trying to find a way to a new life, all risking everything every day. Gracia was protected, she'd be cared for, Rosalina told herself, again and again. Did that mean she didn't weep? Did it lessen her loss? She comforted herself with the thought of holding her baby, told herself, *If it's safe, I'll go get her. When it's safe.*

Gary

He didn't want to risk going over to his mother's, although he'd promised he would. What if she said she wouldn't keep the baby anymore? He'd asked for two days, though, and that meant tomorrow, didn't it? He knew he should at least call.

Maybe he should check with Gus first, and he'd find out that Gus already knew exactly where Rosalina was. The whole thing could be cleared up in a nanosecond, the baby returned where she belonged, and that would be that. He wondered if Rosalina would want child support. That would be tough to manage, and keeping the whole secret, too. He didn't want to see her. Embarrassed that he'd ever fallen into lust the way he had when he was supposed to be doing God's work, not that he hadn't felt for her. He had. He shook his head to clear it, his thoughts thick and lumpy as his mother's tapioca, which he'd always shoved away from his place at the table.

From his desk at the barn that was passable as a church now, Gary used his cell phone to call the sheriff. Dispatch answered. Gary stammered. "Is the . . . sheriff there? Reverend Hawkins calling about a church matter."

"Do you require assistance there now?" Her voice was crisp and official-sounding, as if she were ready to send a SWAT team.

"Oh no, ma'am. This is a nonemergency issue. I just need to talk to Gus."

"All right, Rev. Hawkins, I'll record the request. I'm sure he'll call as soon as he gets in."

Gary hung up and slapped a palm to his face, holding it there. *Idiot!* He shouldn't have mentioned the church, just said it was a personal call. He should have asked Gus for his personal cell phone number in the first place, like a thinking person would have, not called the sheriff's line at all. Now all he could do was wait for Gus to call and hope his mother didn't. He'd call her when he knew something.

The day was not starting out well.

A full ninety minutes passed before Gary's cell phone rang and the screen showed that it was the sheriff's department. Gary had dithered the time away making almost no more progress on his sermon, when he'd hoped to finish it. But each sentence he tried out seemed dangerous, although there was no way anyone could know, was there? Who could possibly stand up and point at him, shouting *Fornicator!*

"Thought you wanted everything unofficial." Gary flinched at the volume. Gus must put the receiver down and talk into it using a megaphone. That was the only explanation. What if someone was outside Gary's office door, even now? The Clean for Jesus Committee didn't come today, did they? They'd be able to hear every word through the door. Gary fumbled on his desk to check his calendar, knocking over the coffee, now cold, he'd brought with him from Sister Martha's kitchen. It spilled toward him, sopping his sermon notes and all the Old Testament passages he'd found, and rolled forward like a muddy river off the edge of his desk and onto his khaki pants. He jerked backwards in his chair, too hard, and as it teetered on two legs, Gary's legs and arms flailed. He dropped the phone.

"Gary? GARY!" Gus boomed. "Can you hear me? Is this a bad connection or what?"

Gary lurched his body forward to right the chair. Coffee still dripped from the desk, but he could reach the phone, which—and he remembered to thank Jesus for the mercy of it—had fallen clear of the stream. "I'm here, Gus," he said. "Just spilled a little coffee. Can you hang on a second?"

"Sure!"

Gary thought his hearing might be permanently impaired, even though he'd held the phone an inch from his ear. He turned the volume control on his phone way down, set it on his desk, and picked up the saturated pages of his sermon to let the excess coffee run off them. The oversized cup had been two-thirds full because his stomach had been off and it wasn't going down well. Nerves. He sopped up what he could with tissues, finally laying the pages of his sermon separately on the floor, hoping he'd be able to read enough to re-create his thoughts. Too bad he'd written in pencil on lined yellow paper, like always.

"Gary! You all right, son?" Even with the volume down, there was no escaping the beef of that voice.

"I'm fine, thanks." Gary picked up the receiver, and thinking to save his eardrum, switched it to speaker, then remembered he'd not checked on when exactly Clean for Jesus was scheduled, and quickly switched it back off.

"I thought I'd just check—unofficially, of course—as to whether you had any leads on Rosalina's whereabouts."

"Looked into that last night. Say, your mother all right?"

"Yes, yes, she's fine, Aunt CarolSue's there, of course, they're both fine."

"Seemed awful tired yesterday, and didn't seem to want supper, which is not like her at all. CarolSue was out when I went over in the afternoon."

"You were there?"

"Stopped by for a visit with Miss Louisa, had myself a break in the day."

Oh Lord. Oh Jesus, please. Please. "All by herself, you say.

Wonder where CarolSue went?" Feigned a level of interest equivalent to a shrug.

"Oh, some ladies' shopping thing, I imagine. You know how they are."

Gary didn't have a clue about ladies' shopping things, but he figured his mother was going to kill him for sure. Carol-Sue would be her accomplice. But they couldn't really do it while the baby was still there, could they? Or maybe they would, and then they'd turn the baby over to Gus, and really, he couldn't let that happen. What if Gracia really was his? He couldn't let her end up in some foster home, or orphanage, or whatever they did now with abandoned babies when they knew there was a living parent somewhere. Gracia had to be with her own parent, didn't she?

He tried to get back to what he wanted to know. "So . . . were you able to find anything?"

"No, I don't know where she went. I left before she got home. Your mother said she was pretty tired, and like I said, she didn't want supper."

Gary thought Gus must be the most aggravating human loudspeaker on the planet.

"I meant about Rosalina."

"Oh. Make the question clear. First rule, son. Ask clear questions. What was it again?"

Gary clenched his teeth. He drew in a breath through his nose, blew it out through his mouth, controlled his tone and said, "I was wondering if you've found out anything . . . about Rosalina . . . where she is, I mean."

"No."

"Will you keep looking? Please. It's important."

"So you said. Yes. Bet she's got false papers. Immigration put it out to local cooperating departments, they'd picked up a guy, regular fake paper factory. Between Elmont and Indy. Round the time they got the convenience store chain that hired lotta illegals. Remember?"

Gary did remember. It had been all over the news maybe six months ago. Immigration attention had ramped up over the past year, as they did every now and then, arrests splashed on the local news as if an international war had broken out. Gary supposed it made sense. Gary saw the logic that refugees should do it the right way, apply, get in line, like the people who'd done it according to the law. That was okay by him. Hadn't Jesus said *Render unto Caesar that which is Caesar's?* This was just about the church not turning someone away, which it wasn't supposed to do. Jesus said to help the strangers and beggars. In a way, it was all pretty confusing. But he was just trying to do right by one person, after all. So maybe he did have something personally to gain; that really wasn't the point.

"You mean she might be using a different name?"

"No way to know, now is there? Could order a police artist sketch, I suppose, give me something to go on?"

"I'm not sure I remember well enough . . ." Gary said, as Rosalina's face appeared, too clear in his mind, the long lushness of her nearly black hair that came to a widow's peak on her forehead, neat sweeps of brows that were as dark as her hair, and wide-set eyes. Broad cheekbones. But a police artist? Wouldn't that make it official? Had he already done that when he called this morning? He didn't dare ask.

"You know, I don't want anything to happen to her," Gary started again. "I mean, not cause her any trouble." He meant immigration agents but didn't know if he should keep mentioning that. He said a quick, silent prayer to Jesus to make that much clear to Gus.

"You said that."

"If you can get me any info, strictly unofficial, I mean, I just want to offer her help. From the church, I mean. Church work."

"I'm doing what I can," Gus said. Not quietly. "Give your mother my best."

And without thinking to say that he didn't want his mother to know he'd asked Gus to look, didn't want her to know he'd spoken to Gus at all, Gary said sure, he would do that, right before he hung up. Then, for the second time that morning, he slapped his palm to his face and held it there as he shook his head and called himself an idiot.

Chapter 13

Gus

Some idiot with Michigan plates who probably had a PhD (Sure thing, Pile it Higher and Deeper, Gus always said about that) but couldn't read a simple map, had run out of gas on one of the iffy rural roads, of which Shandon had plenty, and couldn't tell AAA where the hell he was, so call the sheriff's 911 line.

Gus had been drinking coffee when the call came, so he lumbered out to his black-and-white and went out to find both him and the AAA truck. Good grief. Once he found the motorist by using the landmarks he said were around him (easy, there aren't that many unmarked mailboxes that still have old candy-cane decorations on them from last Christmas. He was in front of the Hamiltons' place, empty since they moved and it hadn't sold), he guided the AAA guy by the motorist's cell phone, turn by turn.

It had brought him within a mile and a half of Louisa's place, and he hadn't gotten to finish his coffee when the call had interrupted his break. He touched her name on his cell phone, thinking maybe she'd put some coffee on and even better, sometimes she'd made cinnamon rolls. Even a cookie with the coffee would be mighty nice. And, of course, there'd be the pleasure of seeing her. She'd sort of hurried him off last night, which she'd not done before. He didn't take it personal, though. She was exhausted, she said, from harvesting the garden and canning. Gus had thought it would be easier this year, what with CarolSue there to help.

He liked CarolSue fine. She and Louisa were cut from the same cloth, he could tell, although she wasn't as rooted in the land, and didn't seem to take to the animals and chickens as deep as her sister, although she and the yellow Lab Jessie were a pack of two now. It was good for Louisa to have CarolSue with her, he supposed, but he did have some concerns about how it would affect keeping company with Louisa. Yesterday, she'd hinted about coming to his place. Whew. That was one terrible idea, not that he was eager to explain to her, but it would be one giant job to make it fit for her to walk in the door. Since Gus's own sister, Rhonda, got that cancer in her pancreas and died so quick, he'd been on his own about cleaning it. Which meant that it was pretty dirty. And a mess, too. Figuring out where to put things in a house was never his strong suit. He heard Rhonda's voice in his head all the time telling him to clean it up.

Louisa answered the phone on the fourth ring, sounding a little breathless. "How's my sweetheart?" He spoke up so she'd be sure to hear him.

"I'm good, I'm good," she said. "I was just carrying in what might be the last nine zucchini. I'll probably need to make some bread for the freezer with it."

"I've got a surprise for you. Got a call from a stranded motorist brought me all the way over here. I'm maybe two minutes from the house. Thought I'd come by. You got some coffee for your local sheriff? He needs it bad, and a glimpse of your beautiful face."

Silence. Gus thought he'd lost the connection. "Louisa? Honey? Louisa!"

"Yeah, I'm here. Well, the thing is, CarolSue's not dressed. At all. She's . . . not feeling well."

"Oh, sorry to hear that. Tell her for me. I won't bother her.

You and I can sit in the living room instead of the kitchen, give her more privacy. How's that?"

A pause. "Uh . . . okay."

"Don't worry, honey. You know, we both got to get used to having CarolSue there, figure out how to live our lives like always. Right?"

"Give me ten minutes to clean myself up," she said. "I'm a mess. You know CarolSue. Fashion queen, hair, makeup. Not only will she not be feeling well, she'll have to rouse herself to kill me if I let you come over looking the way I do right now. Then she'll kill you for having made it necessary to kill me."

"What am I supposed to do for the next ten minutes?" Gus whined.

"Spend it trying to pull up your big boy pants. Ten minutes. Not a minute sooner."

When he arrived, Louisa had set up coffee and yes, a cinnamon bun she said she'd pulled from her freezer, out on the porch, where there was a small table between two white rockers. Late morning sun was on their legs, but not in their eyes, a small mercy. No breeze stirred the leaves of the big maple tree in the small grassy area. A few leaves had already started to turn, early warning flags. It wouldn't be that long before the field corn would be harvested. He hoped Louisa would make good money from her field. Al Pelley kept intimating that she could make more if she'd listen to him.

"Not too hot out here for you?" Gus said, meaning, *It's too hot for me out here, and I'd rather be inside where I won't sweat inside the heavy pants and long-sleeved shirt and tie of this damn uniform.*

"Oh no, it's lovely," Louisa trilled. "I never want to be inside when I can be out, nice and warm in the sunshine."

Gus wondered if she'd gone mad overnight but decided it

was unlikely. He'd heard that older women had hot flashes. Maybe they had cold flashes, too. He wouldn't know, and who could he ask now that Rhonda was gone?

"Good coffee as always," he said, "and even better cinnamon bun. You could make a fortune selling those. I'd go broke myself buying them."

"You're just trying to get seconds, but that was the last one frozen. I'll make more next week. After I get zucchini bread done." She looked pretty to him, her light hair pinned back like that, it made her blue eyes stand out. She always said her sister's eyes were brighter blue, and Gus could see that they were a different, lighter blue, and that CarolSue was more Atlanta-looking with her polished fingers and clothes, and the haircut that Louisa said was like a small animal chewed its way all around the edges right before the wind blew just until her hair looked like a magazine picture. Louisa was more earthy, even when she'd put on lipstick like now. It was CarolSue got her to put on makeup and do her hair, and one time after a nap Louisa told Gus that CarolSue got her a different bra, too, to pull her boobs up higher.

"Well, now that you mention it, I did notice a difference," Gus had said, and she'd slapped his ass in play. Which had led to a second nap that day, a record of which Gus was quite proud, not knowing whether his blue pill would last two naps. But it had.

"I guess I'd best be getting back to work," he said finally, after discussing when the next round of repairs over the Rush Run Creek bridge would start, and the ridiculous detour that annually drove them nuts. "I'm just gonna run in and use your john."

"Oh, wait a moment, and let me check that CarolSue's not in there," Louisa said, jumping up, almost blocking his way. "Hang on."

A moment later she was back. "Oh, sorry, but she's in there. Not feeling well, you know."

"I'll wait," Gus said. "You know. Damn prostate. You don't want me over there peeing into your bushes. Wouldn't be seemly for the sheriff." He grinned at the self-evidence of that one.

"Oh. All right." She sat back down but didn't say anything.

"So, back to the garden when I leave?"

"Uh-huh."

"Canning this afternoon?"

"Uh-huh."

Then she was up again. "I'll check on CarolSue," she said, and the door closed behind her. This time she was gone a good five minutes. Gus checked his watch and waited. He really did have to go. Was CarolSue that indisposed? Maybe he could just quickly use the other bathroom, the one in the part of the house Louisa had closed off. This once.

She was back then, though. "Okay, she's out. You can use it."

The radio was on, tuned to National Public Radio, Louisa's favorite, he knew, and fairly loud, even for Gus. Louisa was always telling him he didn't have to shout, she could hear just fine.

Louisa stood almost outside the bathroom door, waiting for him, which made him very self-conscious. If the radio hadn't been so loud, she'd have been able to hear him pee, and intimate as they'd been, that felt like a bridge too far if a point was being made of it. Why would she want to listen in anyway? He turned to use the towel after giving his hands a cursory rinse and saw a weird plastic thing in the bathtub. He leaned in to inspect it.

When he opened the door, there was Louisa practically pushing him toward the porch again. "What's with the thing in the bathtub? With the yellow duckie in it?" he said.

"Oh, that. Um, well, Marvelle got herself filthy—I don't know, must have been hunting mice. She . . . didn't smell good.

So CarolSue thought a small tub like that wouldn't freak her out. She got it, it was her idea."

"No! You gave Marvelle a bath? She let you do that?"

"I had to talk her through it, uh, you know, it's like soothing a . . . baby."

"You got her a rubber duckie?"

"We thought it might distract her. Well, I mean, a bird-type thing. She . . . watches them out the window."

"Huh. Never heard of that before. So, she's . . . clean now?"

"Oh yes, she's doing great now," Louisa said, all chipper, and took his arm. "Let's go check on her, in the backyard, so you can see."

They talked their way down the hall, through the kitchen, and were in the living room by then. There was Marvelle on the back of the wingback chair, giving him the evil eye. "Honey, she's right here. Looks fine to me," he said.

"Oh good, let's take her outside. Sometimes she needs urging to get some exercise."

"Sweetheart, I've got to get back to work. I'll call you later. Maybe we can . . . arrange a . . . nap?"

"CarolSue's not feeling well at all," she said. "Not at all. Not today. Not here anyway, but . . . ?" And she raised her eyebrows at him, like she was saying, *Well, how about your place?* Good Lord, his dear departed sister would have marched in his place, huffing about how, just to get in the door, she'd had to fight the Board of Health, which was ready to nail up a giant CONDEMNED sign. She'd find a way to die all over again if he let Louisa in there.

Gus went back to work, more than a little worried about CarolSue's health and his future as the King of Naps.

Chapter 14

CarolSue

Louisa waved goodbye to Gus and turned from the front door. We looked at each other, mugging wide-eyed, burst out in hysterical laughter and gave each other high fives. "Holy sh . . ." she gasped.

"Language," I cautioned her. "Little pitchers have . . . and there's a little pitcher in my arms. Holy poop, that was close."

"How'd you keep her quiet?"

"Stuffing her pacifier in her mouth three hundred times. How'd you keep him out there?"

"By pretending I didn't notice it was like a sauna and trying not to faint from the heat."

I'd ventured out of the master bedroom with Gracia and Jessie after I'd heard him leave, finally, after he used the bathroom. "It was a mite tense. But Gracie was such a good girl, wasn't she?" I kissed the baby's head. She burped a good one and spit up on my shoulder. "I need a cloth," I said to Louisa. "And *you* probably need a cold shower, and not for the usual reason."

"You're just lucky he had to get back to work anyway, or you and Gracie would have had to figure out how to climb out the bedroom window. Now *that* I would have liked to see!"

"You mean my desperate illness wouldn't keep him from wanting to nap?"

"You're kidding, right?"

We were laughing about it then, but it had been a rough go. First we'd panicked about Gus coming over, but as Louisa slapped on some lipstick and made it look like she'd used the ten minutes to clean up the way she'd told Gus, I made coffee, scrounged a bun out of the freezer—"Just one!" Louisa yelled from the bathroom, "Or he'll stay longer and eat as many as you put out!"—and then I set up a tray for her to take out on the porch. Meanwhile I grabbed a bottle, the pacifier, the toys, and got Gracie and me in the master bedroom where we just had to desperately hope I could keep her amused and quiet until he was gone.

It went all right until Louisa came in and whispered, "He wants the damn bathroom now," and we had to rush around the kitchen, around everywhere, snatching up all the little evidences of a baby, a sock here, a rattle there, an unfinished bottle on the counter, the duckie book half tucked under the wingback chair. At the last minute, I'd realized the tiny soft hairbrush I'd bought Gracie was on the bathroom counter from when we'd bathed her last night. All of it had to be stashed in the master bedroom, door firmly shut, and I'd have to keep her silent while Gus was in the bathroom just down the hall.

"Turn the radio up," I hissed at Louisa just before she went out. A sensible suggestion from the sensible sister, please notice. She did. I think the Athertons, who live a quarter mile down the road, might have enjoyed the program without needing their own radio on, but I have to say, it helped muffle any other sound.

"I thought he'd never leave," I said then, once Louisa found a cloth and helped me wipe spit-up from both Gracie and me. "Shoot, I'm going to need to change us both."

"You missed the baby tub, and the duckie. I thought I was going to have to make up something ridiculous but I covered. Gary better come get this baby is all I can say," she said.

"What if it had been raining? He'd never have bought the lovely day to sit outside thing. His cheeks looked like tomatoes, he was so hot." She stuck out her lower lip then and blew upward to move the light bangs I'd cut for her—makes her look younger, and they're quite sexy if I do say so myself, not that I enjoy the picture of her with Gus, but *somebody* has to make her look good—off her forehead. I guess that was to make me think she'd been through some great stress. She ought to try keeping a baby quiet while *her* sister makes goo-goo eyes with a puffy sheriff while relaxing and drinking coffee on a summer porch. It's not like there was no shade there.

So she'd noticed Gus was hot, had she? You know what I wanted to say right then about that? *How come you never noticed how hot it was out in the garden when I was falling over from heat stroke, my skin itching me to distraction from vegetation and bugs creeping around my legs, and my back feeling like I'd been lifting boulders for a year?* That's how quickly my feelings turned from our old laughter to jealous irritation. I could bite my tongue because I was going back to Atlanta anyway. I just hadn't had the time to make my calls yet, too busy with the baby, and I didn't really want Louisa to know my Plan. Not yet.

"I think you need to take Gracie for a half hour. I feel a lie-down coming on." I put on the Georgia accent that she hates and laid the back of my hand across my forehead, Southern belle–style. Yes, I knew it would drive her mad. I'm not incapable of taking my own shot here and there.

The day crawled toward evening, Louisa working the garden, and me happily not—rather playing with Gracia, feeding her, changing her, letting her sleep on me. I'd told myself that today I'd definitely call the lawyer in Atlanta, and my real estate agent, but I was either busy with Gracie or hadn't the heart to put the baby down when she was sleeping in my arms and her breathing was so much like peace itself. My elbow was propped on a pillow so her weight felt easy—until my arm went numb and stiff, but I still didn't move, the time was so precious. The picture of my stillborn son was still in my mind, the hour I'd held him after the pain I'd thought about to end, instead of guessing it was the physical prelude to a worse suffering. Here was a perfect living infant in my charge who needed me. I'd not known the hole in my heart was still there, the hopeless tender longing, begging him pointlessly to breathe, breathe, breathe. Much as I cared for my nephew, Gary, who was born nearly the same time as the boy I lost, he was Louisa's, always Louisa's, and I'd had to guard my heart.

Who did Gracia have right now but me?

I held her to my left side so she would hear my heartbeat. I thought maybe she'd remember her mother's and be comforted that I was taking her place. I started thinking about Gracie's mother, tried to imagine what could have brought her to leave her baby. Was it like Gary said, that she just needed some temporary help? The more I thought about it, the more questions I had, the more doubts. Gary said he didn't know where the mother was. Wouldn't a mother say where she'd be, or check on her baby? What kind of help had she come to him for, exactly? Would she disappear and not say where she was going? Was it possible that she'd abandoned Gracie? But then, wouldn't Gary know that he had to call Gus?

Had Gary lied to us? And if he had, why? What wasn't he telling us?

Gracie stirred in my arms. Her eyes opened and locked on mine. I gave her my forefinger to hold. She was wearing one of the dresses I'd bought her, white, embroidered with red strawberries. "Most impractical thing you coulda found," Louisa announced when I showed it to her, trying to act like she is the sensible one, but I'd known how pretty it would

look with her dark hair, and I'd been right, and I remind you
Louisa has less fashion sense than Rosie and Marvelle com-
bined. (You can throw in everything the chickens know
about how to dress, too, and they all beat Louisa.) Gracie lay
loosely folded in a new pink-and-white receiving blanket. I
didn't want her either overheated or chilled as she slept. I
wanted everything perfect for her.

Louisa came into the living room then. "Good Lord," I
said. "What's the deal?" She'd changed her clothes, but a
blind woman could have done a better job of coordinating an
outfit.

"Gus is taking me out to dinner. I can't keep putting him
off. He'll think—well, I just came up with another story and
he's taking me out. I told him I'd meet him at the restaurant,
and you don't even want to know the reason I made up for
that."

"Oh, good job," I said. "Um, you weren't thinking of
wearing that, were you?"

"What's wrong with it?"

"Let me count the ways. And did you fix your hair with a
blender? What happened to the style I taught you, the French
twist with the sexy little strands around your face? Haul me
out of this chair—be careful of Gracie, now—she's just half
awake, and I'll fix you up. I figure I've got a solid fifteen minutes before she wants to eat."

"Well, I need to leave in ten," Louisa said. "I thought I
looked pretty good."

"I swear you do this to torture me, don't you, Sister?"

When she'd left for her dinner with Gus, I fed Gracie on
the couch, knowing I could get up from it unassisted, even
holding her. Don't laugh, it's not as easy as you think. I
played with her feet and tickled her belly lightly, which I already knew she loved, and watched how her eyes tracked
Jessie when the Lab came to nose her. Marvelle, highly suspi-

cious of both Jessie and Gracie, remained perched on the throne she'd created on the top of the wingback chair, with a disdainful expression. I read Gracie three of the baby books I'd bought, plus the one Gary brought, and showed her the pictures. "You're very smart, aren't you?" I said, sure that I could tell. When I saw her rubbing her eyes, I carried her to the back bedroom to change her for bed.

Louisa was so busy worrying about how her time and naps with Gus were derailed by Gracie that she wasn't paying attention to the hole in her own son's story. I wasn't about to point it out. I could see that she was on the fence a bit now, alternating between threatening to kill Gary, and softening, finding Gracie adorable.

I sat on the bed to cuddle Gracie before I put her in the bassinet, but she wouldn't settle down. She twisted and fussed a bit. Then I realized she was looking at Glitter Jesus, hanging directly across from us. I said, "Okay, I see what you mean." Still holding her, I got up and took Gary's artwork down. "I'm not sure Gary's telling the truth, that's the thing, Gracie. Is that bothering you, too? Do you know the real story?" I carried the picture across the room one-handed, and when I propped the picture up against the wall over toward the bathroom, bits of the glitter were still falling off.

"Don't worry, my love," I whispered to Gracie when I finally laid her in the bassinet now that she was quiet. "I'm here. I've got you." She gave me a little smile, even though her eyes were at half-mast on their way to sleep. A bit of glitter was in her hair, and that was fine by me.

Chapter 15

Rosalina

She ended each day the same way in the dark after her prayers, amid the sighs, snores, and mutterings of the other women who slept there, with a sheet of words to cover her anxious mind. Rosalina did her rosary to herself, then mouthed the words, "Good night, my sweet baby. Mama loves you. God with you always."

Her milk was drying up and the pain was nearly gone. It was a relief at work, where she was on her feet all day, but it made her sad, too, the physical connection to Gracia thinning, diminishing as time stretched, now late in the second week. The loss felt unendurable sometimes. She'd remind herself of her own father's sacrifice to save her. But he'd been able to watch her grow, teach her respect and the love of Jesus. Surely that was better than nothing, which is what she'd have of her daughter when the milk was no more.

She was finally able to send some money home, and her father had word that she was safe. She'd not said anything about Gracia to him. Why add to the pain of his sending her away? She could do for him as he'd done for her.

Gary

He felt better after he talked to Gus at the station, even though he'd had to tell Gus more than he'd wanted to—like Rosalina's name—but, Gary reasoned with himself, how was Gus supposed to find her if he didn't even know her name? Of course, he'd had to have that much. It would be fine, and with all Gus's professional training, he'd find Rosalina with practically no sweat, and then Gary would be able to explain that he just couldn't keep Gracia, that she belonged with her mother. Definitely. For sure. He had it worked out in his head and felt like he was walking on God's swept sidewalk again for a whole hour. Then, almost as soon as he got to his office in the church, his cell phone vibrated in his pocket. He pulled it out and was momentarily puzzled: Z Barnes, it read. Oh! Brother Zachariah! He didn't know that Brother Zachariah even had his phone number, but it was fine that the preacher who'd Saved him did, for sure. And Gary answered the call.

"Gary! Brother Zachariah here," the voice came through hearty, even forceful.

"Great to hear from you," Gary said. He meant it.

"Doing the Lord's work, I hear."

"Why yes, Brother, I am. I was so inspired by your work I went and got myself ordained." He sat at his desk, proud, wishing Brother Zachariah could see as well as hear him.

"Did you now."

"I did."

"Heard that, too."

Gary was pleased, wondering if he was starting to be known as an evangelist. It was almost too much to hope for. "That's great. Great. How did word get to you?"

"One of your members, she said she was, well, I guess she was in need of having the holy fire lit inside. Anyway, she was visiting her cousin in Couter County, and don't you know, I'm doing a revival series there, big tent, don't you know, got me a couple gospel singers and they add a real nice touch. Anyway, she came up answering the call to Jesus, all excited about it, too. Thought you'd be pleased to hear." Gary was not. "Afterward, see, she mentioned she'd been comin' to your church. So how's it goin'?"

"It's going pretty well, I'd say. I'd like it to grow faster, but like you told me before, the Lord will provide," Gary said.

"Surprised you didn't ask for some guidance about setting up a church. Disappointed."

". . . Oh. I didn't know I was supposed to. I mean, I didn't know you had one."

Brother Zachariah's voice turned soft and sad. "How long you think I been preaching?"

Gary had no idea. "A long time."

"You imagine I'd know how this is rightly done?" Brother Zachariah's voice was crimped by how he'd been slighted.

"Well, sure. Of course you know. I mean yes, definitely."

"So how did you go about it?"

"I rented a barn and I fixed it up as a church. I talked to people that I knew went to your revival, and—" Gary could explain it all, but Brother Zachariah interrupted, indignant.

"I see. You grabbed people that I warmed up to Jesus and sweet-talked them into coming to you."

"It wasn't like that, Brother Zachariah. I got myself ordained. Like you."

"Not like me, I assure you. You know anything 'bout establishing a church?"

"I just did it." Did that sound prideful? "I did ask the Lord for guidance."

"I see. So you takin' tithes and donations?"

"Well, yes, I mean there's rent on the barn and expenses to pay. And we're small but we want to build a real church down the road someday, so we're trying to set aside a little bit for that."

"You registered with the authorities then, of course," Brother Zachariah said.

"What authorities?"

"Brother Gary, you can't be serious, askin' me that question. You're takin' in money and not registered? You payin' taxes? Renderin' unto Caesar? Not that you have to, bein' a nonprofit, unless you failed to file all the proper paperwork."

"I didn't think I . . ." Gary felt his face getting hot, like he'd done something wrong, but he didn't know what.

"Oh, boy, you got yourself a heap a trouble. Don't tell me you're not proper with the authorities."

"I didn't know I had to . . ."

"See, I'd a thought you'd come to me. You got no idea what you're doin', do ya? No experience, just thought you could do it with no guidance. Now, I suppose I'm gonna have to clean this up since I'm the one that Saved you. You're gonna have to pay the taxes and penalties, y'know, from not being registered proper. I'll take care of the paperwork."

Gary slumped back in his chair, suffused with relief. "I'd be grateful, Brother Zach. I should've come to you when I started up, I just—"

"Never mind. I'll get you right with Caesar. You make sure you stay right with Jesus, y'hear? You figure up how much you've taken in, now, do you have that figure? I'll find out what you owe—interest and penalties, see, and what your tax is—and get you registered right. You get the numbers for me."

"I . . . Do you mean like right now?"

"Better get on this quick. Don't wanna get shut down—"

Good Lord, Gary did not want to get shut down. He'd put everything into this church like a basket of hope that he'd finally picked up after leaving his son's grave wearing the lead shoes of failure. He still wore those shoes, but having been Saved and starting his church was what gave him the strength to lift his feet enough to walk. He couldn't ruin this, too. "Yes, right. Right now. I can look it up right now. I've got the records, see, we keep good records, we're hoping to build someday if we get more people Saved and they donate, and—"

"Just look it up now, so I can get on with it."

"But do you need totals of what we've spent, too? Because—"

Brother Zachariah clicked his tongue. Gary could see him, his hair that started out so high and neat it looked fixed in place, mostly green eyes that grew fiery bloodshot after hours of preaching, and the ripe apples of his cheeks then, too, the inspiring fervor of his shouting, whispering, blaming, blessing, arms waving down the Holy Spirit. The white suit he wore (which Gary had tried to copy when he held his own first revival, with white pants, heaven-blue shirt, and white tie, though he couldn't begin to afford white patent shoes like Brother Zachariah's so he'd settled for new white sneakers). Brother Zachariah made that clicking noise when he was disappointed, when someone was denying his sin. "Do you want the church to be Saved or don't you?" he said now.

"Yes. I'm sorry I did wrong. Please help me," Gary said. He'd learned not to deny it when he'd sinned, to ask for forgiveness.

"I'll see what I can do. Maybe I can fix this. Get me the total amount you have taken in donations. I'll be callin' you back in thirty minutes." And the connection went dead.

Gary did his best to get an accurate total, rummaging through the monthly receipts in his desk. His heartbeat was too fast, he felt sick and sweaty. How had he messed this up so badly? He had the sum ready for Brother Zachariah when the phone vibrated in his shirt pocket twenty-nine minutes later.

"Huh," was all Brother Zachariah said. "I'll let you know real soon what you owe, y'know, taxes and penalties, to stay open. Probably gonna need to be monthly payments. Might hafta take out a loan. Maybe I can cover and you pay me. Gotta keep the Lord's door open."

"I'd be so grateful," Gary said. "Let me know as soon as you can how I make this right."

After Brother Zachariah hung up, Gary laid his head down on his desk, told himself that he had to have faith. There were tears that wanted to come, but he sniffed them back and pressed his jaws together hard to hold them in. He absolutely had to go to his mother's. He'd promised. More important, though, he had to make sure she'd let Gracia stay longer.

His mother was having a conniption. "Yes, son, Gracie is fine and such a good baby, but how much longer?" was what she said each time he either called or went to the house to check on things, and she didn't pick today to give him a break from it. Recently he'd been pleased to see the portrait of Jesus on black velvet that he'd done for his mother back out in the living room, where Gary preferred it. His mother had hung it in the master bedroom a while back and explained it was because it was where she kept her memories of Harold and it was like saying *Bless your heart*. Gary guessed he couldn't disagree with that, though he preferred it in the main room, to be seen all the time. Yesterday, it had been a bit crooked, which wouldn't do, and when he'd straightened it on the wall, a little of the glitter from the halo had flaked off and fallen to the floor. He'd meant to bring some with him today to touch it up but had been upset by Brother Zachariah's call and then concentrated on talking his mother into keeping Gracia longer and it had slipped his mind. He hoped Jesus wasn't disappointed in him, his lack of attention, but then he thought that He would likely find the baby and the church more important and would forgive the oversight. God would be merciful about a small thing, too, having been merciful about Gary's much larger transgression with Rosalina and, he hoped, this tax issue. Plus, there was always that thin line about a graven image, so it was best that he hadn't put that first.

They were in the kitchen now, his mother and CarolSue having tea. Gary asked for coffee, which his mother had made him. The store-bought cookies were disappointing. He'd hoped for some of her homemade ones. She'd started baking again a while back, which he'd taken as a good Sign of something, though he wasn't sure what.

"I'm working on finding her mother," he said now, as he did pretty much every day. "Making progress. It's what God wants." He was fairly sure of that, even now, but he didn't understand why God wasn't helping him out more, because the truth was that he'd made no progress at all. Meaning that Gus hadn't had a thing to report yet. It had put some doubt in Gary's mind, and talking to his mother never diminished that.

"How can you be so sure?" she said again. "Maybe Gracia's mother is a drug addict and God wants the baby in a safe, loving foster home. Which Gus can make sure is what happens." She was relentless, even though he could tell she thought a lot of Gracia. But now, his mother never took her eyes away from his even when she took a drink of her tea, which was disconcerting. He let his eyes follow his hand to the cookie plate as a way not to look at her for a moment.

"It's the sanctuary thing, the confidentiality, Mom. You wouldn't understand, but I have to do it this way. I'll find her. I have to," he said. "She belongs with a parent." As soon as he said *parent*, Gary felt himself redden. He got up abruptly to hide it, went to the counter to pour himself more coffee. While he held the cup, he suddenly thought, *If the church wasn't real because it wasn't registered, like Brother Zachariah said, then there was no sanctuary, and it was just plain old fornicating. But Brother Zachariah would make it retroactively a sanctuary, wouldn't he?*

"Louisa, we're doing fine. The baby's really no trouble." This was becoming a pattern, Aunt CarolSue stepping in to help him. He didn't really understand it entirely because he could see it was annoying his mother, but it was working for him so he sure wasn't going to question it. In fact, he thought maybe it was a Sign that he was right, and finding Rosalina *was* what God wanted. Then, CarolSue pretty much confirmed that by what she said next.

"Really, Sister, Gary is the Reverend. I'm sure he knows how to handle these church matters better than we do. We can help out. I'll take care of Gracie." And then she'd tacked it on again, "She's no trouble. And it's something we can do to help Gary's church work."

"Well, you mean the baby isn't changing *your* life all that much, but I was counting on . . ." She trailed off then, giving CarolSue The Look.

"Mom, if Aunt CarolSue is willing to take care of her, why do you mind?"

His mother put her Grand Finish on The Look then by rolling her eyes at Aunt CarolSue along with a deep sigh and said, "All right. I guess another day or two won't matter. But that's it."

Gary figured out then, a flash of insight, that his mother was mad that CarolSue wasn't helping her in the garden and with the canning because she was doing the baby care. Maybe he could get around that and buy more time. He thanked his mother profusely, thanked CarolSue, and quit the subject for a moment while he was ahead. He could ponder God's various messages and Signs later in private. Now was the time to talk pleasantly about how his mother's canning was coming along, and if Rosie Two was keeping the grass down enough. Last year he'd paid for that kid Brandon she liked so much to mow it, but now she'd gone and gotten another goat. Like she needed more animals around the place.

He was still getting short, irritated-sounding answers from

his mother, when, as if to underline the point she'd made about her disrupted life, the baby started to fuss from the back bedroom, waking from her nap just as his mother was starting to answer one of Gary's questions.

"I'll get her," he said, pushing his chair back from the table.

"You?" It was downright weird how his mother and CarolSue said it at the same time, disbelieving, like a Greek chorus would say *No way!*

"Yes me. You can take a break from baby care." It was genius. "Mom, CarolSue can give you a hand in the garden, and I'll babysit for a couple hours before I get back to the church." He figured it would make his mother happy, get her the garden help she wanted. He couldn't help in the garden himself because he'd do nothing but sneeze. It was that time of year. Ragweed and goldenrod. He didn't last more than ten minutes outside.

His mother sighed again. CarolSue got up and headed toward the master bedroom where Gracie and her stuff were, saying, "Um, honey, Gracie needs to be changed and fed. And then she'll be awake for several hours. She's crying *now* . . ."

"I'm not deaf. I hear her crying," he said, following right behind her. "I'll watch you change her so I . . . remember. I did have a baby once." Gary wasn't about to admit that he hadn't changed Cody's diapers. He'd tried once and gotten a face full of pee, which Nicole thought was totally hilarious, but he hadn't, and after that he'd left diapers to her and his mother. Or Nicole's mother. Anyone but him. "Please. You help Mom with the garden. That'll make her happy. I'll take a turn with the baby. I'll give her the bottle."

"Bless your heart," CarolSue said. Gary thought she didn't sound happy about being able to help her sister, but he was sure he was doing the right thing. He could please both God and his mother, a double win.

Chapter 16

CarolSue

I was doomed. How had this happened? Gracie needed me, I was sure of that, but here I was stuck out in the garden in record-breaking September heat, harvesting sweet potatoes (which I don't even like) with Louisa barking instructions at me, while Gary—who hardly knew which end of a baby to put on his shoulder—had charged himself with taking care of her. I imagined Gracie's little face turning red because she was upside down with her bare foot stuck in Gary's ear.

"I should go in and check on Gracie," I said to Louisa, who was thrilling herself with the astonishing beauty of some of her lumpy produce.

"She's not crying," Louisa pointed out. "We'd hear her. You opened every window so you would. Remember?"

"What if she can't?"

"Huh?" Louisa looked at me as if I'd said something crazy. She can do that and it's very annoying.

"If she can't breathe, she can't cry. Any fool knows that. I'm going to check on her."

"Oh good grief," she said, rolling her eyes. "It's probably good I didn't plant that marijuana I was thinking about before Gus started calling on me. I'd think you'd gotten into it."

"What?"

"The baby is fine. Perfectly fine. Let's get these potatoes dug while we can."

Do you see what I mean about my sister? Much as I love her, sometimes she just doesn't think things through.

Several of the chickens were strutting around the yard, in and out of sight as they pecked at the ground for bugs and whatever else they eat. "Where's Abigail?" I asked. "I haven't seen her all afternoon. I saw JoJo and Beth and Amy a while ago. But I haven't seen her at all." The truth is, I can't tell one chicken from another. They look pretty much alike to me, except for Amy, who's a stunning white with a noticeable black streak in her temperament as well as her feathers, which Louisa would not appreciate my mentioning. I thought she might fall for it. Louisa worried all the time about predators; she was as protective of those chickens as dear Charlie was of me.

She stood up, trowel in hand, and looked around. "You haven't? Uh-oh." And off she went behind the coop, which she left standing open during the daytime so the girls could free-range.

And I was off and running for the back door. Take the "running" sprinkled with salt, of course, but I was moving right along.

Well, fortunately, for once Louisa was right, Gracie was alive. Gary had her lying on the floor on a receiving blanket and was showing her the rattles. Just as I'd told him to, although I didn't think he was doing it in a particularly engaging fashion. And the books I'd put out for him to read her, though, looked untouched.

"Oh, hi, Aunt CarolSue," he said, looking up from the floor. "She didn't seem interested in the book, I mean, she wouldn't look at the pictures or anything."

I knew it! "That's okay. Babies need the sound of your voice, and the more words they hear, the better it stimulates their brains. I read all about it . . . a long time ago."

"Oh." He looked unconvinced.

From outside the kitchen window I heard Louisa bellow. "Sister! I need help out here."

I hurried into the kitchen and called softly so Gracie wouldn't hear yelling. "I'm coming. Bathroom."

I went into the bathroom so Gary wouldn't know I'd lied, and then went back outside.

"Don't 'bathroom' me," Louisa said when I got back to the section where she'd planted enough sweet potatoes to feed all the Pilgrims and the Indians at the first, second, and third Thanksgivings. The sun blistered down, relentless. "I told you Gracia was fine. I know Gary getting mixed up with that cult was idiotic, but he's not totally stupid about everything. He'd yell for us if anything was wrong with the baby."

"People have to grieve in their own way," I said. I'm sure she thought I meant that about Gary, but I was thinking of myself and missing Charlie, and how right then they wouldn't let me hold the baby, and I just wanted to go back home to Atlanta where we'd had our life. He was such a sweet, tender man and so good to me. I wished I hadn't complained about all the time he spent puttering in the garage and how he hadn't worn his hearing aids, which meant the neighbors could watch the same station as Charlie without turning on the sound. When I had a minute alone, I thought about him, and my eyes would start to water. Louisa seemed to have forgotten all about him—or thought I had. She didn't bring up his name. I'd thought she'd wrap me in a blanket of understanding.

"Right," she said. "Listen, this is good. I know we want to let Gary find Gracie's mother—but Gus and I, we're not really spending any quality time together since we've had the baby here. If Gary can babysit here, he can babysit anywhere, so I'm thinking we just ask him to take care of her at the church a couple afternoons a week. And you know, you could even go with them if you were worried. Problem solved." She had a sort of triumphant look on her face and put both her hands palms up, as if to say, *See how simple it is? You can help work out my life now that I helpfully insisted you move in here right after your husband died and*

you couldn't think straight so I could roast you alive digging
up ugly orange potatoes as if it's what you want to do, like
your life is just peachy now and what else could you want?

I could tell her what else I wanted. I wanted to take care of
that baby. And I also wanted to go back home to Atlanta.

I was doomed.

Gus

Something about Gary's story didn't smell right to Gus.
Not the details of what he'd said, which he supposed were
plausible, even though Gary's church was built on shaky
ground. Louisa was right about that much. She sure had a
point about his internet ordination and that money-scamming
cult that he'd gotten involved with after Cody died. That
Brother Zachariah character was a charlatan through and
through, and Gus hadn't ever confided in Louisa that he'd
had a big hand in running him on to the next county, doubtless to bilk sad souls there. For sure, it might get him points
with Louisa in the short term, but he couldn't be a hundred
percent sure that it wouldn't get back to Gary, and in Gus's
limited experience with romance, it was a particularly bad
idea to alienate a woman's son.

The sticking point about Gary was that you couldn't
spend a half hour with him and not know he'd been broken
by guilt as much as by the two deaths. Gus had his own guilt
about Harold—that much he had confessed to Louisa. When
Harold had set out for revenge against the drunk driver
who'd killed Cody, his every intention had been soaked in the
rage of inside-out grief, and half crazed. He cared so little
about what happened to him that a rookie sheriff could have
shadowed Harold as easily as Gus had, to thwart his schemes,
stopping him before he could do real damage and put himself

at risk. Which had been the point, to protect Harold—who clearly wasn't thinking straight—from himself. Not that Gus admitted to Louisa how easy it had been to stop Harold; he wanted to look smart and skilled, after all, but then Harold's inability to get revenge made him kill himself. In a way, did that make Gus responsible? That was the part he felt terrible about.

For a long time, Louisa had blamed him, too. She'd figured that if he hadn't intervened, let Harold get caught, even if he'd been in jail for a few months, revenge would satisfy him and he'd have stayed alive. Gus couldn't argue that point, since there was no way to know if she was right.

Somehow, though, Louisa had come around on her own to understanding Gus's intention, and that there's not always a straight, white thread from the intentions of someone's heart to how something turns out. She'd said that sometimes that thread gets tangled and the way you mean something ends up having nothing to do with how it turns out, and then you feel terrible and say how sorry you are. Sometimes you have a chance to try to make it right. And sometimes you don't, you can't. The other person won't let you, or life won't let you.

Gus was lucky. Louisa was giving him a chance, and he wasn't about to blow that chance by confronting Gary. Dicey as things sometimes were between Louisa and Gary, with him always trying to save her soul and her telling him *Bless your heart, honey, but I plan to be reincarnated as either a Buddhist or a deer* just to torment him, it would still be plain stupid. So Gus needed to ferret out what was really going on with Gary—if it wasn't what he said—but not alienate him, while keeping Louisa out of it. Tricky business, this.

It wasn't that Gary's story made no sense. It wasn't that. Could some poor young woman have asked him for help? Sure. Even the "sanctuary" part, Gus supposed he could buy that. What made no sense was Gary's discomfort, the way he didn't quite meet Gus's eyes when he kept talking about confidentiality, as if he wanted to draw the blinds and keep daylight out. As if he was uncomfortable. Why would he be? It didn't sit right. Call it instinct, Gus said to himself when he thought about it. He tried to figure out what exactly might make Gary so uneasy, why he might be looking for a woman he thought might be in trouble.

There was, of course, another wrinkle. Isn't there always, Gus muttered to himself on Tuesday morning when he sorted through his official email. The one concrete piece of information that Gary had provided—beyond a first name and two possible last names—was the decent possibility that this Rosalina might be undocumented. Well, that was a problem, and one that put him in an ugly place based on the notice that he'd just opened from immigration control informing him that the cooperation of his office was expected in the coming month, as four places of employment would be checked, without notice, for undocumented employees. Gus hit "print," and watched the paper feed into the machine. The noise always sounded like a skeleton's chattering teeth to him. Probably because he was never printing good news. He wasn't a superstitious man.

"Jimmy!" he yelled to his deputy. Of course Jimmy pretended he couldn't hear him, so Gus got up from his desk and knocked on the glass. Jimmy jumped in his chair dramatically. He'd been drinking coffee, reading the newspaper. Ought to have headed out on patrol by now anyway. Gus motioned for him to come into his office.

"Lookit this," Gus said, extending the printout.

This deputy was new, young, and raw-faced, like he'd only recently learned how to use a razor. He'd not been exactly an academic star in high school, according to his record. Gus imagined he'd been overly busy with football and girls. There hadn't been a lot of applicants for the job was the issue. His two part-timers had other jobs and weren't looking to go full-time.

"Cool," Jimmy said. "Can the department get a dog now?"

Jimmy was not going to be a great deal of help.

"No, we are not getting a dog. The point here is that we—and by we, I mean me and Billy—will be expected to cooperate with the Feds, which means that you and Floyd will be covering some more patrols." Floyd was a retired Elmont cop, like Billy, who worked part-time, when Gus needed extra help with a bad accident or dispatch or the like. Both were older and had some sense. Gus figured he'd pay Floyd overtime out of the budget to babysit Jimmy, keep his jets cool, and prevent damage. He'd have to pay Billy overtime, too, but he could charge the Feds for that. Billy wasn't a genius, but he was still strong and fast and not dangerous. If Gus had to be involved in any kind of an immigration roundup, he'd rather have Billy than Jimmy any day.

"How come Billy?"

"Didn't your mother tell you not to whine? Billy's done this before and I need an experienced man." That was a lie. Billy hadn't worked with immigration before, and he'd have to either tell Billy not to blow that cover or just hope it didn't come up. Gus's life experience had suggested that attention to detail was a better bet than leaving something to hope or chance.

"How'm I gonna get experience then?" Jimmy was nothing if not persistent.

"Prove yourself first. Like don't be sitting there drinking coffee and reading the paper when you oughta be out being seen." Gus could come off hard-ass when he needed to. Clearly, it was time.

Jimmy had the sense not to argue. It was only another two minutes before the patrol car pulled away from the station. Gus checked on Connie, the dispatcher on duty, and then poured himself a mug of coffee, spooned in the creamer, dropped in two lumps of sugar, helped himself to the paper off the deputy desk, and settled himself in his office to check out the news. He wondered what thorn was in the Feds' side. Guessed he'd find out soon enough. Gus tended to the *no harm, no foul* side occasionally. When he saw a taillight out and stopped a vehicle for it, there'd been times when there'd be children in the car, a brown-skinned driver wearing an employee identification badge from an Elmont factory. That, and a wedding ring. He'd be respectful, the driver would, but Gus would see fear behind his eyes. Gus would ask the children a couple questions. They'd answer politely, respectfully, about where they went to school, and tell him yes they liked it. Nice kids. Unaccented English. They'd been born here, Gus was pretty sure, although not their father, judging from his accent. But his English was clear and good. Had Gus written the ticket, it would have meant asking for his driver's license. Why destroy a tax-paying intact family, have a man end up deported, because his taillight was out? It was just common sense. He'd told the driver his light was out, and "Get that fixed right away, have a good day," and got back in the cruiser and pulled away, the driver maybe thanking God, Mother Mary and Jesus, or the silver St. Christopher dangling from the chain around his neck, or maybe thinking there was some human kindness or blind luck in the world. Gus didn't know, never would, and didn't need to.

Sheriff right to the bone, Gus was, and not for lack of anything else he could have done. He enforced the law; he believed in the law. The law was right, moral, and just, and not intended to do harm or wreck good lives for no purpose. So once in a blue moon maybe he accidentally forgot to ask for a driver's license. The state didn't lose a taxpayer. A local company didn't lose a long-time employee whose ID badge indicated he was a shift supervisor. Children didn't lose a parent. A wife didn't lose her husband. Just made sense, like a good law. Like a good sheriff who did his best.

Chapter 17

Rosalina

The big garden supply place where she'd been working, along with others from her country, had let them go. The season would be over soon, they said, but if you're still here, come back in March. We'll need help again. What were they supposed to do through the winter? She heard about the meat packing place that didn't look at papers real closely. It kept their costs down not to worry about papers, and they didn't have enough workers with papers anyway. Farms were the best, because they always needed help, but after the harvest it would be the same problem. And she had to guess, they all had to guess, where would they be safe?

She took her chances with the place she thought she'd be most invisible, the chicken packing plant where they'd advertised for help, even though it bothered her, all that death, and she had to dress like its ghost in white coveralls, a white net cap over all of her hair, white plastic gloves, and white shoe covers. But nobody had questioned the I-9 paper she'd given the employment office, the one Maria at the apartment had helped her get, and that was one good thing.

Her job was removing feathers from slaughtered bodies, to undress them, make them vulnerable even when hope was gone. Exposed. She couldn't help but think about the moment the birds had come into the world, unknowing, unsuspecting. Even unafraid. But Rosalina knew enough to be terrified of what life could bring. She'd think like that and then shake her head to banish thinking. Here was what life *would* bring for one: If she didn't get faster, she'd lose the job, and then what would she do? And even if she didn't lose the job, she wasn't safe. None of them were.

Some days, Rosalina daydreamed of Gracia. The daydream wanted to become a hope. The daydream was a voice in her head that said, *Maybe you could go get her, and when she grows up, she will forgive you.* And there was another voice that argued, *You want to expose yourself? To shame her? You think these birds forgive you? What life can you give her?*

It was cold, cold and damp on the processing floor, kept that way so the poultry would stay fresh. Rosalina stomped her feet to try to bring back the feeling. She'd lined the inside of her old shoes with newspaper, hoping it would keep them warmer, but then they were so tight she couldn't feel her toes at all. She'd been taught that hell was fiery. *Wrong, wrong, wrong,* she thought another day, when thinking crept in again, and then she chastised herself. *Be grateful. You are safe, Gracia is safe with the Reverend, her father. You can send money home to your own father. Do not be selfish.* And then she was grateful again. At night she was careful to first give thanks in her whispered prayers, before she asked for love, health, safety, and education for Gracia, for her father's health and safety, to be faster at removing feathers in her job, and the forgiveness of the birds.

CarolSue

Gary kept managing to stretch out the time Louisa had given him to find Gracia's mother. I swear, he had a different reason every time he showed up and instead of flipping out,

Louisa gave in. I'm sure it was because Gracie was so darling that Louisa was like pre-softened butter, and besides, Gus had been all tied up lately with some big "operation," he called it, with the Feds. In the planning stages, he said, sounding important, as men like to.

Louisa was entirely annoyed that he wouldn't tell her what it was about. "Like I'm going to take out an ad in the newspaper," she said. "If I did, though, at least it would be grammatically correct. Not like that idiot editor, who can't write a sentence without inserting an error. How are kids supposed to learn to speak correctly when what they read and hear is riddled with mistakes?" She was off and running on one of her favorite irritations then, forgetting how mad she was at Gus's secrecy. For about three minutes, until she remembered, and got mad at him all over again. And then when she wore out that subject, she started on Gary's inefficiency at finding Gracia's mother. The lack of naps was, I realized, making her cranky.

"Sister, let's make some special tea," I said. "After all, it's four o'clock, and it would be . . . refreshing, don't you think? And seasonal, now that it's a bit cooler outside, too."

Louisa had the back door propped open, and the September air was lovely. Beth wandered through it into the kitchen just then, thanks to the available entry.

"Maybe Brandon . . . or Gary? . . . could put the screen door on? I saw it in the barn," I said, keeping my tone as mild as I could manage. "We could have the nice air without needing to keep the storm door open with a chair."

"Don't criticize," Louisa said. "Brandon's in school, and Gary . . . he'd just start suggesting it's time for him to move me to a *home*, where I'd have all the help and attention I need. Bless his heart, as you want me to say, but you know what I'd rather say. Only way he'll get me out of here is feet-first."

"Gus would do it." I don't usually persist when Louisa gets going, but Beth was wandering toward the living room and now JoJo was approaching the door.

"She's not bothering Marvelle, and for once Jessie isn't trying to play with her. I don't see a problem." Nothing makes Louisa defensive quicker than a negative word about her chickens.

"I was just thinking we have a baby here and possibly . . . I mean, you know, sanitation."

"Place wasn't condemned when I was raising Gary," she shot back. "And I managed not to kill him. Though I may now, if he doesn't find that baby's mother pretty soon. This is getting ridiculous. Pretty soon, she'll be ready for college."

I got up and put the kettle on the stove. "You have to admit, she's a sweetheart. You don't want her stuck in some iffy foster home in Elmont, where we'll never know if she's okay."

Louisa smiled in spite of herself. "Not saying she's not a doll." She scratched her neck and got up from the kitchen chair to pull down the tea bags and get out the bourbon. "Just a splash," she said. "Will you join us, Marvelle?"

"Not like Gus could do anything right now but take her to Child and Family Services. Maybe not even in Elmont. Most likely transfer her to Indy, actually. She'd be a ward of the state in no time. Lost in the system. You know how that goes." I spoke confidently, as if I knew what I was talking about. I was just making stuff up as I went along. I'd learned how to do that from Charlie, who could always sound like an expert on anything. Louisa had pointed out that married men do that all the time to impress their wives. Fortunately, Louisa didn't expect that from me, and she nodded. Or maybe I'd said something that was true and she knew it. I had no idea and it wasn't like I could ask her.

Speaking confidentially, however, the truth was I wanted

that baby with me. Especially then, because I was stuck in Shandon. I'd called my real estate agent. I'd thought it would be easy, that I'd just tell him to take my house off the market because I was moving back to Atlanta and wanted my house. After all, it was mine. Charlie had left it to me free and clear. When Louisa suggested that Gary could babysit—even take Gracia to the church—I figured she was thinking that while she and Gus were napping, I'd be gloriously free to harvest winter squash and pumpkins, or clean out the garden beds (only slightly more rewarding than canning vegetables, which is like saying I'd rather kill fire ants with my bare hands than roll boulders up a hill covered with them). I couldn't tell Louisa that, even though I used to be able to tell my sister anything straight out. That had been on the phone, though. Living together had changed everything.

It felt like a body blow when I heard that I couldn't move home yet. I slumped down onto Harold's old wingback chair and thought, *I'm doomed.* I'd signed an exclusive contract with the agent that put my house on the market for three months. I was stuck there, and I'd have to listen to the muffled soundtrack of a porn movie (what I *imagined* that must be like, not that I knew!) coming from the guest room, while Gary took Gracia to his church and stuck her underneath numerous portraits of Jesus, blond, festooned with a glitter halo, and supposedly walking on water or throwing money changers out of the temple—but in each, looking way more like Elvis in drag and stoned, having lost his guitar. I just knew poor Gracie would be traumatized for life.

But the earth tilted back when Gus got all wrapped up in this operation with the Feds and told Louisa he had to be at the station afternoons and evenings. I thought, *This is a good sign*, and then, *Oh no, bless my heart, I sound like Gary, and that's downright terrifying.* One thing Louisa and I share: We don't believe in signs. Until they suggest exactly what we want. But now I wouldn't be stuck out in the garden. Or inside trying not to listen. *I* would be taking care of Gracia. She was sleeping right then, but I couldn't help myself: I tiptoed into that bedroom to watch her sleep for minutes of gladness, breathing along with her, in and out, in and out with my beautiful Gracie, breathing out what we've lost and breathing in hope, she wearing the pink sleeper I bought her, and with the brown cuddle bear tucked next to her, that too.

Chapter 18

Gary

The timing couldn't have been worse, like a weather map that showed two big fronts colliding. First, Gus had told him that for the time being he couldn't help him look for Rosalina anymore because his department was expected to provide local backup for the Feds, some operation they were starting soon.

"Drugs?" Gary said, although he'd not put much of a question mark on it. The opioid business had mushroomed lately, especially after there'd been the big heroin busts. The other possibility was the human sex trafficking, but Gary hadn't heard too much about that moving through Elmont yet. Maybe, though.

They were at Shandon's one café, and Margo, busty, narrow-eyed, and badly in need of smiling lessons, had already brought their coffee and donuts. Now she interrupted. "That be all?" she said, already tearing the check off her pad. Like Margo, the décor was aging badly, beige Formica tables chipped, and faux red leather chairs splitting here and there revealing dirty white stuffing. But it was Shandon's version of Starbucks and the very big deal was that it now had Wi-Fi. Not that Gary needed it at the moment, though he'd come here to use the internet more than once.

He'd asked Gus if he could join him during his morning break because he didn't want Gus at the church, especially not with that foghorn of a voice, and he didn't want to call attention to himself by going to the station again.

"Nope," Gus said to Margo, because he didn't appreciate being hurried. At the same moment, Gary said, "Yes," not wanting to spend for more than coffee. Margo sighed heavily. "What else you want?"

"Dunno yet," Gus said. "We'll let you know."

"Piece of work, that one. She hasn't caught on yet that I tip her when she smiles," Gus confided after Margo moved on. "Doesn't get a lot of tips from me."

"Huh," Gary said, thinking, *Maybe that's why she doesn't smile*, although he had to acknowledge that he used to tip her regularly and she didn't smile at him, either. He didn't tip anymore, though. The payments to Brother Zachariah for back taxes and penalties were sucking up his and the church's meager funds. He couldn't afford the Wash Away Your Sins Hand Sanitizer he'd been bringing his mother since Gracia had been there in spite of there being an internet special going on. He'd thought that was important for the baby, and it was a big discount, but even so, it was too much now.

"Anyway, that's the way it is," Gus said. "I'll try to give you a hand when this is done, but I don't know how long this operation will be. Maybe not long. Once word gets out, they scatter."

"Drugs?" Gary repeated, assuming again it must be. Later he'd know it was just that he wanted it to be something that simple. Simple for him.

"I can't talk about it, son. Not drugs. And you can't say a thing, understand me? Nothing. Are you . . . uh . . . giving any people . . . shelter?"

"Huh?"

"You housing any . . . needy . . . people in your church?" Gus not only sounded impatient, he put air quotes around *needy*.

Where did *that* come from? Gary wondered. "We don't have that kind of facility. I mean, we could maybe try . . ."

Gus shook his head, used his hand like a broom in the air to flick that answer away. "Not what we're talking about here, son. You'd best step up your own efforts to help that person you're concerned about. That's all. I can't be doing that at this time."

"I . . . uh . . . don't know what, how to do that. To find her, I mean." And Gary had put his palms up, frustrated. He'd closed his eyes then, and had the impulse to let the truth spill from him. Just confess, beg Gus to tell him what to do. It would be such a relief not to carry this alone.

But he stifled the impulse. Because if there was one thing Gary knew for sure, it was that people love to talk. And people love to start a story by saying, *Promise you won't tell anyone?* It's way more satisfying than keeping the promise you yourself made not to tell anyone. And for one, he couldn't delude himself that Gus wouldn't be more loyal to Louisa than to him and blab her son's private business to her right off, for the dating points he'd get for it. And for two, what if Gus said something around the station? Connie, the dispatcher, had come to his church. Twice. What if she was thinking of joining? She knew people. She was on that radio all the time, too. Anyone could listen on the police scanner. He knew that because Brother Randy did it as sort of a hobby. Wouldn't that just be juicy for him to hear Connie drop how the preacher has a secret baby?

The morning light streamed through the café windows now as the sun inched around, southeast, and up toward noon. Gus was seated with his back to the street, and Gary couldn't make out his facial expression, as he was increasingly backlit.

"Well, son, don't you have something to go on? I mean, where is she from? Immigrants usually gravitate to people from their home countries, you know, and to get . . . papers."

Gary was nonplussed for a moment, then he thought he knew. "Oh, like a fake . . . license?"

Gus sighed. "A license doesn't really help them get a job. Look, this isn't an appropriate conversation, given the circumstances with my job right now. I'm sure you can. Figure. It. Out." And Gus had said it just that way, as if Gary should know what he was talking about. Which he didn't. But then he had to pretend he did.

"Oh yeah. Got it. Okay, thanks. But when your project is done, I mean whenever, do you think you'd be able to give me a hand again? If my efforts haven't been . . . haven't worked?"

Another sigh from Gus. He picked up his coffee cup and waved to Margo, who was in no hurry to respond, Gary noticed. While she sauntered in their direction, making a point of stopping at other tables apparently to ask if there was anything anyone wanted. Between tables, she shot Gus a look as dirty as the café windows, which he completely ignored.

"Did you want something?" She flipped her bangs out of her eyes.

"Warm this coffee up, will you?" Gus said to her, then added with slightly exaggerated courtesy, "Please."

That warranted him another dirty look before Margo turned around without responding.

"I took her out. Once," Gus said. "Years ago. Big mistake, as you can see." He chuckled and shook his head. "Big, big mistake. Don't know what I was thinking. Boobies point straight at the ground, for one. Nothing like . . . uh, um . . . anyway . . . you got anything else on your mind? Say, uh, any issue like, uh, parking safety for your services?"

"It's gonna get tight soon," Gary said, "but I think we can get by for a while." If only that were true, there might be more donations coming in. More tithes even. He didn't know how he was going to handle the building fund accounting.

"Okay, well, let me know when you need some traffic control," Gus said. Margo approached with a coffeepot holding what was obviously the last—old—bit of bitterness in it.

"Never mind. We'll take the check now," Gus said.

Gary left the café with a headache and a vague commitment from Gus that he'd help if Gary "still needed it by then." Whatever that meant.

Now he told himself he had to do it and went to his mother's. To his huge relief, she wasn't there, only CarolSue with the baby. "She's at the grocery store," CarolSue explained. "I could have gone with her and taken Gracie, but, you know, it's so cold in there, the way they crank up the air conditioning. Way colder than it needs to be now that fall's coming on."

"Can I hold her," Gary said, not really a question, reaching for the baby. She was on CarolSue's lap in the living room, Jessie the Lab at her feet, and Marvelle, his mother's haughty cat, no favorite of Gary's, staring him down from her throne, the top edge of the blue wingback chair. She flicked her tail at him. Gary did not like Marvelle for the simple reason that she caused him to have thoughts he was sure Jesus would not like if He happened to be paying attention at the moment.

CarolSue seemed reluctant to hand Gracia over to him, but she did. "You're doing a real service to the Lord," he said as he took the baby. Careful to demonstrate that she'd be safe with him, he cupped the baby's head in his hand as he settled her against his chest. "I know this has been a lot of extra work for you, and it must wear you out. I appreciate that you're helping the church, Aunt CarolSue, and I hope you remember the Lord sees good works." His aunt, who definitely looked tired, started to interrupt then, but he talked over her, afraid she was going to say they just couldn't keep the baby longer.

Carrying the baby, who waved an arm and made little sounds that didn't sound like a protest, Gary walked over to the window. He wanted some time alone with the baby, truth be told, but it wasn't like he could say that to his aunt. What reason would he give? But he wanted to study her face. Who knew what the future held? He wished he could bless her on her way. He realized right then: Of course! One thing he could do. He could baptize her. He'd have to check the internet on how to do that with a baby. Probably the full-body dunking wasn't a good idea, but maybe it would be okay if he didn't hold her underwater the usual length of time.

"I'll try to be more help. I'm doing everything I can to find Gracia's mother. I'm sure this won't be much longer." Not that he had any idea if that was true. "But in the meantime, I can pitch in and give you some respite. I can take her, some afternoons. We can find something to do, won't we, pumpkin?" The last he directed to Gracia with a smile. Then he looked at CarolSue and was struck at how bereft she appeared. When she realized he was looking at her, she sat up straighter.

"She's fine here, Gary. Your members need you at the church, I'm sure. Meetings and such. Don't worry about it. We're doing fine."

"That's really good of you. I worry about you and Mom. Tomorrow is supposed to be a really good day. Indian summer. I'll come get her and take her for a walk."

"In what?"

"I'll get one of those stroller-things that looks like an umbrella. Or a regular one. I'll go to the thrift shop when I leave here. They always have baby stuff."

CarolSue's eyebrows went up. "Won't that seem . . . ?"

Gary shrugged. "Someone in the church needs . . . it's true." He shifted the baby to the other shoulder, though he wanted to sit and study her face. Who did she look like? Gary's own high school graduation picture hung on the wall. She didn't have his blue eyes, so like CarolSue's, the same startling color of his lost boy Cody's, that was for sure, but it was starting to look like they did have the same round shape as his. And was her dark hair going to be curly, like his, even if it wouldn't ever be blond? Her high forehead put him in mind of his father, although maybe that was because Harold's hairline had receded some. And then he asked himself if he was seeing what he wanted to see, or maybe what he was afraid of seeing. That was what he called the Brother Samuel question, which he'd hastened to dispatch with certainty one Sunday.

Brother Samuel wasn't actually a Brother, either, but was the skeptical husband of Sister Paula, who'd cajoled him to the service "Just once, please!" hoping he'd see the Light and finally step into it with her. The sermon had concerned miracles, specifically Jesus walking on water. Not-Brother Samuel had—rather obnoxiously, in Gary's private annoyed opinion—challenged him during the Praise Period about the physical possibility of that, narrowing his eyes, which were beady anyway, putting Gary in mind of his mother's irritating chickens, and scoffing, *Pfft. Mighta looked that way from a distance, you know, one of them optical delusions. People sees what they wants to see and think what they want is the way things is.*

Gary had quickly assured his baptized members that Jesus had, in fact, walked on water, and reminded them it was right there in the actual Bible, so they could know it was a true fact dictated by God. What else did he—or they—have to live by?

Now he was uncomfortable, reminded of not-Brother Samuel's words. Gary would feel better if there were something in the Bible that was smack-dab clear about whether Gracia was his or not so he wouldn't have to worry about whether he was seeing what he wanted to, one way or the other. But if she was, how did that tell him what to do, anyway? God wanted him to lead the church, and he couldn't be known as a fornicator and do that. He had to find the baby's mother and give her back, pure and simple.

"Gary?"

His aunt was talking to him. Oh dear Jesus, he had no idea what she'd said to him.

"Oh. Yeah, sure, Aunt CarolSue." He nodded, hoping he hadn't just agreed to clean toilets.

CarolSue broke into a smile. "She sure is. Really good. It's so easy to make her happy, you know? She only cries when she's hungry or just really too, too tired. And then I put her down and bam, she's asleep. Here—you tired of holding her? Want to get yourself a snack and rest before you go back to work?" She stood and held out her arms to take Gracia back. Jessie got up as soon as CarolSue did, ready to follow her.

"No, I'm good. You go take a rest. You deserve it." He still wanted to get to know the baby, though. Nothing wrong with that, or was there? God needed to give him a Sign.

His aunt looked disappointed. "Okay, then." She headed into the master bedroom—his mother and father's old room—but a moment later she was back. "Listen, I'm sure she needs changing now. Let me just put a fresh diaper on her."

"Where are they? I can do it."

"Really, it's easier to do it myself. I have everything organized, and she needs some diaper cream, too. I'll bring her right back," and then she was taking Gracia out of his arms. "Come here, my sweetheart, let's get you cleaned up. We like to be nice and dry, all clean, don't we? No wet diapers for my girl," she crooned, as she disappeared down the hall with the baby.

Gary stood in the living room, his arms suspended halfway to his sides as if unknowing what to do with themselves, and there was a chill where the baby had been nestled against Gary's chest and neck and the heat of his body had mixed with hers.

Much later, Gary would think of how his sweat was like the water of his life, his loss, and how Gracie's head had become sweaty tucked between his neck and chest, so that maybe her loss and his had run together as surely as the water of Rush Run, the creek through the woods that edged this farm where he'd been raised, ran into the greater creeks and rivers that ran to the ocean from which all life rose and rose again. And he would wonder if that had been the Sign. The small Grace that was given. And is given and given.

Gus

Gus left the café as soon as he decently could, still astonished at his own slip. *Good Lord*, he muttered to himself, as he slammed his patrol car door. *You told her son that you'd taken out Margo and you brought up her hanging boobies? You even started to compare them to his mother's? And then you ask him if he needs traffic control for his Sunday services as a way to change the subject?* Well, that last was a ridiculous notion. Gary was lucky to get twenty people at any service, which meant seven cars. There was room around the barn for perhaps thirty, but anyone could bait Gary to talk about his church, so maybe that part had been okay. Gus muttered on while turning the cruiser's key, trying to reason out whether he'd done actual damage to his own cause. *You can't do stupid stuff, that is the damn point.*

The day was brilliant, more fall in the air now, going out in the morning like biting an apple, and the maples edged with scarlet and gold, starting to set themselves on fire when the light came through them. That's how they looked, all upright tall and burning glory when the sun got to a certain angle and shone through them late that afternoon when Gus drove a back road from Shandon in a southwesterly direction, which just happened to be the way to dear Louisa's, and it had occurred to him how she also set his heart and maybe certain other parts of him ablaze.

Possibly today would be a good day for a nap, he thought, and some special tea afterward, then dinner. He'd bring a steak. He could still do that easily—until the time changed back to standard, he had that extra hour of daylight—and neither of them minded eating late. They'd been known to have their special tea in bed, although Gus himself often skipped the tea ingredient.

Damn! What the hell are you thinking? CarolSue is there. Moved in. Gus slapped the side of his face with his palm, something he fantasized about doing to the back of Jimmy's head altogether too often. *This isn't something a man with normal intelligence would forget.* Those last were the exact words he'd said to Jimmy, in fact. Good grief, he must be overtired from lack of naps. He'd heard it could do brain damage.

He drove down Main Street more slowly than usual, scanning the parking meters, which was Jimmy's job, but not trusting him to have actually checked them. They were two-hour meters and the shop owners liked to park right in front of their stores instead of on the side street where they were supposed to, even though there was free parking a block away. Every once in a while, Gus would send Jimmy out to chalk their tires and he could write twenty tickets that morning, easy. Really pissed off the storekeepers but kept the township trustees off Gus's case. It was a balancing act, like Rhonda used to say that his apartment was a balancing act between his need to create chaos and her need to restore order to the universe. He really missed his sister a lot. The big question now was how he was going to balance out this CarolSue thing with his need to be with Louisa. Rhonda would have had some advice, even though he wouldn't have told her about the naps. Too embarrassing and she'd make a big deal out of it. It *was* a big deal, of course, but, well, whatever. He still wouldn't have been . . . specific.

He spotted an expired meter in front of the Supply with an empty spot to slide the cruiser into right next to it. He wrote the ticket so he could claim he'd spent all kinds of time checking meters, which likely wouldn't match with the meter tally, but nobody checked that day by day, only by the month. He'd have to get on Jimmy to do meter patrol on foot again. The town was hardly a blink, and the meters were new. Anything to raise some revenue. Gotta keep the shopkeepers happy, because they're voters, but keep the township trustees happy because they approve the sheriff's budget and salary, after all.

He got back into the black-and-white, pleased with himself. He could do this. Set a task before him and he could do it. Stinking trustees wanted revenue raised, couldn't get their levy passed, okay, he'd raise some revenue. Rhonda had always said he could do whatever he wanted, even when she was mad, like, "You could take care of this place right if you wanted to." So fine. He'd have to maneuver CarolSue out of the way, keep Gary happy, and . . . Louisa, well, Louisa must be tired out from her sister being there and all the garden work. She really must need to get back to regular naps. He'd just have to make that happen.

Chapter 19

CarolSue

Yesterday afternoon was the closest call yet, and I don't mind telling you that I don't think my sister understands the gravity of the situation. I truly think she's gone over the edge. I never thought the day would come when I'd have to say, "Louisa, what's the Plan?" because she used to always cram one of her crazy Plans down my throat so hard and fast I couldn't even speak to object.

Come to think of it, she still does when it comes to something that she really cares about, like getting enough vegetables canned to feed us and the five hundred residents of Shandon in the very likely event that all grocery stores within a thousand miles all shut down forever. That seems to be her notion of a Plan these days. She doesn't seem to think five minutes ahead about keeping Gus from finding out about Gracie.

I've been suggesting to her right along that she should tell Gus she'd like some privacy and a change of scene, and that they should go to his apartment to nap. I don't know if she ever has, but not only have they not gone there, she doesn't seem all that worried about his dropping in again.

Here's what happened yesterday. You can decide for yourself if I'm right.

Gary showed up just as it was getting toward late afternoon, with one of those umbrella strollers. He said he'd been able to talk the Thrift Shop owner into donating it to the church. He seemed pretty pleased with himself about that, and said he'd take Gracia for a walk to give me a break from baby care and so I could help Louisa clean the chicken coop and get fresh bedding in the roost, which she'd said needed to be done. Oh goodie. Nothing more fun for me than cleaning out chicken poop, that's for sure, and I didn't want a break from baby care, but Louisa was tickled three times over because there was still plenty of daylight and we'd be able to get it done that afternoon.

I changed Gracie's diaper and got her dressed for the cooler weather outside—where, yes, it was a good day for a walk, a day of sun so sparkling it made me think of the champagne Charlie brought home on our every anniversary, that sweet, sweet man, a day bright leaves told cheerful lies about the winter ahead. "It'll be all right, my good girl," I whispered to her, or to myself, before we left Louisa's old bedroom that Gracie and I now shared. "I love you." That last was definitely to Gracie, and more true words I've never spoken.

"Be careful," I said to Gary when I handed her over. "Wait, I'll strap her in for you," and I carried her outside to the stroller, which he'd left on the front walk, buckled her in—it wasn't as if she could climb out, but what if Gary tripped?—and tucked a receiving blanket over her.

"We'll be fine, Aunt CarolSue," he said. "You don't need to worry." And just like that, he took off, pushing the stroller down the gravel drive and letting it bump along. I'd have carried the whole kit and caboodle until I got to the road, and I wouldn't have walked her out on that road anyway, little trafficked though it is. There's no sidewalk.

"Watch for cars," I called after him. "Please."

He waved without turning around. I saw Gracia's little hand fly up and down the way it does when she's excited. *Maybe Gary has a good idea after all*, I thought. *I'll get him to leave the stroller here.* And then they were all the way down the drive, trees blocking my view of the road. Gary turned right, and I couldn't see them anymore.

I sighed and headed for the backyard, where I knew Louisa was foaming with excitement about the girls' roost getting all freshened. I've mentioned how she is about those chickens.

I was doomed.

You might be thinking, *Oh come on, CarolSue, that's not so bad.* Well, that's a matter of opinion and maybe you've never had to clean up a roost full of chicken poop. But what happened next was way worse anyway, even though it did temporarily save me from the worst of the coop cleaning.

We'd gotten enough of it started that I was thoroughly disgusted and went into the house to look for rubber gloves, though what I really wanted was a gas mask. Louisa thought that was plain ridiculous, and said as much, but it turned out to be a good thing I was in the house, otherwise I'd never have heard the crunch of Gus's tires on the driveway gravel. Believe me, I raced to head him off at the front door, frantically kicking baby toys under the skirt of the couch on my way through the living room.

"Hi, Gus! What's up?" I said, as casually as I could through my panting, and blocking him from coming in. Jessie was a help with that, straining to get out to greet him.

"Got a surprise for you ladies," he said. "And you can't say no. Had me a surprise of a break this afternoon and got to leave early. Brought you two some beautiful steak and I'm going to grill us a great supper. Didn't know Gary was here, though . . . but the steak's big and it'll do for us all." He held up a package wrapped in butcher paper. Louisa, the vegetarian, would sure be thrilled. As if he'd read my mind, he added, "Thought it was worth a try. I mean, it's not like it's chicken, or goat or venison. She doesn't raise cows."

"Oh . . . my . . . what a delightful . . . thought," I said, almost fainting with panic. "Uh . . . Gary's not here."

"He's not? His van's right there," Gus said, pivoting to

point at Gary's church van, big enough to block out the sun, right there in the driveway. What was I thinking?

"Oh, right, I mean, not right now. He went out . . . for a hike."

Gus broke into a grin that made the rims of his glasses dent the tops of his cheeks. "Gary? Huh. You don't say. Well, hey, can I come in?" He took a step forward. There was no chance I'd scoured the kitchen for Gracie evidence.

"I've got a better idea. Give me those, and I'll stick them in the refrigerator. You walk around the back and surprise Louisa. She's in the chicken coop. I'll meet you out there. It'll be more . . . surprising."

"Sure, love to surprise my honey. I'll just cut through the house," he said. Of course. Gus, who Louisa used to call "that puffy sheriff" when he was her nemesis, long before she was napping with him, had a beefy build that suggested he typically preferred the least possible physical exertion. With the one notable exception involving Louisa, apparently.

"Uh, Gus, to be honest, I handwashed my underwear and other personal . . . items . . . and they're draped over the kitchen chairs because they can't go in the dryer. They were gifts from Charlie, see, and it would be embarrassing for both of us." I have to admit I was proud of myself for coming up with that one on the fly. Picture me trying to be suggestive, to invoke an image in his head of thongs and string bikinis, lace bras, maybe a black lace garter, anything to make him squirm.

My Charlie would have said, "Great, honey. Outta my way." But Gus got satisfyingly red in the face, shoved the steaks at me, and mumbled, "I'll just go 'round the house."

"Good idea, Gus. So, you visit with Louisa, maybe give her a hand, huh?"

I shut the door, leaned my back against it and blew out a long exhale. *Oh God. What now? Think, CarolSue. Think.*

I scanned the living room. A random unused disposable diaper was on the side table. I snatched it up. *Goodnight Moon* on the coffee table. A rattle on the floor—Jessie had claimed that one as her toy and started tossing it in the air and chasing after it. I gathered those and rushed them to our bedroom. The kitchen was a disaster. Bottles, nipples, formula, bibs. What should I do with the formula in the refrigerator? I needed to keep that cold. Never mind. I poured it down the sink and buried the can under other trash in the receptacle under the sink. The rest of it went to the bedroom. Then I tackled the bathroom. Jessie thought all this wild activity was a great game and hounded my ankles, while Marvelle was disdainful, flicking her tail in disgust and planting herself by the back door, wanting to be let out, but I didn't go near that door, afraid Gus would take it as a signal that my unmentionables had been stowed and he could come in.

You see the other problem, I imagine. What if Gary came back? I could only handle so much. I grabbed the landline and dialed his cell phone. Did he answer? Of course not. I stage-whispered into it (since the kitchen window was open), "Don't come back—Gus!" and hung up.

One deep breath. I opened the door and went out.

Gus was being useless, standing and talking to Louisa, who was up to her ankles in poopy straw bedding as she raked out the coop. JoJo, Beth, and Amy were in sight, but Abigail and Sarah must have been spooked by Gus's booming voice and taken shelter behind the barn. Rosie Two was munching the grass, still tall and lush from the wet August we'd had, where the back field sloped down. The feed corn would reach full dent soon and Al Pelley would be here to harvest it for the market. Louisa saw me and glared. "Thought you were helping me," she said.

"Yep, and then Gus came, and you know, I'd washed my underwear, and it was air drying all over the place. Needed to put it all away before Gus came in. You know."

The light dawned. "Oh. Oh, right," she said. And then the

Gary problem must have occurred to her. I saw it cross her face.

I said, "Gus brought such good steaks for dinner, but I'm so sorry, I already have plans. You remember that nice friend I made at the . . . library. Susan. We're going out to supper in Elmont."

Gus stood sweating lightly, his hands in his pockets, while Louisa raked away. "Well, Miss Louisa, that leaves you and me and Gary."

"I doubt Gary will stay. He just wanted to get away from the church for a bit before he went back to work on his sermon," Louisa said. She seemed to have caught on. She must have been wondering what I had in mind. So was I.

"That's what he said. Like I mentioned, he just went for a hike," I threw on, to fill Louisa in on the story I'd spun. I didn't see how Gus could be so thickheaded, but it all just floated over him.

"Well, just a romantic evening for me and my sweetheart, then. It's about time," Gus said, doubtless already planning his nap. No wonder he wasn't suspicious. His skull was filled with hormones instead of brain cells.

"I've got to get going," I said. "I'll just run in and get my purse. You two have a lovely evening. Gus, you please give Louisa a hand, and give her time to shower and dress, will you?" That last was my hint to Louisa to fix herself up and not to wear one of her bag-lady outfits. A little makeup wouldn't hurt either.

"Right, right," Gus said, not moving a muscle.

I hurried into the house. "Feed Jessie for me, will you?" I called over my shoulder to Louisa. "I'm running late now." Inside, I rushed to the bedroom, grabbed diapers, a bottle, a can of formula, a clean onesie, and Gracie's two favorite rattles, stuffed everything into the diaper bag, and grabbed my purse and keys. I looked at the picture of Charlie that I'd added next to Harold's and said, "Help me now, honey," picked up Gracia's baby carrier, and as quietly as I could, snuck through the house, put it all in my car and took off.

I didn't know where Gary had gone, and I'd told him not to come back. I tried to call him again, but still no answer. This time the message I left told him I was waiting in my car about a hundred yards down the road toward the Athertons' and to come with Gracie as fast as he could. He didn't call me back. Surely if he started down the driveway, he'd see Gus's truck. I asked myself if I could count on his not being entirely stupid, and the answer didn't reassure me. I edged my car closer to our driveway, thinking I'd be able to see him approach in time if he was coming from the far side. He'd been gone long enough now that Gracie would be getting hungry and likely to start fussing. Would he know what that meant?

As I sat there alternately checking my rearview mirror and peering ahead, I realized that I couldn't bear the thought of losing Gracia. Gary was looking all over for her mother, and now I didn't want him to find her. Not ever.

Chapter 20

CarolSue

It was an agonizing twenty minutes before Gary appeared in my rearview mirror. I saw him stop and lean over Gracie, and then start pushing the stroller again. I admit, nothing disastrous had happened. She wasn't howling, and her face wasn't red, but I could tell she was letting him know she wanted me. Meaning it was time to eat.

"She's hungry," I announced by way of greeting. "Why didn't you answer your phone?"

"What are you doing out here?" he countered.

"Gus is at the house, which you'd know if you answered your phone." I busied myself with getting Gracie onto the berm and unbuckling, lifting her out. "Did you have fun, sweets?" I murmured into her ear. "I know you're hungry, aren't you."

"Why are you—" Gary had the nerve to start to question me.

"I just told you. It's not like you can take her home." I went right back at him, really irritated about the phone, which my nephew was not accustomed to from me.

"Oh. I'm sorry. I forgot to charge it."

"That can never happen again. I brought all her stuff. It's in my car. I'll take her. I told Gus you just wanted to get away from the church a bit—of course he saw your van—that you had to go back and work on your sermon. You went out hiking."

"Hiking?" He chortled.

That set me off again. "You would have had a better instant idea?"

"Sorry."

"He's going to invite you to stay to dinner. He brought steaks. I told him I'd made a friend at the library and we were going to dinner in Elmont, just for your information."

"Steaks? Does he know my mother? I mean, he takes her out to dinner a lot. What does she order then?"

I gave a half shrug, impatient with discussing Louisa's diet while Gracie squirmed and fussed. "Whatever. That's her problem. I've got to feed this baby. You kept her out too long."

"She was fine, really. She loved it. It's a beautiful day, and I was showing her the leaves. The Athertons' horses are pastured, y'know, and she really liked them."

The sun slanted down fall-gold across us all, and there was tenderness on Gary's face. He reached over and caressed Gracie's cheek with the back of his forefinger.

"I'm sure she did," I said. "That was good of you. You'd better get in and spin your side of the story to Gus—I tried to stick to what you could tell the truth about, you being a Reverend. You really were out walking, and you do have to get back to the church to work on your sermon. But I suppose you could stay to dinner if you want . . ."

"No, how about we all just go to the church. We can pick up something to eat and take care of Gracia there until Gus is gone."

"What if somebody . . . ?"

"You're babysitting and visiting me. True."

"Okay. I'll buy." I knew how tight his money always was.

"You don't need to—"

"I insist." We put the stroller in my trunk, settled Gracia in her carrier, and I gave Gary a fifty-dollar bill from my purse before he headed on to the house. "I'll meet you in the church parking lot," I said. "I'll feed her there, in the car. I don't have a lot of time before she'll melt down from hunger."

"You really know her," he said. "Thank you."

"My pleasure, truly." I don't know what he thought was my pleasure. I meant the baby.

Church parking lot is giving the grassy area in front of the barn Gary uses a lot of dress-up language. It meant a lot to him, though. But it *was* strange to park in front of a banner hung from a barn that read in giant black letters JESUS IS THE ANSWER while feeding a baby whose mother seemed to have disappeared. A baby that I desperately wanted to keep. If Jesus was the answer, how exactly should I frame the question? I was pondering this, burping Gracie and having increasing sympathy for Louisa's issues with the cult Gary had hooked up with, when he pulled up beside me. Carrying two good-sized bags, he beckoned me to follow him into the barn/church. I followed him a couple of minutes later, with Gracie in her carrier, content now, but needing a diaper change.

Gary had stopped. "Why don't we sit out here in the sanctuary section," he said. "More space."

I looked around. The floor was bare. There was no soft place I could lay Gracie down to change her diaper.

"Is there any place with a rug? I don't have anything but the receiving blanket from the stroller. I need something—"

"Can you use the blanket?"

I couldn't figure out why Gary looked uncomfortable. "It's out in the trunk." I gestured with my head, my hands being full of baby. "With the stroller."

"I'll get it," and out he went. Strange as all get-out. I looked around and immediately wished I hadn't. Glitter Jesus paled in comparison to His counterparts here. Mainly because the size here required double the amount of glitter for the halos. One depiction showed Him with an outsized hand raised toward a neon sun. If that was supposed to be a blessing, it looked more like He was about to smite me dead. And had His fiery sequin-centered eyes ever caught his eyebrows on fire from the pupils glowing like live embers??

What I mean is, either Gary was some kind of artistic genius (which I didn't think was likely for any art done on black velvet and glitter, but what do I know?) or these were the worst paintings to ever desecrate a barn. Oh, I suppose it wasn't really his pictures that bothered me so. We were all used to that from his school days. But I stood there a moment shaking my head and thinking, *Gary, Gary, honey. What have you gotten yourself into? You miss Cody and your father, don't you? Louisa misses Harold and Cody, too. I miss Charlie. We all grieve. But this cult, this Brother Zachariah you're so taken with? I don't know, I just don't know.*

Maybe Gracie just needed to burp, but I took it as a sign of both intelligence and good taste that she began to fuss, and I checked around for a spot with less scary scenery. There was a door at one end of the barn and I headed there. I was just stepping in that separate area when Gary came back in. "Uh, that's my office," he said. "I don't think—"

"Oh, look," I interrupted. "If you don't mind, the rug on the floor here will be good to put her down on. Just put the receiving blanket on top of it, will you?"

I could tell he didn't really want to, but I'd had enough of Gary acting weird. I took the blanket and sort of tossed it on the floor. At that, he didn't really have much of a choice. He spread it out, and, awkward as it was, I bent to put the baby down. I wasn't sure I'd be able to straighten up, so I just got down on the floor with her and stayed. "Come on, now. Give me the diaper bag. I'll change her, and let's eat. What did you get us?"

"Burritos. Hope that's okay. I have a lot of change for you."

"Oh my God. Not from the gas station?"

"Well, sort of."

"Just wonderful. Did you at least get me something to drink?"

His face brightened. "Dr Pepper."

"Great. Caffeine. I won't sleep for three days. Open it for me."

I changed Gracie, and Gary and I ate, sitting there on the floor with Gracie, with two pictures of Cody looking down on us, one of him dressed for his first and only prom—Louisa had the same radiant picture of him and his date, both scrubbed and beautiful with their lives shining ahead of them. But there was one, too, of Cody as an infant, and of course all babies look alike but I thought that Gracie reminded me of Cody and then I realized maybe the baby picture of Cody was what made Gary not want Gracie in his office—that it was too hard to bear—and I was sorry I'd been impatient with him. Maybe it was clumsy to try to get his attention on something else, but I asked Gary if there'd been any problem with Gus when he went into the house.

"Didn't really go in," he said. "Just stuck my head in the door and yelled, 'Mom, I'm taking off now. Hi Gus, bye Gus.' Didn't give him a chance to ask me to stay for dinner."

"Probably smart. Ask me no secrets, I'll tell you no lies, right?"

Gary got the same uncomfortable look then and I thought he avoided my eyes for the next minutes. "Gary, you okay?" I said. "Is there something going on? I mean, bothering you?"

". . . Not really. Just . . . got a lot on my mind. Nothing I can talk about . . . not really."

"Okay. But you know, I can keep things to myself."

"No, really, I'm fine. But thanks."

I'd have sworn he wanted to tell me something. But he

didn't. Not then. Everything might have been easier if he had. I'd have told him, *Tell the truth, Gary, ask for help. It'll be a nice shortcut to where you'll end up anyway.*

This might be a good time to fortify yourself for the rest of the story. You might want to use Louisa's recipe for some special tea. I know I found myself in need of it as things progressed. It's plain exasperating how you have to let people work out their own problems, isn't it? Especially if you love them, and you just know they're likely messing up, making things harder and worse than they need to be. But we can't fix others' lives, can we? All we can do is love them. Watch them fall, get up, fall again. Love them and tell them. Love them again and still.

Gary

How do terrible and wonderful coexist, Gary wondered about the afternoon he'd spent with Gracia. His daughter. No, not his daughter, he couldn't let her be. And yet she was, so he'd spent an afternoon with her. Listened to her little sounds, watched her random movements, seen her crane her head to look for him. Not her father. Her father. But she didn't know that, of course not. Or did she have some primal connection to him that she sensed? When Muffin, the Athertons' bay mare, stuck her head over the fence, too big, too close, startling Gracia in her stroller, and she cried, was that visceral tie to him why she'd then relaxed close to his chest when he picked her up? She'd watched, intent, as her not-father but yes, father, stroked the horse's forelock and talked to the two of them, the horse and his not-daughter but then, yes, daughter.

He felt the tie himself and he'd felt love stirring, and that was wonderful. Having had her alone with him, picking her up out of the stroller to show her the horses out in the Indian summer light, when the corn was just starting to be cut in some of the neighbors' fields, oh yes, he remembered his dad on the combine doing that on their farm, and he'd told Gracia about it as he held her. And then, he'd told her, too, that she'd had a brother named Cody, who'd loved horses and maybe she would, too, one day. And he'd been able to bear the memory, perhaps because it was whispered, just between the two of them. She'd met his eyes and not looked away.

But the church had to come first. It was what God wanted. And that was part of the terrible in it, and the other was how he'd filled with guilt over Gracia in his office on the rug where she'd been conceived, while the pictures of Cody stared at him and her like spectral accusations. God had forgiven him for failing his son, but his father never had, and Cody's mother and his own mother never could. And right then his aunt, who was like a second mother, asked him if something was bothering him.

"Oh no, I'm fine," he'd said. He wondered if Jesus was keeping an actual count of his lies. Was he writing them down? Gary didn't see how anyone could keep track of so many, but then he reminded himself that Jesus wasn't actually human and could do anything. It was not a comforting thought.

In the days following, though, after his aunt had taken the baby over again—a strange way to put it, but it did feel like she took possession and Gary was confused that he did not feel grateful—he thought of confessing. *Wouldn't it be simpler? If God really wants the church to survive, then God will make it happen. Or is this all testing my commitment to the church, if I will really put the work of Jesus first? How the hell am I supposed to know?* Thinking in these circles was not conducive to getting a decent sermon written. Not even a mediocre one. And it had to be brilliant because the bills were due, plus another payment to Brother Zachariah. That last was already late.

Gary was still struggling with the sermon on Saturday afternoon when his cell phone rang. He sighed when he checked the screen and realized it was Brother Zach. He'd been hoping to get over to his mother's, to spend some time with Gracia—although he'd tell his aunt and mother that he'd come to see what help they might need—but all he had was a recycled pitch for donations that hadn't worked well enough before. He had to come up with something better. He knew what Brother Zach was calling about, that was for sure. But maybe this was a Sign. He hadn't asked for help when he started the church and look where it got him. Now, here was Brother Zach calling, exactly when Gary was struggling.

"Brother Zachariah, I think you must have known I need help today. Or Jesus does, and had you call me."

"I did feel a message," Brother Zachariah said.

Gary leaned forward in his chair, fingers tight on the phone. It would have been more comfortable to use the speakerphone, but that felt even more dangerous.

"There's something I need to discuss with you. A . . . confession."

"Brother Gary, that's a step in the right direction. I already know the payment is late. You can rectify this and restore yourself and your church to good standing in the eyes of Jesus."

"Thank you, Brother. There's something else and it may, no it *does*, affect the church. I think I need guidance, and since I failed to ask the first time . . . I thought . . . perhaps if I—"

Brother Zachariah cut him off. "You'd best come clean.

What's the problem? You need to pay the tax, you know, I advanced—"

Now Gary interrupted. "I know, I know. And I apologize for being late. I'm working on a sermon, and trying to think, but there's a sin weighing on me, and I'm thinking maybe if I confess, but that might cause people to lose faith, you know, not donate either, but it would be the right thing, maybe it's what Jesus—"

There was a sort of eruption in his ear. "What are you talking about?" Brother Zachariah did not sound patient and kind, like Corinthians said to be. "What the hell have you done?"

Gary shifted in his chair. Took a breath. It was still hardly a whisper. "I . . . fornicated."

"What the hell did you say?"

"Fornicated." Gary cleared his throat. "I fornicated."

"Oh. Well. Did anyone see you?"

"Huh? I mean, no."

"All right, then. Don't tell anyone. I mean all right, you've confessed to me, and in Jesus' name, I forgive you. God forgives you. Don't do it again, hear me?"

"Uh . . . yes. Thank you."

"So, get that payment in now." Brother Zach sounded impatient.

"Well, there's more, see."

"Oh good God, what? She wasn't married, was she?"

"Oh no, not that—" Gary was horrified at the suggestion. Surely what he'd done wasn't quite as bad.

"Tell me it wasn't a male."

Gary shook his head, then remembered he was on the phone and that didn't help. "No. No! It was almost a year ago, and . . . now she's left a baby in the church, with a birth certificate. And the birth certificate says the baby's mine."

Silence. And more silence. Then, ominous-sounding, "Have you told anyone else?"

"No."

"What did you do with the . . . child?"

"My mother and aunt have her. I . . . didn't say whose . . . she is. I feel like maybe I should. I can't find the mother, see, and maybe I should confe—"

"So you're gonna put the burden of your sin on the good people of the church? Stomp on their belief and leave them with nothing? Does that sound right to you? Who is it that didn't register with the authorities? Huh? Those members joined in good faith. You can't let them down. Who you got you can borrow off of?" Gary heard the fire in Brother's voice. He was exhorting him to turn from committing another sin, to fix this. He must be right. Gary thought of the Daily Prayer Callers, all the work done by the Clean for Jesus Committee, the enthusiasm of the hymn-singing on Sunday mornings, led by Sister Ann and Brother Michael, who'd once hoped to make it in Nashville but had that hope crushed by a tone-deaf producer who said their pitch was flat and the lyrics they'd labored over made no sense. They'd found their Purpose with the church. What would happen to them without it?

"Maybe I could ask my aunt."

"Well, Brother Gary, you go do that straightaway. And get that sermon in shape now. You do it. And you say nothing to another human being about this child, hear me? You said you can't find the mother?"

"Not yet."

"Well, look harder and give that child back. Hear me?" Even the daylight outside the small office window was waning. Was it a Sign that he hadn't much time?

"Uh-huh." Gary nodded, straightened his shoulders. "Yes, Brother, I hear you."

Chapter 21

Gus

Something was up with those two, Louisa and CarolSue. Gus had seen the secret looks pass between them, like they were making something up as they went along, and he didn't appreciate being left out. It was like middle school all over again. High school, too, come to think of it. Just like back then, he pretended he didn't notice, and asked no questions. But seriously, CarolSue had dinner plans with a friend she'd met at the library? For one, he was pretty sure that Louisa would have mentioned it if CarolSue had been going to the library, because it was located almost all the way to Elmont, and it might have represented a napping opportunity if he could have shaken free. He'd mentioned repeatedly how extra tired he was of late and Louisa had said yes, she sure was, too, and even a quick nap would have been *something*.

So there was that. And there was weird stuff he'd seen in the house. An actual baby bottle in the refrigerator behind the steak sauce. He'd pulled it out and held it up to Louisa. At first she looked like she had no idea what to say and then she said, "Oh yeah, geez, is that still there? I thought Rosie was sick a while back. She wasn't eating the grass—didn't you mention how long it was?—anyway, and I was trying to get her to take a bottle, you know, like when they're kids and you have to hand-feed them if their mothers don't . . ." and she'd sort of petered out then.

"I didn't know Rosie was sick," he'd said. "You never mentioned it."

"Well, you've been so busy. And anyway, she's fine," and she'd sort of snatched the bottle away from him and emptied it into the sink.

"Huh," he'd said. "Never heard of a grown goat hand-fed."

"You a farmer now?" she'd snapped at him, and he'd had the sense not to argue the point since he wanted the most direct route to a nap.

Almost to the goal, in the guest room, which was now Louisa's room, he was darned if there wasn't a baby blanket, the pale cotton kind, right on the bed. This time she was ahead of him. She grabbed it up and said, "I don't like Marvelle's fur on the spread. I can wash this easier."

Now Gus knew perfectly well that Louisa had never cared a fig where Marvelle plunked herself, and that cat had been known to curl up right on Louisa's pillow. However, Gus caught himself from reminding Louisa of that cat-fact, said, "Good idea," and silently congratulated his own brilliance. His sister hadn't raised an idiot after his mother left them. Rhonda had done her best.

After they were each refreshed by the nap, just lying in the bed with her head neatly in the space his chest and shoulder made for it, no longer testy with each other, Gus almost asked Louisa if something was going on. By then he'd remembered that during the summer there'd been that rubber duckie toy in the tub, and another time he'd seen a book for a little kid on the floor next to the wingback chair. Of course Louisa had said she was previewing kid books for her tutoring, so that made sense. But he held off asking, because it was so nice there, peaceful in the clean white sheets that smelled like Louisa after a shower, with the midafternoon light sliced by the blinds and lying soft on the light coral wall like pieces of fruit. And he held off because Rhonda had always cautioned him about his big mouth and told him to be careful about what he said to women. She said he could go way wrong with saying what he thought because it was so often stupid, and it was way less likely that he'd go wrong if he shut up and thought it over for a while first. So he impressed himself and said nothing. Rhonda would have been proud of him. He wished he could tell her.

When he left after dinner and had a chance to think over what it meant, he was glad he'd kept his trap shut. Rhonda had tried to explain the hormone thing to him several times. Of course that was a long time ago, but it was probably still true, wasn't it? Louisa must be missing Cody and longing for a grandchild again. Maybe this baby stuff around had to do with that, with how much she was still grieving. If he brought it up at all, he'd have to be . . . what was Rhonda's word? Sensitive. He'd have to be really sensitive.

Gus decided to watch what went on, wait a while longer. To make sure he would be sensitive.

CarolSue

Isn't it disconcerting how you can absolutely know something is right, so certain that you'd swear by it, maybe be dumb enough to stake your life on it, and then one day you up and realize you've changed your mind? It's enough to make you wonder if you should follow your own instincts or just go ahead and follow whatever nonsense gets published in that daily horoscope. Or just do what my sister does and make special tea, share it with Marvelle, and ask the chickens what they think. It's all going to come out making the same amount of difference in the end, I figure, because I was one hundred percent positive I wanted to go back home, but this morning I called my real estate agent and told him that he could leave the house on the market when our contract expires soon. At least for the time being. Here's the thing: There's no way I will leave Gracie.

Not only won't I leave her now. I don't want to ever leave her. I want to keep her and raise her.

You might be thinking I've not only lost my marbles, but they've rolled way under the furniture never to be retrieved. But you don't realize how that baby lights up in a grin when she sees me and now she's started to hold up her arms for me to pick her up. She doesn't do that with my sister. Oh, I admit Louisa can get a smile out of her, but it's not the same. She has to work at it. Gracie and I have a bond. She would suffer if I left her, to say nothing of how much I would ache for her.

Yes, I think about her mother—she's like a ghost here always—and I wonder if she's dead or alive, what happened to her, what would possess her to leave her baby. She's a mother; she must be suffering and longing and yet she's done this, and I cannot say I want it undone. Is that selfish? Call me selfish then and I will own it. All my babies were taken from me. Not this one, too. I cannot lose this one, too.

"This can't go on," Louisa announced the day after that closest call yet when Gary and I ended up at his barn-turned-church.

"What?"

"This whole thing," she said, rolling her eyes at me. "You *know*."

We were in the kitchen. She was doing the dishes after supper and she probably figured I was being useless because I had Gracie on my hip and wasn't drying. "If you just let them air-dry, I'll put them away as soon as I put her down for the night. It's starting to get dark earlier and she'll go down easy." That last was pure malarkey. Gracie didn't care about daylight. I was buying time, diverting Louisa from talking about the inconvenience of Gracie. I'd done that a lot, but this time Louisa was having none of it.

Louisa made an unnecessary amount of noise banging a pot into the drying rack. She sighed heavily. Even though her back was to me, I knew another eye roll was going on. Then, abruptly, she wiped her hands on a dish towel and turned around to face me. Confront me, was more like it. I knew something bad was coming; half the dishes were still in the sink.

"You know what I'm talking about."

"Please. The baby . . ."

"It's always the baby."

"Sister. Come on. I'll just go try to put her down a little early, okay? Then you can tell me what's on your mind."

"As if you didn't know." With that, she went back at the dishes with an exaggerated sigh to make sure I got the point.

I picked up Gracie's last bottle, which had two ounces left in it, and headed to the living room talking quietly to Gracie. "It's not your fault, sweetheart. It has nothing to do with you. It's grown-up stuff. Look out the window. See how pink the sky is, it's even turning red, isn't it? That's a sunset. It means it'll be sunny tomorrow, too. You and I will take a good walk. We'll look for deer, okay? You know Auntie Louisa feeds them, right? And we'll talk to JoJo and Beth and Amy, and pat Rosie Two. Jessie will come with us. All us girls together . . ." I rambled on like this, rubbing Gracie's back, feeling her relax toward sleep against my body, ready for those last two ounces when her eyes would open, close, open, search for mine, and finding them, finally stay closed, content, safe, loved. So loved.

Darkness had crept into the bedroom while I walked Gracie. Gary had moved Glitter Jesus in here, to watch over Gracia, he said. It was a sweet impulse, I'm sure, and I couldn't begin to say the truth, which was that it was my room, too, and having Elvis in drag staring at me undressed made me plain uncomfortable. Gracie's nightlight made the red glitter dots in his eyes look creepy. This was why I'd taken to rocking her to sleep out in the family room. I didn't want Gracie to sense another presence in the shadows. She was too young to be anxious about Glitter Jesus—or any ghost. And I didn't want her to feel claustrophobic, but there I was, too, checking that the windows were locked. Oh, I told myself I got that sense because she barely fit in the bassinet anymore. I needed to get her a crib. I could just imagine how Louisa would flip out about that, especially since I knew what she was about to say—and what I was going to answer. You can see, perhaps, how I hadn't been telling her or Gary what I thought, what I wanted. That had been my modus operandi for years. Go along to get along. Once Gracie was well into her good sleep, I left the bedroom door cracked so I'd hear her, and went to the kitchen, bracing myself for Louisa's argument.

I took a breath, squared my shoulders, and used the best defense is a good . . . tactic, which is usually Louisa's specialty. I made the announcement as I walked in the kitchen. "Sister, I want to keep her."

Louisa had been loaded for bear, as I mentioned, and now she turned away from the sink, dried her hands, stared at me, and blinked as if I'd entered the room on roller skates, naked and sporting neon tattoos all over. I tell you now, the look on her face was hilarious. However, don't worry. I wasn't dumb enough to laugh. I just took a mental photograph, thinking I'd enjoy the moment later.

"Keep . . . Jessie?" she said. Now really. Did she seriously think I was talking about the dog? Much as I love that dog and intend to keep her anyway since Louisa already has a menagerie, I didn't see how she could possibly be so obtuse.

"Before I left the room, I believe we were talking about Gracie. You know, the baby I had in my arms at the time." I know that wasn't smart, but I simply couldn't restrain the sarcasm. Everyone thinks Louisa has the true gift for it, but if I wanted to compete, I could bury her.

"You . . . want to . . . *keep* . . . a *baby*? Did you make a batch of special tea all your own? Whatever are you thinking?"

"I'm thinking that I love her, and she needs me, and I can raise her. That's what I'm thinking. Her mother left her and I won't. Ever. Which of those big words are you having trouble with?" I threw that last part on because she was looking at me as if I was using words that weren't in her vocabulary.

She angled her head sideways. Speaking slowly she said, "Do you know how old you are?"

I palm-slapped the side of my cheek. "No! It's lost, like my shoe, and my toothbrush ran away, too. When you find them, can you find my name for me, too, honey? You're a sweet girl. Do I know you?"

"For God's sake, CarolSue. Gary is out looking for her mother every day."

"And quite a fucktacular job he's doing of finding her, isn't he?"

"A *what* job?"

"Never mind." I'd gotten carried away. It was something I'd heard Charlie call a politician's mess once. "I mean, it seems less and less likely that Gary's going to find her. And the idea of Gracie being dumped in some Elmont foster home is . . . well, it's just not going to happen."

"You're not thinking clearly. You can't just permanently hide a baby. In case you haven't noticed, they tend to grow up. Are you talking about trying to adopt her? Then you have to tell someone, and initially that person would be Gus. And he'll have to put her in foster care."

I shook my head. "No way. She has to stay with me."

"And meanwhile, you're going to get caught . . . I mean *we* . . . we're going to get caught. Maybe we're breaking some law. Have you thought of that?"

"Don't be ridiculous. We're still babysitting. Nothing illegal in that. Not you, anyway. *I'm* babysitting."

"We have to tell Gus."

"No!"

"You know, this is also sort of wrecking a good thing I have going with Gus . . ."

"*You* insisted I move here. I didn't get that you wanted slave labor in the garden."

"Are you serious? That's really what you think? I'm trying to give you a purpose."

What? Oh yes, there it was, that homicidal impulse. I didn't even feel guilty when I said, "More like a reason to die now and get it over with."

My sister stood there shocked, her mouth slightly open. She shook her head slightly and then she shrugged, as if all she could do was react with her body, there were no words she could put to her horror. Or bewilderment. Or disgust. Normally I could read her expressions but not this time.

Finally she said, "So you don't want to be here?"

Then it was my turn to shrug. "I didn't. Until Gracie. And now I do because I think she should have some more family than me around, like you if you were willing. But I can take her back to Atlanta with me if you don't want us here. If you're going to tell Gus, I'll do it now. Tonight. We don't need you."

"You don't mean that."

"Yes, I do."

Too late I saw how much I'd hurt her. The early dark had crept up off the ground outside and come in the windows while we'd argued and neither one of us had turned on the overhead kitchen light. The room was dim. I don't know how long her eyes had been glistening before I noticed. Louisa's not a crier, and her voice hadn't betrayed that she was breaking. I don't know what exactly I said that had been too much. I wanted to tell her I was sorry, but at that moment I didn't want her to think I meant I was sorry for insist-

ing on Gracie. So I didn't. "So, what'll it be? Do I need to
pack now? Are you going to tell Gus?" I had to have a clear
answer.

She thought about it before she answered and when she finally did she sounded tired. "No. I won't tell him. But you
could get caught anyway."

"For now, I'll take that chance. While I figure things out."

Do I seem uncaring for Louisa? Or are you thinking I've
forgotten the specter I try to banish from the shadows outside my window at night while Glitter Jesus sheds his halo,
the mother who made this Gracia out of her own flesh and
suffered to give her life? I've not forgotten her, though it's
true I'd like to. If she's alive, some part of her must want her
baby back. Yet, here I am, and I want her just as much. It fills
me with guilt and then it fills me with defiance. Aren't I, too,
giving her life now? I want to say *You left her. I never will.*
Someday Gracia will ask me. What will I say? Can I tell her
that life does not follow clean lines, but ones that stagger?
We limp along, trying to keep up, carrying baskets unevenly
loaded with failures and regrets. We find our joys accidently,
unexpectedly, along the way and must cherish them. Cling
to, remember, and cherish them. (And oh my Gracia, I do
cherish you.) It's the truth. Can I just tell her the truth?

But you're right. I will tell Louisa I'm sorry. I'll mean it
when I say it, because she's cherishing a joy, too. It's something to tell Gracie someday: Don't take away someone's joy.

Chapter 22

Gus

It had been a good couple of weeks at work, which added up to practically no private life—meaning precious little in the way of napping—for Gus, but on the other hand, his re-election ought to be reasonably easy once it was public that he'd gotten a bead on the two guys that were producing the fake I-9 papers over toward Elmont. Not that he'd been after that at the time—if he'd known, the Feds probably would have handled it. No, he'd gone after the clowns making fake community college IDs the high school kids were using to buy booze in the Elmont and Indy liquor stores and clubs. The quality was so good the clerks and bouncers couldn't tell; let them go on no matter how young they looked because the ID said so. When he got an anonymous tip, Gus followed up, not knowing who the forgers had pissed off, but pleased they'd been stupid.

Finding the I-9s in the works was nothing but a bonus. Sheer dumb luck, but he didn't tell the Feds that. Let them think he'd been working on it for months. Let them think he's a freaking Dick Tracy. The good thing was that it accelerated the whole operation, moved it to the front burner before word spread. Even Gus didn't know if they were going to hit the convenience store chain, or the garden supply place—that seemed unlikely this time of year—or one of the meat packing plants. Or all of them. The Feds were tight-lipped, avoiding leaks, but Gus and Billy from Dwayne County plus men from the departments in Couter and Melvin counties would be involved as "force magnifiers." That term just made Gus chuckle and shake his head while muttering *pathetic*. In private. Billy couldn't believe it either.

"Are they fuckin' nuts? That's what they're callin' us? Us and what army?"

Gus shrugged. "We just do what we're told."

"You're the sheriff. Tell 'em no. Anyway, what's the point? We got no problem. When we got a problem, we'll call 'em, and they kin be *our* force magnifiers if they wanna."

Gus shook his head. "Not the way it works, man. Y'know."

Billy sighed. His face and neck were like tanned hide, and deep wrinkles fanned from the outside corners of his eyes. Gus used to tell him that his hat was part of the uniform and to put it on, but Billy didn't like how it felt, and Gus had given up. "Yeah. Stupid," he said.

"Stupid," Gus agreed. "But we're gonna do a good job. This is big."

"Beatin' the bushes. Don't even know nothin'."

"Feds say you don't know these people."

"Right. So . . . ?"

"Makes it better and worse."

"Whatever." But Billy said it with a head shake.

Gus shrugged and put both palms up. "Whatever," he agreed. He took off his glasses, wiped the lenses against the chest of his shirt. After setting them back on his face, he sighed. "Whatever," he repeated. He was tired of this already. "Look," he said. "Not gonna be a whole lot longer, best I can tell. We won't get a lot of heads-up, but I do know the Feds got a private contractor for a detention facility in Elmont. Gotta mean something's goin' down soon."

"No shit?"

"Yeah. Not like I'm on the list to know from them. Got it from Jake Rego."

Billy's face was blank.

Y'know, over t' Dwayne County." Impatience crept into Gus's voice, incredulous that Billy didn't recognize the name. He was talking about chief of corrections at the county jail.

"Oh. Duh. Huh . . . not enough space there?"

"Dunno. Guess they figure there's not gonna be."

"When you think they're gonna let the 'force magnifiers' in on the grand plan?" Billy made air quotes with his fingers and mocked the words.

"At the last possible moment."

Billy shook his head again, muttering, "Damn . . . damn."

Gus nodded. "Damn."

Billy turned and left Gus's office without further comment. It had already been an unusually long conversation for him.

Gary

Gary found himself thinking of Gracia at odd times, like while he was showering, or in the church study staring at his laptop, daydreaming instead of working on his Wednesday night Prayer and Praise message. She'd come into his mind when he drove past the elementary school and had the old familiar Cody grief suffocate him, remembering how Nicole used to take Cody to the playground there even before he was in kindergarten, and how Cody had begged him to go, too. He should have gone with them, way more than he ever had, not left it to Nicole to teach the boy how to ride his bike without the training wheels, which she'd also done.

Now, along with Cody and Nicole, he'd see a little girl on the playground. A flash of red ribbon in dark hair, though he didn't know where that picture came from, but there she was on the swing, then upside down on the monkey bars, then skipping into a crowd of children when he'd lose sight of her, too. It was bizarre and made him think he was losing his mind—as bad as his mother!—the way he wanted to pull over, get out, and run to catch her up in his arms. Not that there was really anyone there. The playground was empty, for heaven's sake. But he had this unbearable feeling: He couldn't lose any more. Not Gracia, too.

And then he reminded himself to get real. His job was to find Rosalina and give that baby back to her mother. To save his church. That was what God wanted. And really, not that it mattered, but it was what Gary wanted, too.

He had to pay attention. Another payment was due Brother Zachariah, and he didn't have the money put together. If the Prayer and Praise message was deeply inspiring, maybe the Brothers and Sisters would come through with extra. Concentrate, he told himself. Stay focused. And pass the collection baskets twice, once after Prayer, and again after Praise. Brother Zachariah couldn't keep covering him. He was risking his own ministry, as he kept pointing out. And there was Gary's sin, Gary's grievous sin complicating the entire situation. Brother Zachariah kept pointing that out, too. But Gary didn't see anything he could do except wait for Gus's help. He'd tried everything; the homeless shelter in Elmont, the churches—adding to his sin list were all the lies he'd told about why he was looking for someone named either Rosalina Lopez or Rosalina Gonzalez or Rosalina Anything. For that matter, she could have made up any name, so his search was as vague and ill-defined as the questions he'd posed, and although he'd started out determined, he'd stuttered himself to a dead end.

The truth was that he was exhausted. He was out of information, ideas, money, and hope. And now he had to finish a sermon. It had already taken him days, way too long.

When he'd drafted the message, given up old words without shine, Gary allowed himself a break. He couldn't help the way his mind drifted to whether Gracia was awake or napping, how the memory of her whole hand clutching his fore-finger came to him. The light was waning, and a shaft of Indian summer sun slanted through the window. Gary rotated his chair to stretch his legs and took it in: how dust motes were dancing on it there, behind him like angels, an otherworldly beauty. It could be a Sign. He sat staring at the movement for a few minutes, then closed his eyes.

Maybe it was a Sign. From Jesus to him. Or, it could be dust in the air. That's what his mother would say. "Son, dust and sunlight are natural, and nature is beautiful, that's all." Gary's eyes were wet as he waited, testing the thoughts.

No, he whispered, when the weight of the death of his son, the weight of guilt and regret, all that could never be undone, the cruelty of such a world was not endurable. *Don't take Jesus away from me. It has to be a Sign.*

Chapter 23

CarolSue

We hadn't seen Gary in several days, which was unusual because he'd been coming around often, to help out. That's what he said, anyway. Louisa thought he was spying on her, and I can't say that the notion was entirely crazy as he did seem to ask a lot of questions about what Gus was up to. "Why should he care?" Louisa muttered. "Unless he's trying to catch us napping. Like it's any of his business." The idea lit her fuse.

"I don't think he has a clue about that," I said to mollify her. And I really didn't. I thought it was something else, but I couldn't offer her any ideas. I went back to folding Gracie's clothes on the couch. The baby was asleep, and I wanted to get the laundry taken care of before she was up again. I'd noticed that she wasn't sleeping as long, so if I wanted to put my own feet up for a while and maybe close my eyes, too, I needed to get this done.

"It's not like we've had any opportunity, anyway," she went on. "If Gary's looking, let him. Ha! He'll find some cold sheets." That was what was really pissing my sister off. Gracie being at the house wasn't such an issue only because Gus wasn't available, so I was thrilled that he was all busy with whatever special assignment was happening at work, while Louisa was more and more crabby about it. I knew that as soon as Gus's schedule was back to normal, I would have to make some other arrangement for Gracie and me. I was going to need to deal with Gary, too. The longer he wasn't around, the longer I could avoid it, quite all right with me. I spent my days loving that baby.

We got around to agreeing that special tea was in order because much as Gary thought he was a big help, Louisa agreed that he was underfoot when he did come. Mainly, he hogged the baby while I got stuck doing bottles or laundry or picking up around the house. I'd have much rather he did those things and leave Gracie to me. Louisa was usually outside with the girls and Rosie Two. Jessie was most often right by me, although she did love dashing around the yard when Louisa was out there, and sometimes she'd amuse herself by chasing the barn kittens, Peace and Plenty, which got Marvelle all annoyed and uppity. Al Pelley, the bandy-legged hired man who used to work for Harold and Louisa, now contracted to plant and cut the fields, had started harvesting the corn, which had reached full dent. Louisa liked to drive him insane by instructing him how she wanted certain areas left for the deer. But then he was off and away on the combine and we could hear it in the distance like the earth turning on its axis toward winter, but slowly, slowly, the sun still warm, still gilding the air and leaves.

Overall, it was sweet, good time when the men weren't around. Does that sound terrible to say? Louisa and I laughed a lot and we shared the delight of Gracie. I'd go out to sit in the Indian summer afternoon with her and we'd talk to the baby and to the girls and each other. Louisa would claim they all talked back to us, even though, of course, she alone knew exactly what they were saying. (I, though, had a lock on Gracie's opinions and she gave me that. Good thing for her she did, too.) Really, it was the couple of weeks that Gus wasn't around that created an interlude when time stopped. I know Louisa missed him. I didn't, though it felt like a time of waiting, but couldn't have said for what, and I didn't want time to start again. I wanted to cling to Gracie, and in a strange way, then hang on to my sister, too, not knowing what the future held for us. But if I had to choose between them, my sister and Gracie, my heart was already packed.

So, as I said, I thought Thursday would be another of those delightful afternoons to savor. We'd agreed on special tea and cookies for our afternoon snack. I'd have ginger snaps and Louisa would have a couple of the bourbon balls that were Mom's recipe. We'd made and frozen those last week when we'd been talking about Mom's greatest hits but gotten into an argument about whether we could have them at the same time we had special tea, based on the total amount of bourbon we'd be consuming, meaning would it be safe because of the baby there?

"CarolSue," Louisa had snorted, all superior. "The entire recipe has a third of a cup of bourbon and makes four dozen balls. How much bourbon is in each one? Do you think you could eat three and remain upright with that tablespoon of Wild Turkey in your tea?" Well, that was just unfair. She knows perfectly well I can't do fractions.

We decided to have tea outside because it was so lovely. Louisa had decided that it was time to start reading *Little Women* out loud to Gracie, which I thought sweet but silly, because even though Gracie was clearly brilliant, even I didn't think that a book without a single picture was really going to interest her all that much. But my sister is quite set in her ways. You should see her wardrobe, which hard as I try, I've hardly been able to update since the eighties, but how she dresses is beside the point right now. (Still, really? At the moment she's in rolled-up jeans and an old shirt of Harold's she absolutely will not part with, and she couldn't have combed her hair this morning because it looks more like a place for the chickens to roost than their own coop does. I'm waiting for Sarah and Abigail—who are young enough to produce eggs—to discover that my sister's head is better than their laying box. Go ahead, picture it!)

Anyway, it was shaping up to be all us girls out in the sun for tea and talk, and it started out just like that. Louisa's chrysanthemums were bright—she had yellows, pinks, rusts, oranges, and a deep purple—around the sunny edge of the yard. The coop was off to the far side, the door open now, as it always was during the day, and the girls strutted about, peacefully pecking here and there for bugs. Gracie had had her bottle and was content, playing on a blanket in the dappled shade of one of the maples. It still had most of its leaves, and they were gold-tinged scarlet. Now and then, one of them would float down near Gracie, who tracked it intently. I had sunscreen and a hat on her, and she was surrounded by her toys, watching the girls and waving her arms and legs with excitement when one of the barn kittens, half-grown now, came near. Marvelle settled herself like a disdainful sentry under the unused extra table, swishing her tail now and then, but watching. Jessie outdid her, of course, by curling up on the side of the blanket itself where Gracie's flailing hand could actually touch her back, which became Gracie's apparent goal.

Louisa and I poured our tea, settled into lawn chairs with the tea and plate of cookies between us on the table Harold had fashioned from a cut tree trunk topped with a piece of slate. We tilted our faces to the sun and soaked in contentment. After a few minutes, Louisa opened the book. She'd read a few lines and then explain to Gracie what was going on. I let her rattle on; the baby was absorbed in trying to grab Jessie's coat anyway.

Have I told you enough that you'll understand the disruption, the disappointment, when Gary suddenly showed up? He came around to the backyard unannounced, no phone call ahead. And that was only the beginning, but I'll get to the rest later. His voice was overly loud and hearty when he called, "Oh, there you all are!" and every one of us startled because none of us had seen him coming. Jessie jumped up and barked, Gracie started to cry. Louisa and I both whipped up, unsure what was happening in spite of the fact that his voice should have been instantly familiar. It was just so unexpected an intrusion into the lighthearted space we'd created.

"Oh . . . Gary, it's you," Louisa said. She didn't sound thrilled. Since Gus wasn't available and the garden was finished, so she didn't need my assistance for that, Gary's "help" just got in our way. It was much more fun for both of us if he didn't show up.

"Well, of course it's me, Mom. Had my Wednesday night service last night—had a hard time getting that done this week, sorry I wasn't around to pitch in—but here I am now. Want me to take the baby?"

"No!" I barked, then realized how that had come out, and he hadn't even been talking to me. "I mean, thanks, honey, but she's fine right now." Actually, she was fussing since he'd scared the bejesus out of her, but I knew I could settle her back down if he'd just go away. "Let's let her be until she needs something. Why don't you take the afternoon off? We're doing fine here."

I'd probably gone too far. He was taken aback.

Gary edged closer to Gracie, still on her blanket, and started rummaging in a plastic bag he held. "Um, well, actually, I brought a couple of things for Gracia, uh, just stuff I got off one of my good internet sites."

"Oh. That's so nice," I said, while thinking *uh-oh*. I'd seen the stuff he'd ordered for Louisa from that internet site he liked so much. When she knows he's coming over, we have to drag it out of closets and out from under beds and put it out so his feelings aren't hurt.

Gary sidestepped me and got to the baby. Down next to her he went and started nuzzling her. Well, she did stop fussing, but don't all babies like attention? Then he pulled what looked like a Barbie doll out of the bag. "It's a Mary doll," he said proudly. "I wasn't sure about the boobies, but that's the way it came, and the internet guaranteed authenticity, so it must be all right. I just didn't think the Jesus action figure was a good toy for a little girl, you know? She doesn't need to be throwing over money tables in the temple yet, but the temple that comes with it is like a big dollhouse. You should see it." Then he shook his head sorrowfully. "But it cost too much, too."

Louisa and I caught each other's eyes, daring the other to speak. I was the first to fold. "Uh, yes, that was probably . . . a . . . good call, Gary," I stammered.

"Oh, and here, I picked these up, too," he said, waving his arm back and extending a small box to me. I was closest to him, but he was speaking to both me and Louisa. "They're just little kid Band-Aids with Jesus's picture on them. In case she ever gets a boo-boo."

I must have looked baffled, or Louisa did.

"To remind her to stick to Jesus." Gary rolled his eyes and filled in what he clearly thought should have been daylight obvious. "Just keep them with her stuff that we got her."

I finally remembered how to speak. ". . . Okay."

Gary, sprawled on the blanket, turned back to Gracie, making fart noises into her stomach and the baby let out belly laughs. Louisa and I looked at each other, both of us speechless until—exactly like Gary had—she rolled her eyes, picked up the pot of special tea, and refilled both our cups to the top. She passed me the cookies. I skipped right over those useless ginger snaps and went for the bourbon balls.

"Gary," I said. "You might as well know. I've decided I want to keep Gracie myself. To raise her. Obviously, whatever you're doing isn't working out. I love her and I can do it."

Gary's head snapped up from where he had it buried in the baby's stomach to make her laugh. He rolled over and sat up, staring at me as if I suddenly had three heads.

"Whoa there, Aunt CarolSue. She has a mother, and I . . . I just asked you to take care of her for a little while. I'll be returning Gracia to her mother."

"Well, then, *where* is her mother, and why haven't you done that all this time? I think there's something you're not telling us. I think you haven't the slightest idea who her mother is or where. That's what I think. So I'm telling you, I'm here and I'll take her for my own."

Gary shook his head. His hair, which is dark blond and curly, actually sort of jumped, he was so adamant. "I mean, she has a father, too," he said. "I imagine, and you don't have the right to just start claiming other people's baby." His face was getting red, and his eyes, which are the same round hydrangea blue as mine—Louise always says that—looked like they were going to pop out of his head.

"Produce the parents," I said, nice and calm.

"This is part of my church work," he retorted. "I'm doing it for my church people!"

"Bless your heart," I went back at him, but still breezy. "Church members have last names and they don't just disappear. Who are the parents and where are they? You're not telling the truth about something."

I decided to risk it, to call his bluff. "Well, maybe Gus ought to be involved now. I can apply to be her foster mother. He'd know how I should do that." I could see Louisa off to the side, and of course, she's freaking out. I held up my hand to stop her. "Don't worry, Sister," I said. "I'll move out with the baby if you don't want us here."

I hadn't really thought that through. I wanted Gracie for sure, but what if Gus had to take her away before she could be placed with me and then the foster placement people said I was too old? Still, I wasn't going to give her up.

At that point, the whole family scene had seriously deteriorated. Gary, who's big, not exactly in good shape and was sitting on his butt, tried to rotate around to pick up Gracie, but I saw what he intended and swooped in to scoop her up. I put her over my shoulder and patted her back. "I'm the one she knows, Gary. I'm the one who loves and takes care of her. We're bonded."

"Don't call Gus," he said. "Just don't."

"CarolSue," my sister started to say.

Whatever it was, I didn't want to hear it. I carried Gracie into the house and stayed there until Gary left. When I went back outside, Louisa and I just looked at each other in tacit agreement to keep our own counsel, although I'm sure she had a lot to say. We ate a late supper because we stayed outside as long as we could, in that exhausted silence after a dispute, when no one can stand to open the subject again and each lets it lie, hoping against hope that it will die and bury itself. Knowing it won't. "No mosquitos," Louisa observed, and she was right. Just the crickets' warning song, while all I wanted was to hold the baby in that golden hour and stop the earth's turning toward winter.

Couldn't we have predicted that would be the evening— fortunately after Gracie was in bed—that we'd hear a car turn onto the gravel driveway? I guess I thought that only so much gets messed up in one day. I was wrong. Louisa checked the front window. "Oh my God, I think it's Gus!" she shrieked.

"What is *he* doing here?"

"How should I know? Pick up the baby stuff. I'll run outside and meet him."

"Maybe you can nap out in one of the lawn chairs," I snapped. "Hasn't he ever heard of calling first?"

"For God's sake—"

"Stay in the dark. You're a mess." I shot this at her as she went out the front door. I was frantic, squatting to pick up the detritus that ends up all around a living room when there's a baby in residence. Rattles, baby books, a receiving blanket. Oh, there on the side table was her empty bottle. Oh Lord, Jessie's toys, too. She loved to snatch Gracie's, so we'd bought her some of her own and they kept trading. I made a run for our bedroom and dropped an armload there, saluting Glitter Jesus on the way out. I wondered what he'd have to say about all this. I was clearing Gracie's things from the bathroom when I heard the front door open and Gus's boom of a voice in the living room. I crept down the hall with the baby tub and bath toys. I'd not made it to the kitchen.

"CarolSue has a bad headache, so we need to keep our voices down," Louisa said.

"Oh, that's a shame," Gus bellowed.

I went into the living room after depositing my load from the bathroom into the baby's room and shutting the door. She was still sleeping soundly. "Keep her asleep," I instructed Glitter Jesus. "Help me out here."

"Oh hi, Gus," I said. "This is a surprise. I didn't know you were here. Nice to see you." What a liar. "I just came out to fix myself some tea. I'm going to bed early. I have a bad headache. Can I fix you two some tea? I'll be in the kitchen anyway." I gave Louisa a meaningful look to signal her to keep Gus out of the kitchen so I could clear it.

Fortunately, Gus had wedged himself into Harold's old recliner, probably not remembering that he always had trouble getting out of it. "Sure, sure," he said. "Sorry about that headache. Louisa told me you were under the weather. You makin' that special tea you girls enjoy? I'll join you in a cup if you are. Got some fine news to share."

"Honey, keep your voice down. Her headache is a migraine and noise makes it worse." Louisa stood to one side of the recliner and put her hand on Gus's shoulder tenderly. She was trying to shut him up so he wouldn't wake the baby.

"Oh, got it, right," Gus said, a tenth of a decibel lower. Louisa turned off one of the floor lamps, too, playing up the part. I beat it to the kitchen, snatching the empty bottles out of the drying rack and stashing the canned formula in the cupboard with the baking sheets.

The tea kettle whistled. I made up a tray, loaded our cups with lemon slices—the fancy version—and honey, and doctored the teapot liberally with the Wild Turkey Louisa always bought in honor of her beloved hens.

"So what's your news, Gus?" I said as I carried in the tray. "I'll join you two long enough to hear that, and then I'll retire with my tea and give you two some privacy." What I intended was to be in the bedroom to make sure I was right there if the baby stirred. This was enormously risky, especially if Louisa and Gus napped, which involved an unfortunate soundtrack. Surely Louisa had better sense. Or not.

"You girls had the news on tonight? If so, you ought to already know!" Gus forgot to keep his voice down in his excitement. Louisa, who'd pulled one of the dining chairs next to the recliner so she wouldn't be more than six inches from him, good Lord, put a finger to her lips, which he missed entirely.

"No, honey, we were outside," she said. "What happened?"

"That big project with the Feds? It's *over*. It's all over the news. Today. It was immigration raids. I couldn't tell you before. It's done, arrested a whole bunch of undocumented, they're in custody, and our part is over. I got a lot of time off coming. That's what I had to come tell you."

"Oh, honey, that's great. I mean that you won't be at work all the time," Louisa said, and kissed him on the lips. Not a short casual kiss, either. She meant it. "We can celebrate! Cheers to you having time off!" And she raised her cup and clinked it against his. "Isn't that great, CarolSue?"

"Wonderful," I said. "Just wonderful." I'm sure I've mentioned my inherited gift for sarcasm. My sister was so caught up with Gus that she had no idea. Charlie would have known right away, though, and it was in moments like those that missing him came over me in a suffocating wave, and whatever I thought I'd set aside was acutely remembered, like the way you remember breathing in the absence of air.

In the bedroom, with Gracie asleep and Glitter Jesus's red-dot pupils looking like little spots of fire above her night light, I lay on top of the bed, not even thinking for once about taking care of the quilt that Mom had made for Louisa, unable to sleep and not only because of the soundtrack running in the next room. Louisa wanted Gus. I wanted Gracie. Gary wanted something else, but I didn't know what.

"Go ahead, Glitter Jesus," I muttered. "You look like you want to burst into flames and it's okay by me."

Chapter 24

Gus

It was the strangest damn thing. He'd been over to Louisa's to tell her the news, and sure, he could tell she was as happy as he was that the project was finished—at least his department's part in it, the force magnifiers' part. And when he'd taken his blue pill last night, she'd called it their personal force magnifier, which they'd both thought was hilarious and then she'd said his force was hugely magnified all the time anyway, and so it had all been great. That wasn't the strange part. He'd gotten a weird feeling, first that CarolSue didn't want him there, which wasn't entirely new, but then, and this was what he couldn't really figure out, something had been poking into his butt while he'd been sitting in the recliner, and when Louisa took their cups to the kitchen, he'd gotten up and taken the cushion out, thinking maybe the chair needed to be fixed and he could do it for her. There was a baby rattle jammed back there.

So he'd pulled it out, and when Louisa came back he showed it to her. She looked weird a minute and then said, "Oh, it's one of Jessie's toys."

"You got baby toys for the dog?"

"She likes to chew on them," Louisa said. She held out her hand for the toy, but before he handed it to her Gus looked at it. No teeth marks.

"We lost that one before we gave it to her," Louisa had

said, seeing where his eyes had gone, doubtless. She was smart, he'd give her that.

Still, it made no sense. The Supply Company in town had racks of dog toys, some of them advertised as indestructible chew toys for retrievers, because so many people around here had sporting dogs. Why would Louisa buy a baby toy? It wasn't like she didn't have more experience than most with animals. Jessie would have destroyed that thing in a hot minute. Plus, it wouldn't have been safe for a dog, not with those little plastic beads inside it. Nope, Louisa wasn't telling him the truth.

Gus tucked what he knew in a pocket of his mind to think on later. He wasn't about to spoil his chance to reclaim his crown as the King of Naps by calling his girlfriend a liar. And she wouldn't lie without reason anyway. He'd figure it out later.

There was one more thing Gus thought he should do, even though technically he didn't even have to be at work the next day. But with Billy being off, it was hardly wise to leave the station to Jimmy alone anyway, so Gus went in the next morning.

"What are you doing here?" Connie said from the dispatch area. She had that big hair thing going on. It must take her forever to rat it out like that. Gus didn't really see the point.

"Jimmy . . ." Gus said by way of explanation.

"Gotcha. I woulda called you if anything big . . ."

"S'okay," Gus said. "Not stayin' all day. Got some stuff to check on anyway."

Gary had told him that the young woman he was looking for, who'd come to his church for help, might be an undocumented migrant. Rosalina Gonzalez. Or maybe Lopez. Before Gus told Gary that he'd tried and come up empty, so he could be done with it, he'd check the names of the women they'd arrested in the raid. He didn't imagine many of them were real names, though. All he could do would be to go by the I-9 papers they'd seized, and he'd have to get access to those from the Feds. Claim he wanted to check the list against local *wanted* names. They'd say immigration took precedence and he'd say, *Yeah, yeah, but I can quit lookin', right?* And they'd probably give him the list.

It took all morning, phone and email, but he was right. It worked. They sent the first list over, the ones that were processed, said the rest would come. The men were being held separately from the women, that was standard. He didn't have any idea where the kids were. The raid had been daytime, the chicken packing plant—which was a big place. Any kids would have been in daycare or school, wouldn't they? Maybe there was family in the area, or other migrants who worked somewhere else. Legal immigrants. The raid had been all over the local news. People must have known to get the kids. Women were being held at the county jail, where there'd been enough room. They'd be processed and most deported. That's what the Feds had said. He and Billy had been perimeter guards. There'd been dogs. Handcuffed men and women led out. Crying. It looked like some were either arguing or begging, but the little he could hear was in English heavily accented and mixed with Spanish, which he didn't understand. He'd been part of it, yet not. If he'd tried to say what had really happened, he wouldn't have been able to. He was an American. He was safe. There was comfort in that, he supposed.

No Rosalina was listed. Gus shrugged, cleaned his glasses on his shirt front, went through his email, read the paper, checked that Jimmy was out being seen, had Connie radio him to write some damn tickets outside town if there are any out-of-state plates over the limit, and told Connie the coffee was too old and smelled bad, could she please make some fresh. He was relieved to have stupid junk to do.

He took himself to lunch at the café. Margo seated him at a dirty table and took her sweet time clearing it, so he changed his order twice to annoy her. She retaliated by putting pickles on his tuna sandwich and upped the ante by spilling coffee into his saucer, leaving the whipped cream off his pecan pie, and overcharging him on his bill. He won the round by grossly undertipping her and left having thoroughly enjoyed himself. He still couldn't believe he'd asked her out, though. What had he been thinking?

He could have called it a day. He had a ridiculous amount of comp time coming, and he'd even put in a half day when he hadn't needed to, so he looked really good. Maybe he just wanted to tell Gary he'd even checked the names of the un-documented picked up in the raid that was all over the news, and that the person he was looking for had just melted into the shadows and he shouldn't expect to find her. Happens all the time. Gary should let it go. Gus hoped there wasn't more to it than what Gary had said, but something about the story bothered him. If Gary was in a mess, then would Gary's mother end up in it, too?

So instead of doing the sensible thing and letting well enough alone, he went back to the station. "Just can't stand to stay away, huh?" Connie said.

"Some adult's gotta check the kindergarten."

"If you find one, let me know. I'm busy running this place."

He liked Connie. She was smart, stayed calm, and had a sense of humor. People didn't know how important the dispatcher was, and he wished his other two were nearly as good at it as she was. When Jimmy had had to fill in for a couple of hours, he hadn't had a clue how to talk a scared kid down. Connie wasn't bad to look at either, except for the big hair thing. Looked like a storm cloud about to dump a heap of mud on her head. He hoped she was done having kids so he wouldn't have to put up with another maternity leave, but

Gus was careful not to mention that, and certainly not her looks, not even on her best days, when she just stuck to a normal-looking ponytail. He stayed five feet away from the dispatch desk; either that, or he called to her over the glass if he needed to talk to her at any length. Better yet, he'd wait until someone else was present. He knew the drill about sexual harassment. His record was clean, and he intended to keep it that way.

He got sidetracked for a bit. Jimmy hadn't done a damn thing he was supposed to, meaning written any tickets. He checked the faxes, went over the quarterly budget report that was due to city council. Then he checked his email. He'd been copied on the scan of the next set of processed names from the raid. The feds had told him at least half would be fake names, based on fake I-9s and that he couldn't assume that local *wanted* either were or weren't picked up based on the list; that he could compare the photos if they had priors. Otherwise it was a crapshoot.

But Gus was looking for one name. Rosalina Gonzalez.

Damn.

She was in custody.

Gus laid his glasses on the desk, rolled his chair back and stretched his legs straight out, his body diagonal, head resting on the chair top. He stared at the stained ceiling, took in a breath and exhaled long, cheeks puffed out. Shit, shit, shit. It would be so much easier if he hadn't found her. Or if he thought Gary was telling a straight story. Now he had to figure out what to do.

Gary

Things were a mess. The last time he'd been at his mother's, CarolSue had dropped it on him that she wanted to keep

Gracia. Of all the crazy ideas. He'd gone over there to see the baby, of course, but hoping he could talk to his aunt in private, to borrow money. Brother Zachariah was breathing down his neck, and hard as he'd prayed on it, nothing had brought in nearly enough. He'd given it his all at his Wednesday night message, the prayer meetings, and his Sunday sermon, during which he'd pulled out all the stops, including a slight dusting of gold glitter in his own curls so the overhead light he'd installed would pick up the glint and suggest to the Brothers and Sisters that Jesus truly was speaking to them in his ministry when he exhorted them to donate. It had been one of Brother Zachariah's ideas, which he said was a godly use of the power of suggestion.

He'd never gotten to even ask CarolSue. She'd gotten all uppity and threatened to call Gus about Gracia. Well, not exactly that, but to ask him about becoming her foster mother. The welfare department couldn't be getting involved with his daughter. No way could he have that, not that he could explain why. Anyway, they'd ended up in a big argument and he could hardly ask her for money.

At this point, he didn't even know whether his biggest problem was waiting for Gus to find Rosalina, preventing CarolSue from calling Gus, or trying to get the money for Brother Zachariah, who'd been coming around to collect, threatening to turn him in because he had failed to register the church properly. Brother Zachariah had reminded him that even Mary and Joseph had traveled on that donkey all those hundreds (was it thousands?) of miles to go get registered and pay their tax. Brother Zachariah said that he was damn tired of Saving Gary, and if Gary didn't come up with the money he owed, Brother Zachariah had no choice but to have the church shut down. Which, he said, would sure increase Gary's guilt for Cody's death in God's eyes. How would he atone without the church?

That last had been yesterday when Gary had said he just

didn't have the money yet. Gary had cried, begged for time and Brother Zachariah said, "You best get it. I'm watching you."

He'd thought on it and prayed on it, and it seemed the best course was to both mollify CarolSue, make sure she didn't involve Gus about Gracia, and to borrow money from her. Not that he had a clue how he could ever pay it back. Maybe she'd make it a donation; that would be the best solution. He knew she had a big soft spot for him, and if he asked in the right way, and his mother could be kept out of it—that would be tricky—CarolSue would likely come around. There was nothing else to try. He'd have to go over there. For sure it wasn't the sort of thing he could work over the phone.

"Please," he said when Brother Zach called again Sunday night wanting to know how much had been in the collections that day. "Give me a chance. I have a Plan." He was home, or what passed for home now, in his bedroom. "I'm going to ask my aunt. She's well-off. Not a church member, see, but we're pretty close."

"And where is this benefactor?" Brother Zachariah had said, his tone an angry challenge around the edge. "Why didn't you go to her before this?"

Gary kept his voice as low as he could. It was an old, well-built farmhouse so the walls were plaster and he had reasonable privacy, but still. He could occasionally hear Sister Martha when she was berating Brother Thomas about his sneaking a third piece of pie when he was supposed to lose weight. Gary wondered why she kept making pies but didn't suggest she stop. He needed a cheap place to live, after all, and Sister Martha hardly charged him enough to cover the hot water he used. The room was plain but she let him put up pictures, his own art, as long as he promised to patch the wall and paint eventually, plus the bed was decent and there was a chair and a good reading light. Gary made do just fine, so he did not want Sister Martha or Brother Thomas getting any hint that he, and therefore their church, might be in trouble.

"Speak up," Brother Zachariah demanded now, and Gary, reluctant, repeated what he'd just nearly whispered.

"She has the baby."

"What?" Brother Zach sounded shocked, like Gary had done something stupid.

"The baby I told you about. She's been taking care of her."

"Where?"

"At my mother's."

"Huh. You told 'em anything?"

"No. Didn't tell them, like you said." Gary hoped Brother Zach would praise him for following instructions.

"Why didn't you get the money from her before?"

He could hardly tell Brother Zachariah about the argument. How would that buy him time? "She's got the baby for me. I didn't want to ask her for more," Gary said, then realized he was whining. "But I will, I will for sure. Tomorrow," he added, adding steel to his voice.

"Huh," came the response. "See that you do."

The morning was dismal, a grudging sky hanging low, full of ominous suggestion, which Gary did not appreciate. With CarolSue and Brother Zachariah threatening him, was God chiming in, too? He wished, as he often did, that God would speak a little more directly, and then he wondered if the thought was blasphemous.

He'd not specified what time today he would approach CarolSue when he'd promised Brother Zachariah that he wouldn't postpone it. He couldn't spare the money to buy himself the big breakfast he would have liked, not right now, so he just had the bread that Sister Martha was kind to always leave out in case he wanted to make himself some toast to go with the last coffee they'd left in the pot. He sat at their kitchen table knowing that Brother Thomas was likely tend-ing something in the barn, and Sister Martha would have gone to visit her mother in the nursing home. The house was empty, giving Gary plenty of space to dread the day.

He gave a deep sigh. This cup was not going to pass from him, but he could avoid drinking from it until the afternoon. The baby napped after her bottle at noon and it was her longest sleep period during the day. His mother had mentioned that, at some point when he'd been over. He'd go then. If the rain held off, maybe he could catch CarolSue inside while his mother was out in the yard.

Chapter 25

Gary

When he pulled the church van into the driveway at one o'clock after dithering through the morning trying to look up convincing Scripture he could cite to CarolSue, but freaking himself out by finding all the wrong Signs, Gary thought maybe it was going to be all right after all. His mother was out in the front deadheading chrysanthemums. She called to him when he got out, gesturing with her chin. "Your aunt's inside with the baby. I'm trying to get this done before it rains. I'll be in in a bit. Did you need anything special?"

"Nope. I'll go see if Aunt CarolSue needs help with Gracia."

"Fat chance she'll let you get your hands on that child," his mother said, and bent back over her flowers, bright smatterings against all the fallen brown of the leaves. He should offer to rake out the garden, but she usually didn't like how he did things anyway because he stepped on stuff he wasn't supposed to. If he had a little extra money, like he used to once in a while, he'd buy her a blower. Maybe he'd be able to do it for Christmas, and it'd be cheaper on the internet than the Supply Company.

Gary's feet swished through the leaves on the stone walk and he let himself in the front door.

"Shhh," CarolSue whispered. She was in the living room. "I just put her down, but she's not asleep. If she hears anything going on, she'll want up."

Gary nodded, pointed to the kitchen and mouthed, "Need to talk to you."

Without waiting, he walked ahead through the dining area and into the kitchen, where he didn't think their voices would carry to the master bedroom. CarolSue followed. Baby bottles were in the drying rack; CarolSue began assembling and putting them away when she got to the sink. But she turned her head to show she was listening.

"I'm sorry," he began. "I know I overreacted when you said you wanted to keep Gracia. You really love her. It means the world that you've stepped in and given her such wonderful care." Every word of that was true. He hoped it would be enough.

CarolSue fixed her eyes right on his. She looked tired, but put together—good grief, she even had makeup on. And her hair was fixed. She did not look like any of the farm women around here, that was for sure. Not even the ones who worked in the Supply Company, the post office, or the bank. Shoot, not even the high school teachers. When Gary went to the community college, a couple of his professors looked like this, ones who came over from the university to teach a class. So maybe it was a city thing.

"I meant what I said, Gary."

"I know you did," he said, ducking the issue. "And we can talk about how that might work." What he meant was, *I'll have to find a way to explain why that's not going to work.* But he couldn't say that now. He had to get past this part. "You know, right, that this is part of the church work."

CarolSue cocked her head. Like she knew he was diverting her and was waiting.

Gary hurried to continue. "I have to do this through the church. That's how Gracia came to me, see? And here's the thing. It turns out that I made a bad mistake. I didn't register the church the way I was supposed to, and now we owe the IRS a bunch of taxes and penalties or we'll get shut down.

I'm worried about Gracia, but about the whole church. Could I possibly borrow the money from you to get the church in the clear?" He rushed the words, to just get it out, trying not to stammer and to look her in the eyes.

"What?' she said, her eyes narrowing slightly and scrunching her nose. "Churches don't pay taxes."

"I was supposed to register, see—"

"So you talked to the IRS?"

"Well, sort of."

"What does that mean?" Her eyes were even more narrow now, as if she were trying to x-ray his mind.

"They were going to shut down the church, see, and I was worried about what would happen to Gracia. So I borrowed, but now the person I borrowed from needs it back, and I have to pay the IRS." It was hard to look at her. And damn if he hadn't just heard thunder. "Can you please just loan me money? I need ten thousand dollars. I'll get a second job and pay you back, and we'll talk about Gracia, as long as I can keep my church open." He really hadn't planned to say it quite this way.

"Gary, it's not the money, but something doesn't sound right about this."

Oh no. Brother Zachariah would be furious. He expected to be paid back and paid back now.

"It's for Gracia," Gary appealed. He'd almost forgotten what it was like to lie on the spot, felt his face betray him again.

CarolSue shook her head. "There's something else going on. I don't know what. I'd do anything for that baby girl, you know that, but something's not right here."

More thunder. If there was lightning, his mother would come in. A few fat raindrops splattered on the kitchen window. The front door shut. "Raining," his mother said, appearing in the dining area.

"We're talking, Mom," Gary said, hoping she'd be tactful and go away.

"What's up?" Louisa said. She was windblown, and her hands were all dirty. She went to the sink and washed them.

"Gary's got a problem with his church," CarolSue said.

"Big surprise there." His mother had never believed in anything he'd done. His aunt at least understood that Gary had been Saved by donating to the Brother's ministry, even if she herself preferred to keep her original Methodist membership and call it done.

"Stop, Louisa. Not now."

His mother sighed, took a clean hand towel from the drawer, and dried her hands. They looked old and work-worn, with short nails, more clean now than during the summer but still showing the effect of all the compost she'd mulched the gardens with. Al had been out on the combine and the kid they hired, Brandon, was away in college now. CarolSue wasn't much use outside. Too late now. His mother likely had it finished. She'd have keeled over before she'd have asked him, her own son, to help her. If he'd offered, she'd have said no anyway. But he should have tried.

"So what's wrong?" his mother said. Weary.

"He's asking to borrow money from me. For the church. Something to do with Gracie."

"Oh no. No, no, no," his mother said right away.

Gary started to put up a hand, to tell her to stay out of it, when CarolSue intervened.

"I was about to suggest that we look into this more," CarolSue said.

"The thing is, I need it right away. So we don't get shut down." Gary was getting desperate but tried to filter that out of his voice. He needed to make a calm, convincing case.

There was a loud, sharp banging on the front door. Jessie went crazy barking. They all looked at one another, wondering who was expecting someone. Gary thought it had to be the worst timing ever. He said, "Hang on, I'll check," heading through the dining room for the front.

Louisa said, "Maybe it's Gus," and pushed to his side to go for the door.

"Shhh. Keep your voices down," CarolSue said, trailing them out of the kitchen, riding herd. "Don't wake the baby!"

Gary looked out the picture window. There was an unfamiliar car behind his van. At least it wasn't Gus. He opened the door.

"Brother Zachariah!" Gary was as shocked and scared as if he'd been caught at something. "I'm dealing with things now." It was the only thing he could think to say. "Please."

The Brother's face was intent. "Thought you might need some help." He stepped over the threshold. "Explaining the importance."

"Uh, no, everything's under control. Stay down, Jessie." The puppy was jumping around, agitated. Gary never could tell what that meant, but this time his mother didn't grab the dog's collar or tell her to settle down.

Louisa said, "What's going on here? Who are you?" As if Gary hadn't just said his name.

"Mom, this is Brother Zachariah. He's the one who—"

"I know." Louisa did not invite him in. "What do you want, Zachariah?"

"Brother Gary here owes some serious money. Else his church is gonna be shut down and he'll likely do some jail time. Fraud and the like. I loaned it to him and he promised it back, but he hasn't paid. He mentioned a family member would help him out today."

"I've just been speaking with my aunt, Brother. If you'll please leave and allow us to finish, I'm sure you and I can . . ."

"I'll just stay so we can take care of it prompt."

His mother took Gary completely off guard then. "Well, if this involves you men and Gary's aunt, perhaps you will excuse me? I'll let you see to your business." Was she really going to cooperate and stay out of it? It was almost as if she was giving CarolSue tacit approval to help him.

Brother Zachariah said, "That's a good idea." He went and sat down on the couch without being invited. Patent shoes and dress slacks, a green, purple, and yellow paisley shirt and a yellow tie. Green socks. His hair was slicked down, shiny as his shoes. Gary had the unwelcome thought that if his father weren't already dead, he would have keeled over seeing that getup on a man in his living room. He stuffed the notion down. Brother Zachariah was a preacher, not a farmer, after all.

CarolSue stepped forward.

"Uh, this is my aunt, CarolSue Davis." Gary extended a hand in the Brother's direction. "Aunt CarolSue, this is Brother Zachariah. He's the one who Saved me, you know, after Cody died, and Dad."

CarolSue hesitated, and then manners won. "Nice to meet you," she said. But she didn't shake hands. Gary noticed that Brother Zachariah didn't stand up, the way Gary had been taught to, and he knew that was a mistake CarolSue would notice. He hoped she'd overlook it.

"Uh, maybe we should sit down?" Gary felt as if his stomach had turned into a frog pond and the denizens were all jumping at once. CarolSue took Harold's chair and Gary the wingback. Outside, thunder and heavier rain. Gary thought, *What if it's a Sign? Oh Jesus, please don't let it be a Sign, please. Please.*

"I'm not sure why you're here, sir," CarolSue said, looking at Brother Zachariah.

"Want to make sure you get a straight story, is all," he said.

"Are you suggesting Gary would lie to me?"

"Might not let you know how serious the trouble is."

"And how serious is that?"

"Real serious. He can still get outta it, but not for long."

"As I was just explaining, Aunt CarolSue, the Brother here has been kind enough to intervene with the authorities and keep the church from being shut down, but now I need to pay him back. He needs the money for his own ministry. Is that right, Brother?"

"That's about it."

"Well, so exactly what would happen if Gary doesn't pay you right now?"

"He gets shut down, and . . ."

"Well, it sounds like you'd get shut down, too, if you don't have the money for your . . . uh . . . ministry. Do I understand you correctly? Exactly what entity have you paid on Gary's behalf?"

"I've paid entirely too much, is that what you mean?"

"Entity. What entity? Who have you paid?"

Brother Zachariah leaned forward on the couch. "Look, Missus Davis. Brother Gary here is aware of all that. The authorities." His voice, usually sonorous, got an edge to it. "Alls I want is to be repaid so I can get about my ministry. And I wouldn't want to reveal some other problems he might have goin' on." As he said the last, he shifted his face to stare hard at Gary.

The cryptic reference led his aunt to challenge Brother Zachariah as to what he meant. Gary knew exactly what the Brother meant, and CarolSue would never give him the money if she found out about Gracie like this.

"Aunt CarolSue, if you'd just consider loaning me the money. I know this is uncomfortable for all of us. I'm good for it. I'll get a second job and pay you back." Gary went on making various proposals to convince her to loan or donate the money. CarolSue looked at him with her head tilted, at least listening, and he'd begun to think there might be hope until he heard the hard, fast gravel crunch of a car coming down the drive too fast and the scraping of tires on pebbles.

A car door slam. Gary started to get up to see what the latest intrusion was, but before he even got to the window, his mother hurried through the room between them all and opened the front door. Gus, in uniform, came in, hand resting on his gun, though it was still holstered.

"Zachariah Barnes, you're under arrest for extortion. You have the right to remain silent." And Gus proceeded to recite all the Miranda provisions in his stentorian voice. Gary tried to protest but Gus ran right over him.

"Wait, wait, Gus, there's a mistake here," Gary said. "Brother Zachariah loaned me money to pay the IRS. I didn't register the church. It was a loan. He just needs me to pay him back."

"Son, that is a load of bullshit. Excuse me, CarolSue, Louisa. Bless your heart, Gary. He's a grifter. Stealing from you. I ran him out of the county once already."

"I'll call my lawyer and be out in twenty minutes," Brother Zachariah said, a splay of red rising on his neck and face. "You betrayed me, Gary. You betrayed Jesus."

"Thanks, Louisa," Gus said. "Come on, Barnes."

Gracia fussed. *No, no, not now. Please, please, just get Gus out of here with Brother Zachariah.* As much as Gary had not wanted Gus to take the Brother, now he desperately wanted them both out. Gracia got louder. Gus, somewhat deaf, didn't seem to notice.

"Brother Zachariah, I'll do everything I can to help," Gary said. "I'll explain."

Brother Zachariah wasn't hard of hearing. A smirk crossed his face and disappeared. Raising his eyebrows, he said, "There's the baby crying. Somebody better go tend to her," his voice infused with innocent-sounding concern.

"What?" Gus chuckled. "Let's go, Barnes. You're crazy, too." He hadn't heard Gracia.

Go, go, go, Gary thought.

But then the baby let loose. The loud voices had awakened her, or the thunder, or a combination. She didn't usually wake screaming, but today she screamed.

"I've got it," CarolSue said, and headed back to the room she shared with Gracia.

"There's a baby here?" Gus said.

"We're babysitting," his mother inserted. "Church work for Gary."

And then it all blew up. Brother Zachariah snorted. "That what he told you? Just another lie. He owes me the damn money. And that there baby is his. He was fornicating again, and the poor girl had his baby, that's what happened. Tryin' to hide it. Wantin' me to cover for him and his church. So y'all just pay me what he owes . . ."

Gus and his mother stood a minute, apparently stunned, waiting for him to deny it. CarolSue came through the hall carrying the baby, who had the hiccups but wasn't crying anymore. CarolSue held a pink pacifier in her free hand and a receiving blanket was draped half over her shoulder and half around Gracia.

His mother erupted at Brother Zachariah. "You are disgusting. That's not Gary's baby," his mother said. "Gus, get him out of here."

Gary inhaled and breathed out. All of it, everything, was gone now. There was nothing left to save except this one small grace. "Yes," he said. "She is mine." He held both arms out toward CarolSue as she approached with his daughter. "I'll take her."

Chapter 26

CarolSue

A reverberation followed Gary's words, as if a gong had sounded and spread, echo after widening echo, into the sudden silence. Zachariah and Gus were by the front door, Gus clutching that con man's elbow to lead him out but stopping in his tracks, as surprised as the rest of us. Zachariah had an ugly, satisfied smirk on his face. I took a step backward, clutching Gracie and intending to take her back to the bedroom. What had I been thinking by bringing her out of the bedroom into this quicksand? I didn't know whether to believe Gary.

But then Gary was right there, and before I could get away, he had his hands on Gracie and was taking her from me. Believe me, I tried to hang on to her. "Let me just . . ." I started to say, and Gary said, "No, give her to me," and I wasn't going to scare her by having a tug of war.

I kissed her head and wrapped the blanket from my shoulder around her and helped Gary get a good grip on her. Gracie didn't cry.

Gus was the one who seemed to get a handle on himself first. He stared hard at Gary and said, "Gary, that true?"

Gary had his chin down against Gracie. He nodded and then found his voice. "Yes," he said.

Zachariah Barnes snorted. "Oh yeah. He makes a great

daddy, don't he now?" Louisa took a quick step and raised her hand. I thought she was going to fly at him and start slapping, slugging, punching. Gus put up an arm to block her.

"Stay back now," Gus said to Louisa. "Still looking?" Gus said then, glancing over to Gary, and I wasn't sure what he was talking about.

"Yeah," Gary whispered on a long exhale, nodding.

"Okay, then. Looks like you all have some things to sort out," Gus said, his face inscrutable. "Louisa, I'll call you later. Time to go, Barnes."

Seeing that Louisa was immobilized again, I managed to get out, "Thank you, Gus," and went to close the front door behind them. I saw Gus put handcuffs on Barnes once they were on the steps, and I was glad.

In the living room, my sister sank into Harold's old recliner. She still hadn't said a word. I can tell you this: For once, she didn't have a Plan. She was usually a half dozen steps ahead of Gary. I couldn't tell from her face how she was taking it. Honestly, I think she was in shock. Well, in fairness, I was too. And then a little bit of quiet jubilation set in. Gracie was my own *family*.

Gus

After Gus had taken Barnes to the station, given him his one phone call, printed and booked him pending arraignment, he turned him over to Jimmy for transport to county. He hoped the judge would deny bail until trial, but it wasn't likely. At least Dalton, the prosecutor, would ask. He hated grifters, and there were already strikes against Barnes.

He guessed it made some sense now, but oh boy, Gary's announcement wasn't going to set well with Louisa. He'd gotten a load of the shock on her face. Had Gary made up some malarkey and asked her, or more likely CarolSue, to babysit that afternoon? Oh wait. Wait. Wait. Exactly how long had that baby been there?

Gus thought all the way back to the bathtub for Marvelle. All the times Louisa had been too tired, or CarolSue hadn't been feeling well. The baby toy for Jessie in the recliner. How he, a sheriff trained to look for clues, had been played. Damn. That baby had been there all this time. She must have known. Must have. He'd thought he could trust her. No wonder she'd been asking if they couldn't start napping at his apartment.

Gary was another matter entirely. Gus had smelled something off with Gary from the beginning, hadn't he? As he thought back, he was disgusted with himself that he hadn't put it together. A baby. Of course. Why else would Gary— with his history, too! Everybody knew why Nicole left him— be desperately looking for a young, vulnerable woman? And here Gary's mother had weird baby stuff around her house, and duh! The great dumb trusting cop had gone on his merry way. It wasn't even as if the pieces couldn't have fit easily if he hadn't been blinded. Had Louisa been laughing at him behind his back?

Probably. If it were anyone else, he'd laugh at them. This was the kind of stupid stuff that was Jimmy's lane, not his. And he'd laugh his ass off at Jimmy. Hell, he'd get rid of him if he could get somebody who could add two plus two.

He looked around his apartment. His underwear was strewn around; he hadn't gotten to the laundry in a while. Dirty dishes, too. Junk mail. The cartons his food had come in. Two burned-out lightbulbs. Rhonda would shit a brick if she saw the place. She'd have warned him to listen to his gut, too. Well, really, first thing she'd say was that Louisa was the best thing to happen to him in years. *Damn.* She'd say, *Clean up this disgusting mess and talk to her. There's two sides to every story.* Yeah, that's what she'd say. Yadda, yadda. That's true, Rhonda, but that baby *had* been there the whole time. He could hear the argument in his head.

So you sure Gary told his mother the truth? Rhonda challenged. *Sons always tell their mothers the truth? You always told the truth? Don't make me laugh.*

So, maybe that was true enough. But why wouldn't Louisa have told me about the baby? She was keeping me at arm's length way before this operation with the Feds came up. She coulda told me what was going on. Talked to me.

Maybe 'cause you're a cop? Or maybe she thought all you wanted to do was nap, not talk?

Gus didn't answer Rhonda's ghost. He used to walk out of the room when she said stuff he didn't have an answer for. She wasn't playing fair. He couldn't walk out of his own head. He never could win with her.

He was mad, and for now he wanted to stay mad while he figured out what to do. He wasn't of a mind to tell Gary that he'd found Rosalina, not when Gary hadn't been straight with him. And he wasn't ready to talk with Louisa. Not yet.

You damn well ought to do something. If you're not going to talk to either Gary or Louisa right now, which you know you should do, then why don't you try just doing your job? Try being a cop. That baby is in your jurisdiction and right now so is the woman who may be her mother. Maybe you better go check this out, huh?

Rhonda could be such a bitch. Since she'd died and taken up residence in his head, the annoyance factor was huge, but at least she couldn't make him tell her out loud that she was right anymore. "All right already," he muttered out of habit.

The Dwayne County Justice Center was housing the women, though Gus didn't know how long they'd be kept there. This was all new, and everyone hoped, temporary, although the way things were going, more likely the new normal. Probably most would be transferred to one of the bigger designated federal places. They were opening all over, in jails that either had or had made room, to get the per diem from the government; and new, private contract ones. There was money to be made. The detainees would have to wait for an immigration court, although most all of them would be deported. They'd cry, they'd beg for asylum. Their stories about what they'd escaped—gangs and violence, drugs, rape, poverty or persecution—were almost certainly true. But most applications would be denied. Some would have been here for years with jobs, families, paying taxes, staying out of trouble. Except their social security cards and their I-9 immigration papers were a hundred percent fake, and that would doom their hope of staying.

Gus didn't know any of this firsthand, didn't know what really happened. One of the Feds had told him this, hard-jawed although his eyes were tired and he shook his head, as if he couldn't decide what to feel. "Whatever," he'd said, raising his shoulders after the raid, the lead of a handsome German shepherd in his right hand. The dog sat quietly at heel while the men watched from a distance. The agent, and two others with dogs at other points on the site perimeter, had waited to see that there were no disturbances while the workers whose papers didn't match were loaded into the busses. There weren't. "Above my pay grade," he said to Gus. "I do my job. My family's gotta eat."

Gus was familiar enough with the Justice Center, though, so going there wasn't any big deal. Not that it was his habit to visit anyone who was incarcerated. Once they were booked, he was typically done, except when he went to court as the arresting officer and for sure, he wouldn't be doing that for any of these cases. He'd had the standard employee tour, years ago, so he'd seen the bunks, the cafeteria, and the rec yard. It was grim then, and no reason to think it had changed. Loud. No privacy. Nothing to see but gray concrete and steel. And other bodies, crowded in, too close. Gus couldn't have worked as a guard there.

Even now, the sound of the door clanging shut bothered him. He showed his ID, signed in and asked for an interview room. Had to leave his sidearm, of course. The woman behind the glass—she wasn't one that Gus knew—punched Rosalina's full name and detainee number into a computer. She pressed a buzzer and Gus proceeded through another set of doors. He was waved through rather than searched and went to the interview room he'd been assigned, to wait. He'd thought maybe they'd make him use one of the booths with a glass separator and speak through a phone, but was gratified that it was a naked room, just a table and a couple chairs. Good. It would be a little easier to read this Rosalina without scratched-up Plexiglas between them.

He waited about five minutes for her to be brought in. She looked young, small, frightened. Her orange jumpsuit was too large, and there were slippers made of something like cardboard on her feet. He noticed this because of the strange scuffling noise they made.

"You speak English?" he said.

"Not great," she said.

"Your name?"

"Rosalina Gonzalez." She had a widow's peak in her forehead, large brown eyes that were listless and dull, high cheekbones under olive skin. Hair pulled into a lank ponytail. Gus tried to see her with Gary's eyes and couldn't. If it was true about the baby, what hadn't Gary been able to resist?

He thought to put her at ease. "This isn't about your case or anything. Not really official. I know somebody who's looking for you. I mean, if I've got the right person. You know a Gary Hawkins?"

She tried to guard it, but he saw the answer on her face.

"You don't need to be scared," he said, trying to be kind. He tried to think how to phrase the next question and wished he had planned it ahead. He was damn good at interrogations and under his usual circumstances would have known exactly how he wanted this to go. "Uh. He maybe has something belongs to you? That you should get back, I mean. Rightly."

She shook her head.

"No?" he asked.

"No," she whispered.

"He doesn't have something of yours?" Now he was incredulous.

Her face was shuttered. "No."

Gus sighed. He closed his eyes for a moment to think. Opened them and leaned across the table. He spoke softly. "Rosalina, did you have a baby a while ago? Because Gary Hawkins suddenly got himself a baby, I guess he's been hiding it at his mother's, see? His mother and his aunt taking care of it. And all this time, he's been searching for you. He's had me searching for you, not as sheriff, but as a family friend. I gotta put two and two together and figure maybe you're the mother of that baby."

She was silent as her eyes filled. Her hands held each other tightly in front of her on the scratched table.

"Am I right?" Gus persisted.

"How is the baby?" she whispered.

"Looked fine to me. Only just saw her the once, for a minute." He nodded. "Fine. Good."

The smallest light of a smile crossed her face and then she closed that, too, into a shadow in Gus's memory. He was sure, but not of what to do.

"She should be with you. A baby needs her mother."

"They will send me back," she said. "After court."

"Where? Your I-9 . . . fake?"

"Honduras," she said, and did not answer the rest. Gus knew anyway.

"A baby needs her mother," he repeated, because he believed it. He'd needed his and he hadn't been a baby when she left.

But he saw her hands shift, the one on the bottom shifted to the top, even though she shook her head. "More . . . needs to be safe." He could see she was trying not to give way to the tears that had made it to her cheeks now. Her nose was running, and of course there was no tissue in the room.

"They'd keep her until you're being sent . . . and then I could bring her to you. I'm pretty sure I could make that happen," he said.

He watched her take that in. Best not to press her more now. Let her maternal instincts eat away at her. It was no big deal for him to come back. "Think it over, Rosalina. I can help you with this. Not as a cop. I'm a friend of Gary's mother, Louisa. That's where the baby is. They're good people. She's getting lots of love, for sure."

"*Gracias*," she started, and then caught herself, nodded. "Thank you."

After he left, Gus would go over the conversation in his head and think maybe he shouldn't have told her about the love.

What if she didn't know about that? If Gus worked on Rosalina about how the baby belonged with her, then maybe his life could go back to normal. Even though CarolSue had moved in, there wouldn't be a baby there anymore.

That what you want, asshole? Gus had thought his way into being plain mad at Louisa. He could stomach CarolSue keeping anything from him. After all, they'd hardly had time to become friends on their own. But Louisa? He'd thought he was more than a good nap to her, that they had trust between them. He wouldn't have, couldn't have hidden something big, something important like this from her. She'd even sort of lied to him, most likely, those times when she'd said Carol-Sue was sick, or she herself was "tired out."

It was the sort of question that Rhonda would have made quick work of. She'd have told him exactly what he wanted, and even though it pissed him off to no end, she'd be right.

Chapter 27

CarolSue

Gus's tires had been loud, chewing the driveway pebbles on the way back out, as if he wanted to be heard. I'd sneak-watched anyway, standing to the side of the living room window to see for sure that Barnes was in custody and in that car, leaving. Then we all slumped into the stunned, reverberating silence, the kind that follows an explosion. As I've said, I feared Louisa was in shock. Gary still had Gracie, and much as I wanted her back, I didn't push it, not wanting to find out where the lines of authority would be drawn. "Hey, sweet baby girl," he murmured into the dark cap of her hair, as he shifted her and lowered himself onto the far end of the couch. "I've got you."

I figured my sister must be split down the middle, dying to blast Gary with, *I tried to tell you a thousand times that "Brother" dude was a con man, but would you listen?* but unable to form that sentence because the words were crowded out by the other ones elbowing their way to the front: *What? All this time that baby is my own granddaughter and you didn't think it would be a good idea to tell me?*

She sat there for a good five minutes, we all did, Louisa definitely giving Gary The Look. She'd learned it from our mother, and it could wither a plant, believe me. I was actually hoping that Gracie would start to cry so there would be an urgent need for me to get her a bottle or something, but no, she just kept looking around and playing with her hands like they were the most fascinating objects in the universe. I don't know how she stood the tension. I was about to break, when Louisa finally spoke.

"CarolSue, can you please make us some special tea? Make it really . . . special." Then, in her steely tone, the one she used to use on unruly fifth grade boys, she spoke to Gary. "You . . . bring me my granddaughter."

I headed for the kitchen but looked back to see Louisa with her arms outstretched, and Gary, who'd gotten up and brought the baby across the room, about to put Gracie in them.

In case you're wondering what's wrong with that, it's this: I was the one who'd loved and wanted that baby from the first day. Not him, not her. Why was I relegated to make a big pot of special tea while my sister was in there bonding with a baby that was already bonded to me? I didn't take well to being shoved aside, but I hid it.

"Did you make the tea extra . . . special?" Louisa said when I carried the tray in ten minutes later.

"We're real low on Wild Turkey now, let's put it that way."

"Okay, then. CarolSue, look." She shifted her face from me to the baby, stretched faceup in her lap. "She does have Harold's chin, doesn't she?"

I nodded but said, "I actually think she looks like Mom. Around the eyes, and eyebrows."

"Ohhh. Hadn't thought of that. We'll have to get out her old albums anyway."

I noticed that Louisa was rather pointedly ignoring Gary, so I spoke to him. "Gary, you want some tea?" Even though Gary always said no because he wasn't sure if it was a Sin, I was thinking he might make an exception, given what was going on.

"I've got to drive," he pointed out.

"Yeah, better not, then." It was just as well. I'd made the

tea and knew if he got stopped he'd get a DUI just for breathing in the vapors. An extra half tablespoon per cup this time.

"Listen, Mom, I am still looking for Gracia's mother. To give her back, I mean. I can't just . . ." He waved an arm in the air, which added nothing.

I thought I had an opening to remind him that I wanted to raise Gracie. "Gary, who is the mother? Have you even heard from her?" It was obvious he hadn't, but he'd need to admit that.

"I'd . . . rather not go into it."

Louisa struggled to get out of the recliner with the baby, and I got to her and took Gracie, sensing what was coming. I moved to the dining room with her as Louisa erupted over Gary. "Oh, really now! You'd rather just screw around, have a baby, lie about it, and then when your charade collapses, say, I'd rather not go into it? I imagine this is all part of your *church work* . . . Extremely holy. Are there extra points involved from Jesus if you found a Virgin?"

I've mentioned, haven't I, that we are Masters of Sarcasm? Louisa was about to go after our annual Best Display Award. Damn, if Gary didn't one-up her, though, and he didn't even have any special tea to help him along. Not a bit, but he managed to stop her cold. He started to cry.

Gary

He was ashamed and shamed. Gary put up no defense to his mother's attack. He was guilty. He thought he should take the baby with him, but she wouldn't let him. "You don't have a thing for her. It's all here. We're the ones she knows," she said. Another truth.

It had been embarrassing, his eyes and nose running the way they had. Using the back of his hand in that little-kid motion to wipe them. Trying the other hand. Best to just leave. He was too upset then to even walk to the door, though. He'd sort of folded in half, like his chest was trying to collapse against his thighs and sank back onto the couch, sobbing like he was five years old. It wasn't only the shame, though, that hit him first, his mother's words as well-aimed as any bullet. The second wave was that she had been right all along about Brother Zachariah. His father had said the same thing before he killed himself, when Gary first emptied his savings to donate so he could be Saved. What did it all mean? He really wasn't Saved or forgiven at all? What about his church? He'd taken his whole life and put it into the faith basket to survive after Cody died. He'd fallen for a scam?

CarolSue came near. He sensed a presence and, head still on his knees, opened his eyes. His vision was blurry, but those sure weren't his mother's shoes. The dark beige carpet looked tired, worn as the earth. It had been there as long as he remembered. Maybe it was really him, though. He felt a hand on his shoulder. She stuffed some tissue next to him, half under one of his thighs. "I brought you some water," she said. "Can you drink some?"

Gary couldn't look at her. He kept his head averted and shook it slightly. But he was getting the sobbing under control.

She patted his shoulder a couple of times. "You'll get through this," she said softly. "Breathe." Gary thought it was the kindest anyone had ever been to him since he'd been married to Nicole. Good God, how he missed Nicole, the black hole of her absence a permanent landmark on his being.

Gracia was fussing, and his mother was soothing her with little tsking sounds. He could hear it mixed in with the noise of his headache and congested air-sucking that was his breathing. CarolSue's shoes left his side and went toward the baby.

"She needs to be changed. And she'll get hungry pretty

soon. Let me take her now. You should . . . you know." She was speaking so quietly he wasn't sure he'd heard right.

Someone sighed. Footsteps crossed the room and went into the hallway toward the bedrooms. Gracia wasn't crying now, or he couldn't hear her.

His mother sat down next to him. He knew it was her, the old, familiar nearness of her body from childhood maybe. A saved memory from when he was not a huge disappointment to both of them.

"I shouldn't have been so harsh," she said. "Please forgive me."

"My fault." His voice was hoarse, a croak.

"I want to ask you questions but I think this isn't the time. Am I right?"

He couldn't even answer that. What right did he have to say no? But he couldn't. And he didn't know, anyway. From under the window, yellow eyes accused him. Marvelle.

She went on without an answer. "Okay. So, leave her here. CarolSue was already nutty crazy over that baby. Myself . . . I'm just going to have to know something about what's going to happen. I can't have another grandchild gone." And he heard her grief rise again, as it had and would again over and over and over, and he took it in and took it on.

"My fault," he said. "Cody. My fault." The weight of it was stone pressing until he could not breathe.

There was a silence between them. It lasted like despair, the distance between the unbearable and the unknowable. Then his mother took in a breath.

"Son, listen to me. We all limp through life. We do the best we can, and it's never good enough. Everyone's got their secret despair, terrible regrets they carry from one year to the next. Everyone. You didn't know Cody was going to be killed. All you can do is to keep stepping back and trying to see as best you can—and know that you're still at least half blind. Try to pay attention when you do something right as well as when you do something wrong. Because there are those times, too, and it'll help you stay sane."

Gary exhaled, a long shudder.

"Sit up, honey," she said. "Here, drink some of this water. Personally, I'd go for the special tea, but CarolSue brought you water." She rubbed his back a couple of times. "I'm trying to figure out myself which we all need first, to be brave— or strong. Take your pick. Maybe either one will do."

Gary raised his head, took the water and drank. His mother put one arm around him, and he rested his head on her shoulder.

"I don't know what to do," he said.

"Yeah. None of us ever do. Guess your best and try it."

He sat that way a few minutes longer and then stood. "I'm going to go now, Mom. I've gotta see about . . . things."

"Okay. Please. We'd like to know. We need to know."

"Yeah."

He went to the back bedroom, where his father Harold was still as present as he'd been in life. His glasses, his shoes. His toothbrush, for God's sake. And here now, a bassinet, a changing table with drawers stuffed with clothes, a basket of toys. Baby stuff everywhere, and his own tarnished Glitter Jesus overseeing it all. He shook his head.

CarolSue was on the bed with the baby, who had a pink pacifier stuffed in her mouth. He saw his aunt had her surrounded by rattles and bright toys. He wondered if his mother knew CarolSue put the baby on her precious spread? What if Gracie leaked? Not only that, the dog was up there, too, curled next to them. The memory would be enough to make him smile, maybe later.

"I just want to give her a kiss," he said. Needing permission.

"Of course. You okay?"

Gary shrugged. He bent and kissed Gracia's head where her hair met her face—was that the start of a little widow's peak?—and smoothed the curve of her cheek with his fore-finger. She was making those little baby babble sounds and smiling when someone played with her. Maybe she did look a little like his father. "You be good for Aunt CarolSue," he whispered. "I love you."

He could have told his mother and aunt about Rosalina. Once he was in the rattletrap church van, with its cracked upholstery and magnetic sign on the side (How had he been so proud?) he confessed to Jesus out of habit as the road stretched between fields of withered, brown stalks of yet-uncut field corn.

It hadn't been the entire truth when he told his mother that he didn't know what to do. He knew some of what he was going to do, and that was talk to Gus. Now that Gus wasn't all involved with extra work, Gary had to ask, even beg, him to help look for Rosalina. For one thing, Gary had seen the news. A lot of undocumented immigrants had been arrested at work. That had been over toward Elmont, and he doubted that Rosalina had been involved, mainly because he'd checked all the churches, all the shelters in the area. He hoped she was nowhere around and feared the same thing. She couldn't just leave the baby like that! Nobody would. How desperate would you have to be to just leave your own child? What could possibly justify doing such a thing? But Gus could double check, couldn't he? Just make sure she hadn't been arrested.

And if she had?

How had this come to pass, that he'd made such a mess? It hadn't started out this way, not at all. He tried to trace the intentions of his heart with Rosalina. He'd started pure. Damn. He'd started pure.

His mind drifted toward Jesus and he jerked it back to the task at hand. He couldn't think about what would happen to his church. He couldn't think about what was a scam to make him feel forgiven, to make him feel hope, and if there was anything that wasn't.

Chapter 28

Gus

Well, it was predictable: Gary was blowing up Gus's phone. Louisa must be shitting a brick—Gus knew she'd not exactly been a charter member of the Brother Zachariah Fan Club. No sensible person ever was. Barnes preyed on the wounded, the grieving, the sick, the dying, making ridiculous promises—oh yes, Louisa said he'd promised Gary would definitely not be Left Behind at the imminent Second Coming, but go straight to Heaven, no detours, and be reunited with Cody as he was suited up playing Football for Jesus. As The Quarterback, doubtless. His father, poor Harold, would watch in the stands with Gary—probably ready to hand him a welcoming beer and catch him up on the score. But all this was possible only if Gary bankrupted himself by donating all his savings to Brother Zachariah's "ministry."

Gus wasn't one to mock anyone's beliefs. He believed in freedom all the way. It wasn't the beliefs; it was the scamming, the manipulating, the advantage taken. Hard to prove criminal intent previously. Extortion would be much easier. Brother Zachariah Barnes had done Gus a rather large favor. The prosecutor was pleased.

Still, he knew that Gary was likely devastated. And what about his little church? It had been his reason for living after Cody. All predicated on Barnes's word. And he'd convinced the people who had joined, too. Convinced them enough that they'd look at glitter art in an old barn week after week, month after month. No harm in that, Gus guessed. But would they find out about Gary's baby? How would that play? For sure, everything was FUBAR, like his father had used to regularly pronounce the state of the world. Fucked Up Beyond All Reason. Or was that Beyond Any Recovery. Gus couldn't remember.

He considered his father's acronym while he let another call go to his voice mail. He'd already taken care of booking Barnes. No reason he couldn't go home and have a beer, wait until morning to listen to messages. Gus didn't see how he'd been pulled into this quagmire. It had all started with the napping, which he now recalled was something Rhonda had warned him could result in a mess.

Rhonda had also frequently advised that "Things will look better in the morning." She'd chirped cheery aphorisms regularly to balance out her dire warnings, and while they popped up in his mind often, Gus had found that occasionally they were dead wrong. Today, for example. Nothing looked better in the least, plus he had a beer hangover and should never even have looked at that carton of Chunky Monkey ice cream after the frozen pepperoni pizza. He belched loudly, glanced at Rhonda's framed picture on his dresser, and gave her the finger for the remonstrations she was aiming his way.

He used an elbow to prop himself on the bed (no top sheet on it since Rhonda died and didn't come over to do his laundry, just a tan puffed quilt he'd had for years), picked up his cell phone from the bedside table, and groaned when he scrolled through the list of messages. "All right already," he muttered. "Let me pee, for God's sake." When he did, he swore off beer. He really did better on Louisa's Wild Turkey. Oh Lord. Louisa. He'd almost forgotten he was mad at her and for good reason.

He needed coffee, which meant he had to get dressed. He

got down three aspirin with water, suited up in his uniform without showering, brushed his teeth, wet down his hair, and headed out into the too-bright daylight.

Coffee and a bagel had done some good. But not enough, apparently.

"You look like death," Connie announced. "What the hell happened?" Her hair looked bigger than usual, but it could have been his eyes not working quite right yet.

"Not a thing."

"Right," she said, giving him the side-eye. "Musta been some party night. That coffee is fresh," she said, swinging in her chair to point at the pot with her chin. Then a call came in on the nonemergency line and he heard her switch to her professional voice: "Dwayne County Sheriff, how may I help you?" He waved a dismissive hand in her direction, poured himself a mug, and walked into his office. He scrolled through his email, almost hoping there was something he needed to attend to, something that would let him avoid a decision. There wasn't.

Instead of his cell, he used the office phone so he could maybe keep it short. It truly was his only reason. And he called the church, not Gary's cell phone, for exactly the same reason.

"Gary, Gus here. Look, the Feds arrested your baby's mother. She's being held at the Justice Center . . ." He left the message, was going to explain more, and then changed his mind. "Just give me a call back when you get to work. I'm in the office."

He'd wait for Gary to call and leave it up to him. But Rosalina kept creeping into his mind. He'd told her that she could think it over, and that he could help her get her baby back. That she should—it was only right. What if they were fast moving her for deportation?

An hour later, he was at the Justice Center signing in. "Immigration lawyer's been seein' the ones that ask," the clerk said, as Gus checked in his sidearm. "Pro bono, like a volunteer?"

Gus rolled his eyes. It was a new kid, early twenties, skinny, with acne. The hours and pay were shit, and respect was an illusion here. As he tagged Gus's pistol, Gus asked to see the list of detainees the lawyer had seen.

"Dunno if we got that."

"Of course you got it."

"Not sure I'm supposed to . . ."

"Screw that. Lemme see." The kid was right, but his uniform didn't even fit, and Gus knew his way around.

Rosalina's name was on the list. So she'd known enough to ask for a lawyer. Or someone had told her to. He told the kid to have her brought to a room.

"She lawyered up."

"Yep. I know. It's about her kid. Tell her that and see if she minds not having her lawyer present. If that's not too many words . . ." He needed to watch how snotty he got. Staff could force you to take the long way most anywhere. But the kid was new enough that he could be pushed around.

"I'll have 'em explain," he said. "But most are getting moved soon. Louisiana, likely. Court, and, y'know, out." He jerked his thumb over his shoulder.

"Y'know, you're pointing t' Canada," Gus said. The kid only looked confused, though.

As Gus had guessed would be the case, a few minutes later, he was waiting in an interview room when Rosalina was let in.

"You remember me?" he said by way of greeting.

She nodded.

"You mind talking about your baby without your lawyer here?"

This time a head shake. She didn't look any better than she had last time. Still the circles under her dark eyes. He shouldn't be surprised by that. "You thought about it?"

"Yes. I will sign papers."

"What? What're you signing?"

"To make sure Gracia can see doctor, go to school. Stay here. I will sign."

"You're not going to take her back?"

"Keep her safe." She could scarcely speak. Damn, he'd not thought to bring either water or tissues and he could have.

"Did the lawyer tell you to do this?"

"No." She was shaking her head and crying now. "No."

"Damn. Who talked you into this?"

"No. She can be safe. No gangs. Not raped or stolen. Have food, go to school." She was breathing in sobs now, but Gus didn't stop.

"I can help you." He kept saying that because surely this was all wrong and he should step in. He wasn't supposed to touch a detainee, but Gus reached across the table and briefly touched her hand. Then he pulled it back, assuming the guard in the hall would be checking through the glass, even though he was a cop. "I can help you," he said again. "You don't have to do it. We can say you didn't understand."

"No," she said. And said it again. "No." She got up and went to the door. Put her face against the glass, as if the cool of it could soothe her. The guard opened the door.

"Wait," Gus said. "Do you just want to see her to say goodbye? I can have Gary bring her to see you. Do you want that? Do you want a picture?" When she saw the baby, surely she would change her mind.

A light came in her eyes for the first time. She nodded, and the guard took her away.

"That was fast," the kid said when Gus checked his gun back out. "Have a good day."

Gus didn't bother with an answer. The kid was earnest and trying. Rhonda would have been disgusted that Gus couldn't bring himself to be nice to him.

Back at the station, Gus tried to figure out what Rosalina

would sign. This was not his bailiwick, even though rural as the county was, too often he had to fill a social service function. But that usually involved a wellness check or a referral. This was above his pay grade. He wasn't a lawyer or a social worker, damn it, nor did he want to be.

It took some time at the computer to even figure out the right question to put in the search bar, and there were several interruptions—routine calls, questions from Connie here and there. And he had to fill in the schedule for the second half of the month when Floyd wanted an extra weekend off for his nephew's wedding at the same time Billy would be on his fishing trip. That meant Gus would have to schedule himself so there'd be a competent adult to oversee Jimmy, who wasn't ready to be on duty alone. Not yet and maybe never.

But when he found a site likely meant for people in something like Rosalina's situation, he began to realize it wasn't unique. Here was a list of options. Sign a child-care power of attorney. But—some hospitals, schools, and doctors won't accept that. Signing over guardianship was probably the best option because she could sign a waiver of service of process for the nearest immigration court, meaning that she'd agree not to be notified by certified mail when an action was taken regarding the child's guardianship. Signing a consent for custody: Well, that was trickier because it had to go through the juvenile court, and if she ever made it back to the States, or changed her mind for any reason, it was very difficult to have it assigned back. It was noted parenthetically that when a child is born to unmarried parents, custody is preemptively assigned to the mother.

And as far as Gus was concerned, that's where it belonged. Not that his father had been as bad as some, but there are a lot of ways to hurt a kid. Rosalina didn't know what she was doing, but Gus did.

Chapter 29

CarolSue

Louisa and I had spent the night almost as if nothing monumental had happened. I took care of Gracie, although Louisa seemed more tender when I brought the baby in, sweet-smelling and damp-haired from her bath, ready for kisses before I fed a bedtime bottle and sang her lullaby while Louisa fixed us a simple supper. I wanted to remind my sister that I'd laid claim to that baby when no one wanted her. I didn't know Louisa's heart yet, but I did know the enormity of her loss and thought she might want Gracie to fill that gaping hole.

If she did, it would be at my expense. Did she believe her losses were larger than mine, or her claim more true?

After Gary left, I couldn't bring myself to ask how she felt. Rather, by taking care of Gracie as I had right along, I thought I was showing: She's mine. And I was relieved that Louisa didn't challenge who would bathe, dress, feed, rock, sing, put her to bed, those ancient rituals of motherhood I'd wanted all my life. After we cleaned up our few dishes and tidied the kitchen and living room, I said I was tired and would turn in early. There was no worry, nothing but peace on Gracie's little face through that night; but I slept fitfully and woke often to check on her, the bassinet two feet away from my bed, as I'd had it from our beginning.

In the morning, I thought I'd best find out if I'd have to fight.

"I'm thinking maybe I should call Gus," I said, when Gracie was down for her short morning nap. Louisa was pulling on her barn boots, getting ready to do battle with Al Pelley about planting something for the deer to eat in the winter—I think she said—in one small area. She liked making her land a haven for wildlife, and he insisted she was insane to reduce the farm's profit margin. Al would be showing up soon, I knew, and I didn't want to allow a lot of time for discussion. I just wanted to get the lay of this land so I could develop a Plan.

"What for?" She countered, as I knew she would.

"Well, you've told me how, out here, the sheriff is practically the social service system, there's so little . . ." I trailed off, waiting for her to agree that she had, indeed, told me about the reduction in services that left too much to Gus to look after.

"Yeah . . . so?"

"I was thinking I should tell him that I want to be named Gracie's foster mother. You know, just in case he has to report something . . . the missing mother . . . to the welfare department, I mean, child services, whatever. You remember how I said a while ago that I wanted to keep her?"

Louisa stopped pulling on her left boot. She was sitting at the kitchen table, a mug with the dregs of her breakfast coffee shoved aside. Sunlight. Another honey-crisp day, the air alive, humming, neighbors' combines bringing in the harvest.

She looked at me, and said, "Huh." Then she finished pulling on her boot.

I waited. She got up and took her cup to the sink.

"Well," I said, "I'm not sure what that deep, meaningful response is supposed to signify. I guess I'll go ahead and call."

"Huh," she said. Again.

Remember those homicidal impulses toward my sister I've had before? Let me tell you, it was damn near uncontrollable at that moment.

"Louisa!"

She had her hand on the back-door knob and had started to open it. I could see the girls—she had let them out of the coop right after she fed them, early—pecking around the yard. Jessie was startled at my sharp tone, and almost jumped to her feet, alarmed. Louisa, though, turned to look at me unperturbed. "What?" she said.

"What do you mean, what? I want to know what you think! Or what you want." This was making a total mess of my plan to casually find out where she stood so I could make a real Plan. So much for that.

"I think it's not going to make any difference what I think or what you think or even what Gus thinks. It's Gary's baby. Gary and some woman we don't know a thing about. For my part, I'm trying not to think anything. Thinking's a sure way to get your heart broken. Now I've got to go make sure Al is doing what I told him to do. Gotta watch that man. He likes to forget whose farm this is." And then she was out the door. Marvelle eyed me, haughty on top of the wingback chair in the living room, blinking lazily and swishing her tail. *Idiot,* her expression said.

I went to the kitchen window and watched Louisa cross the backyard, weave her way behind the finished vegetable and flower beds, past the coop. She conferred with two of the girls, maybe JoJo and Amy—I still wasn't that great at telling them apart, to my sister's disgust—then she walked alongside the barn and headed out toward the first field. She's not a big woman, my sister, and from the back, you could mistake her body for a strong girl's. Thanks to me and Miss Clairol, her hair is blond, and now the breeze raised sunlit strands above her head, crown-like. Queen of her beloved land. Louisa would always have this, I told myself.

I was going to fight for Gracie.

Louisa was out of sight, doubtless in a vigorous argument with Al Pelley over a winter root crop for the deer. I checked on Gracie to make sure she was still sound asleep. I wanted to be able to explain without being interrupted when I called Gus. I didn't have his cell phone number, so I had to call the station and ask for him, which wasn't my first choice.

"Is this an emergency, ma'am?" a pleasant woman's voice inquired. Her tone suggested that she knew it wasn't.

"No, there's not an emergency."

"He'll call you back then. What number would you like to leave?"

Of course, I wanted to talk to him right then, but I had no choice. I gave my cell phone number and hung up.

It was just as well I wasn't on the phone. Sometimes the most frustrating incidents turn out to be for the best. I'd scarcely started Gracie's laundry when a minute later, there came Gary's claptrap church van down the driveway for the second time in less than twenty-four hours, again with its frame about to give way from the weight of upset and worry.

I met him at the front door. I thought—and don't tell me, I know it's selfish and wrong of me—*oh no! He's found Gracie's mother and she wants the baby back!* I should have realized that, had that happened, Gary would be happy, relieved, not slumped over with dread and doom as he was. Hadn't he been looking for her all this time?

"What's wrong?" I opened the door and drew him inside. "Shhh. Baby sleeping. Jessie, off, stay down, good girl." I added that last when I saw Gary knee the dog aside instead of pat her head as he usually did. Something was terribly amiss.

Instead of coming in, Gary leaned back against the living

room wall, as if he hadn't the strength to walk to a chair or the couch. Across the room, his high school graduation picture was still on the wall, smiling at him, full of pride and expectation. His eyes locked on it, and he shook his head.

"They found out," he whispered. He sounded as if he were using his last air.

"Gary, honey. Who? Found out what?"

He looked at me and shook his head. Was this something I should already know? I admit, I was totally confused. Then I took a stab.

"Did something happen at your church?"

He nodded. "They found out."

A light dawned. "Gracie?"

His shoulders shook with his sobbing. He managed to nod. Relieved, I put my arms around him and tried to lead him to the couch, but his feet seemed rooted and his weight was propped against the wall. I thought he might topple over.

When his breath was more even, I asked, "Did you tell them, honey?"

He shook his head. "Clean for Jesus."

That one flummoxed me. "Clean for Jesus? You want to be . . . ?"

"They found out."

That didn't help me. "Clean for Jesus found out?"

"In my office when Gus called. I wasn't there yet. He left a message, but they heard him talk. He said . . ." And then he was sobbing again and I had to wait. I temporarily gave up on finding out who this Clean for Jesus person was, maybe some extra, extra devout member of Gary's church.

"What did Gus say, honey?"

"He said . . . he said . . . my baby's mother had been picked up. He found her."

I felt like I had when I'd found Charlie already dead. That shock of confusion, bewilderment, refusal. "No!" It was all I could get out. I realize it wasn't helpful.

"Arrested. She's . . . undocumented."

"My God, Gary. My God. How . . . did this . . . Never mind. What are we going to do?"

He seemed to think about that, and I thought he was coming up with a Plan for the baby. I started to tell him, "I will take care of her. You know, I've always wanted her. I'll do whatever I need to." Like I could make it happen.

Gary was talking at the same time, sort of mumbling. "I have to talk to them. Tell the truth."

"Gary! Gracie comes first. We need to take care of her."

He looked at me, eyes gone navy instead of our hydrangea blue, and the whites turned pink and watery. "We have to give her back. Her mother. Wrong to keep her away."

"Gary! No! Don't you love her?"

His knees buckled, and he slid to the floor, unable to even stand. "I love her," he wailed. "I love her."

Then I was on the floor crying with him, and that's how Louisa found us.

Chapter 30

Gus

Connie gave him his phone messages when he got back from the café. Margo had been particularly vexing today, but he'd one-upped her by tipping fairly, when she doubtless expected none in retribution. He loved mixing things up like that to confuse the hell out of her. Now the bitch would give him great service out of guilt tomorrow and he'd short her, maybe leave a dollar. On the way out, he'd say, "I left a ten-spot, Margo. Thanks for the great service. Keep the change." All in good fun.

CarolSue had called. He didn't need his years of experience to guess what this was about. He sighed. Might as well get it over with. Got up, shut his office door. Sat back down, leaned back in his chair. Used the office phone in case he needed to document that the call had been returned. Official business and all.

"CarolSue. Gus here. Can you hear me? Everything all right there?"

"Lord yes, I can hear you. Thanks for returning my call."

"What can I do for you?"

"It's about the baby . . ."

"Yes. All right. Well, I have good news. Did Gary get to tell you? We've located her mother, and I'm looking into how to reunite them."

"Uh, well, Gus, Gary says she . . . may be . . . in custody?"

"That's correct."

"Well, I want to make sure, I, um, I want to legally take care of her. I mean, I can keep her. I can be her foster mother, you know, or whatever. I can keep her . . . I mean, I would even adopt her."

"Oh now, CarolSue, I'm sure that won't be necessary. Gary's her father, he says. And he's been looking for her mother, to return the baby."

"Gus, wait . . ."

"You and Louisa have done a real service, a real service, I'm sure. But you really have nothing to say in this. It's a legal matter. In fact, the mother wants to see the baby, so I'll be asking Gary to bring her to the detention center. Or I'll do it." He added the last as a subtle warning not to cross him. It wasn't open for discussion. There was something she didn't know. Gary didn't know, either. Gus didn't know if knowledge would harden their resistance to Rosalina or weaken it, and so he held back.

"But she . . ."

"I'll let you know when to have her ready. I have another call now. Would you tell Louisa I'll talk to her soon?" He hung up. He did not have another call. This was going to be tough. He had a bad feeling he was going to miss a number of naps. Louisa might even have nothing more to do with him, which would break his heart. If the worst happened, he'd just be alone and make himself live with it. Margo was not an option. He had no idea what he had ever been thinking that time he took her out.

What he needed to work on was how to make sure that the baby—he didn't know her name, just that it was a girl or CarolSue had something weird going on by carting a boy around in all that pink, so now he dubbed her Rosalina's baby girl—would be reunited with her mother before Rosalina was deported. At least Gus figured that deportation was the likely outcome. She could come back to the border and apply for asylum in a few years. Maybe she had a good case.

And the baby was a citizen. What difference did that make? Probably a lot legally, in that she could stay, but none as far as needing her mother. Gus was sure of that much.

The search engine was his friend. Again he went to the sites aimed at immigrants. He'd already read through sections about leaving a child behind. Now he looked at Options for Parents Who Wish To Take Their Children With Them When Deported. Under subsections about children who have a parent who is remaining in the States, or children who were born in the States, he found what he was looking for. It was easier, in fact, by far, than leaving a child here. He pulled his cell phone from his shirt pocket and called Gary.

"Gary! Hey, how you doing?"

Gary's voice came, hoarse and spent. "I've been better, Gus."

Another time, Gus would have been sympathetic, and probably asked what was wrong, but he figured it had to do with Zach Barnes, and Gus didn't have any real sympathy on that score. And he didn't want to be diverted from what was important.

"You know, we've got Rosalina Gonzalez, and I know you want the baby returned to her. So I'm going to need you to come sign a letter giving your consent for the baby to accompany her back to her . . . uh . . . home country. Not sure. Mexico? Guatemala? Anyway, this is 'cause baby's got two parents and she's with you. Rosalina's got to tell the court she wants to be reunited, they call it. And she'll need that letter."

"Honduras," Gary said, his voice heavy, weary.

"Huh?"

"She's from Honduras."

"Okay, right. Anyway, it's got to be notarized. If you've got any documents, bring 'em and we'll make copies, huh? Connie's a notary, and we'll bang this thing out, get it all done proper."

". . . Okay."

"Yeah. And she wants to see the baby. How's about I take the baby over, let her visit? I can deliver the letter at the same time, she can see the little one. Don't worry, I'll bring her back safe and sound. She got a name?"

There was a pause. "Gracia. CarolSue calls her Gracie."

"Nice. Like *gracias*, sorta."

"Maybe. Look, I should go. The baby doesn't know you."

"Pfft. I'm great with kids." Well, that was a lie. He was great with dogs, but his only cat experience was Marvelle, who apparently couldn't stand him, and he didn't have any nieces or nephews since Rhonda had never married. Couldn't be that hard not to drop a baby on her head, though, could it?

"Rosalina wants to take her?"

"You think a mother would want to leave her baby behind? Of course it's what she wants. Y'gotta help her, for Chrissake."

There was too much silence then. "Wait," Gary said finally. "I'll marry her. I can marry her and then she and Gracia can stay. It would be the right thing to do. It would be what God wants."

Gus rolled his eyes to the ceiling, then closed them while he took a breath and tried to keep it from sounding like a sigh. "I suspect a lot of things in this here world don't work the way God might prefer. Your situation is one of them. You cannot waltz into a detention center and say, *Oh, hey, that's my fiancée, so let her go, we're getting married today*, and have her released. Nobody gets a green card for being married. Or having a baby. If you'd married her the day you two met, her papers would still be fake. Married makes no difference. Do you not read the newspapers, son? The way things are now? Spouses and parents are deported all the time."

After he hung up, Gus's eyes stung. He blinked a couple of times, splayed his hands on his desk. He still remembered the fight, the sound and shine of glass breaking in the night, a bottle or a window: She'd have taken him with her if his father hadn't stopped her. "She just needed help. For Chrissake," he said to himself and got up.

A lousy typist, Gus prepared the letter himself to make sure the model was followed correctly. Not that it was difficult. Gary showed up later that afternoon, and sure enough, he produced a birth certificate and a social security card for the baby. She was his all right, big as life and twice as real.

"Damn," Gus muttered. "Your mother never let on." He leaned back in his desk chair. Gary still stood, though Gus had pointed to the spare chair on the other side of the desk. The door was closed.

"She didn't know."

Gus shrugged. "She knew she was hiding a baby." His bitterness was leaking out.

"It wasn't like you think." Gary sighed. "It was an argument. She wanted to call you. From the beginning. I was the one who said no. Trying to keep my sin private. Well, the church knows now."

"You tell them?" Gus knew all about this. Brother Thomas had called him, but he wasn't going to let on.

Gary shook his head. "Actually, you did. The ones cleaning my study heard you leaving the message. When you called."

Gus registered disgust, throwing his head back and heaving his shoulders and arms. "Ach! Man, I'm sorry. Real sorry. I didn't mean . . . What's gonna happen?"

Gus knew that too, though: Thomas had asked him about filing charges against Gary. Seems the building-fund money was missing. They were having meetings, he'd said, and wanted Gus to come to one.

"Don't see how we'll . . . go on." Gary's eyes filled. He swiped at his face with the back of his hand and straightened. "So, what do I need to sign?"

"Here," Gus said, sliding the letter toward Gary. "You

gotta sign in front of Connie, but she doesn't need to read what you're signing, so we'll cover it, like this."

"Pfft. What difference? It's probably all over town already."

"Still," Gus said. "We're gonna cover it."

He stood and went to the door. "Hey, Connie, can you come in here for a minute, and would you bring your notary seal?"

In two minutes, it was done.

"Tomorrow I'll do the visit and take her the letter. I'll see if there's any update on court stuff. Good if you can keep the baby until she's moved. I mean, you probably don't want to go the foster care route? In someone else's home, I mean."

"God, no. But . . . should I . . . I mean, should I talk to a lawyer or something?"

"Why would you do that, son? You wouldn't try to keep that baby away from her mother?"

"Not that." Gary looked uncomfortable, like a squirmy teenager Gus might have picked up for siphoning gas from a farmer's pickup truck into a rusty sedan that needed a muffler while a terrified high school girl tried to hide by sliding her butt down in the passenger seat. Only Gary was too old for that, in his forties now, if Gus wasn't mistaken. Old enough to be ashamed of himself.

"What then?"

"I dunno. Just . . . trying to do right." He dropped his head into his two hands. His elbows were propped on his knees.

Gus restrained himself from muttering that it was a little late for that. He wondered, but didn't ask, about the exact circumstances of the sex Gary'd had with Rosalina. He should probably ask her, but then, oh Lord, if she had a complaint, he'd have to pursue it. Was it enough to make sure she had her baby back?

"She wants to be in this country," Gary said.

"Doesn't everybody."

"I mean. Can a lawyer help with—"

Gus shook his head. "Can try in a couple years. Apply for asylum. About ten-million-to-one now." He shrugged. Took off his glasses, rubbed one eye, and replaced them. "So, I'll pick up the baby tomorrow afternoon. One o'clock. All right?"

"Can you do it later? She'd be sleeping, and . . . you know, CarolSue says if her nap is messed up, she's fussy."

Gus sighed. "Two thirty?"

"I guess that'll be okay."

"You got a car seat?"

"Yes. Her carrier. You strap it in."

"I know how to do it." For God's sake, he gave people tickets for not doing it.

"I should go with you. With her."

"Better I just handle it. You wouldn't get in anyway, since you're not married or blood kin." That was a lie, but he didn't know what Gary might say to Rosalina, or if he'd pressure her in the wrong direction. The woman needed to know pure and simple that she could have her baby back.

Gary's skin, normally on the ruddy section of the skin color continuum, was grayish. He hadn't shaved, and his blond hair needed a cut. An errant curl, lacking its usual gel, fell foolish-looking onto the middle of his forehead. His khaki pants rode high due to the sharp bend in his knees, and his mismatched socks were displayed. The plaid of his rumpled shirt didn't hide the stain on the front. He could have been a picture captioned *Defeat*. Gus didn't expect a challenge and didn't get one, which was a good thing because he was getting tired. And impatient. He felt for Gary, he did, but he had work to do, and this mess was Gary's own creation. He didn't truck with excuses. Fathers who kept kids from their mothers: There *was* no excuse.

"So, okay, I'll come by Louisa's to pick up the baby at two

thirty. If you're there, I guess I'll see you then, and if not, I'll let you know how it goes. All right?" Gus said, to signal Gary, who hadn't seemed to get it, that they were done. When Gary didn't respond, Gus stood up and moved from behind his desk. He went around and planted himself in front of the chair Gary was sitting in. Gary still hadn't budged.

"Did you have anything else you needed?" Gus said, and extended his hand as if to help Gary out of the chair.

The light in the room had shifted during the time they'd spent. Gus had intended a quick meeting just so Gary would have his signature notarized, but there had been talk, explanation, Gary's silences, hesitations, so that it seemed much longer. No wonder he was drained. Still, he had the letter now, signed and notarized. The baby's original birth certificate and social security card. Gary had wanted copies, so to be fair, he'd made them, but Rosalina would need the originals. She'd have everything she needed when she went in front of the immigration judge. They'd have to give her child back.

Chapter 31

CarolSue

"No, no, and no."

"We don't have a choice."

"Which syllable of no isn't clear to you? I'll enunciate more clearly. No. Gus isn't taking her to a *jail*." Gary had shown up the next afternoon, looking as if he hadn't slept in at least a week. If it was anyone but Gary, I'd have said he had a bad hangover, but Gary swore off liquor when he was Saved, even though Louisa loved to point out that Jesus himself served wine. But that's what he looked like: red-eyed, unshaven, and he must have slept in those clothes if he slept at all. None of us had had a decent night, truth be told. Louisa obsessing over Gus, me frantic about Gracie, and Gary—well, I didn't know. He hadn't returned my call when I tried his cell phone after I talked to Gus. Louisa said it was all I could do, that Gary was the only one who had any say. "How can you even think about letting that happen? She's a baby! How is that a place to take a *baby*?" I was figuring I could activate some paternal protectiveness. Or something.

He did have the small grace to look guilty, like the failure he was being. "Gus says she wants to see the baby. That she has the right."

"Gary. Think about it."

"CarolSue, it's her mother. And . . . she wants the baby

back. I told you right along I was looking for Gracia's mother. To give her back. And now . . ."

I could tell he didn't know how to say it. I didn't help him. For one, I was too mad. And for two, well, I was too mad.

Gary found the words, though. "And now, I know where she is, and Gus says she wants the baby back. For today, it's just a visit, so she can see Gracie. I said we'd keep her until . . ."

"What? Until what?"

"I think . . . well, see, she's not from here. She's an immigrant, but she doesn't have the right papers."

"So she's going to be deported." It wasn't a question. We were in the kitchen. Louisa was outside mulching her rose garden with straw. The girls were wandering the yard. She had Gracie in the stroller to give her some fresh air, just parked there watching her work. I'd check out the window every now and then, but Gracie was happy so far, as amused by her own hands and feet as much as by the toys I'd tied to the sides for her. Louisa was animated, singing and telling stories while she laid the straw. "I've always been on your side. You know that. But not this time, Gary. You can stop this."

"I signed already."

"You signed? What did you sign?"

"Consent. For her to take Gracia."

"Take Gracie where?" Good Lord, give me some pliers and I could pull teeth more easily than extract his answers.

"Where she's from."

I don't need the pliers. I could do it with my bare hands. "Gary, for God's sake. Where is she from?"

"Honduras."

"Honduras! Aren't people taking terrible risks to escape that country because of gangs and drugs and poverty and violence? Isn't it really dangerous? I read about young girls getting kidnapped and raped, and forced into prostitution. Women are just . . . victimized. Kids don't have a chance. And you want to have her take your baby *there*?"

"Gus says in a couple years she can try to come apply for asylum with Gracie. I can save up and send money, CarolSue. I will."

"You mean if she and Gracie are still alive. And what about your church? Are they going to pay you?"

He closed his eyes and blew out what air he had. "They found out about the baby. Between that and Brother Zachariah . . ." He shook his head. "Doubtful." More head shaking. He bit his lip, his eyes holding sorrow and defeat. "Hafta find some job," he said, and shrugged. "Dunno how I . . ." He kept throwing a line into his brain, casting for words, but there were none he could reel in to use. He gave up.

I summoned the last small bit of kindness inside my soul not to berate him more, not to go berserk all over him. In my mind, I took a step back. I'd develop a Plan is what I'd do. For Gracie. To keep her with me. To keep her safe.

I couldn't take the grief of no Plan, is what it was.

Gary said that Gus was coming at two thirty, so I made sure she was changed and in a pink dress with lace trim and matching bonnet. She'd had a full bottle, but I packed an extra one in the diaper bag with six extra diapers. I put her in a night diaper because what did Gus know about changing a baby? I had no idea what it would be like at the jail. Would it even be clean? Even though she was really too big now, and no longer liked it, I swaddled Gracie in a clean receiving blanket, thinking to keep germs away from her body. Since that struck me as smart, then I put two more in her bag. A book. Her teddy. Her red rattle. Oh yes, her bear. Basically, I packed enough to cover her for a week, although Gus said they'd be there for an hour. Maybe less if he didn't get going.

When I strapped her into the seat and Gus drove out of the

driveway with her in his squad car, I thought my heart had been pulled out of my chest and Gus had run over it on the way. It was all so wrong, so wrong.

Louisa

It was hard, plain hard—even though she had always taught her students that the correct word was *difficult*, as *hard* referred to a physical characteristic, but damn, sometimes life hurt as much as something hard crushing her heart. She didn't know how not to blame Gary. *Here we go again*, Louisa thought to herself. *Well, this time I didn't have all the years invested that I did with Cody. I only just found out this perfect little girl is my granddaughter. I suppose I should be grateful for small favors.* But it wasn't like Louisa was immune to love. Yes, she'd tried to hold back but she'd fallen for Gracia as hard as CarolSue had. The difference was that she'd tried, really tried, not to let it happen. And she'd hidden it as much as she could.

Because of CarolSue. Of course, CarolSue. At least Louisa had had Gary's infancy and childhood, as CarolSue had tacitly reminded her many times, and then she'd had the gift of Cody for seventeen years. CarolSue hadn't, though children had been what she'd most wanted. It would have been cruel to compete with her for time with this baby, especially when they'd believed they'd have her for just a short time. And Louisa had Gus in her bed, too. Not often enough now, but still. How could she deny CarolSue having that baby sleep close to her?

And there was something else that Louisa hadn't brought up—what would it have helped?—but she kept thinking of Gracia's mother. What if she was suffering the way Nicole suffered over losing Cody, the way Nicole still suffered, and

Louisa herself, too? Wherever she'd been, Gracia's mother had never been far from Louisa's mind.

And now, to learn how well-advised her fear had been. How could it be that love ever ended as rain watering the fertile field of grief?

Rosalina

She didn't know how to breathe when she saw him come in with a baby. It was the same big man who'd come before, who'd told her she could have Gracia back, and this time he was holding a little body against his chest, a blanket around her body and a hat on her head, but even so, Rosalina knew. He'd brought Gracia. Her own beloved.

"There's a rule. No touching," he said. "But I've maybe got a way. I'm going to lay your baby on the table so I don't touch you. You pick her up. The guard may come in and make you put her down. But it will give you a minute, maybe more. Understand?" He stood in the small, bare room holding her baby and he looked like he could be a grandfather. How Rosalina's father would love Gracia!

She nodded.

The big man laid the baby on her back on the bare table between them. The cotton blanket fell to the side, and Rosalina saw she wore a pink dress with lacy trim. She had a hat on that matched. Rosalina wanted to see her head, if it was like her own or Rosalina's mother's had been. "Take it off?" she said, pointing, tentative, not wanting to risk a problem.

"Let me," he said, glancing toward the observation window in the door to the hallway. "In case." And he untied it and took it off. Rosalina saw him stick it in his pocket. The jumpsuit Rosalina wore, which was orange, had no pockets.

She was beautiful, her Gracia, more beautiful than Rosalina remembered, but of course time had passed and she had no picture except the one in her mind. Much more hair now, and with curl to it. Her own was straight. But it was dark as her own, and there was the suggestion of the widow's peak that would mirror hers. And the family brows and eyes. The baby's arms and legs moved in an uncoordinated dance, and she moved her head, looking at her surroundings. After a few moments, it seemed the unfamiliarity of it all registered, and her face crumpled into the beginning of a wail.

"Go ahead," Gus said. "Pick her up."

Rosalina gathered her daughter carefully, folding the cotton blanket back over her, and raising her home, to her own chest. The baby quieted some, but kept fussing, and Rosalina whisper-sang the lullaby she'd heard as a child and soothed her with secret words of devotion she did not want the man to hear. Her baby was growing well; Rosalina could tell good health by her sweet breath and her body, plump, in new clothes.

As her baby continued to complain, Rosalina started to walk her, but the lawman jerked his thumb over his shoulder at the door, and said, "Um . . . better not move around. Sorry. Remember. He said to stay at the table," so she came the couple of steps back and stood there, as she had been since she picked up the baby. "Supposed to sit," he said then, like an apology, but reminding her that she was a prisoner. Or detainee, as they were called. One of the guards liked to laugh, *Deportee, ohhh, I mean detainee. Didn't mean to confuse today with tomorrow.*

"She's wet . . . and maybe . . . dirty," Rosalina said. "Is there any . . . ?"

"Oh, yeah. Got a bag of stuff. Gary's family, his mother and aunt take real good care." And although the bag had been thoroughly searched already, Gus unpacked on the far end of the table, away from Rosalina and where any guard observing through the window could see: It was only diapers, wipes. "There's toys and clothes and a bottle in here, too, but I'll only take out what you need. Oh, here's a bag. Maybe for the dirty diaper? What's this?"

A small soft pad. Maybe it was to put the baby on? Rosalina guessed, and pointed to her side of the table. Gus slid it there, and Rosalina laid the baby on it. She was quick getting the diaper off and used the wipes to clean her daughter's soft folds, smiling and speaking in Spanish all the while. She studied the little girl's vulnerability for a moment, the vagina that would put her in such danger, before she covered her with a new diaper.

"Thank you, thank you. Tell them thank you," she said to Gus as she pushed the changing pad and wipes across the table with one hand, while she held the baby, quiet now, against her with the other. She hoped he understood. "And you. Thank you." How could she let him know her gratitude for giving her this, her child's life?

The guard opened the door. He had a nose like a bird's beak and he was skinny all over, but there was a gun on one hip, in a belt. He didn't look at Rosalina, but bobbed his chin up and down and said, "Hey, man. You can't pass nothin' to the detainee."

"Yeah, okay, but it's her baby."

"Facility policy."

"Have a heart . . ."

The guard shrugged. "Better not. Sorry, man." He still didn't look at Rosalina and the baby. Rosalina was glad about that.

Gus looked at his watch. "I probably should take her back anyway. Our time's about up, and CarolSue said she'd be hungry by four. They're not gonna let you feed her, and I shouldn't be the one . . . don't actually know what I'm doing on that score."

Rosalina's eyes watered, never leaving the baby as she put her on the table, tender, kissing and whispering love into her daughter's ear. She fixed the cotton blanket around the baby's body and then removed her hands, raising them to show the guard, who looked when she did, and then left.

"Hey, now, don't cry," the lawman said to her. "Look, I brought what you need. The legal paper, I mean. It's a letter from the baby's father, you know, from Gary Hawkins, giving you permission to take the baby back to your country. See, I talked to him, explained that you needed his permission . . . if they send you back."

"You told him I want to?"

"He's been looking for you all along. Didn't know where you were."

"He doesn't want her?"

"Oh, they're crazy about the baby. CarolSue, that's his aunt, she wants to raise her, y'know, but I told them a little girl needs her mother. He understands."

Her baby started to fuss again. Rosalina made a move to pick her up, but the man said, "I better get her," and he picked her up. He jostled Gracia around and Rosalina's chest hurt with longing.

The lawman kept talking. His voice was kind but very loud and she wished she could tell him to talk quietly around the baby, but she had no right to tell him what to do. She couldn't even hold her own baby. She had no power here, and she never would. It was like being back home. Now he pulled an envelope out of her baby's bag and showed it to her. Her name was typed on the front. He took it out, unfolded it, awkward because he was holding Gracia.

"So Gary, here's the letter he signed. All you have to do is make sure your lawyer gives it to the judge when you go to court. The immigration court. Do you understand?"

She nodded.

"They have to let you take your baby with you. Gary's family will keep her until then. But you can have her back. We'll make sure. Okay? You understand? I have to leave it at the front for your lawyer. I'll do that, but I wanted you to see it."

She nodded.

"Isn't that worth a smile?"

"Yes," she said, and smiled. That was how to be safe.

When he left, she saw the strings of Gracia's pink hat trailing out of his pocket. Her baby was in his arms and her hat was in his pocket.

Chapter 32

CarolSue

After Gus brought Gracie back to us, to me, it felt as if we entered a strange limbo, a purgatory of not knowing when I woke up if this one might be my last day with Gracie. I, of course, was furious with Gary, but then I'd see him that day, witness his heartbreak, and soften. The thought of losing her was as devastating to him as to me. Gus was another matter. I could just blame him, and I did. It was all his idea, I knew, about Gary signing that permission letter. Otherwise, I realized I could have gone to court, *we* could have gone to court to keep Gracie. Now, there was no hope.

Napping had skidded to a dead halt, so I didn't have to see Gus much. But it was because he was mad at Louisa, if you can feature that. She sure didn't. I heard her on the phone defending herself. "No, sir, I did not know she's Gary's baby. You think I keep a DNA kit in the house or something? I told him over and over we needed to call you. He said it was a confidential church matter. Well, sue me, but I believed my son. What would you know about dealing with your own child? Last I knew you never had any, or am I wrong about that, too?" Her voice raised steadily, and on that last shot, she hung up. Not gently.

Have you ever noticed how things can devolve from peaceful and fine to a total mess all around you, when you'd swear you had nothing to do with it? That was the situation I found myself in.

I took Gracie on long walks, suddenly taken with the shining clarity of the air. It was as if the earth had paused, hanging on to the last living leaves, the last warmth and color, even the last few flowers. We hadn't had a hard frost yet. *Look, look at what you're going to lose*, she seemed to be saying. *Take in this astonishing beauty. See how I spread the daylight over the treetops like a gold peach butter before the blue-gray of dusk rises from the ground up? Oh, how you will miss this time soon.*

Gracia hadn't experienced the woods that Louisa and I used to play in, and now she never would. I asked Gary to bring me one of those backpacks you can put a baby in. He looked at me as if I'd sprouted another couple of heads or was babbling in tongues, but the next day he showed up with a used one from the Thrift Store that worked just fine.

Louisa took one look at me, standing in the kitchen with it on as I tried to figure out how to put Gracie in it. "Good Lord, Sister. I'm going to enjoy watching you put Gracie in that backpack now. Go to it, bless your heart."

Possibly you can imagine how irritating it was to have to admit to her that I didn't know what I was doing. I'd seen people wearing these things, carting infants all over and they looked darn convenient. My intent was to take Gracie for a walk out in the back woods, and any idiot knew the stroller wouldn't go there.

Louisa was just having herself a high old time chortling while I tried to twist myself around in such a way that I could get Gracie in the damn thing. Without dropping her. It didn't take long before Gracie was pitching a fit. Jessie barked a couple times, and Marvelle left the room in disgust.

"All right," I conceded. "Louisa. Would you please show me what to do? I mean, if you can stop slapping your thigh with the hilarity of it all."

"Ohhh. Listen to you," she said, amused. Then, I think she

read my expression—not equally amused—because she said, "Okay. First. Take it off."

"I want to . . ."

"Take it off," she said.

I put Gracie down and took it off.

Louisa picked up Gracie and in a couple of deft maneuvers put her into the backpack as it sat on its frame. Then she backed up, slid her arms into the shoulder straps and hoisted Gracie up onto her back. My sister looked at me and said, "Okay, let's get going. Which trail you want? Straight down to Rush Run and stay creek-side, or do you want the big loop? I widened that trail last year."

"I was going to . . ."

"You really think it's a good idea for you, oh Woman of the Great Outdoors, to be in the woods alone with a baby? What happens if you trip? I rest my case. Besides, I want to be with you and my granddaughter."

I could see she meant that last sincerely. I also had to admit she possibly had a point about my survival skills.

And that's how it happened that the three of us set out together on the first of what would be daily hikes after Gracie woke from her nap. Gary had started coming before supper, staying for that, and he liked putting her to bed. Louisa and I avoided asking him questions. He'd had to move out of Sister Martha's, who, he mentioned, we no longer had to refer to as "Sister" (oh, the heartbreak of that, Louisa muttered under her breath) and other than that, he didn't tell us anything except that we could always reach him on his cell phone. There was space for him to move back into his old room with us, but Louisa wasn't a fan of that option and waited to see if he'd ask to do that. He never did. She was relieved when he mentioned that he had "a place for now."

"We're just so different," Louisa said. "Nicole was a saint, you know. Lord, I love that girl. Always did, always will."

"What? You're *not* a saint? Huh. And here I believed

you . . ." I drew the words through Charlie's Georgia molasses, exactly the way my sister most hates.

"Well, of course I am, just not the saint variety that has enough patience for Gary. I mean, how much glitter art can your eyes take?"

She had a point. She definitely had a point.

But, as Louisa says, I digress. We took to walking. As I said, the autumn sun was enough to warm our faces when we'd skirt the edge of the first cornfield if we headed straight back, or perhaps cut to the right, behind the barn and head out in the open, along the edge of the field Louisa reserved for the deer, with its curvy lines that waved into the high grass that provided cover as they emerged from the forest to forage where she'd planted the root crops to help them through the winter. The light was dappled when we got to the trails in the woods, and the leaves that had fallen were pungent, brown, yellow, and here and there, scarlet. I'd forgotten the lovely peace of the woods, and how our wide creek, Rush Run, sings as it rises over and around the rocks of its bed on its way to join the next bigger river, which will join the Mississippi on its way to the ocean. Life, part of larger life, part of even larger life, moving forth, moving on. As we were, as Gracia would. I tried to think of it that way, that she would always be part of me, and maybe I of her. Not that she'd remember me, or Louisa, but that the love I'd put in her would stay.

Louisa, remember, had Gracie on her back. I realized that it wasn't simply that she knew what she was doing and I didn't, or that she was physically stronger than I from all her farm work, which she was. She wanted to be the one carrying Gracie because it felt right to her, to carry her granddaughter. Perhaps it was because she knew she was going to lose yet another grandchild. Not the way she'd lost Cody, but nonetheless, she was going to lose Gracia as part of her life before she'd really had her, and this was her way of having what she could now. It wasn't much, was it?

We backed into talking about it, trying to come up with a Plan. "So, is there some way we can help the mother come here legally with Gracie? I mean, what if I pay for a lawyer for her?" I said.

"Didn't Gary say she has to wait a couple of years?"

"Oh. Or Gus said it. Yes. But we can look into it, right?"

"We've got to find out her name, and where she's going. I mean, where exactly she'll go in . . . Honduras, he said. Why couldn't we go see her? I mean, we get passports and . . . couldn't a travel agent help us?"

"I don't know. We can ask."

"She must want to be here, or she wouldn't have . . ."

"Well, Gary must know more than he's told."

We talked like this as we walked, even when the trail was narrow and we had to go single file. Louisa would be first because she knew exactly where she was all the time. "Watch that vine on your right. Poison ivy," she'd say, in the middle of a sentence. Or, "Shhhh. Over there. See the white tails? Three. Over there," as she pointed to a ridge. By then, they'd be taking off and I'd see the last one as it disappeared soundlessly into the thick underbrush, mainly honeysuckle and still green.

"What's Gary going to do? I mean, what do you think? That church . . ." I said. "I hope they'll . . . I mean, he's poured himself into it. Not my cup of tea, and I know how you feel about it, that Zachariah Barnes and all, but . . ." I gave up. I didn't want Gary to lose any more than he already had.

"I know. I know." She sighed. She'd always figured Barnes for a con man and that Gary had been pulled in by a scam. "All he's said is that there's been a meeting and there'll be another one. I've been thinking, though—how *did* he pay off Barnes?"

I stopped mid-stride on the path. "I never thought of that." Gracie looked back at me.

"Not like nothing else on our minds."

I shook my head. "Sister, did you ask him?"

"Wasn't sure I wanted to know. I mean, what would I do about it?"

"I have it. I mean if he . . . maybe he borrowed it?"

She came close, and Gracie's face was behind her as Louisa dipped her face and laid her forehead on my shoulder. "Thank you. Let's wait and see what happens. You know."

"It's okay, honey. Family."

The only sound that moment was our breath and that of Rush Run, picking up, up, moving on to the next place.

Gus

He'd never been to a church meeting. Well, not since Rhonda had dragged him to Sunday school when he was a kid. She'd intimated that was so he'd avoid the evil of alcohol that had ruined their mother, according to Rhonda. But Gus saw it differently. Liquor was his mother's escape from his father's temper, quick and mean; it was his cruelty that had kept her from them. Rhonda, nine years older, had done her best with the little brother who'd come as an unwelcome surprise, something that had apparently been Gus's and his mother's fault in his father's eyes.

But damn, here he was, in what was likely not Gary's church anymore, invited—more summoned—by the members to "give input" because of his role in the situation with Gary's baby, about which Gary had evidently updated them. And because of what Brother Tom had told him: that their building-fund money was missing. They understood, again from Gary, who obviously never heard of avoiding self-incrimination, that he'd used it to pay off Barnes. Well, in Gus's opinion, that made a steaming pile of cow manure smell attractive by comparison.

And he'd had no idea that there could possibly be this many pieces of glitter art in a church, let alone a barn, even if they were supposed to be Jesus. Was Gary trying to make people go blind to test some theory of miraculous cures? Rhonda would slap him upside the head for even thinking that, he reminded himself. But seriously, he argued with her. Have you *looked* at it? Gus supposed not. Gary would say yes, she definitely had a clear view from heaven, but Gus considered himself a man of science and reason and took into account all the impediments in the way, including trees and the roof of the barn. Nope, he just didn't buy it, even if he did talk to Rhonda all the time and assume she could hear him clearly.

He sat waiting, uncomfortable in the folding chair, and uneasy. Was it embezzlement? Likely yes. Could they bring charges? Well, that would involve the prosecutor and maybe the grand jury, but likely yes. Then Gary would confess. Conviction. Mitigating circumstances? A crapshoot.

How much more could Gary lose? And what about Louisa? Oh God, what about Louisa?

Do the right thing, Rhonda prodded. *Be a good man. If you're with a woman, you'd better love her, you hear? Tell these people the truth, sure, but you also have resources you can use. It's Louisa you'll be helping. Think of it that way. No one has to know.*

That was Rhonda, always one instruction after the other. Like it was just easy-peasy.

All right, already. He swatted Rhonda away. The members were taking seats, Brother Thomas standing in the front appearing to take charge. They must have decided that someone was going to run this thing, and he'd been chosen. Gus waited to be called on. He answered their questions, added his piece, and ninety minutes later when he left the meeting, Gary's fate had been decided.

Chapter 33

CarolSue

I couldn't decide what was the right thing to do. I considered packing Gracie's and my own things and going on the run with her, but as I've told you, I'm the sensible one. I couldn't access my money without my whereabouts being traced, and even though I'm a relative, I figured it would still be kidnapping, and bam! Up would go an Amber Alert. Even if I could hide, what kind of life would that be for Gracie? Here I was, quick to criticize the life she was headed for in Honduras, the one her poor mother had been desperate to escape, yet thinking I could give her a great one outside the law. It was not a workable Plan.

It was the kind of glorious day that is like a hand slowly, slowly pulling the light and warmth away from the earth, letting it linger so you will smell it, feel it, grieve for its passing. Oh, how I dreaded the winter. Gracie, of course, knew nothing of what was coming. She was laughing and babbling, as pretty and delightful a baby as ever lived, I was positive. She was thriving, anyone could see that. We'd been feeding her rice cereal and now were adding puréed fruit, cooked carrots. There was nothing she didn't like. I didn't see how we could go on without her. I tried not to think of her mother, how she must feel the same thing. Everything now was more poignant each day, beauty and impending loss perfectly balanced.

Charlie was on my mind. I would never have even left Atlanta if he were alive. Oh, if he could see me now with Gracie, that good-hearted man would say it was worth his death to give me what I'd wanted. The baby was mourning's bittersweet reward, the bright red berry hidden inside the hard casing that opens in mysterious time. And the season of open yellow hands and red hearts of bittersweet in the woods of our land is glorious, like time suspended in safety, between the heartbeats of beauty and danger. And you might—or I might—be fooled into thinking that this time it might last because time seems to stretch beyond the boundaries of its rightful life. The days with Gracie were like that.

Louisa, Gracie, and I went for our walk. We hiked down to Rush Run in shafts of gold and light, swishing through the leaves still scarlet on the ground, Louisa watching for her beloved deer, both of us talking to Gracie, not knowing, as I've said we never did, if it would be the last time for the three of us. Would this be the afternoon the great hum of the spinning earth would start up again, gunning the earth toward what was to come? Jessie trotted ahead of us, sometimes going on a foray after a squirrel, but generally sticking close.

When we got home, Gary was sitting in the backyard waiting for us, trying to keep the girls at a distance. "Get away, whatever your name is . . ."

"Not an ounce of the farm in that boy," Louisa muttered to me while he still couldn't hear. "No idea what went wrong."

"Shhh. Be nice. He probably just wants to see Gracie."

I was wrong.

Gary stood up, squinting in the brilliant sun. He'd been there a while; his face had already pinked. "Couldn't get in the house," he said in his mother's general direction.

"Huh," was all he got back from her. A while ago she'd gotten in the habit of locking the door when she wasn't there, exactly because she didn't want Gary going through her bank records once she'd found out he planned to build a church on her land, something she was having no part of. It was going to be a wildlife reserve when she died, a little fact that would be the equivalent of a grenade. She'd already signed the trust, which was like pulling the pin. I both hoped I wouldn't be home when she threw it and that I would be.

"Gus called me. He wants to come over. You know, how I told you the church, I mean the members, were having meetings? I guess they had their big one last night and he was there. He has something to tell us. I don't know why him, but . . ." Gary shrugged. "Mom, do *you* know anything?"

"Me? Of course not." Louisa sounded defensive, but I knew she hadn't talked with Gus and it sure wasn't like she hung out with the Daily Prayer Squad callers or the Clean for Jesus Committee that Gary was always talking about.

"Gary, looks like you should get out of the sun, and I need to change Gracie. You want to play with her awhile, while I fix her bottle?" I said.

He was diverted. "Definitely."

"When is Gus coming, though?" Louisa wanted to know as I lifted Gracie out of the backpack. We had this down to a perfect science now. "I'd like to get some of these leaves raked, and start some supper, but—"

"He said his shift ends at four thirty and he'd come over then. I should call him if that's not all right."

"What he wants is an invitation to supper. I know that man," Louisa said, looking at her watch. "We'll see." I'd thought she might be glad. "Guess these leaves aren't going to get raked now," she said. Maybe she *was* glad. I couldn't tell.

"Have we got something nice we can put together?" I asked, trying to sound like that was really what I wanted to know.

"No idea." She wasn't giving up anything. I rolled my eyes when her back was turned and took Gracie into the house.

*   *   *

I checked a couple of times as she was making dinner. The usual enormous salad, a cheese and vegetable pasta casserole and rolls. She'd made a lot, but then she often did, and we'd have the leftovers for lunch the next day. I noticed she didn't set the table.

At a little after five, Gus knocked. It was Gary who let him in. I was feeding Gracie and Louisa was pretending she hadn't heard it. The men shook hands, but as best I could tell, Gus didn't tell Gary one thing except hello before heading straight for Louisa, who was hiding out in the kitchen. She gave him the evil eye—still mad at him for being mad at her—and I thought, oh Lord, this is going to be ugly. But he just put his arms around her and gave her what looked like a sweet kiss. He whispered to her, the first time his voice hadn't been loud enough for the neighbors to hear, and right when I wanted to eavesdrop, too. After that, she raised her face to his, and her face had softened into a smile. Whatever he'd said to her, I sincerely hoped he'd consider selling me the script for the next time she got mad at me because I was mad at her.

Then I realized: Oh! This meant Gus wasn't mad at Louisa anymore.

But nothing had really changed. What had happened had happened. What had been done had been done. Had they both just decided that human beings who love each other are surely going to frustrate and disappoint each other and that the way to stay together is to assume that, and then consider the intention of the other's heart?

Or, on the other hand, maybe he'd told her something new. Could be either. I couldn't wait to find out.

Gus turned and spoke to me in his voice, which sounded as if he were using a megaphone. "So, Miss CarolSue. Good to see you! How's the little one doing?"

Louisa might be fine with him now, but remember, he was

the one who'd told me that I couldn't raise Gracie, so I wasn't feeling all gooey toward him.

"She's doing extremely well, Gus," I said, managing to be civil.

"Glad to hear it. Well, it's Gary that I really need to talk to, but he suggested that he owed it to his family, being as how you all . . . anyway, he just said to come tell everyone at once. That okay with you?"

Louisa and I agreed, of course. "But the baby—"

"We can keep things under control," Gus said. "Maybe we could all sit down? In there?" He pointed to the living room. "I don't suppose you have a bit of that special tea made up, Louisa?"

"I can fix it," she said.

This was ominous. We needed to be sitting down and have special tea. Gracie gurgled at me. "Let me finish feeding her and then I'll give her the bottle in there," I said. "You don't think this should wait?"

"S'all right," Gus said. Which would have been reassuring if he hadn't added, "Hey, honey, I'll take my special tea without the tea, just the special if that's okay with you. Gary? You want the same?"

We all knew Gary didn't drink, so I almost fell off my chair when Gary said yes.

Louisa made herself and me some special tea the right way, and by the time it was all set up in the living room, Gracie was finished. The worry and dread I carried was far heavier than the baby as I carried her in.

"So," Gus began after dramatically clearing his throat. I would have thought he was enjoying this except that he looked so awkward, so uncomfortable. "Gary's church asked me to come to their meeting last night to answer some questions for them. Gary said it was all right with him, so I did." He looked at Gary. "I thought I might be able to help. Provide information, you know. Like about Barnes, as best I could." Gus shifted his weight and took in a breath. "See, they were wanting to find out if they could press charges against you, how to go about that. About their building fund money. Embezzlement."

Gary's head went down into his hands, face-first.

"They were looking for information. I answered their questions."

"For the love of God, Gus! Are they pressing charges?" Louisa erupted from the couch, where she was next to Gary. I was in the wingback chair so I could set Gracie's bottle down on the little side table when I needed to burp her. Gus was over in Harold's recliner. Louisa didn't like it when he sat in that chair, but she'd never asked him not to, so how would he know that was something else connected to Harold that would always be sacred? Sometimes I wondered if I was grieving the right way, when I compared myself to my sister. I guess we go on the way we go on, though, and maybe there's no right way.

Gus held up one palm. "Whoa," he said. That kind of response is guaranteed to light my sister's fire, but instead of flipping out, she shut up. "Okay," he said. "I don't think so. They can, and they still may, but I think they've come to a resolution that, if Gary agrees to it"—he faced Gary and paused, waiting for Gary to take his face out of his hands and look at him—"it may keep this whole matter out of the court system."

Gary's voice was hoarse. "I already said I'd get a second job and pay it all back."

"Well, son, they're not willing to wait for that. From their point of view, see, that's their money that should be in the bank and drawing interest. You know how that works. Anyway, to cut to the chase, a donor came forward last night and contributed all the money to replace what's missing. Plus the lost interest."

Louisa's mouth dropped open. It was almost comical the

way she gasped, except that I imagine mine had too. Gary's expression was complete disbelief.

"None of my members have that kind of money," Gary said.

"Well, I can't speak to that. And the person doesn't want his identity known."

"Wait a minute," Louisa said, wrinkling her face, narrowing her eyes. Skeptical. "There's more to it. There's got to be."

Being the sensible one, normally I'd be the sister to say that, but Gracie had just spit up on me and Marvelle, behind me on the top of the chair, was taking random paw swipes at Jessie's face when the Lab put her front paws on the arm of the chair and stood on her hind legs every now and then to lick Gracie's face. All Louisa had to do was pay attention. I was surprised she didn't let Rosie Two and the girls in the house tonight and expect me to manage them, too.

Gus sighed. "I'm afraid there is a catch. It seems they want to keep the church going, but they're not entirely sure about you, Gary. Uh . . . they think you, well, to rephrase their concerns, they aren't pleased with your recent . . . uh . . . moral leadership."

Gary said, "They're kicking me out . . . of my own church, aren't they."

"No, no. It's not that, not exactly. They want you to take a sabbatical. An unpaid sabbatical. They can see their way to maybe having you back after that."

"How long? I can get by for a month, anyway."

"A year. Minimum."

"A year? Who's going to run the church?"

"Don't know that, son. Won't be you. Brother Thomas seems to be sort of taking charge right now. Since I have a connection to you because of, well, your mother, I guess, and the legalities about your baby over there"—he gestured at Gracie who was nodding off on my shoulder now—"I was asked to just fill you in. The not pressing charges, well, it's all tied to you agreeing to this. That was the church's condition—"

"But they got the money from that person," Louisa objected. "I don't understand." She'd reached over and put her hand on Gary's knee.

"The donor could have put the condition of not pressing charges on it . . . There was a lot of talk about options," Gus said. "Anyway, the point is that, Gary, you've got to decide if you think you can beat this in court and you want to let them go that route. Might go to mediation, but not likely a prosecutor would go for that. Court'll order restitution even if all you get is probation and community service. Make it hard in the job market later. Or, you can take their offer, and maybe even come back to your church. If you think you want that. But now it's all between you and them. Brother Thomas wants you to call him."

Gary sat still, as if he was trying to absorb it. In the way of human beings everywhere, I suppose, my sister—who'd loathed everything Zachariah Barnes stood for and the bill of goods he'd sold Gary after Cody was killed—well, now she was working herself up to fight for him to keep the church that she'd always considered crackpot. I saw it on her face before she spoke.

"But it's Gary's church! They can't—"

"Sister," I interrupted her. "Give him time to think. He'll know what to do."

She didn't like my inserting myself, I could tell, because she started with what was going to be *Shut up, CarolSue* in only slightly nicer words, but Gary stopped her.

"She's right, Mom. I gotta think." He stood up. "Thanks for coming, Gus. I'll take it from here." He stood and crossed over to me. "She's sleeping? Too early for bed, though, isn't it? Give her to me. I want to hold her some."

I transferred Gracie to his arms. She roused and whimpered, and Gary offered her the pacifier. Then he took her

THE BOOK OF CAROLSUE 263

blanket out of her carrier, wrapped it around her and went out the front door. I admit, it scared me. Louisa, Gus, and I all sat quiet, still in our places, nothing to say. Emotion drained slowly from the room along with the remaining daylight, replaced with uncertainty.

Maybe five minutes passed like that. Then Louisa got up and switched on the floor lamp. "Gus, honey, would you like another special tea without the tea? CarolSue? How about a refill?"

"Sure would," Gus boomed. And I allowed as I'd have a touch more myself. As we were coming back to life, Gary came back in with Gracie. Louisa reached for her, and he put the baby in her arms. "I'm going to get going. Thank you, Mom and CarolSue. Thanks, Gus. I'll be in touch with Brother Thomas in the morning."

"I thought you'd stay to supper," Louisa said.

"Not tonight, Mom. But thanks. Jesus loves you."

"Okay, son." This was a typical exchange for them.

After Gary left, Gus said, "I'll be on my way, too."

"Not on your life," Louisa said. "What'll I do with all this food if you don't stay to supper? Don't you irritate me now."

"Wouldn't dare, honey."

Everyone was trying to act and sound normal, as if we still weren't waiting for the moment we'd lose our Gracie, and now, to find out if Gary would be either charged with embezzlement or accept being banished from the church he'd started with the only remaining hope of his life.

Later, after we'd eaten, Gus had gone home, and Gracie was asleep, Louisa and I did the dishes. At supper we'd all talked about Gary, but briefly, so as to not reawaken the terrible worry that Louisa, especially, was tamping down. We agreed that it was up to him entirely, and it was best not to advise him one way or the other. "Who's giving the money?" Louisa said. "And how much is it anyway?"

"Person wants to remain anonymous. I imagine they've got their reasons," Gus said. "As to the amount, I guess you could ask Gary, but maybe it's best to stay out of it, honey. He's a grown man."

I agreed with that, and then we let it drop.

And once Gus was gone, I could ask her: "So . . . Gus was mad at you, and you were mad at him for being mad at you. He comes in and whispers in your ear, and all of a sudden, you are no longer shooting death rays at him? What did he say?"

"He said, 'I'm an idiot, sweetheart. Let's take a nap.' "

Chapter 34

Gus

It had gone about as well as it could have at Louisa's, he supposed. God, he hoped Gary would have the sense to take the deal. Oh, it was Gary's mess, and in Gus's world, he should pay the consequences, but damn, he couldn't abide standing by while the woman he loved lost her son to prison and her granddaughter to—was it Guatemala? Someplace dangerous, anyway—after losing her grandson and her husband. He couldn't do anything about losing the baby, which sounded like the baby, too, was dying. Gus didn't mean it like that, but he knew it might feel that way to Louisa. He could keep Gary out of prison by making the money contingent on no charges, but the decision was up to Gary. Gus hoped Gary would think of his mother. Part of Gus wanted to shake some sense into him on that score, but best to stay at some distance and have only Rhonda and Gus himself know what he'd done.

He was sitting in his office at the station, replaying it all over his second mug of coffee, when he backtracked and noted, with some surprise, that to himself he'd thought of Louisa as the woman he loved. Huh. Well, maybe so. Maybe so.

"Connie," he called through the open door, which drove her insane. She said he should quit being a lazy ass and walk out there to talk to her like a normal person. It wasn't exactly respectful, but she was easy to like, so he didn't really care, and he kept right on doing it anyway. "Did you give me all my messages?"

No answer. She was pretending she couldn't hear him.

Gus sighed and got up, walked around the partition and out into the short hall area. "Connie!"

She turned from her phone board and flipped her headphones down around her neck. "Oh! Goodness. Were you speaking to me?"

"Did you give me all my messages?"

"No, I sold the ones I didn't care for at a garage sale up the street. What do you think I did with them?" She rolled her eyes. Did all women do that?

Gus sighed and hoped she would mess something up someday and that he'd catch it. He'd thought Gary would have called him by now. Or Brother Thomas. Or, not that he hoped this, the prosecutor. It was pushing noon and nothing, though.

He checked his email again. Nothing there, either.

The phone on his desk buzzed. "Line two," Connie said. "Someone named Juan Ramirez, I think he said."

Nobody Gus knew. "I'll take it," he told Connie and switched over. "This is the sheriff," he said. "Can you hear me?"

"Loud and clear. Connection is fine, sir. This is Juan Ramirez. I'm an attorney with Legal Aid, presently representing Rosalina Gonzalez. She said you had visited her, and I got your name from the log at the detention center."

"And?"

"Miss Gonzalez asked me to call you. I believe you have the ability to bring her daughter to the detention center?" It sounded to Gus like he sighed. "An immigration judge is coming to Indianapolis, so they'll be bussed there for court rather than transferred to a federal facility first."

"They're going to let her take the baby to court?"

"Arrangements will need to be made if Ms. Gonzalez is deported. But maybe you could bring her for a visit again? Her court assignment will be either tomorrow or the day after, I believe."

"It's not a great time for the family."

"It's a worse time for Ms. Gonzalez."

Gus leaned back in his chair and looked at the ceiling. The lawyer was right, but damn. Damn. If she was deported, it would be right after court. Likely from Indy. "Understood. All right. I'll call them and try to bring the baby today."

"The schedules are capricious. What we are told is not always reliable. Please do it as soon as possible."

Gus said he would, hung up and spoke to Rhonda in his head. *I don't care. No one should keep a child from its mother. You were good, Rhonda, but you needed her, too. It wasn't fair. It wasn't right.*

As he expected, Louisa and CarolSue didn't take it well. "Today? And you mean she could end up deported—like tomorrow or the next day? From Indy?"

The undressed answer to that was *yes*. He'd tried to explain it clearly, even made sure he spoke slowly and loudly so Louisa could take it in and tell it correctly to CarolSue. She had, because Gus overheard what she said and CarolSue's reaction. And then, worse, he had to say he was coming to pick Gracia up to take her for a visit. Yes, today. He'd be there at one o'clock. No, later really wouldn't work and he was sorry about the nap schedule. Louisa's voice was breaking when he hung up. "Love you," he whispered, after the phone was in the cradle. He couldn't let Connie hear that, certainly. He wondered if Louisa would forgive him, especially since he saw no chance that CarolSue would.

At 12:55, Gus pulled into Louisa's driveway slowly, not wanting to make noise on the gravel, meant to convey that he was sorry. Likewise, he knocked quietly at the front door. It had rained earlier, and he wiped his feet carefully while he waited. Louisa came, and let him kiss her cheek. "I know this is really hard," he said. "I'm sorry, honey. Her lawyer called this morning."

"We want to go with you," she said as he stepped into the house. "We're ready and so is Gracie."

He wasn't prepared for this. Maybe she didn't understand what Justice Center meant. "Honey, it's a jail. No place for—"

"We know. CarolSue wants to know Gracie's mother, and so do I. We're her family. We're all family now."

"I guess . . ." He wasn't happy about it. "But you're not going to—" He was going to say *pressure her to change her mind*, but he stopped himself because she was handing him something.

"Here." A piece of paper. She'd written out her full name and address and phone number and then written *(grandmother)* and then she'd written CarolSue's name with the same address and CarolSue's cell phone number and *(aunt)*, and Gary's full name, Gary David Hawkins *(father)* with his cell phone number and her own address as an *in care of* one to use. "I want to give her this," she said. There was a phone card good for international calls clipped to it. "CarolSue went out this morning and got the card for the phone. That was her idea."

"Have to leave it at the desk. I'm not allowed to pass anything to a detainee. But her lawyer will get it to her. I'll make sure he knows about it."

"Can we find out her address? Or where she's going? Is there a relative's phone number at least?" CarolSue spoke up from the other side of the room where she was strapping Gracie into her carrier. She'd been crying. Gus could tell by her voice. The baby was making happy baby sounds, which somehow made it all harder.

"We'll ask. I believe it's information Gary has a right to

have. I'm not a lawyer. Look, I'd rather you two not do this. Let me handle it."

"We're going," Louisa and CarolSue said in almost perfect unison. CarolSue was clutching the carrier with Gracia in it now and he could see there was pretty much zero chance of taking it anywhere today without CarolSue attached. And he figured he was just getting back on the nap track with Louisa. No point in messing that up.

"You look nice, honey," he said. "I like your hair like that." Capitulation, conciliation.

"CarolSue put makeup on me," she said. "My hair's the same."

Well, he'd tried.

Louisa

It didn't matter how gaping the hole of absence was going to be. Not anymore. Louisa hadn't believed she could live through losing another grandchild, not after Cody. But she'd brought herself around to this: She wouldn't let it happen. She would form a relationship with Rosalina herself. Hadn't she loved Cody's mother? Didn't she love Nicole still? She could love and support Rosalina, and if Rosalina would let her, she would help Rosalina bring Gracia back to Indiana, to the farm where she could grow up safe and unafraid. She and CarolSue would find the best lawyers to help them. And meanwhile, they would write, they would call, they would learn how to do that sky-peep thingy that Gary talked about, so they could see the baby and share her life, and she wouldn't forget them. CarolSue said she would make sure Gary had enough money to get Rosalina the right kind of phone so she could do the sky-peep thingy on her own.

CarolSue was right about one thing. They were family now, and Louisa wasn't about to let go, not when she had any part of a choice, not when there was something, anything, she could do about it. She hated it when CarolSue was right. Fortunately, it didn't happen all that often.

CarolSue

She was thin, the way someone who hasn't had enough to eat is thin, I thought, but what do I know? If someone with brown skin can look pale and washed out, she did, maybe thanks to the ugly orange jumpsuit and the fluorescent overhead light in the cement-block room. She looked young, scared, and resolute all at once. Her eyes were big, brown, shadow-ringed, under black arches. High, wide cheekbones. A widow's peak of dark hair on her forehead. I could already spot the ways Gracia would resemble her mother. I smiled at her right away—and I think Louisa did, too. Whatever cold hurt I felt about her taking Gracie away from me, from us, had begun to thaw when I first took her in, and it melted when she wasn't allowed to hold Gracie but had to stand back and watch while we laid her on the table and unwrapped the blanket so the guard could inspect her (again) for contraband. Tears, but no sound came from her.

"Showoff asshole," Gus muttered at the guard's back as he left. "Not necessary." Then he spoke in his normal tone to Rosalina. "It's okay now. You can pick her up."

And the baby, my Gracia, was in her arms and my heart was breaking for all of us. I'd thought we'd talk, that Louisa and I could hear and understand her story, that part of Gracie's history. Now I know it was naïve of me, to think that we could grasp how her life had brought her to this juncture in the brief time we had, and later I wondered how much time the court would give to listen before her future was decreed. Whether we could have understood or not, there wasn't much talk. "*Te amo, hija*," Rosalina said over and over as she held Gracia to her body, her eyes locked down on that little girl, and rocked her, talked, smiled, poured love on her as if her soul was a pitcher full of it and her baby the waiting receptacle. And maybe that was so.

The talking we did was to tell Rosalina what Gracie liked to eat, when she'd first rolled over, her favorite lullaby, what makes her laugh. I could tell she wanted to know those kinds of things, because she asked. Other than that, I tried to shut up and let Rosalina have her time with Gracie. It felt like the right thing to do.

I was aware that the guard kept looking in the window of the interview room—Gus had been able to get the room, and I understood it wasn't the usual visiting area. I don't know how long we were allotted, but it didn't seem long enough before he came in and said "Time!" Then he had to see Rosalina break down as she had to set her baby on the table, where in haste I put the pad and blanket back on the hard surface. Then she raised her hands so the guard could check that nothing had been put in the baby's clothing, and I wrapped and lifted her. "I'm sorry," I whispered to Rosalina. "Try not to worry. I love her so much. We're taking good care of her for you." I was crying, too.

"We're leaving all our contact information for your lawyer," Louisa said to her. Her eyes were full, too. "So you can stay in touch. Please. We want news. And we'd like to try to help if you want to . . . come back."

"I will help," I said. I realized we were assuming she was going to be deported. But maybe she'd win and then . . . I needed to tell her. "If you don't get sent back now, you can come stay with us. We'll find a place nearby for you and Gracie. Gary loves her. He's a good father." I looked at Louisa, signaling her to back me up.

She did. "You're wanted," she said. "You and Gracia. We'll help."

The guard was there. "You'll have to leave," he said. Rosalina just stood there, alone, as we were led out. I carried her baby.

As we left, Rosalina was crying. "*Se fuerte, hija,*" she said. "*Te amo.*"

Chapter 35

CarolSue

We heard nothing after that. My nerves were raw. Louisa seemed edgy, too, although the second afternoon, she wondered how I'd feel about maybe taking Gracie on "an outing" by ourselves, since it was such a beautiful day. She didn't want me out in the woods by myself, though. "Maybe a shopping trip?"

"Where to?"

"Anyplace but here."

"Why, you have some Plan?"

"No."

"Oh. Right. Bless your heart. Let me take a wild guess. Gus has some personal time coming and thinks he might take the afternoon off because things are nice and quiet at the station. And oh my, you are both so extra tired that you may just need the house extremely quiet because you may want to take a nap."

"Well, if you put it that way."

"Tell Gus Gracie and I will leave at two thirty. But I am darn well bringing her home at four thirty and you two better have some special tea made."

I took Gracie to Meyer's in Elmont and bought her more clothes. I didn't know how much Rosalina would be allowed to take, but surely a diaper bag. I bought a new one, the biggest I could find. I'd cram all the clothes I could in it, as many diapers as would fit and a few toys. Then I started thinking about formula. How would she feed her? Powdered formula would be more practical. I got her a pre-paid credit card, too. I should have thought of all this earlier, I realized, so this trip was a small grace. As was every hour with Gracie.

When I got back—it was four forty-five, as I didn't want to risk walking in on anything—I turned the baby over to Louisa to feed while I opened and washed and packed everything I'd bought. "Gus, would you make sure that this gets to Rosalina? It's for Gracia."

"That's a real kindness, CarolSue," he said.

"Thank you, Sister. I can share those expenses," Louisa said. "I should have thought of packing things. I was distracting myself."

"No need."

"She's my granddaughter. I want to."

I'd not meant to leave her out. There was suffering to go around. I'd seen Rosalina with Gracie. I hurt for her, too.

It wasn't an hour later that Gary showed up, unannounced. He came in like an energy field, without knocking—which Louisa couldn't stand—and disheveled, breathless. He had an envelope. "The church forwarded my mail. Look!"

At the moment, I was changing Gracie's diaper, which was a certifiable mess, so Louisa overcame her annoyance that he'd burst in without knocking and said, "What is it, Gary?"

"You've got to see!" He was worked up for sure. I thought maybe the church was taking him back early or something, but, no, it couldn't be from them if they'd forwarded it.

"Louisa, just do it, honey," Gus said. He sometimes took Gary's side like that.

She did. "What is . . . Gary? What does this mean?"

I'd finished changing Gracie and with her in my arms I

went over to where they were gathered. Louisa lowered herself onto the couch. She handed me papers. Gary took Gracie from me so I could read them.

What I held took my breath. "Oh my God," I half whispered, half gasped. Rosalina had signed guardianship of Gracie to Gary. Gracie's birth certificate and social security card were in the envelope. Louisa, Gus, and I were all open-jawed with disbelief.

"She wouldn't do that," Gus said.

"It's notarized," Gary pointed out. "And witnessed by her lawyer. Look," he said, holding another piece of paper out, "her name and an address in Honduras. And this must be her father's name, too, with a phone number."

"We can send her pictures and write to her," I said. "We have to."

"I can do better than that," Gary said. "I'll pray on it." He kissed Gracie's head. She was squirming and starting to fuss, gnawing on her hand in her mouth. "What is it, honey?"

"She's getting hungry. Why don't I give her the bottle now?" I said. "Give her to me, okay?"

Really, I wanted to get out of that room, because I didn't know what I felt, and I didn't want to advertise my confusion. But maybe Louisa and I were feeling somewhat the same joy and relief that Gracie would be making her home with us. (Oh! But would Gary let her stay with Louisa and me? A new worry. I didn't ask.) At the same time, I hurt for Rosalina, sure that she had decided out of pure love to give Gracie what Rosalina believed was the better life. Celebrating would be wrong, as if it would be at her expense.

Gary seemed to be overcome. Now he, too, had sunk down into a seat. His head was down and he was shuffling the papers, reading them over and over as if new words might appear. And I thought Gus was upset, though I couldn't have said why.

"I'll head out now and give you folks some time to absorb this," Gus said. "You all right, sweetheart?" He said that to Louisa, going to where she sat and bending to kiss her cheek.

She got up and gave him a hug. "You don't need to leave."

"Oh, best I do for today."

"Are you all right?" she said. I knew what she was getting at. There was something he wasn't saying.

"Fine, I'm fine," he boomed. "I'll talk to you later. G'night, all." The last sun angled low through the living room window and glinted on his badge as he turned around. And then his back was at the door and he was gone. All the things I'd bought for Gracie were in the backpack by the door. Later I'd unpack it all in the room we shared.

Gus

Gus pulled out of Louisa's gravel driveway, which faced west, and headed southwest on the highway, which didn't help a bit with the blindness caused by the setting sun. He pulled down his visor and put on his sunglasses.

Damn. He couldn't believe that Rosalina, a *mother*, would leave without her child. Not after he'd made sure she could take the baby with her. For God's sake, he'd brought the letter from Gary, signed and notarized. Rosalina had seen it. He was sure she understood. She loved that baby. She wanted that baby—he'd seen it, he'd felt it, it was as old and familiar as his own beating heart. He'd made sure it was logged in when he left it for her lawyer, so he knew the lawyer had gotten possession of it.

The lawyer! That was it. Her damn lawyer. He was the one who'd decided not to let it happen. Maybe Gus could still intervene. Maybe it wasn't a done deal. That lawyer was going to get a piece of his mind.

It wasn't that Rhonda had never said, "You know, Gus. Maybe Mom did what she thought was best for us in the long run." Oh, she'd said it plenty when she put him to bed at night, back when he still had tears for lost toys and people, for bandaged knees, and for anger, young enough that he'd still talk of it to her if only his night-light illuminated the room. But Gus knew his mother loved him, so that couldn't be true.

Now his old anger rose back to the surface like debris on deep water. He watched it float all evening, prodded it here and there, considering whether to call or to visit in person. He decided to call only because he wasn't a hundred percent sure he'd control himself well and it was important to protect his job. If he could intervene and stop this travesty, he'd probably need to still be sheriff.

He didn't sleep well.

In the morning, he didn't even get coffee and a bagel on his way to the station. He'd rely on Connie's coffee and pick up something midmorning at the café so he could make the call from work first thing, let the lawyer see it on caller ID. It was bright and clear, and there was some frost on his windshield. It would warm up later in the day, but Indiana was teeing up winter and Gus hated winter, all the extra work of it. Already accidents were way up because the deer were starting into rut season.

Connie's coffee. One thing to be grateful for. Occasionally she reminded him slightly of Rhonda. "Jimmy gone out?"

"Hasn't been in yet."

"Sheesh. Tell him I said Main Street tickets today, and that's an order." He remembered to thank her and shut the door to his office, not that it always helped much, and then called the lawyer before he could put too much more thought into it.

After introducing himself and having the lawyer say, yes,

he knew who the sheriff was, that they'd met twice in court—embarrassing—Gus started in.

"I'm assuming you did not give Rosalina Gonzalez the notarized permission to take her child with her if she is deported, since she mailed guardianship papers to Gary Hawkins." Gus wanted him to know he was pissed off. "I'd like to know what's going on. I made sure she knew she could take her daughter with her. I brought the baby to see her twice and—"

"Wait a minute," the lawyer Ramirez said. "Excuse me. You are mistaken. Of course I provided her with the notarized permission that was left at the detention center. It would have been a serious ethical breach not to do so. I also translated it into Spanish, as her English is fair but not her first language. As is also my ethical obligation, I informed her of the legal options should she choose to have her child stay in the States with her father. That's my only role, I assure you." His voice was calm and factual, not defensive. Damn, Gus thought. He'd make a good witness.

"So you didn't *advise* her to—"

"Let me put it clearly. Ms. Gonzalez will be deported or already has been. You are right if you perceived that she loves that child deeply. She decided it was best for the child to be here. That she could not keep the child safe nor provide for her well-being, and that came first."

In Gus's mind, Rhonda whispered, "See? I *told* you."

Still gruff, but pulling back, Gus said, "All right, then. You say she's gone? I'd like to inform the family. She provided contact information. They'll stay in touch about the baby."

"Gone, yes, probably as of yesterday, but I don't know for sure. Our Indy office took over when these detainees were moved for court. And about contact. She wants that. By the way, she said you were kind."

"Tried to help is all."

"She knew. Sheriff—Honduras. It's bad there. Especially

for girls and women. Really bad. I didn't advise her what to do, but there's more than one way to be a good mother."

Rosalina

After court, there was one day in another place. Then the law people gave the deportees back the clothes they'd been arrested in, but chained their feet and hands when they walked them out in a line to climb stairs onto a plane. How could she have held her baby if she hadn't signed over guardianship? she wondered. Would a lawman have carried Gracia? Rosalina thought the baby would have been scared, crying, and what could she have done?

She rubbed her wrists when a lawman took the chains off, after the door was shut and locked. Rosalina had never been on an airplane. As it rose, the noise filled her ears like a hurricane. There were no babies with them, just a few older children. One cried, and one slept against his father. Most faces were exhausted, blank.

Her father did not know she was coming. He would be disappointed, so disappointed. All he'd sacrificed to save her, gone for nothing. She had the phone card the Reverend's mother or aunt had given, so she would be able to call, but she did not know how she would get home. She shouldn't use the credit card they'd given her. That had been for the baby. The baby she didn't have with her.

She was a good mother; her baby was safe. She closed her eyes to hold the river of tears underground. It was the water of life that would take her back to Gracia. *Se fuerte, hija*, she whispered. *Se fuerte, madre.* Be strong, daughter. Be strong, mother.

Chapter 36

Carolsue

Louisa and I felt ourselves in a holding pattern for days after Gary left that night. We knew something was in the air, some Plan being set in motion, and that made Louisa especially nuts because, as I've mentioned, Louisa is always the one concocting a Grand Plan. Gary came each afternoon to spend time with Gracie and left either before or after supper, sometimes bringing something extra useful for Gracie like a plastic crèche with BPA-free manger animals so she could suck on them, the shepherds, and the wise men without poisoning herself. He said he'd prefer we not let her teethe on the holy family, however, but since Louisa and I doubted she could be quite that discriminating, we put them away. She seemed to like the donkey best anyway, doubtless because it put her in mind of Rosie Two, as it did look more like a goat than a donkey and she's a very bright baby. Not that either of us said that first part to Gary because we are also bright and didn't care to start something.

When Louisa asked Gary what he was doing about a job, he said, "I've got something in the works. Trying to do the right thing, Mom." But that's all he'd say. Just as importantly, he said nothing about taking Gracie out of Louisa's house to be with him. Maybe that wasn't practical where he was living, or maybe he couldn't support her. Thanks to Charlie, I certainly could, but I didn't want him to think I wouldn't take care of her financially if he needed help with that. When I told him, he smiled and thanked me, but that was all.

As a fountain of information, Gary's spigots were completely shut off.

Tentatively at first, we moved things around. It was Louisa's suggestion. "Look," she said, one morning at breakfast. "Let's redo Gary's old room into a room for Gracie. You shouldn't be sharing a room with her. This is silly. She needs her own room. She's going to need more furniture. We've been playing make-do for a long time."

"That makes sense," I said, getting up for more coffee. "But what about you? How about you move back into your old room and I take the guest room?"

"And give up napping?" Nobody can scoff at an idea like my sister. "I wouldn't be comfortable in Harold's bed with Gus. Think about it, Sister. I love the guest room, anyway. It's airy and light, and I might redo that, too. But I will pack up Harold's things now." She sighed. "I'll need help with that. Maybe you'd like to pick a new color? Gus would paint it."

I pulled her eyes to mine and covered her hand, resting on the kitchen table, with mine. "Are you sure?"

"It's time. I'm ready. But you get to keep Glitter Jesus. Or put Jesus in Gracie's room, let him watch over her."

"The eyes traumatize her, and they bother me at night, too."

"Well, Gus and I can't . . . it's creepy to glance up and be watched by Glitter Jesus."

"Gary checks every day or we could just put him in the garage," I said.

"Don't I know it! Bless his heart."

"Then for the time being, it's back to the living room, I guess. We can stick it behind the couch when he leaves after supper."

"Gotta be careful to put it up after lunch, though."

"We'll remind each other."

But of course, it only took us two days until Gary showed up at three thirty and we'd forgotten to replace Glitter Jesus on the living room wall. Not only that, Louisa hadn't locked the front door when she went out to sweep the dead leaves from the stone walkway. Not that she'd ever refuse Gary entry, but I don't blame her for guarding her privacy after how she found out he wanted to get her off her land to build a church on it. That happened a couple of years ago, but some betrayals are never forgotten, and a section of our hearts gets fenced off and guarded forever after, even with people we truly love.

So Gary walked in, which put Louisa in a quiet smolder right away. I tried to smooth things over, but Gary made it worse by asking, "Where's Jesus?"

Now, that's always a bad question to ask Louisa, because she has a whole repertoire of smart-ass answers depending on where we actually stashed Gary's painting. I hurried to cut her off.

"Oh gosh, look, it fell off the wall again! We've got to fix that hanger, Louisa!" I said, retrieving Glitter Jesus from behind the couch. As usual, glitter fell off and glinted from the couch as I pretended to adjust the perfectly fine adhesive hanger on the back of the lightweight black velvet surface and affixed the monstrosity to the wall again.

"I can touch up that glitter and bring a new back for it. I'm thinking I'll do one for the baby's room."

"Oh, she can enjoy this one," I said, before Louisa said something worse.

"I'll get to it," Gary said. "But I have a job. I came to tell you. And to ask you to take care of Gracia. She'll need you both." He took Gracie from my arms. I'd been playing with her while Louisa fooled with peeling vegetables in the kitchen.

"Get back from where?" That was Louisa. She was wiping her hands on a dish towel.

"From what?" I chimed in.

"Honduras. I'm going as a missionary."

"Bless your heart!" I'm serious, Louisa and I said it at exactly the same time.

"I signed up with an ecumenical religious charity. They send both lay people and ministers, but since I'm ordained, I can go as a minister." He was extremely proud of this. Louisa must have been thinking exactly what I was. Did those people know how Gary had gotten himself "ordained"?

"I figure I can see Rosalina, and while I'm working there, I can help her find a way to come back. Legally."

"Are you crazy?" That, of course, was Louisa.

"Isn't that dangerous?" I said. "What about Gracie?"

"None of their workers has been killed. Yet, anyway." He thought he was amusing when he said this. "And I'm doing the right thing. I have to at least try. For Gracia. Rosalina tried to do the right thing. I have to, too. If you'll take care of her."

Louisa grew serious and did an about-face. "I think I can see your point. You're trying to fix things. Of course we'll take care of her."

"I've told you, I'll always be here for her. How long will you be gone?" I said.

"Well—there's that. I signed up for a year. That's the commitment they need for them to provide living expenses. And, you know, the situation with my church—"

"We know," Louisa said.

"I can call and if you'll learn how, we can Skype so I can see Gracie. And I can fly home for some visits, too."

"I can do that Skype thing," I said.

And he applied for an expedited passport. Within three weeks he was gone.

Gus seemed to appoint himself Gracie's protector. Whatever had upset him about Rosalina seemed to be gone. He was as tender toward the baby as he and Louisa were toward each other, especially after he knew Gary's Plan.

Our land tilted farther from the sun and the darkness came earlier and earlier as we four settled into comfort. Gus was around more and more, and I took Gracie on outings so we wouldn't "wake them up" while Gus and my sister napped. During an unusually warm week right before Thanksgiving, Gracie and I went walking by ourselves. I insisted on learning how to manage the backpack. I always carried my cell phone, though. I owed it to Rosalina—and Louisa—to keep Gracie safe. At the same time, I thought about the illusion that we can protect children from the dangers of the world, even from their own wild, dangerous hearts and the firecrackers they'll light using their precious lives as fuses. Louisa and Harold hadn't been able to protect Cody from a drunk driver. And look how Rosalina's father had tried to get her out of harm's way and now she was back, directly in its path.

I would just have to do the best I could with what was left of my life. We all would. And so would Rosalina. In the woods, I talked to Gracie as we went along. I told about her mother and father, her grandmother, her grandfather Harold, and my dear Charlie. And I told her that she and I together would learn our land and these deep woods that are like sentries around our sanctuary, guarding us and the animals who are refugees here.

We didn't go far; we weren't ready for that and couldn't risk getting lost. Jessie was with us, too, and she knew the way, but I stuck to the wide, main trail I remembered from walking it with Louisa and Gracie. It led us to the source, to Rush Run, the creek that has run strong and clear through the farm for generations, carrying on still, ready for the next.

Acknowledgments

Abiding gratitude to Stacy Testa, who supports me and my work with steadfast, caring expertise. No author could hope for more attentive, skilled, or loving representation. Special thanks to Tara Gavin, who acquired and first edited this novel, and to Elizabeth May, who finished the work of bringing it out when Tara left Kensington prior to its publication. First readers are always especially helpful; in this case, as with all my work, Stacy's editorial feedback was invaluable. Authors Patry Francis and Donna Everhart also contributed their good insight.

I'd like to express my gratitude to the members of the Kensington Publishing Corporation team, with special appreciation for the people who have worked with such care on the preparation of the manuscript, especially Tory Groshong, copy editor, and Carly Sommerstein, production editor. Vida Engstrand, director of communications, handles publicity with enthusiasm and creativity, with Crystal McCoy. Kristine Mills is responsible for the beautiful cover and book design.

My husband, Dr. Alan deCourcy, continues to regularly save my computer from an unnatural, possibly violent, end. His love and faith have sustained me through this and multiple books as well as life itself. My sister Jan is practically a one-woman Southern publicity department, and that's only one of the hundreds of reasons I adore her, as I do Alan and our family, who are dear to me beyond words: Brooke, Matthew, Andrew, Alyssa, and Ciera. It is they who keep me going, along with the support of our extended and still-growing family. My love and gratitude to each of them.

THE BOOK OF CAROLSUE

Lynne Hugo

ABOUT THIS GUIDE

The suggested questions are included to enchance your group's reading of Lynne Hugo's *The Book of CarolSue.*

DISCUSSION QUESTIONS

1. If you have a sibling, did you have roles in your family? For example, was one of you supposedly the smart one? Or the social one, the athletic one, etc.? How do you see CarolSue and Louisa acting in, or sometimes breaking out of, the roles they have played in their family? If you have a sibling, has any of this happened in your family?

2. How did you react to Gary's relationship with Rosalina? Did you feel he took advantage of her? Did she take advantage of him?

3. People grieve in many ways. How would you compare and contrast CarolSue's grieving with Louisa's?

4. What do you see as the role of animals in *The Book of CarolSue*?

5. If you have read *The Testament of Harold's Wife*, how do you compare the two novels? A third book may be coming, to complete a trilogy. What characters from the first two, other than Louisa and CarolSue, would you most like to see again? Why?

6. What do you imagine as the best futures for these characters? Was the ending satisfying?

Reminder: the author is available by Skype or FaceTime, or in person if you live in the greater Cincinnati area, to join your club for all or part of your discussion or just to answer questions. You are invited to contact her with your individual or group thoughts about any of these questions, or anything related to her work, through LynneHugo.com. Thank you so much for your interest!

Keep reading for a special excerpt of Louisa's story.

THE TESTAMENT OF HAROLD'S WIFE
A Novel

From award-winning author Lynne Hugo comes a witty, insightful, refreshingly unsentimental novel about one woman's unconventional path from heartbreak to hope . . .

After losing her husband, Harold, and her beloved grandson, Cody, within the past year, Louisa has two choices. She can fade away on her Indiana family farm, where her companionship comes courtesy of her aging chickens and an argumentative cat. Or, she can concoct A Plan. Louisa, a retired schoolteacher who's as smart, sassy, and irreverent as ever, isn't the fading away type.

The drunk driver who killed Cody got off scot-free by lying about a deer on the road. Harold had tried to take matters into his own hands, but was thwarted by Gus, the local sheriff. Now Louisa decides to take up Harold's cause, though it will mean outsmarting Gus, who's developed an unwelcome crush on her, and staying ahead of her adult son, who's found solace in a money-draining cult and terrible art.

Louisa's love of life is rekindled as the spring sun warms her cornfields and she goes into action. But even the most Perfect Plans can go awry. A wounded buck, and a teenage boy on the land she treasures help Louisa see that the enduring beauty of the natural world and the mystery of human connection are larger than revenge . . . and so is justice.

**Look for THE TESTAMENT OF HAROLD'S WIFE
on sale now.**

Chapter 1

Larry

Sometimes in the shower he'd think of it. Or it would get going in his head at night if he got up to pee and didn't fall back to sleep quickly. Like a movie rerun with no stop on the remote. Blinking and shaking his head sometimes worked, but he had to do it right away. If the movie got past the thud, the steering wheel fighting his hands, he had to let it play to the end to hear how he'd shouted, "There was a deer! It was a deer," at the back of the do-gooder woman who'd stopped at the accident.

"Honey, what's the matter?" LuAnn said once when he hadn't known she was awake, and she went up on her elbow and wiped his face with her finger. "It's okay to cry."

"What the hell are you talking about," he said, not a question. "Shut up, will you," not a question, either. He'd been looking at porn to get his mind on better things, but then he long-armed the magazine under the bed, switched off his lamp, and shimmied down with his back to her. If he hadn't, she'd have kept talking.

She'd made it worse saying that crap when he might have still been able to get it to stop. And then he'd had to let it play to the end again, to hear what he'd yelled, even though he'd seen the movie, hell, he'd made the damn movie, and he knew how it went:

A heavy thud, and then another, something recoiling off the hood. He jerked the wheel to an overcorrection back across the center line, off the shoulder. Get the truck under control, get it stopped. Goddamn, he'd dozed and hit something.

Prob'ly a deer. Rut season. They were all over the roads in the damn early dark. He'd never hear the end of it from LuAnn. Not his fault, dammit. He hadn't had that much, not that much, he'd get Chuck to tell her.

Don't just sit there, get out, check the truck. Shit. Front end a mess. Headlight and . . . oh Jesus. Jesus. What *is* that? Oh Jesus. No. No way. Don't look. A random sneaker and papers is all that is.

Gotta be a deer, there's deer all over the roads now. Rut season. Gotta be a deer. Truck ought t'drive okay. Get outta here, then figure what to do. Lose the empties outta the truck first, walk 'em t'the other side of the highway, other side, throw 'em in the brush. Lotta highway trash. Farther away. Don't trip. Wipe 'em clean. LuAnn'll see the truck. Probably look inside. Thinks she's smart.

Okay. Cross back, get t'the truck. Go, steady. Keep your eyes open.

A long lull in traffic. Lucky.

He was just checking the truck so he could get it straight to tell LuAnn what happened.

Wouldn't you know the damn do-gooder in a six-year-old blue Civic would pull up right then. "Are you all right? Oh my God! Did you get 911? Have you checked him? Where's the other car?" Bitch freaking out, holding a cell phone to her ear, running toward what lay crumpled on the gravel shoulder of the highway, the sun bleeding all over the blackening sky by then.

"It just now happened. Call 911! It was a deer! There was a deer!" He yelled at her back, yelled it twice, then followed her.

He could make the replay finally stop if he turned up the volume on how he yelled it again, too, as he caught up to the woman with the cell phone, to get it right in his head: "It was a deer! There was a deer!"

Chapter 2

Louisa

I am Louisa, Harold's wife. Or I was. Now the last best friends I have are Jo, Beth, and Amy. The four of us still mourn Meg. I'm the only one who's finished *Little Women*, but when we have tea out in the yard, I read it aloud to them from the battered copy I bought at the library sale. I have all the classics now.

They don't care to hear more than a paragraph at a time, but so what? They're beautiful, my friends, my comfort. My looks are closest to Beth's, a brownish blond, but hers are wholly natural while mine are compliments of Miss Clairol. Amy is purely white but for a couple of stunning black streaks that also run in her otherwise cheery temperament, while Jo is a quick-eyed, pretty, russet auburn, like my sister down in Georgia. All of us are old, I suppose. My mind rebels at the word. Old is something that I once thought I'd never have to worry about because time took forever to pass. I won't think about it now, and you shouldn't focus on it, either. None of what's happened had to do with age anyway. It was all set in motion by two selfish men, one of them my son and one a stranger to us both, neither more than half my years, so if you're one of those people who think it's youth that matters, you've been warned.

I thought about changing my name to Meg, after my husband killed her, which was right before he killed himself.

That doesn't sound good, does it? Well, it was quite the right thing to do. She was sick and it's wrong to allow suffering. We all miss her terribly. I didn't change my name, even though it would have made us a more coherent group again, because I thought my sainted mother would be upset. That's an expression Mom used to indicate someone was dead, calling them sainted. My sister, CarolSue, and I say it now as a joke. But my son, Gary—a name I would surely reconsider if I had the opportunity since I've learned it means "spear carrier"— would claim his departed father is definitely *not* sainted because he died on purpose. He would say it as a black-or-white fact, too. After everything that's happened, he cannot stand to look in the shadows. I'll never be able to count on him to kill me when my time comes. But I can take care of myself.

"This is crazy. They're chickens, Mom. They're chickens, and they don't belong in the house." Gary had dropped by without calling and caught me having tea in the living room with the girls. It was raining outside, and much as I love them, I don't sit in the rain to have tea. *That* would be crazy.

"They have names, son. Please be polite. You were raised better. Look, here's my pretty Beth. Say hello, Beth. You know Gary." Beth was already clucking quietly. She's quite the conversationalist. "Gary, tell Beth how pretty she is. Notice how my hair is the same color as hers?"

"Mom, no, I came to check on you, see if you need anything. I'm not talking to chickens. I'm going to get them out of the living room and back into the coop. Besides, Marvelle will kill them." Marvelle is a retired barn cat who looks like she's wearing a fluffy tuxedo. She came to us complete with her unfortunate name. Once a living legend mouser, I brought her inside to the soft life after she quit caring what the mice did. As the words spilled from Gary, she was curled up under my green ottoman, ignoring the hens *and* him. I thought it gracious on my part not to point this out. Gary started to chase down JoJo, which was a terrible way to start since she's the fastest, but I wasn't going to tell him. He wouldn't have a clue how to round them up anyway. All the farm has long leaked out of my boy, who no longer sees the life spark in creatures or feels its force in the land. You'd think, perhaps, that had to do with the way his son, Cody, died, because of that terrible drunken stranger, and Gary's fault in it, too, but it had happened well before then.

"Technically they're all hens," I said, very calm. I crossed my legs at the ankles as if I were entertaining the Prince of Wales, not that Gary looked all that royal in those baggy khakis. "You know, your father never did get another rooster after Bronson died. The girls were past their prime. I'm thinking of enlarging the flock again now, though, and then I might get one. Do you think a rooster would understand if I name him Laurie?"

My son was not looking engaged in this subject at all as JoJo flew up to the hanging light fixture in the dining area to escape him. "Don't you remember that male character named Laurie in *Little Women*? I read you that whole book—how old were you? Gary, please, will you please just sit? You're getting the girls stirred up. There's room next to Beth." I pointed to the couch. "Move over, Beth." Beth, obliging girl that she is, flapped her gold wings and half hopped, half flew up to the couch back on the other side. She couldn't have possibly created more room for him without entirely abandoning the couch.

"Mom! What are those holes in the wall?" Gary, who'd backed off his silly chicken roundup attempt and started to sit when Amy advanced toward him in a menacing way—she and I like to play good cop, bad cop, and she'd certainly not appreciated his comments—hoisted himself back up, and scrambled behind my chair away from her. I had to crane my neck to see him finger two small holes chest-high in the wall to the right of his high school graduation picture.

Oh crap, I thought. Well, it's my own fault. I could have fixed those a long time ago, and at least he hadn't noticed the ones under the window. For a moment, I wished he'd notice that the walls need painting—once a cheery buttercup color, now they're more like a dying dandelion—but on the other hand, if he noticed he might do it, and that would mean he'd be here in my house, and we haven't been getting along that well lately. He worries about me all the time now and it just brings out my worst side.

"Those have been there since last summer. Will you please sit down and have some tea?" I pointed to the china teapot in the cozy my mother knit. "Shall I get you a cup or a mug?"

"You know I don't like . . . Never mind. They *look* like bullet holes. Do you have something to tell me?"

"For heaven's sake. Were you raised on a farm or weren't you?"

"This is hardly a working farm, Mom. The chickens don't even produce eggs anymore. You need to get rid of them."

"I don't produce eggs anymore either, son. Are you going to get rid of me?"

"Mom!" he said, and put on his shocked look.

"You just don't remember all we did on this land. Your daddy hoped you'd take over, but he always suppor—"

"Wait a minute. How did those holes get there?" Gary was raised not to interrupt, but he does regularly. I stopped talking entirely to make a point, but it didn't sink in.

"That's just a couple BBs," I finally said, because he wouldn't let it go.

"*What?* What happened? Was someone breaking in?" Gary's face reddened deeper than its usual shade. He thinks all my business is his to know.

"Four or five deerflies were in here so I took them out. Back in August. I couldn't find the flyswatter. I wish you'd put things back where they belong when you come over."

"Jesus, Mom. I didn't move your . . . wait a minute. You

were shooting deerflies? That's *insane*. You could kill yourself." He stopped for a few seconds, his mouth hanging open and his eyes widening as the idea took hold. He gathered steam and blew. "Wait a minute. Wait just a minute here. *Were* you trying to—?"

"Gary. You of all people shouldn't take the Lord's name in vain, I'm sure. I occasionally miss a deerfly. If I were aiming at a person, *any* person, I assure you I wouldn't miss."

Do you see what I mean about my worst side just popping right out? CarolSue gets all over me about it. "Stop, Louisa!" She says it all the time. "You're not helping him or you heal."

Gary's oval eyes went down to mail slots. "What's that supposed to mean?" he said, all this time standing over my chair, looming. I could feel my neck stiffening looking up at him at that bad angle, and I didn't appreciate it.

"Nothing, son. Would you like to give the girls some grapes? They'll eat right out of your hand. They love their grapes." Very glad to rest my neck by having a good reason to look away from him, I picked up the plate of green grapes I'd cut in half. Amy hopped into my lap right away, proving my point. Gary backed up, knocking the floor lamp into the wall and startling everyone. It hit the wall, and he caught it before it hit the floor. The rag rug might have kept it from breaking, but I think the shade would have been toast.

"Mom," he said louder, enunciating as if I was hard of hearing. "We need to think about getting rid of the chickens. They're too much for you now. They can't be in the house. I've been thinking about the farm anyway. This place has gotten too much for you to handle."

"Gary, I love you, son, but over my dead body will my girls leave." I wouldn't dignify the rest of his opinion.

"Is that a threat, Mom? If you feel like you might hurt yourself, I'll put you on the crisis prayer list and take you to the hospital until God makes things right. It sounds like a threat to me. I'll find a safer place for you." He felt around the holes again, stared at me, and without saying anything more turned and went down the hall toward the bedrooms.

Oh crap, I thought. Here we go.

Within a clock minute, he was back. He didn't loiter getting to the point.

"Where is Jesus?" he said, his whole self in agitation. I was going to get smart with him about how being a reverend, he should know, but I decided to be kind and give him a straight answer.

"Jesus is in the closet."

"Jesus is in the closet? You cannot be serious."

"I think maybe it's why he never got married," I said. Poor judgment on my part, but I couldn't stop my worst side. She does love the openings Gary gives her.

"That is *blasphemy*. Something *is* wrong with you. Why is the *picture* of Jesus in *your* closet?"

Here's the story on that picture: last year, after he became Reverend Gary, my son gave me a painting he'd done himself. He got offended almost to tears when I said Elvis looked good as a blonde in drag. I had to apologize many times and explain that all the paintings involving glitter that I'd seen before were of Elvis, which was why I didn't know this one was Jesus. I pointed out that no one knows what Jesus looked like. This hurt his feelings because the glitter halo was Gary's creative depiction of holiness, which was the point I was supposed to get. He is so sincere it would never occur to him that glitter might not be a good idea. Mollifying him backfired, though, because he carried out his plan to hang it in my bedroom, to be "the first thing I saw in the morning and the last before I closed my eyes."

I knew where that idea came from, and it's an example of chickens coming home to roost. My Harold would say Glitter Jesus on my bedroom wall now is exactly what I deserve for what I made *him* suffer (he claimed damage to his retinas) during our son's adolescence. Gary was miserable as a teenager, bony wrists and knees and ankles all going in wrong directions, plus he had trouble making friends. In ninth grade, after writing a report on Van Gogh, he decided his isolation was related to an artistic temperament. He'd always enjoyed art class, too. Like any mother, I ignored his father and evidence—anything for your child to have self-esteem, right?—and built him up with praise as gaudy and ill-conceived as his projects. What else would I do? I loved my son then, and I do now. Different as we are, I know I mustn't lose sight of all that is good and kind in him, and you mustn't, either.

Anyway, while death threats from me kept Harold's mouth shut, I'd display Gary's dreadful pictures in our bedroom, telling our boy I wanted his art to be the first thing I saw in the morning and the last thing at night. (Anything to keep them out of the living room.) You should have heard Harold when Gary applied to LaGrange Community College to "jump-start" his professional career with an Associate in Studio Art degree. "Now, there's a surefire moneymaker," he said in private, way more times than I cared to hear. That man could roll his eyes as well as any woman. Remembering little things like that crumples me inside like the wadded-up tissue that's stuck in my every pocket to fight the sneak attacks of memory.

Harold had to admit it turned out all right, though he never did give me any credit. After one semester, Gary's tactful instructor redirected him: had he ever thought about the amount of artistic vision computer graphics required? I'd hoped he'd get a Bachelor's, and Harold wanted him to study Agriculture, but at least Gary eventually got an Associate in Computer Science degree. And a job. When he married Nicole and then our grandson, Cody, was born, Harold and I thought we'd run the big bases and were home, safe. Life was finally so good that Harold and I joked how great it was that Nicole, not Gary, had decorated their house; we could visit without being blinded.

But I digress. The point is, now I was a widow and had this Glitter Jesus on my bedroom wall, as if arthritis and a double dose of grief weren't enough to make a body tremble and cringe. I'd never tell Gary that I wanted to remember Harold there beside me, especially horny and passionate and tender, the way he used to be. That I couldn't possibly, what with Jesus' hand raised up like a stop sign and a dot of glitter on the pupils of his eyes, giving a woman absolutely no privacy for trying to remember the best times. We all went over the edge after Cody died, but Gary thinking Glitter Jesus was a great gift shows a lot of his brain cells drowned in his tears. Once I even had the thought of getting another goat in hope that an accidental kick to the head might bring Gary to his right mind. Does that sound bad? When you live alone you have thoughts like that and you stop bothering to chide yourself for them.

How *could* any sane mother tell her son who's pushing forty-five that she was trying to give herself a little satisfaction, and Glitter Jesus' eyes staring her down were an inhibiting factor? It would have been about as natural as mentioning it to a stranger stocking shelves in the grocery store. Gary and I have never been alike, but back when we were all of us a family, all of us living our real lives, I'd watch and listen to him and smile, recognizing myself and Harold and our parents in him, the sum different from the parts, yet adding up to our son with an acceptable, even beautiful, logic. Now I couldn't find anyone or anything familiar in him. Ever since Gary got religion after Cody died, sometimes he looks like Glitter Jesus himself, little pricks of fire centered in his eyes.

On the other hand, what mother *should* tell her son anything about herself and sex? Even if he hadn't become Reverend Gary, I'm not that far gone. So I did the next worst thing to telling the truth. I stood up, gave him a kiss on the cheek, and lied. "Gary, this has been a lovely visit," I said.

"Bless your heart." (CarolSue taught me to say that.) "I'm so glad you stopped by. I hope you remember to call first next time, because you know I've started to get out quite often with my friends. I really need to be getting my supper in the oven about now, and CarolSue is calling at five." As I said this, I was moving toward the door with my hand on his elbow. His face was a kaleidoscope as I talked, but I never let him get a word in. I might have been actually pushing him to the door. I realize that great mothers don't do that, but I'm trying to be honest and let the chips fall.

He called the next morning a little after ten, but I didn't answer the phone. I love that Caller ID gadget. And wouldn't you know, it was Gary who signed me up for it. I know he really tries to be a good son.

I wasn't surprised at all when the sheriff's car bumped down my driveway soon after I didn't answer Gary's call. My son is nothing if not predictable. He was probably up until midnight hot-wiring the crisis prayer lists. But I was ahead of him: the hens were in the coop, the yellow kitchen was scrubbed, floor swept—even the cabinets wiped down—dishes out of the drainer. This isn't easy to do because so many things in my kitchen—oh, say, the red-handled paring knife, the cast iron skillet, the daisy spoon rest, the good spatula—were my mother's, and I remember them all the way back to when Harold and I were engaged. My mother was making me learn how to cook, and Harold would come early to sit in our kitchen, which just made me nervous because Mom would correct my every other move. Later, he'd praise what I'd made so lavishly that I knew it must have been terrible while he managed to hang around until Mom and Dad couldn't stay awake anymore. Oh, his kisses were so gentle, like he was afraid I would break. Believe me, I convinced him I wouldn't. And not that I could say it, but it would have been all right with me if his hands had wandered farther than they did before we were married. It was plain embarrassing, the way I wanted him touching me all over.

Anyway, I'd prepared everything today for unwanted company, even made my bed, and picked up the bedroom in case of a prying glance in there. But I left Harold's good shoes where they were, still half under his side of the dresser. Really, I should donate them to the Goodwill in Elmont, but the idea of someone filling my Harold's shoes, well, I just cannot. The bathroom's cleaned, and I remembered to move Harold's straight razor from its place on the side of the sink where he'd left it that last morning. I'd replaced it there practically the minute CarolSue left for home after we got through Harold's service and settling his affairs and she'd satisfied herself that she'd boxed up his things so I wouldn't have to look at them.

Never an electric shaver for my Harold, not ever since we were first dating did that kind, good man give me beard burn. He'd shave a second time before we went out. He used to bring me daisies because he thought they were my favorite flower. I let him think that: he could pick them for free from the side of the road on his way to our house. Really, I love the scent of Peace roses and when we bought the farm and I ordered a bush from the Burpee catalog, Harold planted it for me. It's strong and healthy, fragrant with a tinge of lemon like his cologne I loved to breathe in. Oh God, where is my sweet Harold?

The usual ghosts appeared when I dusted the living room, each object reminding me how it came to be part of Harold and me. The pewter-base lamp that was a wedding present from Harold's aunt Elsie. A polished wood picture frame my parents gave us for our tenth anniversary. The picture of us in it is long faded. The green ceramic bowl I made in a college ceramics class for my father; my mother gave it to Harold when Dad died. And there's the white afghan that his mother

knit for me; I refolded it over the back of Harold's empty
chair. Everything in my house tells the story of what's gone
forever.

Holes in the walls are filled with toothpaste and touched
up with yellow highlighter. No, you're right, it didn't match
the walls that well, but men don't notice something like that,
now do they? I made sure that I had a calendar out on the
kitchen table with some fake engagements written in. My hair
pinned up with little tendrils left out, and even a makeup job:
eyebrows, a touch of shadow, mascara, blush, lip gloss. Carol-
Sue isn't my sister for nothing. I do so wish she had told her
second husband that she hadn't signed on to leave her family
and no, she wouldn't move to Georgia with him. It's almost a
thousand miles from southeastern Indiana.

I opened the front door and stepped out on the porch
when I heard the patrol car tires crunch on the gravel as Gus
put on the brakes too hard. He is really full of himself. A mistake to go outside, though. I wasn't thinking of the heady scent
in the air to bring *When lilacs last in the dooryard bloom'd* to
mind and then, *O Captain! my Captain!* even though it's a full
year now. Or will be next week. The first dark purple buds
formed two weeks ago. Another thing I do wish is that
Harold hadn't killed himself in April, right when the earth
was rising up a hopeful pale green, bursting into pink and
white and lavender, awash in yellow sun after the darkest
winter we'd ever known, the winter I was surprised to out-
live. It was the insult of spring Harold could not abide. It
made me feel guilty that I could, and now I feel guilty that
I've gone on a year without him, though every day I find another corner of life empty. *O Captain.*

I can stifle tears. Gus, maybe two hundred sixty pounds of
him, labored out of his patrol car. *Sheriff* was emblazoned
along the side of the car in black and gold on a white panel,
and I couldn't help but notice how it contained the word *riff*.
Shorthand for "reduction in force," the *Elmont Herald* ex-

plained, as half the county was laid off or let go in the past couple of years. Why couldn't Gus have been? Yes, I blame his interference for driving Harold to kill himself. But maybe it was my fault.

"Morning, Gus. Thought I heard a car out here." I threw my voice in his direction from the porch as I cleared up my eyes and arranged my mouth into a welcome.

"How're you doin', Miss Louisa? You're lookin' fine!"

Miss Louisa. That's rich. "I *am* fine, Gus. How 'bout yourself?"

"Can't complain." All the while Gus kept coming, right on up my worn porch steps.

"What brings you, Gus? Something wrong?"

"Just comin' by t'see how you're doing is all. Know it's comin' up on the anniversary."

Puffing fat men don't pull off casual all that well. He was wearing his glasses today, and they looked tight on his face. I remember when Gus was almost too skinny and not bad-looking even if he did have some acne. Oh, didn't we all. Even the boys in Vietnam then, like my Harold.

"Well, that's nice of you, Gus, but I'm okay. Of course it's hard. I miss Harold and Cody like both my legs have been cut off, but what can you expect when you lose your husband and grandson within six months? I'm doing all right."

Gus didn't say a word about how Gary had called him and sent him out here to confirm I belonged in a lunatic asylum. Probably told him that his poor mother was clearly losing her marbles, triggered by the anniversary of her husband's suicide. Out here the sheriff is the law and the social service system. We don't have a great tax base in this rural township. What Gus said was, "Mind if I come in and visit a minute?"

I made a point of staring at his waist. "Not comfortable with that gun coming into my house, Gus. Perhaps you can understand since I've lost both Cody and Harold." Now, no gun was involved in either Cody's or Harold's death, but I doubted Gus would think that fast. I truly think Gus showers with that gun on. But Gary probably told him he needed to see for himself that the house was filled with guns, chickens, and wanton disrespect for Holy Glitter. I was starting right out by throwing him a curveball about the guns.

Oh, how the struggle wrote itself across his face. It was just like teaching my fifth grade again when one of the boys was looking for a loophole to wriggle through. "Well, now, Louisa, you know it's my job to be armed. I can assure you I won't touch . . ."

"Then we can just visit out here, Gus. Nothing nicer than a porch on a spring day." I felt the seat of the painted rocking chairs, then turned to the door. "No worry, chairs are nice and dry. I'll bring us some coffee. Be right back," I trilled over my shoulder.

"I think it's kind of chilly for you out here. How about I just put the gun out in the car while I come in. I'll be on my own time without it, of course," he said. The agony of defeat.

"Oh my! Bless your heart, I thought you already were. Anyway, I appreciate that."

I waited while he lumbered back to his car and watched him put the gun in the trunk. When he returned, I opened the door and let him follow me inside. I couldn't wait to see his face.

"How about that coffee?" I said. I was going to let him have a good look at the house and try to figure out where I had stashed the ungodly menagerie. "Come on into the kitchen and I'll put on a fresh pot. It'll only take a minute."

"I'd love a cup. That's a glorious picture. Is it new? Don't remember seeing it when I was here for Harold. You an Elvis fan? I always thought he had black hair. . . ."

His mentioning Harold, meaning how he kept coming here to arrest him—not that there was ever one indictment, not in this county—set my teeth on edge. "Oh yes, it's a beauty," I said. "Bless your heart. Gary painted that for me after Harold died. That sweet boy, bless *his* heart, too, hung it in the bedroom for me, but I'm just not in there all that much, and I decided to put it out here in the living room where I'd see it all day." Marvelle twitched her tail in amusement from her throne on the back of Harold's recliner. She and I share a sense of humor, something my son sorely lacks. Sometimes it makes me doubt everything I learned about genetics in biology class.

Gus followed me too slowly to the kitchen. He must have been scouring the place with his X-ray vision while I started coffee in the four-cup electric pot Gary got me for Christmas. Gus got to the kitchen table and sat down. He thought I didn't see him inch my calendar closer to himself and pretend he wasn't looking at it. The FBI missed a brilliant operative. I don't understand how he was able to thwart Harold's schemes to get revenge on the man who'd killed our grandson, but he did. Or what made him so determined. Did he have to prove that he was a big man because he didn't go to Vietnam and Harold did? What would Glitter Jesus have to say about that?

"You sure look pretty. Haven't changed in forty years. You been keeping busy?" Gus said.

This was just too easy. "Oh my, bless your heart. Well, I have my girlfriends and activities. Actually, I've been thinking about doing some volunteer tutoring back at the school. Those farm boys still need to learn to read." I put on my ultra-sincere face, and brushed the hair CarolSue had taught me to leave loose on my forehead to the side as I pretended to worry what to say. "I didn't work over Christmas at the Toys! Store. Too hard to go back there after, you know, getting the call about Cody. Hard on the legs, too, all that standing, too far to drive to Elmont. Not that my friends don't keep me running. But I need a solid focus."

"Seems like a fine idea."

"So, how have you been? What's been going on? I know

you've got a big job on your hands. Practically a one-man force. I haven't really seen you since . . ." Believe me, I didn't care how he was. This was to divert him into talking about himself so he'd think he'd learned all about me. And if the slant reference to Harold's funeral made him uncomfortable, so much the better.

"Oh now, I do have a deputy, and some part-time help. But you know, we have more DUIs than we used to, and you'd be surprised, I don't know what we'll do exactly to manage, more drugs coming in. People don't realize. Even our own, you know, couple smart alecks growing . . . Hey, you don't want to hear this stuff. Would you mind if I use your bathroom?"

"Not at all. Down the hall, first door on the right." So he felt he needed to check the rest of the house to see if I was keeping the zoo—or maybe growing pot—back there. I know I can't grow pot, though. Not without buying grow lights first. I wonder if they're difficult to install?

After a ridiculous amount of time, the toilet flushed and the bathroom door opened with unnecessary loudness. I wondered for just a few seconds if Gus had really peed, and if his was like my Harold's had been, damn prostate pee, he called it. I used to lie in bed and listen: a tiny stream, then silence, then a little more. Fits and stops. Sometimes I'd fall back to sleep before Harold even made it back to bed. If I was awake, he'd take my hand and apologize. He didn't need to. After that bad fall he took in the dark making his way to the bathroom, I'd made him start to put on his glasses and turn on the bedside light when he had to get up in the night.

Gus's coffee was cooling on the kitchen table.

"See everything you wanted?" I said as he re-entered the kitchen, my tone innocent.

"Oh sure. Nice bathroom. Real nice." Blocks of sunlight rested on the table then as the earth turned toward noon. That morning they looked almost solid, like something I could use to smash him, this man who'd come to spy on me, doing my son's bidding. But it had been our Cody and my Harold who were smashed. Wishful thinking didn't do a thing to Gus.

"Miss Louisa, perhaps you would go to dinner with me sometime at the Lodge? The hunting club has a dinner, you know, the second Friday of the month, and we bring the ladies to that." Luckily for me, I don't have a partial plate like Harold did, because I'd surely have swallowed it when Gus invited me out in the middle of my murderous thoughts. Some men have an astounding inability to read women, don't they? Thank goodness.

"That's a . . . lovely, Gus. That you bring the ladies, I mean . . . I'm sure they are very . . . honored."

"For sure. They love it. So, what do you say?"

"Thank you for asking me, but it just wouldn't be right so soon after Harold died. It wouldn't be respectful, Gus. It's hardly a year." And it would take me a hundred years to want to go out with you, I added to myself. Make that a thousand.

"I can wait," he said with a chuckle, and wiped a faint sweat sheen off his forehead with a chubby ringless hand. "You just call me when you're ready," he said with the great confidence of the clueless.

I changed the subject and we discussed the riveting topic of his arthritis (he has a bit of it in his knees that worries him). Then I had to be fascinated by his speculation about whether the county would patch or repave the rural route leading to the bridge that's out again before he went on to guessing how long the bridge will be out this time. Later, when he'd finished his coffee and left, Glitter Jesus stuffed behind the couch, I was tickled knowing Gus was burning up the phone line to Gary. He had to be secretly thinking Gary the least credible eye witness who'd ever asked for an *unofficial* official investigation in the twenty-seven years since Gus had first been elected sheriff of Dwayne Township. Miss Louisa was not only normal, she was kind of hot. Maybe CarolSue's remedial lessons in hairstyle and makeup for the harried woman who lived on a farm and taught fifth grade hadn't been entirely wasted.

There was one true thing I'd said to Gus, though. It was about needing a solid focus. After a year at a standstill, something about having to rev my engine to put one over on him gave me an idea. Something I could do for my Harold, in Cody's name. Sometimes you finally see something down the strangest, most out-of-the-way back road and you know it's time to take that route. So while Gus was trying to find a smooth way to tell voter Gary that maybe *he* was the crazy one because his mother is just as fine and normal as pot roast, I got on the phone to CarolSue to say, "I need your help because it's time to pick up Harold's cause and get revenge on Cody's killer. Only difference is we're going to do it right. We're going to have a Plan. None of that haphazard crap that didn't work."

And CarolSue said to me, "Well, of course we will. And I've been bored to tears lately. Charlie's always out in the garage, not that I want him underfoot, and I've already got the garden mulched. Annuals go in so early down here."

"Thank you, sister. I knew I could count on you."

"You have nothing to thank me for. You and I have to take care of each other, don't we? I'll be there. Haven't I been saying you've got to find something to take hold of? And maybe there's a little spark between you and Gus—"

"Have you lost your mind? That just pisses me off, I mean—I am Harold's wi—"

"Okay, okay. I just thought . . ."

"Well, don't think about anything but a Plan."

It was the middle of the night, too late to call CarolSue again, when a different thought came to me.

After Gary's visit, I'd reassured the girls that everything he said about getting them out of our house was nonsense and they absolutely shouldn't trouble their minds. We laughed and drank a toast to what good company we are. And you know how the next morning went with Gus. I'd taken care of everything. I didn't replay what Gary had said until my eyes opened in the blackness of my bedroom and The Thought was there, like one of those insights that you get with total clarity before sleep, but it fades in daylight and then you forget it until it's too late. Months later I'd remember how Marvelle's yellow eyes glinted at me from Harold's side of the bed and The Thought had been sudden, strong. *Gary wants me out.*

I lay there with The Thought. I could have saved myself a lot of trouble if I'd paid more attention to my instincts. Too late, I'd remember that I hadn't been able to sleep for fretting. This is my farm, my land. Harold and I made it sing out its good heart year after year. Our sweat has been its best rain. Corn was its song and it sang and sang, through seasons of planting and harvesting. It fed our mouths, and through years of sunsets and dawns, it fed our souls. The animals we raised and loved are buried here. My Harold's ashes are in this ground, with some of Cody's that his mother was kind to give us. The land sings the only notes I still hear. And I hear, I still hear.